the PROPHECY *of* WIND

JAYNE THORNE, CIA LIBRARIAN BOOK FOUR

TWO TALES PRESS

NEW YORK TIMES BESTSELLING AUTHOR

JOSS WALKER
AND R.L. PEREZ

PRAISE FOR THE JAYNE THORNE, CIA LIBRARIAN SERIES

"Vivid world-building, a page-turning mystery and a smart, adventurous heroine in the process of discovering her own power and learning from her mistakes makes for another great addition to an outstanding urban fantasy series."
— **Jayne Castle,** *New York Times* **bestselling author of the Harmony series, on** *Master of Shadows*

"Light-hearted books can get a bad rap, as though making readers smile is somehow a weakness on the author's part... Walker has a light touch with [her] prose, and the likable characters breeze through many of their interactions. Which isn't to say that Tomb of the Queen lacks gravitas. No, there's a good story here with real edge-of-the-seat moments... It's fun from start to finish, and I'm going to keep my eye out for more from this "new" author."
—**Charles de Lint,** *The Magazine of Mystery & Science Fiction* **on** *Tomb of the Queen*

"Writer Joss Walker brings the magic back! It will take a witch with heart, humor, and book smarts—plus some killer kickboxing skills–to save the world, and Jayne Thorne is the witch we need now. Hold on tight, you urban fantasy fans, because once you open *Tomb of the Queen*, the action doesn't stop until the last thrilling page."

— **Laura Benedict, bestselling author of the *Bliss House* trilogy, on *Tomb of the Queen***

"A librarian gets recruited by the CIA to help track down rare and magical books... Jayne Thorne has just discovered that magic is real, and the CIA needs her help. After a crash course in Magic 101 she's sent to Ireland to investigate a rare manuscript. The start of this series is everything I love about urban fantasy: a wise-cracking heroine who diffuses tense situations with a joke, plenty of adventure, and an interesting magical world that exists alongside our own. I can't wait for more adventures with Jayne!"

— **John McDougall, Murder by the Book, on *Tomb of the Queen***

"Joss Walker's debut had me completely under her spell. Part cleverly plotted fantasy and part thriller, I was drawn in by her charming bookworm of a librarian with magical powers, dashing Irish rogue, and the complicated battle between 'good' and evil. Addictive and utterly delightful, this is a book to treasure."

— **Paige Crutcher, author of *The Orphan Witch*, on *Tomb of the Queen***

"*Tomb of the Queen* is a relatable, fun romp of a thrill ride! The characters are lifelike and well fleshed out, and the magic is done in a unique way that I have never seen before. I loved this book, and I'm sure that I will read it over and over again!"

— **Julie L. Kramer, *USA Today* bestselling author of *Of Curses and Scandals*, on *Tomb of the Queen***

"This book was just my cup of tea! Or perhaps, my slice of pie? 😊 Jayne Thorne, CIA Librarian is a relatable, lovable, and smart heroine dead set on vanquishing evil. A genius mythology twist, swoony budding romance, and gorgeous library imagery, paired with non-stop action, makes *Tomb of the Queen* a winner for fans of urban fantasy. Stop everything and read this book!"

— **Ashley McLeo, author of the bestselling *Starseed Trilogy*, on *Tomb of the Queen***

ALSO BY JOSS WALKER

Jayne Thorne, CIA Librarian Series

Tomb of the Queen

Master of Shadows

The Keeper of Flames

The Prophecy of Wind

The Book of Spirits (2024)

A Betrayal of Magic (short prequel)

The Eighth Road (short prequel)

Discovery of Magic (bundle)

The Guardians Mini-Series

Guardians of Silence

Guardians of Fury

Guardians of Power

Writing as J.T. Ellison

Standalone Suspense

It's One of Us

Her Dark Lies

Good Girls Lie

Tear Me Apart

Lie to Me

No One Knows

The Lt. Taylor Jackson Series

All the Pretty Girls

14

Judas Kiss

The Cold Room

The Immortals

So Close to the Hand of Death

Where All the Dead Lie

Field of Graves

The Wolves Come at Night

The Dr. Samantha Owens Series

A Deeper Darkness

Edge of Black

When Shadows Fall

What Lies Behind

A Brit in the FBI Series,

Cowritten with Catherine Coulter

The Final Cut

The Lost Key

The End Game

The Devil's Triangle

The Sixth Day

ALSO BY R.L. PEREZ

Timecaster Chronicles

Twisted by Time

Devoured by Darkness

Bound by Blood

Nightcaster Chronicles

The Cursed Witch

The Fallen Demon

The Lost Phoenix

Bloodcaster Chronicles

The Demon's Kiss

The Angel's Vow

The Reaper's Call

Ivy & Bone series

Ivy & Bone

Thorn & Ash

Oak & Ember

For those who believe in magic,
and those who fight to make it so.

PROLOGUE

With the power roiling inside her, sometimes Ruth Thorne couldn't even remember her own name. This moment, this threshold she stood upon, was the rare occurrence when her mind was lucid and she recalled her purpose: acquire the Masters' totems. Unleash the power of the Torrent.

Free the dark master.

She was becoming one with the monstrous presence inside her. She had been warned about the costs of dark magic, of channeling power from the Torrent. Of coveting, touching, subsuming, using the cursed magic for herself. She'd had no idea then what that would cost, but now...

The battle lines were being drawn, and if she had any hope of winning, she had to be more aggressive. She'd started the Kingdom to rid the world of nonmagical creatures, to rule among those who were blessed with magical genes. A cleansing was needed, a return to the ways things were supposed to be, when the Torrent wasn't trapped in a river of stars accessible to a very few powerful magicians, as it was now, but flowing in the very air they breathed, the sky they watched, the trees and the streams and the clouds and the rain. When the sun rose and set

1

on magical creatures who did not need spells, did not need to battle amongst themselves. Harmony. That's what she had always sought. She was willing to do whatever it took to find that peace for her people.

And, in so doing, had unleashed a monster much worse than anything they could have conjured with the darkest necromantic texts.

She was changed. Her mission was perverted. She was being used, a puppet unable to break free from a master so dark, so unforgiving, he would see the world burn before he let his enemies win.

Under his rule, there would be no harmony. Only cruelty, darkness, hate. She was bringing the monster to the world, and she was helpless against it.

There were moments of softness in her memories. Gentle smiles from the men she'd cared for. The possibilities of the children who grew inside her. The simple pleasure of a good meal, a beautiful work of art, a magnificent view.

But her drive wiped them all away. Her quest for power trampled the realities she found herself attached to.

She needed the grimoires. The grimoires led to the totems. The totems led to ultimate domination. For her. For the beast within.

And time was not her friend.

Her second, Lars, stepped to her side. "Ruth? Is all well?"

His Dublin schoolboy accent made her cringe. A pinwheel of images danced through her brain. The coast of Ireland, raising Queen Medb, the death of Alarik, and the decimation of the Irish faction of the Kingdom by the very people she was about to slay—it seemed so far in the past, though it was mere months ago.

Behind her stood the remaining followers loyal to her cause, ready to act, thirsty for blood, prepared to unleash hell on their enemies. They were powerful, yes; as the Torrent became easier to access, their powers were growing. But to win this battle, they needed her to be their amplifier. She could now boost their magic, make them true soldiers of the cause.

Her chest swelled with lethal energy, driven by the powerful presence that grew with each passing day. She had once feared it. Feared allowing it to take over. Now, she knew it was inevitable.

The time is now, the presence seemed to say. *Find the totems. Slay our enemies. Free me. Or you will be the first to suffer.*

Ignoring the disorienting dizziness clouding her mind and the cold, clammy sweat clinging to her palms, Ruth turned to Lars and gave him one firm nod.

"We await the signal. As soon as it happens, we must be ready to move. Prepare the troops."

He gestured to the soldiers behind them, and as one, they all reached for the Torrent. Magic swarmed in the air like bees buzzing against her ears. A shimmering portal appeared, and Ruth would be the first to step through.

Her daughters and their weak TCO compatriots would feel her wrath today. They would rue the day they decided to challenge her.

To challenge the master.

CHAPTER

ONE

BACK TO THE FUTURE

Geneva, Switzerland
Henry Thorne's Time Catch

Jayne Thorne stared at her long-lost father, trying, and failing miserably, to understand the words that had just left his mouth. The time catch was going to his head. Magicians were known to go mad in Time Catches, and as far as Jayne's limited but harrowing experiences with them, that was entirely understandable. So when her father said that there were people trapped in the Torrent, including his mother, Alexandra, and Jayne's *daughter*, the only logical interpretation was he'd gone potty. Jayne had no daughter. She didn't even have a boyfriend.

Clearly, her father was bonkers. Along with all the emotions from the past few weeks, Jayne's fear and frustration and joy and pain intermingled, and, no, she wasn't proud of it, but it was inevitable. She blew a gasket.

"You don't get to just appear back into our lives like this and drop bombshells like I might have some daughter out there floating around the universe in a time-space continuum like some sort of *Star Trek* episode. No, sir. Absolutely not."

Sofia touched Jayne on the arm. "Jayne. Let him explain."

"No. We almost died finding you, Dad, and here you are, alive, and people are dead, or sucked into the Torrent according to you, and Mom has been possessed by some sort of monster, and I want an explanation!"

Henry fiddled with his glasses. "I can't explain properly, not without creating all sorts of conundrums for you, my dear. Just trust me. Can you do that?"

He looked so earnest she took a breath and thought about it.

"Nope. Are you saying you've met my daughter from the *future*?" Jayne asked, trying not to shout the words. Her father couldn't be serious. After years and years of believing this man was dead, she got this instead of a teary-eyed reunion full of hugs and kisses and murmured words of affection. Henry Thorne was raving mad. It was heartbreaking, really.

"Erm, yes."

"Bonkers," Jayne said, stalking off. She bumped immediately into a metal shelf, knocking a hundred small glass jars from their resting places. With a flick of his hand, Henry tossed a Repair spell at the mess, which uprighted the shelves and caught the jars, setting them back in precise rows. It was pretty cool magic, but Jayne was too incensed to appreciate it fully.

"Dad," Sofia said, her voice eerily calm. "Back up a bit. What happened to you? We thought you died. Have you just been... here, this whole time?" She gestured to the chaotic science lab around them, the makings of the Time Catch Henry had been hiding in. Her voice broke, betraying what she wasn't saying: *Why didn't you come find us? Why did you abandon us?*

Henry scratched his head, ruffling his brown curls. He dropped his arms, then crossed them, as if unsure where to position his hands. "I, uh..." He pinched the bridge of his nose and huffed out a huge sigh. "I'm so sorry, loves. I would never have left you if I had a choice. Surely you know that. But your mother—Ruth—held me prisoner for years. I was in a Time Catch, unable to do much of anything but think. It happened during the fire in Yosemite, do you remember that?"

"Yes, we remember," Sofia said carefully.

"Well, that burst of power trapped us both behind the lines, and the only recourse was a very hastily created Time Catch. Your mother understood that I was not going to willingly be separated from you for long, so when she conjured it, she added a lovely little loophole—she could leave, but I couldn't.

"I was stuck there for years, my darlings. All I could do was watch you from afar and hope you'd find the clues I'd left behind in the notebook. A...friend finally discovered where I was and helped me escape. But I couldn't exactly march back into your lives, not without making you both targets."

He adjusted his glasses, his voice growing thick.

"I would do anything for you girls. You must know that. Once I got out...I only wanted to keep you safe. I thought by staying away, I could protect you. I knew Ruth would eventually find out about the Guardian magic in your blood and try to use you, too. I couldn't risk it. She was too volatile, still is, and you —you were both too precious to me." Tears sparkled in his eyes.

Jayne felt her own eyes grow hot, and she glanced at Sofia, who was weeping openly. Her white-blond hair fell in a curtain around her face. Jayne could only imagine what she was thinking. Ruth had tried siphoning Jayne's powers when she was only six years old, and Sofia had witnessed the attempt. Though Jayne didn't remember most of the event, it was still traumatizing for Sofia—it had triggered her defensive nature toward Jayne, bringing out the protective lioness inside her.

They both knew what Ruth was willing to do for more power.

"We needed you," Sofia whispered, the tears streaming

down her face. "God, we needed you so much, Dad. We had no one."

"You had each other," Henry said. "I know things were hard for you both, but I knew you were together. I'm so sorry for what you had to go through on your own. Truly sorry."

Sofia heaved a shuddering breath, crossing her arms over her chest. She looked like she wanted to dive into Henry's arms and squeeze him into the tightest hug but was restraining herself.

Sensing the need for a subject change, Jayne cleared her throat. "So, uh, daughter from the future? Can we circle back to that, please?"

Henry pressed his palms together, focusing on Jayne like a professor would turn attention to a responsive pupil. "Right. Well. Unfortunately, I can't answer that. There just isn't time —"

Jayne huffed a laugh. "We're in a Time Catch. There's time."

"Ah. Yes. But it's fairly complicated, and—"

Jayne took a step closer to him. "We didn't wait seventeen years to track you down just for you to say it's complicated. We're adults now. It's been long enough. Please, Dad. We deserve to know." Her blood thrummed with impatience and anticipation, and she had to fight the urge to bounce on the balls of her feet or grab her father by the collar and shake him for answers.

Henry rubbed his forehead and groaned. With a sigh, he let his hand drop against his thigh. "You're right. Of course, you're right. I, uh... Lord, where to begin..." He straightened, then cleared his throat. Jayne was once again reminded of a professor about to dive into a lecture. Everything about Henry Thorne was just so scholarly, from his thin, wiry frame to the glasses he left on the table to his quirky mannerisms.

"My mother—your grandmother—Alexandra Thorne was sucked into the Torrent thirty years ago," Henry began. "It was an accident. She got too close to a powerful source of Torrent energy, and it sensed her Guardian magic and pulled her in, then shut, disappearing entirely. I've been trying to find a back-door access point to the Torrent. I need something more powerful than the Guardian pockets, but not volatile enough to break the Torrent itself, to let her out."

When he paused, Jayne found herself nodding. "Okay. We're with you so far." She still had no idea what this had to do with her future daughter.

"I've made several scientific breakthroughs." Henry's face brightened with excitement. "So many discoveries! I can't wait to share them all with you." His expression smoothed, and he cleared his throat again. "Right. Another time. One of those discoveries is something I've been working on since college. It's a way to manipulate time. I've developed a capacitor that theoretically will temporarily allow someone to reach through the time vortex with a specific destination in mind. Now, it's very sensitive, and there are strict rules, inviolable rules. This is an alternate reality we're talking about. Just like the Time Catches exist in another plane, the Torrent does, as well."

Jayne's brow furrowed. *Time vortex? Capacitor?* She felt like she was talking to Doc Brown from *Back to the Future*.

Oblivious to her confusion, Henry plowed on. "I didn't test it as thoroughly as I should have. I—I was just too excited! I thought I'd found the key to rescuing my mother at last. But when I turned on the capacitor and entered the time vortex, I used the coordinates calculated based on my blood type and the Guardian magic inside me. I input the destination to thirty years in the past, but something must have malfunctioned, or I calculated wrong, because the vortex took me to thirty years into the future. I believe it recognized the signature of your daughter's magic, Jayne. It matched my blood type and Guardian magic to something closer to your grandmother's." He grimaced sheepishly as if admitting he'd committed some small offense like finishing the last bit of milk from the carton instead of accidentally yanking Jayne's daughter through time and space. "Once I realized my mistake, I tried to release her, to send her back, but my capacitor short-circuited and didn't have the power to complete the cycle, and the Torrent was already open, and she—fell in."

"Fell in...the Torrent," Jayne repeated numbly.

Henry nodded.

Jayne's brain hurt. Was this man serious? Or was this some lunatic dressed like her father, spewing nonsense just to mess with her?

Sofia raised a hand, her face contorted with part incredulity, part bewilderment. "I'm sorry, are you saying you've unlocked the secret to time travel, and you were using it to find your mom, but instead you trapped Jayne's daughter in the Torrent?"

Henry's eyes lit up, clearly pleased Sofia had caught on. "Yes! Exactly."

"What does that even mean?" Sofia sputtered. "I—you— Jayne doesn't have a daughter! What if telling us changes everything? What if she doesn't even end up having a daughter now? Will this random woman in the Torrent be erased from existence?"

"I think we're missing the bigger picture here," Jayne said. "Time travel? There's no way." She glanced over her father's malnourished body and wondered if he had just been on some strange drug trip and concocted this whole story in his head. "Someone would have discovered it by now. The TCO, the CIA, the worldwide Adept community... Are you telling me that you alone have discovered time travel and no one else knows about it? I just—find that very hard to believe. No offense," she added quickly. "We love you, Dad, but we haven't seen you in seventeen years. It's a little difficult to swallow."

After all, when Ruth had shown up after being presumed dead for so long, things hadn't turned out so great. Jayne wanted to believe her father was the same man she'd known as a child, but her experience with Ruth made her overly cautious.

Henry rubbed his eyes, suddenly looking very tired. "You're right. And I—I don't blame you at all. I've had to keep this secret locked up tight. Ruth, the Guardians, everyone would use this for the wrong reasons."

"What are the right reasons?" Sofia asked. "Who gets to decide what those reasons are? Aren't you trying to use time travel to get your mother back? Instead of, I don't know, changing the world for the better?"

"This *is* changing the world for the better," Henry insisted. "There is something powerful living inside the Torrent, and the longer those two are in there, the more it will feed off their energy and grow into something monstrous, something unstoppable!"

This lined up with what Vesta had told Jayne. The white-haired fire goddess had implored her to stop this darkness from spreading, to use the power of the totems she had received to set things right.

"Show me," Jayne said.

Henry shrank away from her as if recoiling from her demand. "What?"

"Show me your capacitor. Show me your discoveries. I want to see them. It will help me understand." What she didn't say was *Prove it. Prove to me you aren't insane.*

She was willing to listen. She was willing to entertain the notion that time travel was real. After all, just last year, hadn't she believed magic to be nothing more than a myth? How far-fetched could time travel be, by comparison?

But what had solidified her belief in magic was actually experiencing it. She needed a measure of proof to help her rational brain understand it. Quantum physics was just scientific magic, right? But provable. Definable.

"I can't," Henry said, wringing his hands together, a look of helpless frustration on his face. "The capacitor is too unstable. I had to dismantle it, just to be safe."

"Well, can you at least tell me about this daughter of mine?" Jayne asked. "Who is she? What's her name? When will she be born? Who's the father?"

Please, for the love of God, don't say Tristan Lowell...

Henry spread his hands in a placating gesture, his face crumpling with regret. "I can't. I'm sorry."

Jayne sighed. "You've got to meet us halfway, Dad. We can't help you if you can't give us any more information."

"You don't understand," Henry said. "The time vortex is a living, breathing entity. Anything I tell you about the future could jeopardize the timeline and unravel everything that holds the universe together. Even the smallest change can cause massive disasters over time."

"Chaos theory. The butterfly effect," Jayne said.

Henry pointed to her, wagging his finger in the air. "Yes. Exactly."

"Then can you at least come with us to the TCO?" Sofia asked. "Show them your findings. Let their research team work with you. You clearly can't do this alone." She gestured to the lab.

Henry shook his head so forcefully Jayne worried it might fall right off his neck. "No. No. I absolutely cannot include anyone else."

"Dad, if what you're saying is true, then you singlehandedly managed to tamper with the future all on your own," Jayne said. "Sofia's right. You're in no position to tackle this by yourself. You need help."

Henry ran a shaking hand through his brown curls again. He really had the crazed scientist motif down pat. It would be comical if it weren't so horrible.

"No. I can't bring in strangers. I don't trust them. I don't trust anyone except you two."

Even after seventeen years apart? Jayne had been six years old when he'd left. He hadn't seen her grow up. He had no idea what kind of woman she'd turned out to be.

She wished she could say she had the same level of trust in him.

"They're the good guys, Dad," Sofia said, inching closer to Henry and taking one of his trembling hands in hers. "I can introduce you, one at a time, to only the most trusted officers. I've worked with them myself and can vouch for them."

Jayne immediately thought of the mole within the TCO. Now would *not* be a good time to bring that up. But if they started by introducing Henry to Ruger and Amanda—who were both rock-solid in the trust department—then Henry's secrets would be safe.

Baby steps. That was what her father needed.

"Just meet my handler," Jayne offered. "And my boss. You don't have to unload all your secrets at once. They need to know you're alive, though. There's a war brewing out there, Dad. And we need you on our side."

Henry was silent, his body restless. He shifted his weight from one foot to the other. Rubbed his nose. Scratched the inside of his wrist. Chewed on the edges of his fingernails. Overall, he was quite a fidgety person. But Jayne supposed if she'd been cooped up in this lab on her own for Lord knows how long, she would be a little kooky, too.

After a groan of frustration, Henry said, "Fine. All right. I'll go with you to the TCO."

CHAPTER

TWO

I SMELL A RAT

TCO Headquarters, CIA
Langley, Virginia

Mother needs eggs, but we can't afford them.

A manda read the text over once more. Even after putting it through several cipher keys, she couldn't make sense of it.

It was the latest message her assistant, Pierce, had received. His response:

Doc has no eggs at the moment. If Mother purchases some, this would be a good time for a visit.

The messages were clearly coded, but it wasn't a standard encryption that could be cracked. Whatever code they had was already established. *Mother* and *eggs* represented something, but Amanda didn't know what. She needed more context.

A knock sounded at the door.

Amanda looked up, hastily pulling up a document to cover

the video feed of Pierce's apartment. She'd only just finished having Ruger bug his home and phone lines. She thought she'd been discreet enough for Pierce to be none the wiser, but he'd been covering his tracks for so long that she couldn't be sure. So far, nothing incriminating had popped up, except for that strange exchange of messages. She couldn't take chances, though. If Pierce figured out she'd made him as the mole, that his former chipper, do-anything-for-his-boss nature now seemed smug and cruel and she recoiled from him, she'd never find out who he was working for.

"Enter," Amanda said.

Ruger stepped into her office, his massive frame vibrating with agitation. "They found him."

"Found whom?" She sat back in her chair, surveying Ruger's wary expression, his dark brows knitting together and his lips turning down into a disapproving scowl.

"Henry Thorne."

Goddess, had Jayne and Sofia actually done it? Had they truly tracked him down? Amanda had begun to believe the man was dead—as they'd all thought for so long.

"Alive?" she asked. Her heart shuddered at the thought of what the girls would go through if they found nothing but a corpse.

"Yes. He's been in a Time Catch, working in some sort of lab." Ruger's scowl deepened, the old burn scars on his face twisting. Amanda heard what he wasn't saying: *The coward has been hiding.*

But she wasn't one to pass judgment. Not until she had more information.

Ruger went on, "They've just brought him in."

"Willingly? I never envisioned him offering himself up to the TCO."

"Apparently the girls talked him into it."

She gestured to the chair in front of her desk, and Ruger

took a seat. "I'm remarkably impressed. Those two are quite a team. Good. Bring him in. We'll debrief him. Find out what he knows and how he can be of use to us. But first, I need to discuss something highly sensitive with you." She took a breath, rapping her knuckles on the polished surface of her desk as she deliberated how best to approach it. Because he wasn't going to love this.

"I want you to handle Henry Thorne while I deal with Pierce."

"Babysitting, Amanda? Seriously?"

"Not babysitting. Protecting. And watching. We don't know where his loyalties lie, and I don't know who Pierce is working for. I must ensure that Thorne isn't a massive Trojan horse from our many enemies. Especially now that we know who the mole is."

"You think Henry could really be working for Ruth and the Kingdom after all? Or La Liberté?"

"Unknown. Which is why I need you to gather as much information as possible on what he's really been up to." She sat back in the chair. "We're in uncharted waters, Ruger. Knowing who to trust is everything right now."

"I agree we need to use this information to our advantage, and the fewer people who know, the less likely it is Pierce will suspect his cover's been blown. But you need me watching him, not Thorne. I need to protect you, Amanda. That's my job."

She smiled at her old friend to soften her next words. "Your job is what I tell you it is. And I have a feeling about Henry Thorne. Besides, I do have safety precautions in place. Every six hours, I deactivate a scheduled encrypted message before it's sent out. If something should happen to me, and I'm unable to deactivate it, all the information I've acquired will go straight to you. You will step into this role, assuming you're willing, and carry on the mission. Am I clear?"

Ruger's jaw worked back and forth. The frustration in his eyes told Amanda he didn't approve of this.

Too bad.

Ruger exhaled through his teeth. "Very well. Please keep me informed. And let me know if there's anything else you need me to do." His eyes took on a lethal edge, and Amanda could once again read the violent intent on his face.

She couldn't blame him. Pierce had been a seemingly loyal employee for seven years. That he would betray them so callously was a heavy blow. She'd grown to care for the man, and he'd seemed genuinely eager to help their cause.

All of that had been a lie. A deception. A cold-hearted manipulation.

And Amanda had fallen for it.

Shame warred with anger in her chest, and she took a steadying breath. "See that a portal is set up for Thorne. Make sure Tristan and Vivienne are on deck if we need them. I'll send you my notes and you can prepare some questions. Hopefully, he'll have the answers we're looking for."

Ruger shot her a doubtful look that she ignored. He rose from his chair and lumbered to the door. As he opened it, he turned back to face her.

"Be careful, Amanda. I don't relish sitting behind your desk anytime soon. Understand?"

CHAPTER
THREE
NEGOTIATIONS

"I can't share anything with you unless I have your word you'll help me," Henry said.

Jayne sat across from her father at a table in a small room within the TCO. Next to her was Sofia, and pacing the length of the room like a rabid animal was Ruger. They had been arguing for the better part of an hour, trying to convince Henry to turn over his equipment and research to the TCO.

"Help you break open the Torrent and rescue two people supposedly trapped inside?" Ruger said, incredulous. "Even if I believed you, our entire mission is to protect the Torrent and ensure its power doesn't cause destruction or chaos. What you are suggesting could have catastrophic consequences."

"There will *be* catastrophic consequences if we do nothing!" Henry insisted.

"According to whom? What research? What proof? All I have is your word. We have decades of studies and experiments that tell us tampering with that amount of power is deadly and could end thousands of lives. Possibly millions. My superiors would never agree to it."

"Well, I'm afraid that means we are at an impasse." Henry sat back in his chair, crossing his arms like a petulant child.

Jayne rubbed her temples. "This is getting us nowhere, Ruger. What if we agree to work with him, to test if his theories and claims are valid? If the TCO acquires proof of their own, maybe that would be enough."

"I still can't guarantee the director will sanction a rescue mission within the Torrent, even if we *do* have proof," Ruger said, scratching his chin. "No matter how important they are to you, Thorne, the CIA would never jeopardize so much just to save two people."

Jayne's insides squirmed. This was one thing about the CIA she disagreed with. They were sometimes too willing to sacrifice a few in order to save the many. To Jayne, everyone was important. Everyone deserved saving. Why else had she been gifted with this power, with these totems, if not to save people?

And if her father was correct, this was her family they were talking about. How long had Jayne waited before finally getting permission to track down her father? Would she have to wait for this, too? If her grandmother and daughter—God, she still couldn't wrap her head around that—were trapped and suffering, every moment counted. While the CIA twiddled their thumbs and deliberated over this, actual human beings were stuck in the Torrent, enduring any number of horrors while some dark, sentient being was feeding off their energy.

Jayne shuddered, yanking on her hair tie, letting the dark mass spill down, then putting it back up into a bun. Beside her, Sofia squeezed her shoulder, trying to alleviate her distress.

"We have to start somewhere," Sofia said, adopting her reasonable big-sister voice. "The TCO should explore these theories to see if there is any validity to them. If something dark and powerful is living and feeding in the Torrent, it affects us all. It's worth looking into."

Ruger ran a hand down his face. He had scars, burns, from

his many battles, and Jayne was reminded again that he'd been doing this far longer than the rest of them.

"With all the threats we are facing, all the work we have to do, it will be hard to convince anyone to make this a priority."

"Ruger," Jayne said firmly, "we owe it to my dad to at least investigate. If the TCO wants my help with future missions, they have to prove they can make my family a priority. This isn't just some side mission that's unrelated to our work. It's important. For months, I've worked my ass off using my powers to help the TCO. This is the least they can do in return."

Ruger dropped his hand with a sigh and paced to the end of the small room. After a moment, he said, "I have to ask—why now? Why come to us now?" He turned, his dark eyes fixed on Henry.

Henry straightened in his seat. "My daughters." He said it like the answer was obvious.

"What about them?" Ruger asked.

"I left a trail for them to follow," Henry explained. "I needed to know they could piece the clues together on their own, that they could read between the lines in ways that Ruth never could. If they managed to track me down, I knew they would be able to help me with this, too. That they would die on the right side of this war."

"So it was all some elaborate test?" Jayne asked. "We were looking for our missing father, who was presumed dead, and you were just concocting these series of hoops for us to jump through?"

"Yes. Well, no. I mean—" Henry exhaled and drummed his fingers on the table. "You have to understand, Jayne, that I couldn't reach out to you through conventional methods. I was being watched on all sides. I *did* want to be reunited with you both. More than anything. But I had to be certain you were trustworthy. That you wouldn't follow in Ruth's footsteps. There is too much at stake for me to risk that."

That was...reasonable. How long had Ruth tried to convert Jayne and Sofia to her way of thinking? To draw them to her side? If she had succeeded, Henry's worst fears would have been confirmed.

"The journal," Sofia said suddenly, her eyes lighting up. "You left the journal to us on purpose."

Henry nodded vigorously. "I infused it with my Guardian powers, ensuring only someone with my blood could access it."

It had taken both Jayne's and Sofia's blood to crack open the code encrypted in his journal—a code Ruth had tried and failed to unlock.

As Jayne thought of the journal, she recalled something Sofia had shown her. "What did you mean about Ruth's secret?"

"Pardon?" Henry asked.

"In your journal, you mentioned a contingency plan—a way to end her. What is it?"

Deadly silence filled the room. Ruger stopped his pacing, and Jayne felt every pair of eyes on her. But she stared at her father, waiting, holding her breath.

"You didn't finish decoding the page?" Henry asked at last, his voice a low murmur.

"Not that one," Sofia said. "The ink was badly smudged. We couldn't piece it together."

Henry chewed on one of his fingernails, his gaze growing distant. "I—I can't say."

Jayne kept herself from groaning loudly. "Dad... You haven't seen her recently. She's dabbled in something dark. Something unnatural. It's frightening. It's like nothing I've ever seen. We need that contingency plan." She resisted the urge to scratch at the patch of skin on her arm that was dark and leathery, just like the skin of the strange gargoyle creature that had possessed Ruth. Jayne was always careful to wear jackets or long sleeves to cover it up, but even without seeing it, she still knew it was there, festering like an open wound. A tangible promise of how things could go badly for her if she weren't very, very careful. As a Master, she wouldn't burn if she overstepped her powers, like a regular Adept. No, her power meant she would be transformed. She had to ensure this poison didn't turn her into something dark like it had her mother.

"I won't reveal it until we are certain there's no way to bring her in peacefully," Henry insisted. "I knew her when she was good, back when she hadn't been corrupted by darkness and power. I won't give up hope that we can bring that woman back."

"You're an idiot, Thorne," Ruger spit out. "She's not worth your loyalty. She's evil."

"She's the mother of my children," Henry said softly. "She wasn't always bad. I know in my heart I can reach that woman."

Jayne exchanged an exasperated look with Sofia, whose eyes swam with sympathy. They couldn't fault their father for his loyalties. It was admirable, really. But if he'd been in hiding this whole time, desperate not to draw Ruth's attention, then he had no idea what she was like. What she was capable of.

Jayne knew firsthand there was no coming back from that.

Baby steps, she reminded herself. Perhaps, after working with the TCO, Henry would see sense. He would give them the answers they needed.

"All right, fine," Ruger said, harnessing his anger. "First things first. We'll set up a team to work with Thorne and analyze his research to determine the threat to the Torrent. Thorne, you agree to comply? To cooperate with our people if we cooperate with you?"

Henry said nothing for a long moment, and Jayne resisted the urge to groan. *Please, Dad. Extend the olive branch.*

Finally, he nodded. "Yes, I will supply all pertinent research and information. Anything sensitive, I reserve the right to keep to myself until I have your word you'll give me the assistance I need."

Ruger grumbled something unintelligible. Jayne forced a smile, knowing it was the best they were going to get. "Thank you, Dad. You won't regret this. I know working together is the right thing to do."

Henry nodded, dropping his gaze and scratching absently at his chin. Jayne couldn't imagine what he was going through right now. He had been a loner for the past seventeen years, and now he was being asked to turn over everything he sacrificed so much to protect.

Jayne stretched out her arm and took his hand in hers, ignoring the twitch that signaled his discomfort at being touched.

"Sofia and I are with you, Dad," Jayne said earnestly. "We aren't going anywhere."

Sofia placed her long delicate fingers atop Jayne and Henry's, offering a gentle and reassuring smile.

Henry's shoulders slumped, and he relaxed slightly. "I know. It's wonderful to be with you girls again, to see the strong women you've become. I just feel—"

A low boom shook the ground. The walls trembled, and the lights in the ceiling flickered. A blaring alarm began to echo through the room.

Jayne shot to her feet. Those alarms could only mean one thing: the TCO was under attack.

CHAPTER

FOUR

AMBUSHED

With a grunt, Tristan Lowell found himself flat on his back on the mats in the training room. Again.

Standing over him with a satisfied smirk on her face was his sister, Vivienne. Seeing her like this, her dark curls floating, smug and proud, and *here* in the flesh, Tristan couldn't find the strength to be frustrated. Even if she had just bested him for the tenth time that morning.

"I didn't realize being stuck in a magical grimoire allowed for much sparring," Tristan said in French, their native tongue. His ribs ached, and he knew he'd have bruises after today. But he'd wanted to see what Vivienne had learned under the tutelage of the fire goddess, Vesta.

A lot, as it turned out.

Vivienne's grin widened as she stuck out her hand to hoist him up. Tristan winced, clutching at his side as he stood beside her.

"Vesta was a wonderful teacher. But maybe you're just rusty," Vivienne replied in her charmingly accented English, nudging his shoulder.

Tristan barked out a laugh. Between his missions with La

Liberté and working undercover for the TCO, he would hardly call himself rusty. "You must teach me what Vesta's shown you. I'm sure we could all benefit from the training of a *goddess*." He still couldn't quite wrap his head around the concept. His own sister had been mentored by the bringer of fire.

Then again, Jayne had bonded with Medb, the earth goddess. And she'd received both the goddesses' totems, Earth and Fire. Surely, this shouldn't be too far-fetched by comparison.

Vivienne wound up her hair, which had come down during their last bit of sparring. "*En Anglais, s'il vous plait.* In English, Tristan. I told you I want to practice the words for the bond with Jayne so we can easily slip between languages. She still thinks—and dreams—in English. Under duress, I assume she will do the same. I cannot be a detriment to her if the language spell fails at the wrong time."

Jayne dreams in English. Vivienne could see Jayne's dreams, and that made him feel weird. His mind immediately closed off any further thoughts of Jayne. Since their kiss—and her blatant refusal to acknowledge that anything had happened between them—he hadn't allowed himself to dwell. They were partners. Nothing more. She made it clear how much she detested him.

Even so, his chest tightened and his stomach clenched as he remembered that burning heat between them. She'd felt it, too, surely. Otherwise, she wouldn't have responded as she had, pressing her body against his...

"Your face is redder than a tomato," Vivienne said, arching an eyebrow at him. "Did I hurt your feelings that much?"

Tristan cleared his throat, feeling his cheeks grow even hotter. In deference to his sister's wishes, he replied in English. "Of course not. I'm just flushed from the exertion. I think I need a break before you snap my bones in half."

Vivienne laughed. "Are you truly that fragile?"

"Like a delicate rose. You must handle me with care."

He smiled at the sound of her chuckles as he strode to the benches that lined the training room, taking several gulps of water from his bottle.

Vivienne trailed after him. "Vesta taught me a lot more than just fighting tactics, you know." She unscrewed the lid on her own water bottle and took a long sip before continuing. "There were certain things she was forbidden to discuss with me, but over the years, I was able to piece together a few tidbits."

Tristan frowned. "You're being quite vague."

Vivienne huffed a short laugh. "Yes, well, so was Vesta. I think she is bound by a powerful spell that seals her lips when she gets too close to revealing the truth."

"The truth about what?" Tristan was growing impatient. It was clear Vivienne took pleasure in drawing out the suspense. That much hadn't changed about her.

Vivienne took another infuriatingly long gulp of water. "The truth about Vesta. And the other goddesses who—" She broke off, her spine straightening as she whirled toward the door, her body suddenly on full alert.

"What is it?" Tristan tensed as well, sensing her Rogue magic flaring.

"Something's wrong. I can sense Jayne. She—"

Alarms began to blare, and a heartbeat later, the doors burst open, and several unfamiliar figures surged toward them, all wielding various weapons from daggers to handguns. Real weapons.

Tristan summoned a Shield spell, draping it over him and Vivienne just as a gunshot rang out, ricocheting off his barrier. Another invader invoked an Attack spell. Jets of green light speared toward Tristan, cracking through his Shield.

Real *and* magical weapons. *Merde.*

But Vivienne was ready. She gathered a ball of fire in each hand and shot one after another toward the enemy. An attacker fell, his chest taking the full impact of the flames. Another dived out of the way, narrowly avoiding getting burned. Vivienne weaved her hands together and crouched, slamming her fists into the floor. The ground rumbled, and fire shot upward like a geyser, burning the assailants closest to them to ashes. The weapons in their hands melted from the extreme heat, and their screams echoed in the vast training room as they disappeared.

Tristan could only stare, stunned at this magic he'd never seen before.

"Come on! I need to get to Jayne," Vivienne said urgently, snapping Tristan out of his shocked stupor. "I can't shift without her yet."

An attacker reached them, and Vivienne slammed her fist into his jaw. The man was twice her size, and the blow barely fazed him. She elbowed him in the chest, then the gut, then kneed him hard in the thigh, as Jayne had taught her. As he crumpled, she twisted and thrust, the bottom of her foot connecting with his skull in a vicious side kick. He went motionless, hitting the floor with an audible thud.

"Jayne's teaching you Krav Maga, I see," Tristan said, flaring an Attack spell layered with a magical kick of his own into the chest of the last man standing. He went down in a heap.

"And she's teaching you layered spells. This is good. More power."

Three more strangers appeared in the doorway, and Tristan swore under his breath. What the hell was happening? How had these people breached the TCO headquarters?

They couldn't get to Jayne if the enemies kept pouring in. Tristan grabbed Vivienne's elbow and jerked her against him. "On my mark, summon your flames as high as they'll go."

Vivienne nodded, her sharp gaze pinned on the newcomers. Tristan reached for the Torrent, snatching the spell he needed. When one of the attackers conjured magic, Tristan unleashed his own and shouted, "Now!"

Vivienne released jets of fire from her fingertips, spearing them toward the attackers like liquid flames. Tristan clenched his fingers into a fist and punched the air. Just in time, he flung another Shield over himself and his sister as gasoline poured from the ceiling.

The flames roared, igniting, spreading along the floor as the gasoline continued to rain down on them. The attackers were drenched in it, the fire consuming them completely.

"Damn," Vivienne whispered, clutching Tristan's arm tightly. "Impressive."

Tristan's mouth spread in a thin line as he watched their enemies go up in flames. The screams were dreadful, echoing in his mind. To be burned alive was a terrible fate.

Above them, the fire-suppression system shuddered to life and tried to deluge them in foam. It was too late.

But it was either them or us, Tristan reminded himself. It was something he often thought of during his time working undercover within La Liberté. Some choices were difficult, but they had to be made.

This was the exact type of thinking that made Jayne hate him.

Gritting his teeth, Tristan reinforced the Shield protecting him and his sister as he steered her around the flames and foamy residue and out of the room.

FIVE

TIME AFTER TIME

Ruger, Sofia, Jayne, and Henry burst out of the interrogation room. Down the hall, Adepts and other officers hurried past, some shouting panicked orders.

Ruger grabbed the arm of one officer Sofia recognized. "Secure Thorne. Immediately."

"No," Henry protested. "I'm fully trained."

"That's an order," Ruger said, his tone lethal.

"I'm staying with my daughters." Henry threw his shoulders back, and though Ruger dwarfed him by nearly a foot, he managed to hold his own in a staring contest. Jayne couldn't deny there was something formidable about her father with that steely, determined glint in his eye, all the mad-scientist quirkiness gone. In this moment, he was a powerful Guardian, the golden power of their ancestors flowing through his veins. Looking at his resolve, Jayne saw only a magician tasked with protecting the Torrent at all costs, a true member of the magical secret society passed genetically from magician to magician. Sofia and Jayne had gotten their Guardian blood from Henry—and Ruth had tried everything in her power to take it from all three of them.

Ruger seemed to sense it would only waste time to argue. "Stay close and don't fall behind."

Henry nodded as they continued onward, breaking into a run. In the distance, sounds of shouting and gunfire peppered the air. Jayne didn't know if it was La Liberté or the Kingdom or some other foe, but she was ready. Already, her magic thrummed in her veins, eager to be unleashed. For the briefest of moments, she thought of Tristan. Were he and his sister safe?

But she pushed the thought from her mind. They were both trained. They could handle themselves.

And Jayne didn't need her new Rogue. She could fight just fine on her own.

Keeping her battle staff by her side at all times had already become second nature; though she'd been gifted it recently, pulling it from the Torrent the last time she'd fought her mother in her altered form, it had become an extension of her being. She'd trained in the dojo with a staff, but this one was special. It had belonged to Medb; her name was carved into it with runes, and it was imbued with power of its own. It quivered in eagerness for the fight.

They flew past the entrance to the TCO library, and Jayne said a silent prayer of gratitude that their enemies hadn't made it this far. At least Katie Bell—and all those precious books— were safe for now.

When they rounded the corner to the atrium, they found a swarm of chaos and spells. The air was thick with magic and some kind of eerie lime-green smoke. Beside her, Sofia choked, covering her mouth.

"Don't inhale it directly," Henry warned. "It's poisonous. Your magic should protect you, but it'll still slow you down if you ingest too much of it."

Jayne shot him a sharp look. "How do you know that?"

"Because I developed it. And your mother abuses it. This is the Kingdom we're dealing with."

Shock and fury raged inside Jayne, but now was not the time to address it. Gritting her teeth and holding her breath, she surged forward, wielding a Shield spell around herself and Sofia as she ran.

An invader dived for her, but Jayne slammed an Attack spell straight into his chest, knocking him flat on his back. Three more surrounded her. She reached for the Torrent and twirled the staff. Where her fingers met the weathered wood, power burned, and her forehead prickled with awareness.

Medb's power had awakened.

And with it...Vesta's.

Jayne found herself grinning as she weaved a Block spell with a Blood Choke before swinging her staff into a wide arc. The weapon swept under the legs of all three attackers. As it made contact, they flew backward, clutching at their throats from the force of her spell. She raised her palm, and a ball of flame rose from her fingertips. With a grunt, she launched it at another assailant. The fireball collided with his face. He screamed, clutching at the scorching flesh before collapsing.

A roar echoed nearby, and Jayne looked up to find Cillian in wolf form, fighting side by side with Sofia. *Good,* she thought. At least Sofia had some backup.

But where were Tristan and Vivienne?

"Over here!" shouted a voice. "I've found her!"

Jayne whirled to find a Kingdom thug waving frantically, gesturing at...*her.*

Several attackers moved away from the fray and toward Jayne.

Shit. Jayne counted at least a dozen coming for her. No matter. She could take them.

More soldiers flooded the atrium, streaming toward her. Bottlenecking her. Jayne found herself backing up several steps, reinforcing her Shield spell. Her hands grew slick with sweat as she clutched her staff.

Let them come, she thought savagely. *I'm ready.*

She was about to summon another fireball when a burst of green smoke filled the air, penetrating her shield like a knife through butter. She recast the protective spell but not before some of the smoke entered her lungs. Tiriosis was definitely part of its makeup; she could feel her magic weakening. It scorched a path through her nose and throat, burning and boiling her from within. She choked, spitting, struggling to get the foul taste out of her mouth. Spots filled her vision just as the crowd of enemies closed in on her.

She swung her staff and felt a satisfying *crack* as one of them went down. Then, hands were on her, pinning her in place. Her staff was wrenched from her grip, and she cried out, slamming her forehead against the skull of the nearest thug. One hand released her, and she twisted away from the other, ducking down low to avoid being snatched again.

Fire erupted on her fingertips, but her vision was spotty. She couldn't see. Fatigue crept into her bones, dulling her magical senses. The flames flickered and died, and she felt Medb's power receding as well.

No, she thought. *Come back! I need you!*

"Jayne!" cried a voice.

Tristan. The sound of his voice sent a bolt of clarity through her hazy mind. Her foot connected with someone's shin, and she kneed another in the thigh. Elbow to the gut. Punch to the throat. One by one, the attackers went down as Jayne cleared a path, desperate to get out. After years of training, she was a lethal machine, with or without magic.

An explosion of red light filled the air, and four men went down at once. Several yards away, Jayne saw Tristan standing shoulder to shoulder with Vivienne, wielding a tapestry of glowing red magic between his fingers.

"Jayne, now!" Vivienne shouted, her loud voice commanding as it pierced through the chaos.

Jayne focused her thoughts and energy on Vivienne and the Rogue magic flowing through her. Sluggish, but it was there, a thread between the two women. Master and Rogue. She closed her eyes. *Shift.*

An almighty roar echoed in the atrium, and Vivienne was now in lioness form, swiping her mighty claws and taking down three attackers at once.

But the foes kept coming, a relentless colony of fire ants that just wouldn't die. There were still at least fifty members of the Kingdom standing, and more kept pouring in. Panicked, Jayne gazed around, searching for allies. But they were outnumbered. Severely outnumbered. Dozens of their officers were either on assignment or otherwise detained. They were unprepared for an attack like this, in their own headquarters, one of the safest places in the world. They couldn't win.

And then a figure entered the room, her graying blond hair flowing, storm-cold gray eyes, the Water totem gleaming on her forehead.

Ruth Thorne.

She looked thinner and more skeletal, as if something was eating her from the inside. Her cheekbones jutted out against her skin, her face a contour of severe edges and sharpened fury. Shadows lined her eyes, and her skin was sallow and sickly.

Despite her emaciated appearance, power still rippled from her, making the air quiver.

A mixture of rage and fear burned in Jayne's blood, and she found herself drawing closer to Ruth, eager to end this fight once and for all.

Ruth's cold eyes assessed the throng, drifting over them almost lazily as if she were bored with the situation. When her gaze landed on Henry, something shifted.

Oh no, Jayne thought. Her heart seized in her chest as she followed Ruth's eyes to where Henry fought. They couldn't lose him. Ruger had been right, he should've gone somewhere safe. Ruth wanted Henry desperately. If she got him...

Henry grappled with an assailant, his wiry frame surprisingly strong against his opponent's brawn. With a deft move that made Jayne proud, Henry blocked a strike, then hooked his leg under the man's ankle, bringing him crashing down. As soon as the thug was on his back, Henry's eyes locked onto Ruth, and he froze, his whole body going taut with awareness.

Ruth moved forward with purpose, her eyes on Henry like a predator closing in on their prey. For the briefest of moments, his eyes flicked to Jayne. Something sparked in his gaze. Panic, resignation. He reached into his pocket and withdrew a small device that resembled a remote control.

Just as Jayne was wondering what the hell he was doing, Henry pushed a button on the device. The air around her completely halted. A searing, ringing noise filled her ears, and everything went eerily, deadly still. All sounds quieted. All figures froze like statues. Jayne's breath sounded loud in her ears, her heartbeat thundering in the open, silent space. It was as if someone had pressed the pause button on the fight. Ruth was still and unmoving. Across the room, Sofia was frozen, midstrike, against her opponent. Cillian, in wolf form, was suspended in the air, claws out as he lunged.

Jayne tried to move forward, to investigate and find out what was going on, but her own body was frozen, too. Or rather —not frozen, but sluggish. She could move her legs, but they felt ten times heavier than normal, like she was wearing a snowsuit weighed down with bricks. The ground felt like molasses, beads of sweat forming on her forehead as she struggled to move.

"Don't fight it," said a quiet voice.

Jayne jumped—or she would have if her body was responding normally. She was startled to find Henry suddenly next to her, that strange device still in his hands.

"Did you do this?" she asked, grateful to find she could still speak. At least that part of her hadn't been altered.

"It won't last long." Henry's voice was quick and urgent as he placed his fingers around Jayne's wrist.

As soon as he made contact with her skin, Jayne felt a disorienting *whoosh* sensation, the feeling of gravity pressing in on her, squeezing the air from her chest. She gasped, her inhale a shaky, rattling noise that sounded like the breath of life.

And then, she was moving. Henry guided her through the still-frozen atrium, dodging the stiff bodies and motionless forms of those around them. Her legs moved effortlessly. Whatever had been blocking her before was now lifted as she allowed Henry to guide her across the room.

"Dad," Jayne breathed, finding her voice at last. "What's going on? What did you do?"

"I froze time. But I need to reset it in about"—he checked his watch—"ten seconds."

Ten seconds? Jayne made a noise that was somewhere between a laugh and a choked gargle. She wanted to scream, to shout that he was crazy, but how could she deny this proof?

Did this mean everything he'd said was true? That he could manipulate time? That her *daughter* was trapped in the Torrent?

God, she couldn't think of all that right now. Her head was about to explode. She needed to focus on the here and now.

Henry positioned her directly in front of Tristan, who was a perfect marble statue, paused in the act of slamming a red spell into someone's face. His expression was a mask of determined fury, and he looked like a warrior from some epic painting that Jayne could stare at all day. Beside him, the lioness Vivienne stood on her hind legs, claws poised to strike.

"As soon as I reset it, you and your Rogue will portal out of here," Henry said in a rushed whisper.

Jayne's gaze snapped to his. "What? I'm not leaving."

"They are after *you*, Jayne."

"Exactly why I can't leave! I'm not abandoning my team. They need me."

"With you gone, the Kingdom will retreat. They'll be frantic, searching for where you've gone. Your team will be safe."

"You don't know that! Dad—"

"There's no time!" Henry shouted, his voice sharper than Jayne had ever heard it. "Do not fight me on this! Your handler would agree with me, and you know it."

Jayne clenched her teeth, determined to argue, but he was right. Ruger would insist Jayne get out before the enemy took her. And they nearly had—she thought of that swarm of people crowding her, smothering her, cutting her off from any escape.

"But Sofia," Jayne said, gesturing to her sister across the room. "And you... Dad, I can't just leave you both here! Not with her!" She gestured wildly toward Ruth. "They have Tiriosis, they can hurt you badly."

"We can take care of ourselves. Besides, I've locked onto your signature." He waved the small device still in his hand. "I can track you. When this is all over, I'll find you and we'll continue our work. I swear it, Jayne."

Henry's watch beeped, and he swore. "Time's up."

Before Jayne could react, everything slammed into her all at once. A roar of noise filled her ears—shouts, grunts, the clang of weapons, the explosion of spells... Green fog wafted in the air, circling around her. She barely remembered to hold her breath in time before she got another mouthful of it.

A bright red light burst in front of her, followed by an alarmed "Jayne!"

Tristan had just taken down his attacker and was staring at Jayne with wide, disbelieving eyes.

"Portal her out," Henry ordered. "Now. Take the Rogue, too. It isn't safe."

Tristan's thick brows furrowed as he glanced from Henry to Jayne. Somehow, he managed to duck as another thug came for him. Tristan landed a blow to the man's gut, knocking him down.

"He's right," came Vivienne's voice in Jayne's head. "I saw the way they zeroed in on you, Jayne. You are what they're after, and they won't stop."

Knots twisted in Jayne's chest. She glanced at Ruth, whose fierce gaze was now fixed on her. Her nostrils flared, and she moved with surprising speed toward Jayne, as if she knew her window of opportunity was closing.

"Jayne!" Henry said urgently.

Every instinct told her to fight, face Ruth, remain alongside her team. "I can't—"

A hand grabbed her wrist. She raised her free arm, prepared to strike, only to find Tristan in front of her. Conflict and anger warred on his face.

"Sorry, Jayne," he whispered.

He waved his fingers, and a shimmering gold portal appeared.

Jayne tugged, trying to free herself from his grasp. "Tristan, don't you dare—"

With a snarl, Vivienne leaped through the portal first. Jayne had just summoned her fiercest Attack spell, prepared to knock Tristan on his ass if she had to, but he had already shoved her in after Vivienne. A searing bright light filled Jayne's vision, and the portal sucked her away from the TCO headquarters.

CHAPTER
SIX
HOUDINI

S ofia felt the air shift, something brief and subtle that made her ears pop. She couldn't pinpoint what had happened, but as she gazed around the hectic battle, she realized Jayne had vanished.

Her heart jolted in her chest, and she whirled, her eyes scanning the area more thoroughly in case she had missed it. Perhaps Jayne had crouched down low or was blocked by a taller figure. But no...her sister was gone. Disappeared like Houdini.

"I sense it, too," Cillian said aloud. "Something is off."

"Something good...or something bad?" Sofia muttered, knowing Cillian's acute wolf hearing would pick up on her voice. Did this mean Jayne was safely hidden away...or that she had been captured?

But if she had been captured, why was the Kingdom still attacking?

Sofia's eyes locked on Ruth. Her mother's face contorted with fury, her gray eyes burning.

Muffled shouts rang out, and several thugs spun around in

confusion. One of them shouted, "Where is she?" and Sofia heaved a breath of relief.

So, Jayne had escaped. Sofia didn't know how, but this was good news. Her Houdini act had fooled everyone, including the Kingdom.

With the enemy distracted, Sofia aimed a strike in the chest of the one closest to her. She struck, blow after blow, her attack relentless as unencumbered magic flowed through her. The man tumbled and fell, unconscious, and she moved on to the next one.

Take as many down as we can, Sofia thought. *The more they leave behind, the weaker they'll be...and the more we can interrogate later.*

"Agreed," Cillian thought back with a growl.

Anger surged within her as she pushed onward, spelling with anything that came to her, using her body, too—ramming her fist into a skull, a throat, a gut... Her knee jerked upward, her foot slammed into a shin. She threw a Drop spell at a woman rushing toward her, tossing her backward. Cillian took her cue and pounced from one person to the next, claws swiping and fangs flashing.

Sofia didn't realize she was making her way toward Ruth until only a few yards separated them. The determination fueling her fight thrummed in her blood, urging her onward.

You won't defeat me today, Mother, Sofia thought, slamming an Attack spell straight into one man's chest, then slicing her hands through the air with a Cut spell Seo-Joon had taught her. A ribbon of blood blossomed on his shirt from Sofia's phantom cut. Blood dribbled down his chin as he collapsed.

In no time at all, Sofia faced her mother, their eyes boring into one another. Cillian's mossy scent tickled Sofia's nose, and she knew he stood alongside her, ready to fight with her.

Ruth raised her arm and shouted, "Retreat!"

Sofia froze. *Retreat?* What the hell was Ruth doing? "I never took you for a coward, Ruth!" she shouted.

Ruth's lip curled, baring her teeth. For a brief moment, utter blackness took over her eyes, and Sofia took a hesitant step backward.

But the moment passed, and Ruth's gray eyes returned. With one final sneer in Sofia's direction, she turned and followed her people toward the exit, a portal she'd created that wavered green and gold.

No, Sofia thought, enraged. *She won't get away that easily.* She bounded forward, prepared to tackle Ruth if she had to—but a hand fell on her shoulder.

It was Ruger. A long cut bled freely above his eyebrow, and the shoulder of his shirtsleeve had been scorched to a crisp. He shook his head slowly. "Don't, Sofia. We were losing that battle. We need them to retreat."

"And just let her leave?" Sofia hissed.

"Yes. For now. They came for Jayne." He scanned the room, and Sofia knew he'd already registered Jayne's strange disappearance. "Let's just hope our librarian was clever enough to find a hiding spot far, far away from here."

"Jayne isn't one to hide," Sofia said with a mixture of pride and fear. Hiding was Sofia's mantra. But Jayne? She liked to be in the thick of it, plunging headfirst into danger.

The thought was not a comfort. Especially right now when the Kingdom had almost overtaken them.

"She's smart," Ruger said. "She knows when she's outnumbered."

"Does she?" Sofia raised an eyebrow. Her greatest fear was losing Jayne, who was known for biting off more than she could chew. Past experience had shown that Jayne was capable and could handle herself in any situation, but what if there came a time when she couldn't? When the situation was too dire, and she lost the battle?

Sofia didn't want to think about that scenario.

Her adrenaline faded, and her body sagged from exhaustion. A haziness clouded her mind, and in a flash of white light, Cillian stood next to her in human form.

"Is it over, then?" he asked breathlessly, his Irish accent more pronounced than usual. His steely blue eyes surveyed the room, his fists clenched. Sofia knew he was still in attack mode.

Ruger spread his arms, conjuring a Locator spell. Sofia sensed his energy spreading through the room, creeping along the floor. He closed his eyes briefly, then grunted something unintelligible. He dropped his arms. "It's over. The last of them have left the premises." His eyes opened, and he looked to Sofia. "You and Cillian find the injured and triage them as best you can. Medics will be here shortly. I'll track down Amanda and re-establish our wards. We've got a hell of a mess to clean up."

SEVEN

YOU CAN'T HANDLE THE TRUTH

J ayne fell face-first onto a tan rug as coarse as sandpaper. A bland mocha sofa stood next to her. Spitting carpet fibers from her mouth, she jumped to her feet. She stood in a small living room with minimal furnishings. It looked like a cheap and dirty hotel room, drab furniture and barely any decor.

She reached for the Torrent, intent on summoning a portal to get back to the TCO, back to her friends, her family...

A hand closed on her wrist. "No you don't."

Seething, Jayne looked up to find Tristan, his hands on hers. His long hair was disheveled, and a bloody cut ran along his jaw. Perspiration coated his face and neck, but he had a calm, level look that Jayne knew all too well.

"Let me go," Jayne growled. "Or I'll have you flat on your back."

Tristan arched an eyebrow. "Kinky."

The heat in his eyes threatened to scorch her entirely, but she clung to her fury, determined to hold her own. If it came to a fight with Tristan, she knew she could win. She'd done it before. She wrenched her hand from his and drew back, one foot behind the other, taking up a fighting stance.

"*Beurk!* You two are insufferable." Vivienne stepped into the room, equally as disheveled as Tristan, but she somehow carried herself like a queen. "Jayne, if you try anything stupid, you'll regret it. We aren't letting you go back."

"They need me!" Jayne protested. "Our people are under attack, and you expect me to just sit here and hide? Where the hell even are we?"

"A safe house in Takoma Park, Maryland," Tristan said. "One of the more...unassuming ones. We usually save it for undercover operations. I've stayed here before. We will be comfortable enough."

"I don't care about comfort. We have to go back. We need to help."

Vivienne drew closer, her brown eyes fiery. "Jayne, I want to go back and fight as much as you do. But they were after *you*. And they almost had you. Even a Master isn't invincible. The Tiriosis in the gas was impossible to avoid for much longer."

"And if our team gets slaughtered because we didn't stay to help?" Jayne challenged. "How can you have that on your conscience?"

"That's war," Tristan snapped. "You have to make tough decisions. You want to talk about horrifying hypotheticals? Here's one: The Kingdom captures you. Ruth Thorne finds a way to extract the *two totems* you possess, and she wipes out the entire TCO, including your friends. Your sister. Your father. What happens then? How would *your* conscience fare, knowing you could have done the smart thing and fled when you had the chance?"

"Bastard." Jayne surged toward him, her fingers curling into a tight fist.

Vivienne snagged her arm, preventing her from slugging Tristan in the face. "Easy now. He's only making the same point you were." She shot a sharp look at her brother. "Albeit in a callous manner."

"She doesn't need to be coddled." Tristan crossed his arms over his chest. "She needs the truth."

"And what *is* the truth, pray tell?" Jayne snarled.

"The truth is, you are a valuable asset. You aren't just an officer on our team anymore. Priorities are different around you, and you need to understand that. You are a capable fighter, yes, but you are not without weakness. We know that, and the Kingdom knows that. But do you? Do you understand that you can still be killed? Injured? Captured? You have two totems, and if the TCO loses you or your power, we're screwed. We value you as a fighter and a friend, yes, but it's more than that now. Be smart about this, Jayne. You remember your training. What do we do when an asset is at risk?"

Jayne gritted her teeth. "Protect the asset at all costs." The training had indeed been ingrained in her. But in those scenarios, an asset was a high-ranking government official with valuable information, someone who needed protection because they were unable to defend themselves.

That wasn't Jayne.

You are not without weakness. The words circled through Jayne's brain, making her feel tired and angry all at once. She envisioned the crowd of Kingdom operatives, the never-ending horde that enclosed her. The enemies kept coming. They surrounded her, cutting her off, smothering her...

Jayne jerked her arm free of Vivienne's grasp, closing her eyes with a groan. "I can't just do nothing." Her voice broke, betraying her weakness. The weakness Tristan had so bluntly reminded her of.

Vivienne seemed to sense Jayne was no longer a flight risk. She plopped down on the sofa and propped her legs on the coffee table with a heavy sigh. "We won't be doing nothing. We'll be training and plotting. I don't know you very well, but I do know you despise being helpless. Well, we aren't. We have skills to develop and knowledge to sift through. We can make a plan of attack."

Jayne's ears perked up at that. She sat next to Vivienne, eager to cling to any semblance of purpose, of strategy, to keep her afloat. Anything to prevent her from envisioning her sister and father's brutal deaths because of her absence.

"Vivienne is right." Tristan sat down in the armchair on the other side of the room, which looked rock-hard and deeply uncomfortable, its crimson cushions stiff as boards. "What did this attack tell us?"

"They've grown in numbers," Jayne said.

"Have they?"

Jayne frowned at the shrewd look in Tristan's eyes. She thought back to when the Kingdom had been flooding into the atrium, their numbers massive. And yet...

She sat up straighter. "Oh. They weren't all Adepts. Some of them used normal human weapons." She'd thought that was odd, but at the time, she hadn't truly considered it.

"Hired thugs, perhaps?" Vivienne speculated.

"It tells us they're desperate," Jayne said. "*She's* desperate."

"Desperate to get to you," Tristan said, leveling a hard look at her. "To get to your totems."

"Something *has* changed." Jayne rubbed her chin thoughtfully. "Something to move up her timeline. She was never this bold, this reckless before. Hiring those extra bodies must have been a huge expense for her."

"She did not look well," Vivienne muttered. "She seemed to be at death's door."

"Because of the Wraith," Tristan said darkly.

Jayne nodded, her hand absently rising to the spot on her forearm where her shirt sleeve hid the dark leathery patch of skin. *At death's door.* She thought of Ruth's new alter ego—the Wraith, a dreadful gargoyle-esque creature she could shift into.

The indestructible winged body that couldn't be pierced by magic.

The thing Jayne would turn into if she wasn't more careful with her own magic.

So why hadn't Ruth broken out that party trick?

"Ruth has bonded herself to a powerful Master magician living within the Torrent," Jayne said, her shoulders relaxing. "She's nothing more than a puppet now. We need to know who is pulling the strings. And why."

"I may know something about that," Vivienne said, dropping her legs from the coffee table to sit forward, bracing her arms on her knees. "From Vesta."

"Ah, yes, good old Vesta, the fire goddess who mentored you," Jayne said. "No big deal."

Tristan's mouth twitched, but Vivienne shot Jayne a murderous look. Jayne raised her palms in surrender. "Ooookay. Not a fan of Vesta jokes."

"Vesta has been bound by a powerful magic that prevents her from sharing certain truths with anyone," Vivienne said. "But I was with her for years. I was able to pick up on bits and pieces."

"'Sharing certain truths'?" Jayne repeated. "Like about the Master living in the Torrent? She was able to share that with me." She recalled Vesta's words: *The creature who roams free is powerful enough to destroy gods and goddesses like myself. It's how I was injured in the first place. Be wary, Jayne Thorne, for this creature is no match for you. This Master has lived in the Torrent for a very long time, trapped by my own people many years ago. But it has since been unleashed, and its demonic essence only grows. Now that it is tethered to this world, no one is safe. Not you. Not even me.*

"Yes, but she cannot speak his name," Vivienne said. "None of the gods or goddesses can. They cannot direct us to where he can be reached or detail the history behind his entrapment."

Tristan rose to his feet and snatched a notepad and pen

from the desk against the wall before returning, perched on the edge of the seat. "What do you know?"

"These necromantic grimoires we've been searching for," Vivienne said, "they are all linked to a god or goddess who helped bring down the Master."

"So, Medb and the Master of Shadows...," Jayne said slowly.

"They betrayed him, yes. Just like Vesta."

Tristan was scribbling furiously on the notepad. "He punished them by binding them to grimoires," he muttered.

"Yes. And I believe I know where the next book might be. But unfortunately, I believe he knows, too. As do his servants."

Ice crept into Jayne's chest. "Ruth."

Vivienne nodded solemnly.

"Then, we must get to it first," Tristan said. "Where is it?"

"Vesta was unable to explicitly tell me where it was located, but I could tell where her power was often directed. These gods and goddesses can communicate to one another through dreams."

Jayne's mouth turned dry. "And with me, too. I've been visited by them through dreams multiple times now."

Vivienne arched an eyebrow, and she looked so much like Tristan with that expression that Jayne almost laughed. "That might be helpful. Can you control it?"

"No. I can try, though." She thought of the crazy-ass dream she'd had with the goddess trapped inside the firestorm. Ruth had been there, too—because she also had a totem, and God knows what kind of power because of her Wraith.

"Vesta was often in communication with a powerful presence living in Zagreb, Croatia," Vivienne said. "Based on *Maman*'s extensive research and some digging of my own, I was able to link it to the Liber Linteus."

"The Liber Linteus?" Jayne asked, her brain snagging on something she'd encountered in her own research. At Tristan's blank look, she said, "The ancient Etruscans wrote a sacred book of rituals, possibly a calendar of sorts, on linen strips, and it ended up being used in a mummification for Nesi-hensu, the wife of a tailor. It's one of those fun historical controversies: whether it was part of an Etruscan burial custom, or if the people doing the burial just grabbed the closest pieces of linen and they had no idea it was a priceless piece of history." She looked at Vivienne, eyes wide. "Are you telling me those linen strips—the stuff that bound the mummy—is a necromantic grimoire?"

Both Vivienne's eyebrows lifted, her dark eyes alight. Jayne could tell she was impressed, and she tried not to feel too satisfied. "Yes. But, unfortunately, there was a terrible earthquake in the region a few years ago. The exhibit is still closed, and I'm not sure the grimoire is even in the Archaeological Museum in Zagreb anymore, though I suppose it will be easy enough to discover its whereabouts."

"Then we need to contact the museum immediately. Surely they'll give us access if we explain it's a matter of life or death."

"We can contact them, yes. But there's no guarantee they will work with us. We must move quickly."

"Well, let's do that," Jayne said. "And if they won't cooperate, then we'll steal the damn thing."

Tristan spit out a laugh, and Jayne's temper flared again.

"Don't mock me, Lowell. I'll make you regret it."

"Not mocking, m'lady. Simply amused by your dive to the dark side."

Jayne cast an entreating look toward Vivienne, but the woman was already walking toward her room, a phone in her hand. Fine. She squared off with Tristan, trying, and failing, to ignore the fact that he was bloodied and battered from the fight. That he'd gotten hurt saving her. That she wanted to crawl into his arms and weep.

"Let me make this clear. I will do anything necessary to save my family and my loved ones. Anything. And if you get in my way again, or portal me out of a fight, or put one toe out of line, I will walk away from this partnership, and do this myself. Am I clear?"

"A simple thank-you would have sufficed," Tristan said.

"Am. I. Clear?"

"Yes, Jayne. Crystal." And without a second glance, he stalked away after his sister.

EIGHT

A FALSE TRAIL

The TCO had lost ten officers in the Kingdom's attack. Fourteen were injured, three of them in critical condition.

Between re-establishing the wards—and reinforcing them —tending to the injured, accounting for anything missing or damaged, and sweeping the place for bugs and lingering magical essence, Amanda had her hands full.

> Mother needs eggs, but we can't afford them.

> Doc has no eggs at the moment. If Mother purchases some, this would be a good time for a visit.

The messages had cycled through Amanda's head nonstop since the attack on the TCO. They were related; she was sure of it.

Which meant Pierce was in communication with the Kingdom.

Mother could easily mean Ruth. And with so many of their tactical teams out on assignment right when the Kingdom attacked, Amanda could infer that *eggs* meant manpower or soldiers.

Mother needs eggs, but we can't afford them. Mercenaries, perhaps? The flood of attackers in the atrium *had* seemed like far too many, based on the intel they had on the Kingdom's organization and growth.

This was an utter disaster. If Amanda had been able to decode this sooner, maybe she could have prevented the attack from happening.

But the logical side of her couldn't deny this was the perfect opportunity to feed Pierce false intel. She had to be smart, though. If she started too big, Pierce would know right away that she was on to him.

So after twenty-seven straight hours of cleanup, when Amanda finally sat down at her desk to start the mountain of paperwork that was waiting for her, she pulled on the Torrent. Her Ink spell awaited her, something she had crafted years ago to assist with forgeries. With delicate precision, she altered pieces of data on the documents, changing coordinates, rewriting addresses, and erasing the names of the officers who had perished. The words on the pages shifted and twisted, moving in sync with the motions of her fingers as they followed the spell.

Once she was finished, she looked over her work. If Pierce fed this information to the Kingdom, they would believe the TCO's sample of Tiriosis, the deadly magical poison, had been stolen, and that only eight officers instead of ten had died. Amanda had also altered the coordinates of their closest safe houses, just in case that was where Jayne was hiding.

"Let's see what you do with this," she said under her breath, stacking the papers together. A knock sounded at her door. "Come in."

Ruger ducked through the doorway, looking just as haggard

as Amanda felt. "The building is secure. Thorne says he has a location on Jayne. We can portal there, with your permission."

Amanda shook her head. "Not yet. The Kingdom has proven they have tricks up their sleeves. Wait until our research team sweeps over Thorne's tech before we trust it. We can't risk the Kingdom using some untraceable tracking device or spell that we can't yet detect."

Ruger inclined his head. His dark eyes shifted slightly. "Amanda, I have to ask... Do you think our mole was behind this attack? Because if so—"

"I don't know," Amanda said in a clipped voice. "It's likely that's how they got in."

"Then we need to arrest the traitor. We lost people today. We can't play his game any longer."

Amanda shot to her feet, her blood roaring. "Are you implying this attack was my fault?"

"Not at all. But it might have been prevented."

Amanda's chest swelled with indignation. His words stung more than he could know because she'd been thinking the same thing. *I could have prevented this.*

She shoved away the thoughts. They weren't helpful. And they were illogical. "By the time I found out who the mole was, this attack plan was already in place. I understand we sustained losses, but this is *war*. There will be casualties. At any rate, this provides us with an opportunity to feed false intel and see where the trail leads."

Ruger's gaze was a dark storm, but he said nothing. The tension in his jaw indicated he still disagreed with Amanda's decision to keep Pierce's identity as the mole under wraps.

With a sigh, Amanda scribbled a few notes on a sheet of paper and handed it to Ruger. "This is the false information I'm leaking. Follow it. See where it leads or if the Kingdom acts on it."

Ruger nodded stiffly, taking the paper from her. "And what about Sofia and Cillian?"

"We need to send units to all the Guardians. It's no longer safe for our allies to be isolated like this. Time to prepare for battle."

Ruger's brow furrowed. "But their pockets...the Torrent will be vulnerable."

"I know. But the secret of the Guardians is out now. There is no turning back. It's dangerous to have other Adepts around such a volatile pocket of energy, but we have to risk it. This was always a possibility. It's time to go on the offensive. Sooner or later, the Kingdom or Hans Kaufmann—or both together, Goddess help us—will seek out those pockets, one by one. The Guardians are no longer safe protecting that magic all on their own." Her hand went to the necklace at her throat, the powerful trinket her husband, Karam, had given to her. It possessed a modicum of Guardian magic, and it allowed Amanda to channel it like he had. The metal felt warm against her palm. "Have Sofia make contact with Xiomara and anyone else who pledged loyalty to us."

He nodded again, then turned to leave.

"Ruger?"

He paused without glancing back, his hand on the door handle.

"You used to trust me." Amanda's voice was gentle. "I need that trust again."

Something clouded over his expression. "Trust is earned. You've been keeping secrets from me, and I can't let that go. Not overnight."

"I'm your superior. There will always be things I can't disclose to you."

"No, not state secrets." Ruger turned to face her, his expression tormented. "Personal secrets. Secrets that, as your friend, I deserved to know. There is nothing I have kept from you."

Amanda's chest tightened at his words, a fresh wave of pain and guilt spilling through her. Goddess, he was right. Amanda knew all of Ruger's darkest secrets. Yet she hadn't told him about her daughter or the Guardian magic lingering inside her before it had leaked out in Patagonia. He was upset, and rightly so. She'd told herself it was for his protection, but that wasn't completely true. She knew firsthand that Ruger would take his secrets to his grave; he had proven that time and time again.

No, Amanda had kept these secrets to protect herself and her heart. To keep that pain buried deep.

She took a shuddering breath, her eyes growing hot. All she could manage to whisper was "I'm sorry. I should have told you sooner. You must understand, Ruger, it was something I never thought I'd have to reveal, to anyone. Not even you."

Ruger's expression closed off. Without another word, he opened the door and left the room.

NINE

THE WEIGHT OF THE WORLD

Sofia sank onto the bunk in one of the TCO's spare rooms. She'd been ordered not to portal to her apartment just in case the magical doorways were still compromised. Regardless, she couldn't bring herself to leave. Not after what had happened. The clash of weapons and spells still echoed in her mind. The faces of the dead. The feral, tormented look on her mother's face.

With a groan, Sofia rubbed her eyes. She was so damned exhausted, but her mind was spinning. She couldn't possibly sleep. All she could think about was Jayne. She couldn't bear to be away from her, not knowing if she was safe. For years, it had been the two of them against the world. Sofia had always protected her little sister, always made sure she was safe. Not knowing where she was at all times was like a festering wound that wouldn't heal, constantly throbbing and pulsing.

She went to the mini-fridge, which had been stocked with sodas and snacks, and grabbed a turkey rollup and an apple. She needed to talk to the team responsible for catering—they'd been eating like fifth graders, and she was in dire need of some proper food. Maybe a salad. After several bites, she felt less drained, but her emotions still weighed heavily on her. She turned on the small TV positioned on the far side of the room, hoping to distract herself with something trivial. Instead, she found herself staring, horrified, at the news report.

New York family exhibits massive wave of supernatural energy. Civilians not safe, asked to evacuate immediately.

Sofia's blood ran cold as she listened to the news anchor relay the story of how a small child being punished had set fire to a school—without any sort of starter. Thankfully, no one had died, but the incident left the community in a panic. Confusion about how the fire started was compounded by claims from the other students that she'd done it with only her mind. When the child's parents exhibited similar paranormal tendencies trying to protect their young daughter, school authorities called for their arrest, for the safety of the public. The family ran and were still at large, but their photos were being plastered all over the news and social media. They would be found, sooner or later.

"Amanda says it will only get worse."

Sofia jumped, dropping the remote with a loud clatter. She found Cillian standing in the doorway, his gaze solemn, his hands shoved into his pockets.

"What will?" Sofia asked.

"These incidents. With the Torrent opened up again, magic manifests itself more violently every day. It's unstoppable. And it's emerging from people who we assumed were nonmagical. These poor, ordinary humans are finding themselves overwhelmed by powers they didn't know they had. I can empathize. When I turned the first time, I thought I was going mad. They must, too."

Sofia blinked tears from her eyes as she gestured to the television. "She's just a small child! This isn't some adult we're talking about, someone who knows how to lie low and protect themselves. She's practically a baby."

Cillian stepped into the room, his face drawn and marred by

fatigue. He looked terrible. Then again, everyone did. No one had slept since the battle.

But he also looked older. There was something ancient in his eyes, something weathered and haunted. He was no longer the happy-go-lucky kickboxer Sofia had first met.

"I keep thinking of those Guardian kids," Cillian said softly. "How lost and confused they felt. So fragile. It just...it takes me back to when—to when—" His voice broke, and he shook his head.

He didn't need to finish. Sofia knew Cillian had had a rough childhood, often beaten by his drunk of a father. Cillian hated being helpless. He was a lot like Jayne in that sense.

Jayne. Thinking of these helpless Adept children only brought Sofia back to that horrifying memory all those years ago when Ruth had almost succeeded in siphoning Jayne's powers. Jayne had been a defenseless child. The very woman who should have protected her from danger was attacking her.

Luckily, Jayne had Sofia. But these new Adept children? Did they have anyone to protect them?

"I wish we could do something," Sofia said, wiping tears from her face. It was all too much—the battle, Jayne's disappearance, the friends who had died, and now this, the knowledge that children and families were out there suffering simply because they didn't know how to wield their magic safely.

Cillian closed the distance between them. He took Sofia's fingers in his, his large hand dwarfing hers. With his other hand, he caught a tear before it trickled down her cheek. His calloused finger brushed against her skin, and a shiver rippled over her.

"I know," he whispered. "I know." His blue eyes were weighed down with grief and anguish, his face so broken that Sofia couldn't help herself. She stepped closer and drew his body against hers in a tight embrace as if she could squeeze the sorrow right out of him. His arms circled around her, and for a moment, she focused on his heartbeat against hers, the steady sound of his breathing, the familiar and comforting scent of him filling her nose...

"You didn't say anything about a Wraith."

The loud voice pierced through the hazy comfort of Cillian's arms around her. With a jolt, they jerked apart, and Sofia found her father standing in the doorway, his eyes blazing.

Without waiting for a response, Henry stormed into the room. "You never said anything about Ruth becoming a Wraith."

Sofia blinked, her mind taking a moment to catch up. "I— we weren't allowed to. Besides, we only recently found out."

"This changes everything." Henry ran his hands through his hair, giving him that familiar mad scientist look.

"How?" Cillian asked. "We knew she was into some manky shite."

"Yes, but this is different. If she is connected to the Master living in the Torrent, if she's been possessed by this evil, then... then..." Henry shook his head and began to pace the length of the room, dodging the two cots.

"How did you find out?" Sofia asked.

"I saw her. My Tracer picked up on Torrent residue that matches what I've been researching all this time. She's covered in it. She has been dabbling in dark magic for decades now, and she's never looked like that. This is different." Henry raised his hand to his mouth, chewing on his fingernails as he continued to pace. "If we can apprehend Ruth, if I can run tests on her blood, on skin samples, I can cross-reference them to my own findings and—"

"Hold on." Cillian raised his palms. "Apprehend Ruth? Run tests on her? It's impossible to capture her because of the power she has. I hate to tell you this, but I don't think that's going to happen."

"You don't understand!" Henry waved his hands in frustration. "With those samples, we can discover the Master's location within the Torrent. We can find him and anyone he's captured, and free them. Then we can end him once and for all."

"Would it stop magic from turning on in all these poor people who have no idea how to handle it?" Sofia asked. "Will it help those who don't have tolerance and understanding find it for those who do?"

"I don't know," Henry said grimly, "but if we don't try, he could use all of the new Adepts to fight for him. Ruth knows how to make her power look very seductive to newcomers. It's how she built the Kingdom in the first place. With the Master's help, she could turn them all against us."

CHAPTER

TEN

MIDNIGHT ENCOUNTERS

A firestorm surrounded Jayne. Lightning flashed, illuminating the blazing inferno around her. The wind whipped at her hair and clothes, bringing with it the stench of burning flesh.

Her mind was foggy with disorientation and fear. She tried sifting through the panicked thoughts circulating within, but it was like she was only half-conscious.

Perhaps she was.

"I'm dreaming," Jayne said. Her voice echoed in the vast space. The realization sent a bolt of clarity through the muddled confusion of her brain. "I'm dreaming," she said again, and the fog of her thoughts completely dissipated. She tucked her windswept hair behind her ears and squinted at the burning flames before her.

The fire swirled, forming a massive tornado of amber lightning. She stood atop a cliff overlooking it all.

She remembered this place. She'd been here before when Vesta had been trying to speak to her.

Ruth had been here, too.

Sudden alarm shot through her as she whirled, expecting to

find her mother's cruel sneer and cold eyes. But Jayne was alone, a solitary figure on the bluff.

"Why am I here?" Jayne asked. She remembered Tristan asking if she could control her dreamscapes, to try to communicate with the other gods and goddesses. "Vesta? Medb? You there?"

No one answered.

Well, of course, it wouldn't be that easy.

Jayne took a breath and focused her energy on the totems within her. She closed her eyes, summoning that raw, ancient power. Her forehead prickled with awareness.

The air shifted, growing heavy with the presence of something otherworldly and powerful. Jayne opened her eyes, expecting to see Medb or Vesta...instead, she faced a woman she had never seen before. Her flaming orange hair was framed by the fiery storm behind her. Her amber eyes flashed with the burning intensity of a thousand suns. She wore a bronze helmet and matching armor. In her hand was a long, sharpened spear.

Jayne took an uncertain step backward. "Um. Hi."

"I have a prophecy for you, Jayne Thorne." The woman's voice rang like a massive bell, piercing through the roar of the storm behind her.

Apprehension rippled over Jayne, making her insides coil with dread. A fearsome warrior goddess who looked ready for battle had come to deliver a prophecy? Jayne didn't particularly like the sound of that... Why couldn't a prophecy have come from someone delicate and angelic, someone who *didn't* look like they were going to bring about the apocalypse?

Jayne squared her shoulders. "Okay. I'm ready. Lay it on me."

The woman's harsh expression didn't change. "I am bound by his chains. You must free me for the prophecy to be revealed."

61

Jayne suppressed a sigh of frustration. "All right. Where are you? How do I free you?"

"My secrets are kept in the tombs of the dead. But be wary, Jayne Thorne. He knows you draw closer. And he will fight to keep you from discovering the truth."

"He who? *What* truth?" Jayne recalled what Vivienne had said about Vesta being bound by some spell, unable to reveal secrets. But she was getting really tired of having to sift through all this vague nonsense.

The air shifted once more, and Jayne's vision blurred. The warrior goddess flickered in and out of view.

"No!" Jayne shouted, but her voice pierced through the dreamscape like a blade cutting through fabric. The firestorm dissolved, and she bolted upright, her hair clinging to her sweaty face and darkness pressing in on her. Her breaths came in short gasps as she assessed her surroundings.

She was in one of the safe house's dingy bedrooms, sitting atop a lumpy mattress. The blackness outside the window indicated it was probably the middle of the night.

Still unable to catch her breath, Jayne tied her hair back into a messy ponytail and covered her face with her hands, struggling to calm her racing heart. The dream had been so vivid. It had never been like that before—so crisp and *alive.*

And who was that warrior woman? Jayne had been expecting to meet one of the goddesses she'd already bonded to, but perhaps these dreams were a way for the *other* deities to reach her. She already had a direct link to Medb and Vesta.

This new goddess said she was waiting for Jayne to free her. *My secrets are kept in the tombs of the dead.*

Vivienne had been right—the grimoire had to be the Liber Linteus, the strips of fabric surrounding a mummy. Unless this was an Egyptian goddess and they needed to go scope out the pyramids...

Jayne took a few steadying breaths and reached for her copy

of *Dune* on the night table, hoping that diving into the desert planet of Arrakis would take her mind off things. But after rereading the same sentence seven times, and still only seeing the firestorm from her dream, she knew her efforts were useless.

She ripped off the blankets and climbed out of bed, still a bit dizzy from the intensity of her vision. She pulled on a pair of yoga pants and wrapped a sweater around her shoulders. Though she was covered in sweat, her skin was chilled to the bone. She shivered as she emerged from the bedroom, hoping no one else was awake. She needed to be alone with her thoughts and her research, free to sort through the raging chaos of her mind in peace.

No such luck. In the living room, she found Tristan sitting on the sofa and working on his laptop, dressed in nothing but a pair of shorts that clung low to his hips.

Jayne froze in her tracks, caught off guard not only by the sexy, disheveled look of his hair but also by the sculpted muscles of his chest on full display. Heat roiled inside her, and she found herself scowling.

Tristan glanced up, then smiled. "Do you frown in your sleep, *mon amour?*"

My love. A ripple of pleasure washed over her at the sound of the words, but she quashed the sensation. *Damn it, Jayne, get ahold of yourself.*

"When sleeping involves nightmarish visions of warrior goddesses, then yes." She tried to keep the bite out of her voice, but it didn't work.

"You had a vision?" Tristan sobered immediately, sliding the laptop onto the coffee table. "Tell me."

Jayne wanted to argue, but with the laptop no longer blocking his abs from view, she was a bit distracted. Gritting her teeth, she stepped farther into the room, making her way to the kitchen. Thank God this house had been stocked with food.

Once she had grabbed an apple and a slice of fresh peach pie, she sat down on a bar stool at the counter and told Tristan about the dream in between bites.

Tristan was silent for a few moments. He scratched at his chin, his eyes contemplative. "I'm not sure who this could be. But I could wake Vivienne. Perhaps she knows." He started to rise from the sofa, but Jayne stopped him.

"No, don't."

Tristan paused, arching an eyebrow. "Why not?"

Jayne's face burned from the look he was giving her. His eyes seemed to say, *You want to be alone with me, don't you?* But she felt the opposite. She was afraid of being alone with him, but if he rose from the sofa, he would have to come closer to her. And she didn't trust herself when he was near.

Swallowing hard, Jayne slid off the stool and said, "I really don't want to dive into anything tonight. I just needed a minute to gather my thoughts and grab a snack. Since you've already set up your own midnight research station here, I'll just go back to bed."

She headed toward her bedroom, but the softness of his voice halted her.

"Jayne."

His smooth voice was like a warm caress. Jayne found herself closing her eyes just to relish it, to savor the sensation. She sensed movement behind her, and she turned to find him approaching her slowly as if worried she might bolt like a startled deer.

Fighting to keep her voice level, Jayne asked as innocently as possible, "What?"

He faced her fully now, only a few feet separating them. Jayne kept her eyes on his, though she was painfully aware of the rise and fall of his bare chest. If she took one step, their chests would be flush against each other, and her blood boiled at the thought.

"Did I do something to upset you?" Tristan asked.

Jayne hadn't expected that. "I'm sorry?"

"Are you angry with me? You just seem so much more hostile around me as of late."

As of late. Meaning *since we kissed.*

Shame swept over her, momentarily cooling the heat scorching her veins. Damn. She *had* been a bit of a bitch to him lately. Deflating slightly, she said, "No. I'm not angry with you."

Tristan spread his hands. "Then I'm at a loss. One moment, we're sharing this passionate kiss—which was one of the most intoxicating moments of my life—and the next, you're treating me like that guy you hate but you're forced to work with. Again. You're giving me whiplash, *mon amour.*"

One of the most intoxicating moments of my life. God, did he really mean that? Shaking her head, Jayne muttered, "No. I mean, yes, you're right. I'm sorry. I don't know how to process how I feel when I'm around you. It's maddening."

Tristan offered that lopsided grin she loved and hated so much. "I'm maddening?"

"Very."

He inched closer to her. Jayne could feel the heat emanating from his chest, seeking out hers. "But you do feel something when you're around me."

"Maybe." Jayne's breathing turned ragged.

"Then what is there to process? We are attracted to one another. That much is clear."

"Yes." Jayne felt like she should argue another point, but all coherent thought had left her as Tristan's chest brushed against hers. His vanilla-and-soap scent washed over her, crisp and inviting.

You're a damn Master, Jayne Thorne, she told herself. *You will not be cowed by this gorgeous, shirtless Frenchman!*

Her thoughts broke through her lustful daydreams of being wrapped in his arms and tangled with his body. She took a sharp breath and drew back a step. "Yes, but I still don't like you."

Tristan's brow furrowed. "Your actions say otherwise."

"I'm attracted to you, yes. But as a person, I don't like you. I don't like the things you've done. And I swore to myself I wouldn't get involved with a colleague again. Things got messy with Cillian, and that's the last thing we need right now."

Hurt and frustration flashed in his gaze. "So, what? You'll just shove aside these feelings like they don't matter? Keep pretending you despise me?"

"It's not *all* pretend," Jayne mumbled.

"Why are you so determined to hide from the truth?" He stepped forward, his fingertips brushing against her, trailing a path of fire as he dragged them up and down the length of her arms. Though Jayne still wore her sweater, the touch felt as intimate as if she stood naked before him. "You were fated to bond with my sister. Which means you were fated to be involved with me, as well."

He leaned in, his lips brushing her ear as he whispered, "Why deny yourself what you truly want? Why are you punishing yourself?"

His breath tickled her skin, sending a jolt of electricity through her. Her skin was suddenly on fire, and she wished she could take off her sweater—and all the rest of her clothes, too.

"You flatter yourself," Jayne said, her voice coming out a bit breathless. "How do you know what I truly want?"

Tristan's hand lifted to her face. His thumb traced the line of her jaw. His long fingers cupped her face, drawing her closer. "I can feel your desire in your magic, *mon amour*."

God, those words. That damned French accent. It turned Jayne's insides into a puddle.

For just a moment, she allowed herself to dream. To envision what it would be like to close that small distance, to bring his mouth to hers, to taste his tongue. To feel his body pressed against hers in all the right ways.

Heat pooled between her legs, and she gasped, startled by the intensity of her imagination. She wanted him. She wanted him desperately.

Her mouth opened to argue with him, but as her lips parted, he angled his face, his mouth lining up perfectly with hers. She could taste his breath. Feel his heat. All thoughts of arguing fled her mind, leaving an emptiness in its wake. She could hardly remember her own name.

One of his lips brushed hers, soft and smooth and delicious. It unraveled her completely. A low, soft moan rose up her throat as her restraint snapped.

To hell with it.

She wrapped her arms around him, her fingers tangling in his beautiful hair. Just before their mouths collided, a door opened, echoing in the living room.

Jayne's whole body lurched as she jerked away from Tristan. On the other side of the room, Vivienne stood with her hands on her hips, her hair a wild mane of brown curls. She wore a tank top and shorts, her face still marred by lines of sleep and exhaustion. Despite her disheveled appearance, her eyes were blazing.

"*Beurk!* What the hell is the matter with you two? You can't go one night without boning?"

Embarrassment mingled with indignation as Jayne felt her face grow hot. "We were not—"

"What do you want, Vivienne?" Tristan asked in a tired voice, running a hand through his hair. Jayne couldn't help but remember how that hair had felt between her own fingers just moments ago.

"I want to go back to sleep!" Vivienne protested, waving one hand toward them. "But the lust between you two woke me up!"

Cold dread seeped into Jayne's bones. "Our *what* woke you up?"

Vivienne let her hand drop. "The Rogue bond, Jayne. I can feel everything. Hear everything. See everything."

Everything. Oh, God, no... Jayne wanted to bury her face in her hands. She hadn't even wanted this moment with Tristan. Now it was being broadcast to his sister as well? This was like a nightmare come to life.

Move past it, Jayne. Take control of the situation. She squared her shoulders and took a long step away from Tristan. "Okay. Well. This is utterly mortifying. So...I will figure that out in the morning. Since you're both up, we might as well get to work. I had a vision, Vivienne, and maybe you can help me decipher it."

Vivienne's face slackened in surprise as she glanced from Tristan to Jayne. "I, uh... Well. All right then." She took a seat. "Let's discuss it."

ELEVEN

ANSWERS

Like she had every week since Patagonia, Amanda stopped by her apartment to drop off her computer and then headed in a zigzag direction toward the suburbs of McLean. She took a cab across the Key Bridge to the Georgetown University campus, then an Uber to Falls Church, then another cab to the gas station at the intersection of Spring Hill and Old Dominion, from which she made the rest of her journey on foot.

Convinced no one had tailed her, Amanda inserted her key into the redbrick safe house on Northwoods Trail and walked inside.

"Hummingbird," she announced at once.

Peters emerged from the kitchen, his graying brown hair stark against his pale skin. Each time, Amanda marveled at how much older he looked from the hardened soldier she'd known in her early days of the CIA, back when they roamed London looking for Adepts to recruit.

"Any trouble?" Peters was always no-nonsense. Straight to business. It was what Amanda liked best about him.

"No." Amanda set her bag down on the coffee table. "But this will be my last visit for a while. With the mole still in play, it's too risky." Technically, she shouldn't have even risked it tonight.

But she couldn't stay away. She had to explain, once and for all. She couldn't let the truth fester inside her any longer.

"How's Betty?" Amanda asked.

Peters adjusted his horn-rimmed glasses and sighed. "No change. She's resting now."

Peters's wife had been ill for a long time, and now her health was declining even more. Betty was a beautiful soul, and Amanda couldn't imagine what Peters was going through.

Nor Rebecca. She was losing the only mother she'd ever known, and to top it off, had just discovered her birth mother was actually alive, the leader of a magical branch of the CIA, and that her father, who'd given her Guardian blood, had sacrificed himself protecting the pocket in New Delhi before she was born...it was a bit much for a child to take in.

"I'll pop in to check on her," Amanda said. "See if there's anything that can be done."

Peters offered a sad smile that told Amanda he saw right through her attempt. "There's nothing to be done. But thank you. We've made our peace with this."

"And Rebecca? Has she made her peace with it?"

Peters's lips formed a thin line, a wrinkle developing between his thick brows.

Of course not. Rebecca was a child, and from what Amanda had seen, she was stubborn. Naturally, she would fight tooth and nail against the hard truth that her adoptive mother was dying.

I did this, Amanda couldn't help but think. *I put this on Peters. On Betty. It's because of me they've had to endure this.*

"I know that look." Peters sat on the plush sofa and gestured to the seat next to him. "You can't blame yourself, Newport. We knew the risks when we took this on."

Amanda ignored his invitation to sit and squared her shoulders. "It was still my burden. And I dumped it on you."

"We offered. Gladly. It's not like you abandoned that baby girl on our doorstep without another word."

Amanda flinched at his phrasing. In her mind, that's exactly what it had felt like: that she'd abandoned Rebecca with no word of explanation. Of course she hadn't, of course she'd had no choice but to do anything in her power to keep her daughter safe, to keep her from their enemies. Peters understood the truth, but would Rebecca ever understand?

As with Ruger, Amanda told herself it had been Rebecca's safety she'd been thinking of. But that wasn't entirely true.

And it was time to come clean about that.

"Is she awake?" Amanda asked, clasping her hands behind her back.

Peters nodded. "She stays shut in her room most of the time. I've found it's best to give her space when she needs it."

Amanda nodded tersely, trying to view this as another assignment, another obstacle to overcome. But her emotions got the better of her, twisting in her chest and climbing up her throat. Her shoulders sagged. This wasn't just another assignment. That wasn't why she was here.

"It's all right to feel sometimes." Peters's mouth curved into a knowing smile. "You're only human, after all. Despite what you might think."

Amanda's mouth quivered, and she took a steadying breath. "If I feel one thing, I'll feel everything."

"Would that be so bad?"

"Yes." Frustration burned inside her, and she clung to it, desperate to push out this crippling weakness that threatened to claim her. "My job demands that I make hard decisions, and I can't do that if my emotions are running wild."

"Emotions keep people alive. The love you feel for your

team and colleagues pushes you to do whatever it takes to protect them. That's not a weakness, Newport. It's a strength."

"It *is* a weakness. It's a liability. This, here"—Amanda gestured to the room at large—"is my greatest weakness. And if my enemy discovers it, they will have me. They will have the power to trap me, to destroy me."

"Yes, but your enemies are human, too. There is no escaping it. You cannot simply bury that which you care about and expect to emerge from this war unscathed. We all suffer loss. But it makes us stronger."

Amanda's eyes burned. *Loss.* What would she do if she lost Rebecca? Or Ruger, or Jayne, or Sofia? Much as she wanted to deny it, she saw her team as family. She tried to keep them at a distance, to remain aloof. She was only their boss, after all. There was no reason to get attached.

But these were all lies. Lies Amanda had to keep closely guarded.

Perhaps Peters was right. Perhaps it was time to let go. To accept her frailties and move forward. To trust the people she cared most about.

"Oh, it's you."

Amanda turned and found Rebecca perched at the top of the staircase, her hand on the banister and a cold look in her eyes. Karam's eyes. She had Amanda's flaming red hair, but everything else about her was all Karam.

For one moment, Amanda struggled to breathe as she took in this girl, this Guardian child, who had so much of her husband in her that it made her heart ache.

"What do you want?" Rebecca asked in a bored voice, not moving from her position on the stairs.

"Rebecca," Peters snapped. "Manners."

"I want to explain everything to you," Amanda said. "I won't be able to visit again for a long time, and I think you deserve the truth."

"What else is there to know? You gave me up to keep me safe. I understand that. I'm not an idiot."

Peters huffed in exasperation and rubbed his forehead.

"Please," Amanda said. "I want you to know everything. From there, you can make your decision about whether or not you want to see me again. Whatever you decide, I'll respect it. But you deserve to know about your father. About what he sacrificed."

Rebecca's eyes sparked with interest. She dropped her gaze and clenched the banister tightly. After a moment, she said, "All right. But I want Dad to stay."

Dad. A knot formed in Amanda's throat, but she nodded. Peters knew everything anyway. It would do no harm for him to remain for this conversation.

Slowly, Rebecca descended the staircase. When she reached the bottom, Amanda marveled at how tall she was. She was only ten, but in this moment, she seemed like a mature teenager.

And with everything she had been through, Amanda couldn't blame her for growing up a bit too quickly. With the frightening developments of the world and the magic around them, children were asked to do too much too soon. Rebecca should be attending school, making friends, living her life without a care in the world. Instead, she'd been abducted by a terrorist and, once rescued, was now forced to live in this safe house, isolated from everything and everyone she knew.

"You can sit." Amanda gestured to the seat next to Peters.

Rebecca crossed her arms and lifted her chin. "I'll stand."

Amanda chuckled. This girl was a force to be reckoned with. "Suit yourself." She took a moment to collect her thoughts, her instincts demanding she separate her emotions from the situation.

But no. Not this time. This time, Amanda allowed herself to

feel. It was the only way to ensure Rebecca got the entire truth —not just the facts, but the feelings as well.

"You already know your father was the Guardian of the New Delhi pocket in India. He loved it there. He created a sanctuary for magical and nonmagic people alike." She paused as she recalled the light in Karam's eyes, the pleasure he took in bringing peace into people's lives. He had been such a kind, pure soul, and was taken from this world far too soon.

And so, Amanda told Rebecca everything. She spoke of Karam's meditation classes, how he used the power of the pocket to calm and heal those in need, of the life he'd built in New Delhi. She told the story of how they'd met and fallen in love, two officers from different countries and backgrounds.

By the time she reached the part about Karam's death, she and Rebecca had ended up sitting in armchairs across from each other, though Amanda didn't remember moving. She explained about how a Guardian ally had betrayed Karam— which they now knew to be Hans Kaufmann. The Kingdom had come for the energy surrounding the pocket, and Karam had died protecting the city.

"I found out I was pregnant the week after he died." Amanda's voice was thick, her eyes shimmering with tears that she didn't bother to hide. Rebecca, too, was teary-eyed as she stared at Amanda with rapt attention. "He gave me this." She lifted the necklace around her throat that bore the three overlapping triangles—the sigil of the Guardians. "If I hadn't been pregnant with you, I would not have been able to wear it. But you...you infused me with some of Karam's power. It's because of you that I can still channel that power. That I can still summon Guardian magic.

"I knew the Kingdom wouldn't stop, that they would keep hunting Guardians and the massive power they were tasked with protecting. And you were so small and innocent. So fragile. I—I couldn't risk it. I couldn't lose someone else. In truth, I *was* trying to protect you, but I was trying to protect myself more. More than anything in the world, I wanted to keep you and raise you and watch you grow. But if I did that, I knew you and I would constantly be targeted. We would live a life on the run, always looking over our shoulders. And the thought of losing you..." She broke off, her grief choking her, making it hard to breathe. She closed her eyes and a tear trickled down her cheek before she continued.

"I don't know what will happen when all this is over," Amanda went on. "I don't know how long this war will last—it could be months, or it could be years. And after the dust settles, it's possible there will be no more Guardians. No more pockets to protect. But one thing is clear: you are *powerful*, Rebecca. Powerful enough to grant me power when I needed it, even when you were just a small presence in my womb. I know you haven't been properly trained or prepared, but I have a feeling the Torrent will call to your power one day. It will sense your potential and will summon you. I just want you to be prepared. And I want you to choose the side of light, like your father did."

Amanda fell silent, her mind and body drained as if she'd been wrung out, her emotions now puddled on the floor for everyone to see. But she also felt a sense of weightlessness, as if a massive burden had been lifted from her. She was a sticky mess, her makeup smeared and her skin blotchy, the tears still streaming down her face. But she was free of this weight. And now, for the first time in years, she felt like she could breathe.

"I—I don't know what to say," Rebecca said, her voice cracking, her cheeks also stained with tears. She shook her head, her face crumpling as she wept some more.

Amanda pulled out several tissues from her pocket and handed some to Rebecca. They both blew their noses and dabbed at their eyes. Even Peters, sitting silently on the sofa, sniffled now and then.

"What would I need to do?" Rebecca's voice was clearer now. Stronger. "To find out for sure about my Guardian magic?"

"We would need to run tests on you and get you in touch with other adult Guardians we know. I'm not as familiar with their process, with all the training involved. But I know there is a technology that can assess the magical presence inside you and estimate its potential. If that echo of the Torrent is strong enough, you may start to feel a certain pull to whichever pocket you'll be tasked with guarding. A true Guardian would be able to train you from there."

"How does it work? For normal Guardians, I mean. When do they find out?"

Amanda had asked Karam this same question when they'd discussed having children. Remembering the light in his eyes at the thought of having a child made her want to burst into tears all over again. "When the Guardian magic within a child comes to life, it bonds with the parent's magic, solidifying into something they can both channel together. As the child grows, both will be able to nourish that power and decipher the Torrent's intentions. Without that bond, I'm not sure how it works." From what Amanda understood, the connection between a Guardian parent and child was critical to a Guardian's training.

"The Torrent's intentions?" Rebecca's brow furrowed. "Is it alive? I mean, does it have a brain?"

Amanda shifted slightly in her seat. "It *is* alive. And that's what's so frightening about all this. We have no idea how it will react to this war. How the Torrent—and all the magic of the world—will be affected."

Rebecca fell silent, her gaze dropping to her hands clasped in her lap. "You're really fighting a war, aren't you?" She closed her eyes. "That's a stupid question. I saw it. I saw the battle with that man." She spat the word, and though Amanda knew Rebecca recalled his name, it felt fitting that he was just that—a man. Nothing more.

Rebecca met her gaze. "I understand now. And I know how hard this has all been for you."

Relief filled Amanda's chest, but before she could speak, Rebecca raised her hand.

"But that doesn't mean I forgive you. Or that I still want to see you. I just need time."

Amanda expected this, but that didn't stop the words from slicing right through her. She forced herself to nod, to plaster a stiff smile on her face. But it felt as though she'd been cracked wide open. Her normally stoic facade, the armor she'd worn for so long, had been shattered, and she couldn't reassemble it. Here she was, flayed open and laid bare for all to see. And it was terrifying.

"I understand," Amanda said at last, rising to her feet. "Peters will know how to contact me if you decide you want to talk."

Rebecca jumped to her feet, her eyes wide and full of panic. "You're leaving?"

"I have to. As you said, there's a war to fight."

Rebecca licked her lips, then glanced uncertainly at Peters. After a moment, she threw herself into Amanda's arms, clutching her tightly. Amanda gasped, startled and touched and so full of affection and love for this child. Her arms circled around Rebecca as she held her close, relishing the feel and warmth of her, safe and alive and whole. She smelled like morning dew and spice and just the subtle hint of Karam. Nostalgia and grief welled in Amanda's throat, and her eyes were moist again. Goddess, would she ever stop crying?

Too soon, Rebecca released her and raced up the stairs without a second glance. But her loud sniffling indicated she, too, was crying once more.

Amanda pinched her nose, closing her eyes to calm herself. When she sensed movement, she dropped her hand and opened her eyes to find Peters approaching her.

"I'm proud of you, Newport. That couldn't have been easy."

Amanda offered a watery smile. "No, it wasn't. But Karam would've wanted it."

Peters nodded, gazing wistfully up the stairs. "I think this will really help. She needed something real. Something true. There is so much I can't tell her, and she knows it. She understands. But it still puts a wedge between us." He smiled. "She has always wanted us to treat her like an adult. And just now, that's what you did. Thank you."

An adult. Amanda wanted to scream. Rebecca wasn't an adult at all, and she shouldn't have to face adult things.

But that was the way of the world. And Amanda couldn't shelter Rebecca from the harsh truths she would have to face.

All she could do was prepare her.

CHAPTER

TWELVE

DISCONNECT

J ayne, Tristan, and Vivienne stayed up the rest of the night discussing the possible identity of this mysterious new goddess. Vivienne was convinced it was Minerva, the Roman counterpart of Athena, the goddess of war—known to wear a golden warrior's helmet. Jayne had to admit the theory fit perfectly. A little too perfectly.

When she suggested this was a bit on the nose, Vivienne had fixed her with the signature hateful glare Jayne had come to know and love.

Tristan offered to do research to see what he could uncover about warrior goddesses. Which was helpful, but Jayne was antsy to get started on another assignment, return to the TCO, and get back to work. But Tristan said it was standard for the team to go silent after an attack like this, just in case they were being monitored or tracked. He expected Ruger to show up in a day or two.

Which felt like a million years to Jayne.

They took a short break when their stomachs were rumbling too loudly for them to concentrate. Tristan made peach crepes, and Jayne had to admit they were delicious. It also made her wonder who'd made the peach pie she'd enjoyed in the middle of the night. Surely it wasn't him? Still, the image of Tristan working at the stove? Damn, the man was sexy. And apparently, he could cook as well as he could throw intricate battle spells at an enemy.

Jayne was in serious, serious trouble.

After breakfast, despite how exhausted she felt, she decided to train. She fully expected Vivienne to reject her offer, given the Rogue didn't seem to like Jayne too much.

But, to Jayne's surprise, Vivienne nodded seriously. "You're right. We should train. We are both still new at this."

Jayne waved a hand in Vivienne's direction. "You don't seem too new at this. You shifted like a pro during that battle."

"Shifting, yes. I can do that without difficulty. But I have never been bonded to a magician before, let alone a Master. It feels...different."

Jayne considered this. Her temporary mentor, Hector, had told her Rogues couldn't perform their own magic, that they couldn't shift without bonding to a magician first. But that had proven to be untrue. For starters, Gina Labelle could shift at will. Plus, Vivienne's family had strong Adept ties; she wasn't an ordinary Rogue. And based on what Sofia had told her, Cillian had unlocked his own brand of Rogue magic recently as well.

So much was changing. So quickly. Everything Jayne was learning about Rogues proved to be vastly different from what she'd been told. Not that she was surprised...as a research librarian, she knew firsthand knowledge always trumped suppositions.

"Yeah, bonding can be an adjustment," Jayne said. "Then again, my only experience was with a Rogue who hadn't bonded properly with me, so..." She trailed off awkwardly. Thoughts of Cillian no longer plagued her with guilt and unease, which was a relief. But it was still an uncomfortable topic since their breakup.

"Ah, yes, the kickboxer you were sleeping with?" Vivienne raised her eyebrows.

Jayne choked on a half laugh, half cough. God, this woman was direct. But Jayne kind of liked it. "Um, yes. Him." Her cheeks heated, and she forced herself to keep her eyes forward and not look at Tristan, who was on his laptop in the corner. She could feel his eyes drilling into her.

"Oh, don't start, you two," Vivienne grumbled, pulling her long sable curls back into a messy ponytail. "I can already feel the tension brimming. Let's shut it down now before it goes too far."

"Lord, help me." Jayne pinched the bridge of her nose. It was difficult enough navigating through Vivienne's constant dance between hostility and general bluntness. But now she could read emotions from Jayne, emotions that were better left private. Jayne didn't consider herself to be a closed-off person or anything, but even she had her limits. She didn't like the idea of every naughty thought about Tristan being aired out for the world to see.

Jayne and Vivienne pushed the furniture against the walls, clearing a large space in the living room. Tristan migrated to the breakfast nook, his eyes dutifully fixed on his laptop screen, though Jayne knew he would be watching their training closely.

"Okay, let's start with a few simple spells, just to see how our magic meshes together," Vivienne said, standing taller and looking as regal as a queen.

Jayne bristled at the idea of taking orders from her, but she nodded slightly, hoping to keep the peace between them for as long as possible.

"Block," Vivienne said.

Together, they reached for the Torrent and summoned a Block spell. It was fairly standard, except Jayne recognized a subtle new feline scent mingling with her usual roses-and-woodsmoke fragrance. She inhaled deeply, committing the smell to memory, embracing it, welcoming it. She didn't want her magic—or the magic of the totems—to think Vivienne's magical presence was a threat.

But as Jayne gathered the spell in her hands, something shifted inside her. She felt another presence, not unlike Medb and Vesta's presence with the totems. The spell faltered in her hands before fizzling out completely.

"Whoa."

Jayne staggered, disoriented as the Torrent vanished and she was thrown back into the living room. Across from her, Vivienne wielded a brilliant green ball of energy, but it was much brighter and stronger than a normal Block spell. Vivienne's eyes were wide as she stared at the shimmering lights weaving between her fingers.

Jayne lifted her own hands, trying to conjure the Block spell again. Instead of returning to the Torrent, the ball of energy in Vivienne's hands twisted, spiraling toward Jayne before it bounced effortlessly into her palm. Warmth coated her skin, heating her blood and coursing through her with an almost violent fervor.

Alarmed by the intensity of her magic, Jayne released the spell, and the room became significantly dimmer. She and Vivienne exchanged equally startled looks.

"So our magic feeds off one another," Vivienne said slowly. "Not just with shifting."

"That's new." Jayne scratched her nose. "I wasn't even trying to project my magic toward you, and you just absorbed it."

Vivienne nodded. "You hesitated."

Jayne's eyes narrowed. "I was caught off guard."

"That hesitation could get you killed. Be confident and precise with your casting. It could save your life."

Jayne groaned. "God, you Lowells are all the same, aren't you?"

"What's that supposed to mean?"

"Nothing. I could do without a patronizing lecture today."

"I'm just trying to help."

"Right. I know. Sorry." Jayne spread her feet apart, wiggling her fingers to prepare herself. "Let's go again."

They tried several other simple spells—Shield, Attack, and Birth (which was a hoot, especially when Vivienne took on the appearance of a cranky old woman). Each time, their spells merged of their own accord, sometimes funneling to Vivienne, and other times to Jayne. It was an impressive blend of their powers, but it was frustrating because no matter what they tried, they couldn't control it.

"It's like the magic has a mind of its own," Jayne grumbled after their fifth attempt. They had just tried to feed the magic to Vivienne but it had all gone to Jayne instead.

"Of course it does," Vivienne said matter-of-factly. "The Torrent is alive, and we are wielding pieces of it."

Jayne gritted her teeth, quickly losing patience with Vivienne's practical and abrasive manner. "I *know*. But that doesn't help us if we're in the middle of a battle. What happens if a psycho is about to chop off your head and you summon an Attack spell, but it goes to me across the room? You're headless, that's what."

Vivienne rubbed her forehead, looking just as exasperated as Jayne felt. "Let's take a break, *oui*? Rest, get some water, and we'll try shifting next."

"Fine." Jayne wiped sweat from her brow and went into the kitchen to grab a bottle of water. She had just downed half of it when she realized she wasn't alone. Tristan was leaning in the doorway, infuriatingly handsome. He seriously looked like he belonged in a French fashion magazine, his collared shirt unbuttoned, his arms crossed and muscles bunching the fabric.

His hair was soft and wavy as if he'd had it professionally styled.

Stow it, Thorne.

Jayne shot him a scathing look before turning away and sipping more of her water.

"What was that for?" Tristan asked with a laugh.

"I didn't say anything."

"You didn't have to. Your withering glare said it all."

"I'm not in the mood, Tristan."

He lifted his palms and stepped away from the door frame. "As you wish. I'll just keep my comments to myself."

Jayne cursed under her breath. Tristan and his sister might be condescending, but their suggestions *did* tend to be helpful. They'd both grown up in the magical world, whereas Jayne had been sheltered from it until adulthood. Was she powerful? Yes, very. Knowledgeable? Still learning.

Regardless of whether Jayne was in the mood, it was clear she needed help.

Before he could leave the kitchen, Jayne said, "Tristan."

He glanced over his shoulder, arching a single eyebrow. *"Oui, mon amour?"*

God, she hated that term of endearment. Mostly because of the way it heated her blood and made her toes curl. But also because of the knowing smirk that always spread on his face, like he knew exactly what it did to her.

Jayne crossed her arms. "Let's hear it. What do you have to say?"

"You're sure you won't rip my face off?"

Jayne snorted. "No promises."

He stepped into the kitchen to face her fully, his expression sobering. "You're trying too hard to remain in control."

"What does that mean?"

"It means you're reluctant to relinquish power to someone else. You like having it for yourself. Being behind the wheel."

"Well, of course. No one likes to be powerless."

"This isn't about being powerless. This is about *sharing* power. If you want Vivienne to share her power with you, you need to be willing to let go of your own in exchange." He stepped closer. "As with most relationships, it's a give and a take. A test of trust. A leap of faith." His voice had grown soft, a low murmur that made Jayne's mouth go dry.

Suddenly, it didn't seem like they were talking about Master and Rogue anymore. "I may not be ready to take that leap," she said quietly. "As I said to Vivienne, what happens if I'm face-to-face with a threat, and this bond *takes* when I need it to *give*? Or, what happens when I give but get nothing in return? What happens when I pour everything I have into this and it ends up destroying me completely?"

Damn it, he made her say the most outrageous things aloud. Fear curled in her chest, but she forced herself to meet his gaze. Affection gleamed in his eyes as he lifted his hand, trailing his fingertips up and down her arm. She inhaled a shaky breath, enjoying the feel of his touch.

"It isn't without risks," he whispered. "Nothing is. If we lived without risk, that wouldn't be living at all."

His hand slid behind her, finding her waist and bringing her hips flush against his. She was so startled by the motion that her hands lifted to his chest as if to push him away, but she didn't. She could feel the firm muscles underneath his shirt, the way his heart raced in time with hers. She licked her lips.

"Stop your flirting and get out here!" Vivienne called from the living room. "We don't have time for this."

Jayne clenched her teeth, stepping away from Tristan and the intoxicating heat of his body. "Your sister is—"

"Invasive? Infuriating? Blunt?"

Jayne offered a sarcastic smile. "A classic Lowell."

Tristan laughed as Jayne stalked from the room, trying to shake the lingering haze of his nearness from her body.

THIRTEEN

FEELING A BIT...HAWKISH?

Vivienne was bent at the waist, stretching lithely like a ballerina. She glanced at Jayne, then scowled. "Can you two not go five minutes without trying to jump each other?"

Jayne rolled her eyes. "God forbid you find yourself someone who gives you the hots. Because when you do, I'm going to make your life a living hell."

To her surprise, Vivienne grinned, her eyes dancing with amusement. She straightened and waved Jayne forward. "Let's try shifting, shall we?"

"Sure." Jayne reached for the Torrent, but Vivienne's voice cut her off.

"Wait. We need a plan first."

Jayne blinked, and the shimmering river of stars disappeared. "What?"

"What will you have me shift into?"

"I was just going to start with a lioness, since we're both familiar with that one."

"Yes, but *why*?"

Jayne blinked. "I don't understand. Why *not*?"

"If we are in battle, there must be a logical reason to shift and a purpose behind the creature I shift into. It helps me bond with the mind of that creature. For example, a lioness is helpful in big battles because of its strength and agility. But in other circumstances, a different animal would be better. Imagine if we are at sea, or in a desert. The surroundings also affect my power as a creature. You would not make me a lion if we were surrounded by the ocean. A shark, though..."

"Oh, God." Jayne dropped her hands, resisting the urge to collapse. "This is just training, Vivienne. We are practicing. If you question every little thing like this, we won't get anything done."

"Training will prepare us for real scenarios. If I shift without a plan, the shift might not stick. I could be yanked back to my original form."

"Has that happened before?"

Vivienne nodded. "If the magic isn't strong enough, I will revert back to a human."

"Okay." Jayne bounced on the balls of her feet, determined to get through this training session without punching her Rogue in the face. She cracked her knuckles and took a deep breath. "Scenario: There's been a breach in the TCO headquarters. A flood of enemies comes pouring through the door, catching us all off guard. Lioness form, yes?"

To her immense relief, Vivienne nodded and closed her eyes. Jayne reached for the Torrent and found Vivienne standing alongside her. She suppressed a yelp of surprise, trying to remain focused on the task at hand. She sought out Vivienne's now-familiar magic, the feline scent mingling with woodsmoke and roses. Ever so gently, she coaxed it forward and commanded, "Shift to a lioness."

White light illuminated the room. With a roar, Vivienne's body elongated and sprouted fur, forming the majestic lioness Jayne had seen before. The Torrent vanished from view, returning them to the living room. Vivienne sat back on her hind legs and casually lifted a paw to lick it.

Jayne crossed her arms and raised her eyebrows. "Comfortable?"

"It *is* one of my preferred forms," Vivienne's voice echoed in Jayne's head.

Jayne laughed at the sight of this massive lioness sitting there grooming herself. "You're nothing but a house cat, are you?"

In a flash, Vivienne's claws were out, her dark, lethal eyes pinned on Jayne. "Don't test me. Flesh tears so easily."

Jayne shuddered. "Yep. Okay. You're scary again." She spread her arms, calling on the Torrent once more. "Let's try something new. Uh, here's the scenario: A pair of attackers has cornered us in an alley."

"Are there any civilians around?"

Jayne's brow furrowed. "Nearby. But none in the alley."

"Let's do something smaller. Less obvious. A hawk."

Jayne stared incredulously at the lioness. "A *hawk*?"

"A bird of prey, yes. They are predators, too, you know."

"Yeah, but how do you expect to do some serious damage as a bird?"

"We need to balance power and subtlety if there are civilians around. Trust me, Jayne. Let's try it. Call Tristan over, and I'll show you."

Jayne sighed. "Fine." Raising her voice, she said, "Tristan! We need you to be our punching bag, please."

As Tristan rose from his seat and approached, Jayne reached for the Torrent, gathered her magic, focused on Vivienne, and said, "Shift to a hawk."

A flash of white light, and Vivienne's large gray wings were spread, her shrewd yellow eyes gazing around the room. Jayne was surprised by how big she was, especially with her wings fanned out. She looked just as majestic as the lioness.

Jayne waved a hand at Tristan. "Attack."

Tristan rolled up his sleeves, his mouth twisting into a long-suffering smile. He summoned a spell, and his magic twisted in the air. Before he could cast it, Vivienne surged forward, talons out, and flew straight toward his face.

"Argh!" Tristan's strangled yell was the most undignified thing Jayne had ever heard him utter. He dropped the spell, hands waving frantically to fend off Vivienne. Her wings flapped wildly, talons flashing. Jayne winced as she saw one make contact with Tristan's face, raking a fresh cut along his cheek.

"*Merde*, Vivienne!" Tristan finally blasted her with a Block spell. Vivienne careened backward only to fly for him once again.

Jayne doubled over with laughter at the sight of Tristan, this suave and capable magician, being outmatched by a *bird*. The longer the two of them fought, the more her laughter intensified, until she was on her knees and tears streaming down her face. "God, this is better than prime-time television."

"Are we *quite* finished?" Tristan roared as he hit Vivienne with another spell that slammed her against the wall, pinning her.

"You've made your point, Vivienne," Jayne said, wiping tears from her face. "I was mistaken. A hawk is the most badass nuisance I've ever seen."

Before Vivienne could soar for Tristan again, Jayne reached the Torrent and commanded, "Shift to a human." In a flash, Vivienne stood before them, her hair a bit more disheveled than before and a satisfied smirk on her face.

Tristan shot her a furious look, wiping a fresh streak of blood on his forehead.

Jayne, still laughing, said, "Come here. I can heal that."

Shaking his head, Tristan drew closer, and Jayne raised her hands to the wounds on his face. His intoxicating musk surrounded her, wrapping her in a soapy vanilla fragrance, tinged with sweat and exertion, creating a devastating scent that she wanted to fall into. She closed her eyes, allowing herself a moment to savor the combination, before reaching for Medb's power. The goddess's familiar ice-cold magic crept into her chest as Jayne summoned her healing powers.

"Easy now," Tristan murmured. The softness of his voice drew goose bumps on her skin. His hand clasped her forearm—the same spot marked by the dark leathery skin.

Everything inside Jayne turned cold. Tristan was worried about her burning out. They had speculated that for most Adepts, burnout meant bursting into flames and dying. But for Masters, it meant becoming a Wraith.

This couldn't be proven since Jayne was the first Master in ages to come along. But the spot on her arm was enough to cause concern.

Clearing her throat, Jayne nodded and coaxed only a tendril of her magic forward. Her fingertip glowed white as she pressed it against the bloody marks on his forehead and cheek. In seconds, the cuts disappeared, leaving only faint trails of blood.

Dizziness overcame her, and she stumbled backward in a daze. Her skin felt warm, despite Medb's lingering magic.

"Hey." Tristan's arms were around her, steadying her. "I've got you. Viv, will you get her some water?"

"I'm good," Jayne insisted, but Vivienne obediently handed her a bottle of water. After taking a few sips, Jayne's head started to clear and her body temperature returned to normal.

"From now on, leave the minor scrapes and cuts, okay?" Tristan smiled. "It will take more than that to mar this master-piece." He gestured to his face.

Jayne knew he was only trying to distract her, and it was working. She snorted loudly and saw Vivienne rolling her eyes. It didn't take long for her worries to come creeping back in, though. She used to be able to heal even fatal injuries without such consequences. What did this mean, that merely healing Tristan's small wounds impacted her this way? She knew it had to be more than just being wiped out from training.

Was Medb's magic fading? Or had Jayne's powers become tainted by the mark on her arm?

FOURTEEN

A NEW PROJECT

After gathering her emotions and assuring Peters she was capable of maneuvering in the world without tearing it apart, Amanda followed another circuitous route back to Langley. Jayne wasn't the only Master who needed a mission; it was time to send Cillian and Sofia back into the field as well.

The hallway still smelled of gunpowder and bloodshed, weighing heavily on Amanda as she strode to her office. She forced herself to nod amiably at Pierce as she reached his desk, though all she could think was *This is your fault, you bastard.*

He was responsible for the lives they'd lost. She just needed a few more incriminating pieces of evidence, and he would lead her to his masters.

"Are Officers Thorne and Pine here?" Amanda said in a tight voice, keeping her hands curled into fists to contain her rage.

"Oh!" Pierce jumped to his feet. "Yes, they are in your office waiting for you, Ms. Newport." He cocked his head, ever chipper. "Are you all right? You look like you've had a rough morning."

"I am fine. Thank you, Pierce."

Inside her office, Cillian and Sofia were huddled together,

their chairs scooted close, their knees touching as they murmured to one another. The dynamic would have appeared romantic if not for the solemn grimness on both their faces. Whatever they were discussing, it seemed quite serious.

At Amanda's entrance, they both shot to their feet. Sofia's cheeks turned a bit pink as if she'd been caught doing something scandalous. She nervously clutched a stack of papers in her hands, twisting the pages together.

"Thank you for coming in." Amanda wasted no time as she crossed to her desk and took a seat, sifting through files and documents before she found what she was looking for: information on the Guardians and their pockets. "For your next assignment, you'll be—"

"Actually, we had something we wanted to run by you first," Sofia said, glancing quickly at Cillian, who nodded.

Amanda faltered. "All right. What is it?"

Sofia set the papers on the desk in front of Amanda. They were crinkled from Sofia's fidgeting, but Amanda smoothed them out and easily read the headlines on the news reports: "Magic Is Real—and It's Claiming Our Children" … "Houston Child Arrested for Attacking Teacher with Supernatural Force" … "Teenager Summons Fireworks from His Hands in Central Park"

Amanda frowned as she skimmed over each article. "What is this?"

"Cillian and I have been doing some research," Sofia said. She wrung her hands together, clearly still nervous, but the lift of her chin and the spark in her eyes revealed the determination Amanda knew so well. "With magic becoming more prominent in the world, there are still people out there who need our help. Children. They are defenseless against this, and the public views their abilities as something demonic, something to be feared. They don't have anyone to help or train them because, for them, magic didn't exist until now."

A knot formed in Amanda's throat as she thought of Rebecca and how frightened she must have been when her Guardian magic first manifested itself. She took a steadying breath and said sharply, "What's your point?"

"We'd like to help them," Sofia said simply.

"Help...the children? Which ones?"

"All of them."

Amanda sighed and set down the papers on her desk. "As worthy an endeavor as that would be, it's a fairy tale, Sofia. It's impossible for us to track down every Adept child in the world."

"I thought you would say that. Cillian and I are working on a spell. With my Guardian magic able to seek out other Guardians, and his Rogue magic able to project to other Adepts, we think we've found a way to combine those abilities into a sort of radar that can scan nearby areas for high magical activity."

Amanda froze, her mind snagging on something similar Quimby Cain, their tech expert, had been developing. Already, the pieces were sliding together in her thoughts, formulating a more solid plan. "You know," she said slowly, "that just might work."

Sofia's jaw went slack. She clearly expected Amanda to outright refuse her suggestion. And perhaps, a few weeks ago, Amanda would have.

But everything had changed when she found Rebecca. That girl had cracked open the worn armor surrounding Amanda's heart, opening her eyes to the tragedies of the world she had bluntly refused to see.

"Hans Kaufmann was abducting children," Amanda said, her voice full of steel. "He may try to do it again. You're right. They are defenseless, which makes them targets. Hans won't be the only one trying to siphon their magic. I'm sure our other enemies will catch on that these rising Adepts are ripe for the picking. I will send your request up the chain of command and see if we can get a team assembled for extraction and proper training for these young Adepts."

"I—no," Sofia sputtered, gesturing between Cillian and herself. "*We* want to do it."

"You're needed elsewhere, Sofia. We are at war. Your powers are too valuable."

"These kids are caught in the crossfire," Cillian said, his eyes blazing. "Between me and Sofia, we're more powerful than any team you could put together. Protecting your future soldiers seems like a smart move to me."

Amanda pursed her lips. "And just what do you plan to do with these children once you rescue them? Tear them away from their families without permission? Hide them in your apartment, or in the spare rooms at the TCO?"

"No," Sofia said, her eyes sparking with frustration. "I think we should open a school."

For the second time, Amanda was caught off guard. She simply stared at Sofia, not comprehending.

"Like Hogwarts," Sofia offered, as if that provided any clarification.

She couldn't be serious.

Impatience and anger roiled in Amanda's chest. She did not have time for this. "We just suffered a major loss. Our headquarters were attacked. We still haven't fully recovered. Our enemies grow closer, causing more acts of terror every day. And you want to pause everything and pour money and resources and officers we don't have into creating a school? I'm sorry, Sofia, but that is *not* what the TCO is meant for."

"The TCO is meant for protecting magic and magic-users," Sofia argued. "This falls under that umbrella."

"But we do not have the funding or staffing for a project like this! Do you know how difficult it is to get a school up and running? We are struggling enough as it is, trying to balance our assignments and fighting the threats that come our way."

"Which is why Sofia and I want to do this ourselves," Cillian said. "All of it. We'll track down the children, talk to their parents, offer safe refuge and a protected space to train."

"Where is this protected space, pray tell?" Amanda snapped. "Are you going to build a fantastical castle on a Scottish loch and portal them all there?"

"No. We're going to build it in a Time Catch," Sofia said.

Amanda slammed her hand flat on the desk. "*Not* an option. The last time we used a Time Catch for nonmagical persons, we accidentally trapped an officer inside for days. Our simulators aren't strong enough to—"

"Not the TCO Time Catch," Sofia said. "My father's."

"The one in Geneva?"

She took a deep breath. "He has others as well. They are tethered to his magic and his research. He has safeguards in place. They are far more advanced than the Time Catches we're used to."

"This isn't just a charity project," Cillian added. "If we rescue these kids and give them a chance to develop their powers, not only will it keep them safe, but it will bring them to our side. As you said, we don't have the manpower for everything. But as we train and prepare these kids for the war that's coming, we'll be creating more soldiers to use."

"If they enlist, of course," Sofia added.

Amanda's mind was buzzing. Her irritation surged to the surface, eager to keep arguing her point. But it seemed Sofia and Cillian had thought of everything. "And the teachers?"

"We can alternate between whichever officers we have available," Cillian said. "While Sofia and I are in the field, we can leave the kids with Seo-Joon. When we return, we can train them ourselves."

Amanda tapped a finger against her lips. Proper training from a Master with Guardian powers and a Rogue who had his own unique brand of magic... The idea was tempting, but also volatile. These two had only just discovered their magic.

But if someone more experienced was on board to supervise? It *could* work.

And they weren't wrong. She'd seen the news and felt the reckoning of all the new souls accessing the Torrent. They needed guidance, and she needed them on her side. Because if she didn't command their loyalty, too many other factions would try.

"All right. I'll put Hector Ortolan on this assignment as well," Amanda said. "He can oversee the training and ensure the safety of the new recruits."

Sofia's expression brightened. "You'll let us do it? You'll let us start a school?"

Amanda nodded. "It's a worthy effort, and all the points you make are valid. I can send units to the Guardians myself while you two work on this. Get with Quimby and see what technology she has available. I'm sure there's something you can combine with your spell that will enhance it."

Sofia's face split into a wide grin, making her look years younger. She exchanged a gleeful look with Cillian. "Thank you, Amanda. This means a lot to us."

"Don't make me regret trusting you on this," Amanda warned. "I was going to send you to your sister, to start ferreting out the rest of the Kingdom members who attacked us, and end Ruth Thorne for good. But you've convinced me. You must be careful, though, Sofia. It's true that our enemies may be closing in on the same idea. They will want the children's magic for themselves. You will encounter threats along the way."

Sofia straightened, her expression hard and fierce. "Then we'll be ready for them."

FIFTEEN

RAVENOUS

R uth Thorne's mind had become a cloud of darkness, one she seemed to emerge from for only seconds at a time to take care of her basic needs. Her master couldn't use her if she starved or wasted away entirely.

But she was no longer herself. And each day, she became something less and less recognizable.

You have failed me, he often reminded her. *I am hungry and must be fed. If I cannot feed off others' magic, I will feed off yours.*

Always hungry. Always ravenous for more power. More energy. More fuel.

It would never stop. Ruth was a fool to ever think it would.

"Drink, darling. Please."

Ruth blinked back into reality, her head a garbled mess of disembodied voices and lethal threats. Something warm touched her lips, and she almost choked on it before realizing it was broth, filled with spices and seasonings that made her frail body feel alive again. She had once cared for the finer delicacies in her meals, and this rich broth was expertly prepared. Her tongue sifted through the various flavors and sensations, trying to pinpoint which spices she recognized. The mental effort sharpened her mind. The corners of her vision, which had grown dark, now brightened with clarity. She sat up straighter, realizing she was huddled on the floor of her flat in London. Hans crouched above her, gingerly feeding her spoonfuls of the delicious broth.

Ruth took a large swallow and gasped, the sound rattling and haunted.

"How long?" she rasped. "How long have I been gone?"

Hans's brows were drawn, his face tight with worry. "Four days."

Damn. Her blackouts were lasting much longer than usual. How long before she disappeared entirely? Before her Wraith completely consumed her?

"Ruth." Hans sighed, dropping his head for a moment before feeding her another spoonful. "We must find another way. We cannot go on like this."

Ruth was automatically shaking her head. "The bargain—"

"I know. There is no escaping the bargain. But there must be something we can do. Something else you can feed him. Think of the Kingdom, of your cause, of your magic. He is eating away at you one bite at a time, and soon there will be nothing left. You have too much at stake to give in to him. *We* have too much at stake."

Ruth thought of her devoted followers, who had once filled her with a sense of pride. But all emotion and determination seemed to have seeped out of her, used as sustenance for her master just like everything else.

"Tell me what he requires of you," Hans pleaded. While Ruth had not shared the details of her bargain with the dark Master, Hans knew enough. It was hard to live with her and not piece things together.

"Magical nourishment," she whispered. "As he grows, his form requires more and more fuel. Powered only by magic. *Raw* magic. He needs Jayne. He will consume her and let me go."

Hans frowned as he considered this. While he deliberated, Ruth raised shaking hands to take the bowl of broth from his grasp. She lifted the bowl to her lips and began to take larger gulps, moaning with satisfaction as the warm liquid scorched a path down her throat. It was hot—too hot, really. But the sensation only brought her more clarity, which was exactly what she needed.

"We can't use the totems," Ruth said, wiping her chin on her sleeve. God, she had truly become a slob. But there wasn't time for refinement right now. She was on the brink of death. "I've already given him the power of the water totem, and it's clear accessing Jayne's powers will be time-consuming. He is displeased we did not achieve our goals in the attack on the TCO. He needs energy *now,* and he'll take it from whatever source he can get."

"I might have an idea," Hans said slowly, his blue eyes calculating in that way that reminded Ruth of why she had been so drawn to him in the first place. Potential. A clever mind. A mind that could generate ideas and strategies when she couldn't. A willingness to deviate from what was meant to be his fated course in life. Hans had become more to her than she cared to admit. He'd given up his Guardianship of the Geneva pocket when it killed his little sister and had cleaved to Ruth's cause instead. He was a visionary, a leader among the Kingdom faithful—and, unlike her ex-husband Henry Thorne, their visions coincided nicely.

Henry was with the TCO now. He had turned against her completely. She would confront him soon enough. His little time trick was something she could use.

"Tell me." Ruth sat up straighter, feeling stronger than she had in days.

"It will require us to cross lines," Hans warned. "If our followers found out…"

"This stays between us," Ruth vowed. The Kingdom was

still in the dark about her predicament. They simply believed she was traveling, pursuing a top-secret lead on a powerful source of magic.

Well, except Lars. It was impossible to fool her second. He definitely suspected something. Announcing she was possessed by a Wraith wasn't going to endear her to the troops.

"There is another source of raw magic we haven't yet considered," Hans said. "One that is fragile and vulnerable and should be fairly easy to take." His gaze latched onto hers. "I think this is our solution, Ruth. This is how we free you."

Ruth nodded, her blood pulsing with anticipation. *Free.* The word was such a foreign concept to her.

But as she listened to Hans's plan, she realized she would do anything—sacrifice *anything*—to buy her own freedom.

Even if it meant crossing every last line.

SIXTEEN

HONOR AMONG THIEVES

Jayne, Tristan, and Vivienne had been at the Takoma Park safe house for three days when they finally received word from Amanda. Jayne was going absolutely mad being cooped up, waiting.

"Can we just go to a library? Any library? I've already read all the books here."

"*Ma cherie*, you 'just going' to a library tends to end up with international incidents. You must learn patience."

Jayne shot him a look. "Patience. You do realize I am a research librarian. I eat patience for breakfast."

Tristan laughed. "That may well be true, but the answer is still *non*."

"How about a bookstore? Or let me go online, I'm desperate enough to get something delivered. Oh, I know, let me use the portal back to headquarters. I can go visit the TCO library. Katie Bell always likes my company."

"When you aren't setting the world on fire, I too enjoy your company. *Je suis désolé, ma cherie*. We follow orders. We stay here until we are summoned."

To make up for disappointing her, Tristan made them a

lovely lunch of *croque monsieur* and salad, and they were just finishing up the meal when a coded message came in to Tristan's phone indicating Amanda would be arriving via portal in the next ten minutes.

"See?" Tristan waved a dish towel at her triumphantly. "If I'd let you go off wandering, and she arrived to find you gone, she would have had my head."

Jayne shoved the last of her sandwich into her mouth before hurriedly straightening up the kitchen and the rest of the small house. What compelled her to tidy up before her boss arrived was unknown. Stress cleaning, definitely.

But it wasn't just Amanda who shimmered into existence in the middle of the small living room. The golden doorway also revealed Ruger and Henry, who stepped through behind her.

Amanda wrinkled her nose at their drab surroundings, then shot Tristan a quick nod of approval. "Abysmal. The perfect cover. Well done, Lowell."

Jayne almost laughed. *This place is a shithole. Job well done, Officer.*

But before she could make a quip, her eyes met her father's, and she rushed into his arms, clutching him tightly. Her worry and fears from the past few days had wound themselves into tight knots in her chest and stomach. All she could think about were the people she'd left behind while fleeing—Sofia, Cillian, Henry, Amanda, Ruger—and what might have happened to them.

"Thank God you're all right," Jayne breathed before releasing him. Then, she lightly punched him on the arm. "How dare you have them whisk me away like that?"

Henry rubbed his arm, grimacing, though Jayne hadn't hit him very hard. "I had to keep you alive and stop the battle. Wouldn't you have done the same for me or your sister?"

Jayne scowled but made no argument because, well, he was right. If the Kingdom had been targeting Sofia, she would have gotten her the hell out of there. Pronto. Regardless of her sister's arguments.

She deflated, her anger vanishing. Truth be told, she wasn't angry. She had just been terrified. If after all they'd been through, having just found him after so long, something had happened to Henry—something Jayne could have prevented—she never would have forgiven herself.

"Is Sofia all right?" Jayne asked. "And Cillian?"

Henry nodded. "They're both fine."

"Enough pleasantries." Amanda perched on the very edge of an armchair, her back stiff as a board. "We have a lot to catch up on." Her gaze sharpened as it landed on Henry. "This device you used to rescue Jayne... I would like to be briefed. Please."

Henry wrung his hands together, his expression uncertain. "I, uh..." He faltered, looking to Jayne imploringly as if she might deliver him from this awkward situation.

Jayne lifted her hands. "Hey, you're the one that used the thingy in broad daylight, in front of witnesses. You owe us an explanation."

Henry dropped his hands and paced the length of the living room. Ruger took a seat next to Tristan and Vivienne on the sofa, his dark eyes full of suspicion and doubt as he watched Henry.

"I call it a Time Jumper," Henry said at last. "It's similar to the capacitor I developed, but on a much smaller scale. It's portable, obviously. More manageable and less volatile. And less dangerous to the time vortex."

"It seemed to freeze time," Jayne said slowly as she remembered the disorienting sensation of the world around her becoming still as a statue while only she and Henry remained in motion.

Henry nodded. "Yes. When I select a single target, they are the only thing immune to the time freeze. Plus myself, of course, since I'm holding it."

"When you used it before, Jayne was the target?" Amanda inferred.

"Yes. But the target can only maneuver so much. It needs direct contact with the caster, which is myself. Jayne was aware of everyone else being frozen, but she couldn't move."

"'Caster'?" Ruger repeated in amazement, his baritone rumbling through the small space. "It's a spell? I thought it was a device."

"It's a combination." Henry withdrew the small remote from his pocket, which Jayne recognized from the battle in the atrium. "I call it a Time Jumper. It's fueled by Guardian magic. I crafted a spell that links to it directly. When I conjure the spell, it activates the Jumper. It's got a built-in laser pointer, and whoever I direct it to when I cast the spell becomes my target."

"How many targets can you have at a time?" Tristan asked, his eyes alight with interest. He looked positively fascinated by this, like a Star Trek nerd talking about wormholes. Jayne made a mental note to tease him mercilessly about this later.

"Right now, only one." Henry seemed to gain confidence the more he spoke. He had stopped pacing and was now gesticulating with his hands like an enthusiastic college professor. "But I'm still tweaking it. I'm hoping to add more targets, but it's a delicate formula I'm toying with. After what happened with the capacitor, I have to use a more thorough testing process before I employ it."

Ruger rubbed the back of his neck and exhaled through his teeth. "Good God, you really did it, didn't you? You tapped into time travel."

Henry nodded. "It's something I've been working on since my days at Oxford. I've only mastered it in the past few years. It's...personal, for me."

"Which is why we need to help support his research," Jayne said. "The TCO needs my father."

"Thank you, Jayne," he said.

"We'll make those determinations once the full implications of this device can be assessed," Amanda said, her voice sharp and commanding. "Now, we need to discuss your next assignment. It's clear the Kingdom got the upper hand on us. We need to get it back."

"We have a suggestion that might help," Jayne said, glancing at Vivienne and nodding.

Vivienne sat forward, her chin lifting. "I believe I know the location of a necromantic grimoire. We must access the Liber Linteus. It lies within the Archaeological Museum in Zagreb, Croatia. But there was an earthquake a few years ago, and the museum sustained heavy damage. It was quite a sad disaster. Because of this, they have secured the exhibit, and we cannot get to it as tourists. I've reached out to them, posing as an archaeologist who needs access for research, but they have declined. Vehemently. Because of this, and knowing that even if we explained our purpose, they will not hand it over willingly, we must steal it for our cause before another can reach it and use its power."

Jayne snorted and disguised it as a cough. *Vivienne's bluntness to the rescue.* Ruger, Amanda, and Henry all gaped at her.

Amanda recovered first. "I admire your fervor, Miss Lowell, and am very glad you are on our side."

Vivienne tossed her hair over her shoulder in triumph.

"But I don't think our counterparts in the Croatian government would take kindly to us storming the castle and stealing their ancient linen-wrapped mummy."

"But—" Vivienne started, but Amanda held up a hand.

"At least allow me to try diplomatic avenues before we go *Ocean's Eleven* on Zagreb, yes?"

Jayne gawped at Amanda, who winked. "What? You think I don't watch movies? Great heist films are my favorite. Ruger and I have popcorn and discuss the lives of crime we should have embarked upon instead of trying to uphold magical law for the world and contain the enthusiasm of young Adepts."

"Come now, that's just embarrassing," Ruger said, and they all laughed, the tension broken. Jayne was still in shock—Amanda, making a joke. It was unheard of.

"I'll see what I can do about this possible grimoire."

While she stepped into the kitchen to make a call, everyone relaxed for a few minutes. Jayne crossed the room to Ruger.

"How goes it, Rug?"

"Just fine, Agnes," he replied. Ruger was the only person on the planet Jayne would allow to call her by her given name. Now that she had access to her father, she really needed to get the parental reasoning behind it. "You holding up okay? You and pretty boy over there getting along?"

"Never," she replied, feeling Tristan's eyes locked onto her back. "He is insufferable, and his sister..."

"I can hear you, Jayne," Vivienne called out.

"We've been working on our shifting bond. It's intense, Ruger. Getting her to shift is much easier than anything that I could ever do with Cillian. Is he okay? Are he and Sofia..."

"Working on a special Guardian project together, and if you're asking if they're playing kissy face, I have no idea."

"I am not asking that! I just want to be sure he's okay."

"He seems quite fine. Quite taken with your sister, if you want the truth."

Jayne felt a knot unfurl in her chest. "Oh. Good. That's good." Nothing like hoping your ex and your sister were getting it on, but she wanted them both to be happy, and now that they were bonded as Master and Rogue, she doubted Sofia would be able to resist Cillian's appeal. He was quite the Irish charmer when he wanted to be, and in his wolf form, quite the formidable partner, too. Unlike Tristan, who was more of a smoldering mess. That dark hair, the laconic voice, the look in his eyes when he said *mon amour*...

"Jayne, for heaven's sake," Vivienne snarled.

"Our thoughts and emotions are linked," Jayne explained to Ruger. "We need to figure out a way to have a little privacy. We're working on it."

"Block spell, maybe. A Shield? I could talk to Hector—" Before he could finish, Amanda returned, looking flustered.

"They politely declined our offer of help to secure the Liber Linteus. Emphatically."

Ruger's brows furrowed. "Has someone gotten to them?"

"Possibly. It was...a confounding conversation. They said the exhibit was guarded by a strong magical spell and there was no chance of nefarious or malicious access. The man I spoke to, though...he sounded familiar somehow. I certainly have never spoken to our counterparts in Croatia before."

"It's possible they've already been infiltrated," Ruger said.

"Well, wouldn't that be a kicker?" Amanda eyed Jayne thoughtfully. "Okay, team. Back to work." They all took their seats in the living room, and Amanda crossed her legs, all business again. "Would you please explain more about this warrior goddess you believe is trapped in the Torrent?"

SEVENTEEN

NO, THANK YOU

With Jayne and Tristan filling in the gaps, Vivienne outlined what they knew from her discussions with Vesta as well as Jayne's freaky firestorm vision.

"Croatia is on my list of possible destinations," Henry said when they finished. "I've done my own research on the Liber Linteus. Ancient Adept texts claim the grimoire there holds a backdoor access point to the Torrent itself. If I can use that back door to slip into the Torrent without disturbing it, then I can rescue the people trapped inside."

Jayne's eyebrows lifted. A back door to the Torrent? Well, that was a bonus. "Maybe that's why this goddess wants me to find the grimoire. Maybe the back door isn't just the key to saving those in the Torrent, but the key to defeating the Master who lives there as well."

"Yes, this goddess from your vision..." Ruger was stroking his chin. "Do we know anything else about her?"

"We think it may be Minerva," Vivienne said, her voice full of confidence. "She is the goddess of war, after all."

Jayne bit her lip. She didn't have anything to support her idea, but it didn't feel like Minerva was the one communicating with her. She suspected it was someone else but had no idea who that might be. It would be a hell of a lot easier if these goddesses could just introduce themselves like normal people.

"Minerva isn't known for prophecies, though," Henry said, backing up her thoughts. "I think that's what we need to be focusing on—not her warrior ensemble. When a people are at war, everyone wears armor. And as we know, these deities are at war with whatever Master is living in the Torrent."

Jayne smiled. "How do you know so much about mythology?"

"I'm a researcher," Henry said plainly. "It's what I do. These aren't just stories of old, lore, or myths. After your encounters with Medb and Vesta, it's clear they're real."

"Regardless of which goddess is trying to communicate with Jayne," Ruger said, "you are suggesting we waltz off with an ancient mummy's wrappings. There will be consequences."

"Then we must hope the museum will listen to reason, and allow us access," Vivienne said. "You must try speaking with them again, Amanda. The grimoire is at great risk in non-Adept hands."

"Not to mention that if the Kingdom knows about it, they'll be planning the same thing," Jayne said. "If not something worse, like breaking in and blowing up the whole building."

That horrifying idea was enough to end the dithering.

"You both make excellent points," Amanda said solemnly. "After the reaction I got when I asked for access, something is definitely rotten in Denmark. I agree that we need to take the offensive with this. If the Liber Linteus allows us an approach to the next totem, then we must get to it before the Kingdom does."

"What about La Liberté?" Jayne shot a glance at Tristan and Vivienne. "Are they still a threat?"

Tristan followed on. "More importantly, what about *Maman*? We have not heard from her in many days."

Amanda nodded. "I'm not surprised. Before I left Langley, I received word that Gina had been taken into custody. She will be tried at The Hague for her crimes."

Jayne couldn't help pumping her fist in the air. "Good job, International Magical Court!"

Amanda's mouth quirked into the ghost of a smile. "It seems the stunt you pulled at the Vatican Library put her in the crosshairs of the magical law enforcement office at Interpol. Not only was it illegal for her to break into a public place and use a frightening display of magic in front of non-Adepts, but the incident in Fontainebleau has been brought to light as well. For now, La Liberté won't be a problem."

"That won't last long." Tristan's gaze had darkened at the mention of Fontainebleau. Though he looked calm and collected, Jayne could see through it. That incident still haunted him. "There is a clear chain of command within my mother's organization. Someone else will take over while she's being tried."

"Pierre," Vivienne said with distaste.

Tristan nodded, his expression souring.

"Friend of yours?" Jayne asked wryly.

"We've loathed each other for years," Tristan said. "He's impulsive and reckless. More so than *Maman*. He's dangerous and should not be underestimated."

Amanda nodded. "Send us all the information you have on him so we can be prepared. In the meantime, I will continue trying to make inroads in Zagreb." She narrowed her eyes. "And just in case we are not sufficiently persuasive, the rest of you start making a plan to infiltrate the Archaeological Museum to retrieve the grimoire. Thorne, you will help them. You too, Ruger. I need plausible deniability. The director will have my head on a platter if I tell him I've sanctioned this mission."

Henry straightened, his face slackening. "I, uh... What? I thought your research team was going to work with me on—"

"Yes, and we will continue that work," Amanda said with an air of impatience. "But if we must go through with this in a... less than legal manner, your Time Jumper will be useful for the mission. The nonmagical security will be difficult enough to get past, but I have no doubt there are magical measures in place as well. If we strike, we need to be decisive. We cannot afford to fail. Time is of the essence."

"Pun intended?" Jayne asked.

Tristan smirked. Vivienne rolled her eyes, and Ruger sighed. Amanda ignored Jayne completely. It *was* a bit much to expect her to enjoy two of Jayne's jokes in one day.

"I—I—the Time Jumper wasn't meant to be used this way," Henry sputtered, his face turning slightly pink.

"And what, exactly, was it meant to be used for?" Amanda asked, eyebrows raised.

"For science! For furthering my magical research. For saving lives. Not petty theft."

"This is not petty. You saw the Kingdom. You saw Ruth. This is war, and the enemy is growing stronger. This is what we need to beat them. You have an impressive mind, Henry Thorne. Use that brain of yours to see logic and sense. If you want to fight on our side—on the side of your daughters—and we need to make this move, you will help us."

Henry's lips grew thin, his eyes darting quickly to Jayne and then back to Amanda. "This wasn't part of our deal. I told you I wouldn't share this kind of sensitive technology until after—"

"The attack has changed everything." Ruger jumped in, crossing his arms and leveling a hard stare at Henry. "Amanda's right. We need to make our move. Now. Are you with us, or not?"

Silence filled the room as every pair of eyes fixed on Henry expectantly. He shuffled his feet, scratched his chin, then chewed on one of his fingernails. Jayne's stomach twisted with anxiety. *Come on, Dad. Don't be an idiot.*

At long last, Henry dropped his arms. "Fine. Fine. You're right, of course. I'll help. But—but there are rules."

"You'll go over all that during training." Amanda waved an idle hand. "Our officers are professionals. If you clearly highlight the risks to them, they'll be cautious." Her eyes found Jayne.

"Why are you looking at me?" Jayne asked, pointing to her chest in mock offense. "I feel so attacked."

"Jayne," Amanda said sharply.

Jayne raised her palms in surrender. "Right, okay. I'll follow the rules, I swear."

Tristan choked on a laugh, and Ruger shook his head slowly.

Jayne scowled at their obvious doubt. "What? I can be responsible."

"Really?" Tristan challenged. "Because I've been keeping a list..." He fished through his pockets as if to retrieve this list.

Jayne felt her cheeks heat. *He's bluffing. He has to be.* Tristan caught her eye and winked. A coil of heat spiraled through her, and she averted her gaze. *Not now, Jayne, you horndog. Focus on the task at hand.*

With a cheerful grin, she clapped her hands together. "Okay, merry thieves. How do we steal this grimoire?"

CHAPTER

EIGHTEEN

THE NICK OF TIME

Tristan held Henry Thorne's Time Jumper in his hands, the device so small and seemingly insignificant. Just a black remote with two buttons, one red and one blue. But Tristan could feel the power emanating from it, solid and thick like syrup sliding into his fingers. The sense of the magic was strange, but he knew it was because it was Guardian magic—something he wasn't yet familiar with.

Across the room, Henry visibly fidgeted, clearly uneasy with his device in Tristan's hands. Well, he would have to get over that. Tristan could tell the scientist was uncomfortable working with others. This whole task would take some adjustment for all of them.

Amanda had already departed, leaving the rest of them in the safe house to finish planning before they portaled to Croatia. Everyone agreed it was safest to iron out as many details as possible first before traveling. Portaling that far was bound to alert other Adepts; once they arrived, their time would be limited.

"I felt something when you triggered this," Tristan said,

114

glancing up at Henry. "Some small shift in the air. It was very subtle."

Henry nodded. "Yes. It's impossible to mask it. Once we use this, other Adepts in the area will be aware of the change. But our advantage is they won't know what caused it."

"Because to them, time travel isn't real." Vivienne stood behind the couch where Tristan sat, her arms crossed. He could tell she didn't fully believe in it herself.

"We don't even know if we need to use the Time Jumper," Jayne said, sitting at the desk, her eyes fixed on the screen of her laptop. "According to the museum's website, the Liber Linteus is located in its own room on the third floor of the Archaeological Museum. Maybe we can simply use spells to break in."

Henry shook his head so vehemently that his brown curls bobbed around his face. "No. There are magical wards surrounding it and a motion-censored explosive device attached to the display. If it's removed or tampered with, a shield will slam into place, and the device will be detonated. It is a specially designed shape charge, which will blow outward. It will not destroy the rooms around it, but it will take out any intruder foolish enough to try and steal the grimoire."

Tristan blanched. "*Merde*. Really? That seems a bit extreme to me."

"What about the people there?" Jayne asked. "I'm sure someone goes in to inspect or clean this room and the grimoire. Will they just be blown to pieces when they get close?"

"It's triggered only by Adept magic," Henry said. He leveled a knowing look at Jayne.

"Oh." It all clicked. "But Guardian magic...and Medb's earth magic might be able to get through."

"And Vesta's," Vivienne piped up.

"Right," said Jayne. "Plus, the magic in your device is fueled by Guardian magic as well."

"This is all just speculation, though," Henry said. "It's why I haven't entertained the idea of grabbing the Liber Linteus myself. Our magic is still rooted in our Adept blood. They weave together. We have no idea how sensitive the calibration is in this explosive device. If it even catches a whiff of Adepts, it might trigger it."

Ruger was spreading out blueprints on the coffee table. "Let's start from the outside and work our way in. All our speculation won't mean anything if we can't get inside that room."

"Where did you even get those?" Jayne asked with an impressed chuckle.

"Amanda sent them. We are the CIA, you know," Ruger said simply. He traced a circle around the large perimeter on the blueprints. "This is the Vranyczany-Hafner Palace in Zrinski Square, where the Archaeological Museum is located. There will be the usual security precautions when entering a museum of priceless artifacts—metal detectors and bag inspections, and security will be tight because the entire museum isn't open, just some of the ground-floor displays. Now, that shouldn't be a problem for us because our most powerful weapon can't be detected by human methods." He pointed to Henry. "Are there any magical security measures in place to keep us from entering that you know of?"

Henry shook his head. "All my research indicates the only magical security is in that isolated room."

"Who even put those protections in place?" Tristan wondered. "Who would be protecting this grimoire—without wanting to utilize it for themselves?"

Silence followed his question. "It would be one thing if our magical counterparts in the Croatian government had put up the wards," Jayne said. "But if that were the case, they're allies of the TCO. Right?"

"You'd think. But clearly, that's not the case or they would have agreed to work with Amanda from the get-go."

"It can't be the Kingdom or La Liberté," Jayne said. "They'd just take the grimoire for themselves."

"Are there more enemies at play?" Vivienne asked. "A threat we haven't considered?"

"There are always new threats," Ruger said darkly. "They spring up from nowhere and blindside us when we least expect it."

"It's likely whoever put this magic in place will be waiting for us to strike. Do you think we could come to an arrangement with them?" Jayne asked. "I mean, we aren't trying to *harness* the dark magical energy like Ruth and Gina are. We're seeking the grimoire to *free* the goddess trapped inside. Surely, whoever is protecting the book would want the same thing."

"We can't assume that," Henry said. "Magic has many uses and dangers. There's no way to know for sure why someone is invested in a powerful piece of magic. Perhaps they have the same knowledge we do and want to keep the goddess trapped instead of setting her free."

"Henry's right," Tristan said, earning a surprised glance from Jayne. "We have to assume the worst-case scenario—that there's an unknown enemy protecting the grimoire who will try to thwart our efforts."

"In addition to the other enemies who will likely do the same thing," Jayne added. "Well, I suppose it's no fun unless there are a dozen evil psychopaths standing in your way. It would be far too easy without those obstacles."

Tristan smiled. Trust Jayne to make light of a dark situation.

"Okay, getting inside the museum should be easy," Vivienne said, redirecting the conversation. "I think we should station someone on the outside to keep watch."

"Me or Ruger," Tristan said at once. "Vivienne, you need to be with Jayne to access your bond as easily as possible, and Henry isn't field-trained. Besides, he needs to be close by to assist if something goes awry with this." He raised the Time Jumper.

"You do it," Ruger said. "You blend in much better as a tourist than I do." He offered a wry grin.

Tristan shrugged one shoulder, trying to appear modest. The big man was right—a huge dark-skinned man with burns on his face would draw more attention than a tall Frenchman with a nonchalant attitude. Ruger couldn't do nonchalant if you paid him. He brimmed with intensity and purpose.

From her desk, Jayne scoffed. "Don't look so pleased with yourself." She turned to Ruger. "He really doesn't need his ego inflated any further."

Tristan laughed again. She could hide it all she wanted, but he could easily read the heated desire shrouded by her insults. She was either lying to herself, or everyone else. He couldn't tell. But with each barbed comment, he only grew more certain that she was using it to disguise her feelings for him.

If only he could get her to admit it.

"Vivienne, Jayne, Tristan, and Henry will go into the Archaeological Museum," Ruger said, following a path with his finger on the blueprints. "Tristan will remain on the lower levels as a second watchman while Jayne, Vivienne, and Henry go to the third floor where the Liber Linteus is held." He pointed to a small chamber located on the third level.

"That's pretty far into the museum," Jayne muttered, rubbing her forehead. "We'd have to get past a lot of hallways and security to reach it, and who knows if the staircases are safe. There was a lot of damage to the city." Her eyes drifted over Henry and Vivienne. "And we aren't exactly inconspicuous."

"Well, you *are* a Master magician," Tristan said with a smirk, just to infuriate her. "I'm sure you'll devise some genius way to go about it. Perhaps you can channel your powers and learn to levitate?"

Jayne's eyes narrowed.

"If you two are finished?" Vivienne said impatiently, waving her hand toward the blueprints.

"We'll need to practice in a simulated environment," Ruger said. "It may take some time, but we can get a team to re-create this isolated room and replicate all the spells Henry knows about that might get in our way. And then we can focus on *that*." He gestured to the device still in Tristan's hands.

"Right, well, at first, I should be the only one to touch it." Henry snatched the device away from Tristan, cradling it like it was a small child.

"Dad, you're gonna have to get over that paranoia real quickly if we're to make this work," Jayne said.

"I know!" Henry snapped, sounding like an ornery toddler who didn't want to share his toy. "I'm just a little gun-shy, after what happened with the calibrator. And I'm accustomed to working alone. I do trust you. All of you." He even glanced at Vivienne, who straightened in surprise. Henry didn't know her or Tristan very well, and yet he claimed to trust them.

Tristan wasn't sure if he believed it. But from the plea in Henry's eyes, it was clear the scientist wanted it to be true, even if they weren't quite there yet.

"But I need time before I can test that trust," Henry said.

"That's fair," Tristan said. His eyes were on Jayne as he said, "Take all the time you need. We'll be here."

Her gaze found his, sharp and honed to a point. The death glare in those eyes was a warning that Tristan chose to ignore.

I'll be waiting, he silently said to her.

One thing he had learned in his line of work was that there might not be a tomorrow. And the more time he spent with Jayne, the more he wanted to reserve all of his tomorrows just for her. Just to memorize the look and feel of her, every compli-cated facet and imperfection, every fear and desire, every thought and memory. She was a treasured book he was desperate to read, to devour every page again and again, always finding something new within the story that he hadn't seen before.

Ruger rolled up the blueprints. "I'll get these to the TCO and get a simulation room in place for training. In the meantime, Henry, you need to teach them what you can about your Time Jumper. And Jayne and Vivienne, you need to work on solidifying your Rogue bond. We can't afford any hiccups on this mission."

Henry's lips thinned, but he nodded. Vivienne and Jayne exchanged a heavy glance. Jayne's was a mixture of hopefulness and apprehension whereas Vivienne's was full of agitation.

Tristan frowned. It was clear his sister didn't have any great love for Jayne. But was it because of the Rogue bond—the fact that ultimately, Vivienne was being controlled by a stranger—or because of whatever simmering tension existed between himself and Jayne? Vivienne had never been the overprotective type, but then again, she'd been trapped in a grimoire for so long that Tristan almost didn't know who she was. What kind of sister was she to him? What kind of brother did she need? The fierce protector, or the sibling who stood back and let her pave her own path?

In a sense, almost all of them in this room were strangers to one another. Ruger and Jayne had an established relationship as mentor and student, but Henry was new to everyone—Jayne too, since she hadn't seen him for almost two decades—as was Vivienne. Even Tristan and Jayne didn't have their usual dynamic because of the complicated emotions swirling between them.

One thing was certain: there was ample opportunity for this mission to end in a complete and utter disaster.

CHAPTER

NINETEEN

SO DOPE

Cillian was getting antsy. Sitting in a reclining chair in the CIA lab made him feel suspiciously like he was at the dentist. Behind him, Quimby Cain was shuffling around the counter, opening and shutting cabinets and drawers as she muttered to herself. Sofia sat in the seat against the wall, back straight and face taut with nerves as she watched Quimby's fussing.

"How much longer?" Cillian asked uncertainly.

"Almost there!" Quimby offered a nervous chuckle. "Sorry, I'm just looking for my—ah, there it is." Metal clinked, and then she faced him, holding what looked like a huge brass helmet. "Here you go! Isn't she a beauty?"

Cillian eyed the helmet doubtfully. It had various wires tied to it, dangling from the inside to no doubt attach themselves to his skull. He suppressed a shudder. "Is this going to make me go bald or something? Like Professor X?"

Quimby barked out a surprised laugh. "Not at all! Here, try it on."

The helmet slid over his eyes and blocked his vision. "Uh... not sure if—"

Quimby was laughing her head off, and Cillian pushed up the edge of the metal to see her and Sofia holding their sides, giggling.

"Ha bloody ha," he said. "If you two don't stop, I'm going to wolf out all over you."

"Your face," Quimby gasped. "Priceless." She took the helmet from him, set it on the table, then turned back with a large needle.

"Have you ever heard of blood doping?"

"Yes, I have, and no, you are not sticking that thing in me."

"Are you afraid of needles?" Sofia asked him.

"I'm not afraid of anything," he said. "I'm just not keen on having sharp things pointed at me."

"Well, it might be hard for me to work my magic without it. I need your blood, Cillian. I think I can enhance your natural tracking skills—I mean, wolves are canines, and canines are excellent trackers, and—" At the look on his face, she blanched. "I mean, I'm not saying you're a dog, like some bloodhound, not at all. You're a seriously majestic creature who can hunt through the wilderness—"

"Stop, lass. I get it. You've figured out a way to enhance my senses when I'm in wolf form?"

"Yes," she breathed, relieved. "Exactly. Athletes benefit from enhanced red cell counts, which increase the oxygen moving through their muscles, making their performances better and allowing them to recover faster. Same idea here. I believe this will allow you to project your Rogue magic farther and sense any responses you might receive. You should be better attuned to magical signatures and will be able to find young Adepts whose magic has just turned on. And they should be able to reach out to you, as well."

"That's what I don't understand," Sofia said. "How is he supposed to receive responses? That's never happened before."

"Well, we haven't really tried," Cillian said. Between the

THE PROPHECY OF WIND

battle with Hans and the Anti-Guardians, and then the attack on the TCO, there hadn't been a lot of time for him and Sofia to train and work on this new ability of his.

"That's just the thing," Quimby said eagerly, adjusting the glasses on the bridge of her nose. "This will amplify your powers so that what once might have been a difficult or impossible task will now be more achievable. It can help accelerate your training, because you'll know exactly what a specific sensation feels like. If your senses are enhanced, it'll be easier for you to seek out that same sensation. I think what you're doing is some sort of telepathy, but we need much more experimentation to prove it."

Cillian still had his doubts. "Yeah, but...what if I hurt someone?"

"I built in fail-safes. This formula—once you let me take some blood and create it—will be tethered to Sofia's magic." Quimby gestured to Sofia with a grateful smile. "Like a true Rogue and Master relationship, she'll be with you the entire time. If you go too far, she'll be able to bring you back."

Cillian's eyes found Sofia's only to realize she was already staring at him, her gaze full of emotions he couldn't begin to read. *She'll always bring me back,* Cillian thought with a surge of affection. *She is my anchor. My harbor during the storm.*

Something heated stirred in Sofia's expression, and she averted her gaze before Cillian could decipher it. "How does this work?" she asked.

"I'll take some blood, spin it, add my special formula, spin it some more, then transfuse it back into the wolf here," Quimby answered. "Once it's all inside him, we'll go to the training room—or I guess, the makeshift training room? I don't know what to call it while they're fixing the damage from the attack and all." She winced. "Anyway, we'll go there together, and I'll oversee everything to make sure it's working properly. If, for whatever reason, Sofia is unable to call you back, I have this doohickey." She raised her wrist, and a silver watch rattled as she shook her hand. "There will be the tiniest bit of extra iron in the blood, and if it's necessary, this will act as a magnetic kill switch. Just in case."

"Smart," Cillian said, and Quimby beamed.

Quimby approached him with the needle, and he instinctively drew back. Her eyes lifted to his dark blond hair, which had grown so it curled in front of his eyes. "You aren't super attached to your hair, are you?"

He blanched, and Quimby burst out laughing. "Kidding, kidding. I swear it's safe. I've tested it several times on other Adepts. I mean, it hasn't done what I think it will do with you, Cillian; none of them have Rogue blood. But it's made their magic stronger." She grinned at Sofia as if any normal person would find this hilarious. Sofia, however, only crossed her arms, her leg bouncing with anxiety.

"Fine," he said, slapping his arm down straight, inner elbow exposed. "Get it over with."

"Okay, now just hold still," Quimby said. "Try to relax."

"Right." Cillian took a deep breath and looked at Sofia, allowing himself to fall into the cool depths of her blue eyes. She was a steadying presence, and as their eyes met, he felt something settle inside him. Something that felt safe. Like home.

He almost didn't feel Quimby stick the needle in his arm. Once it was in place, she gently attached the tubing to an empty IV bag.

"I won't be able to stand this for long," Cillian warned. "Otherwise, I might faint."

"Just pretend you're dating a vampire who needs a healthy snack. It will be over soon."

"Not funny," Sofia and Cillian said at the same time.

IT TOOK Quimby an hour to enhance the blood and transfuse it back into Cillian.

"How often will you have to do this?" he asked, turning green as she slid the transfusion needle into his other arm.

Quimby frowned, snapping a finger against the tubing to hurry it along. "Well, I don't know. The Adepts I've tried this with tend to lose the enhanced power after a week or so. Your genetic code is totally different. Sofia's, too. It could last an hour, it could be permanent. That's why we call this an experiment."

"You're a funny gal, you know that?"

Quimby sketched a bow. "I try."

"It's a nerd thing," Sofia added. "Like Jayne and her never-ending quips."

"It's a defense mechanism, actually," Quimby said. "When you're the smartest person in the room, and your brain moves faster than your mouth, you trip over your words and almost always say the wrong thing. Humor helps diffuse the tension. That's why Jayne's so snarky and silly. She's just trying to find common ground with her team."

"Was she always like that, Sofia?" Cillian asked, plainly fascinated. "The smartest girl in the room?"

Sofia laughed. "Oh my God, you should have seen her as a kid. She'd walk up to strangers and tell them all sorts of random facts, about the history of the street we were on, the phases of the moon, whatever had captured her interest that day. She was too smart for her own good."

"And now, she's the reason we're going to win this war," Quimby said fiercely. "Jayne's powers, your powers, Cillian's powers...even Tristan and his sister are going to play a part. Five people with special abilities unlike anything we've seen in my lifetime. And now you've managed to bring Henry Throne back to the fold—his PhD paper on theoretical quantum mechanics laid the groundwork for his time travel contraption. *Time travel,* you guys. A secret society of Guardians with magnified powers has been revealed... Magic is back, and the latent gene that runs through the veins of the Adepts is turning on. We're living in a sci-fi movie. This is a brave new world. I'm proud to be a part of it. I kind of hope..." She ducked her head, and Sofia nodded.

"You're hoping you have the latent Adept gene?"

"Absolutely," Quimby said, eyes shining. "Though it seems like it brings nothing but trouble." She grinned at them. "It's one thing to do theoretical magical work, but if I could experience that sense of power for myself? It would be amazing."

"Did you try this blood doping on you? See if you could turn on the gene?"

Quimby blinked at Sofia. "Well, no. It didn't feel ethical to me to try and use another Adept's magic to transfuse myself. If I make myself part of the experiment, it might taint my results. What if I become my own monster? I—"

"Erm, Quimby? I feel a bit queer."

A warmth was spreading through Cillian's body, and while he hated to interrupt the two women, he wasn't sure this was how he was supposed to feel. Heat, everywhere, burning inside him, almost like the night he turned the first time, on the sidewalk in Dublin, with Jayne looking horrified by his side.

But he didn't shift. Instead, the heat peaked, and like the relief of a fever breaking, his body was suddenly filled with a vibrant harmony, building to a crescendo, the apogee of a song only he could hear, a high C sung by a phantom soprano which turned into an army, a field of people, marching up a hill, all singing the same note, their voices ringing through his body and filling him until he thought his ears might burst, his brain might explode. He put his head in his hands, fighting as the song built to a crescendo within him.

"Gah, make it stop!"

Wave after wave of sound crashed through his body, and just when he thought he would die with the intensity, it stopped. The noise receded, leaving behind the faintest whisper of song, tendrils that he could sense somewhere near.

He looked at Quimby and Sofia in turn. Quimby was staring, hand over her mouth, aghast. Sofia, though...when he laid eyes on her, he could sense a vibration coming from her, tuned to the note of C, deep and resonant and perfect, as if she were a cello string plucked. He looked at Quimby again, and the song faded. Back to Sofia, and it strengthened.

"Oh my God," he said. "I think it worked!"

CHAPTER
TWENTY
THE SYNESTHETE

"We won't train for long," Sofia assured Quimby. "We'll just test it this time and see how it goes. There's a whole building of Adepts we can search. It will be awesome. I promise."

Sofia extended a hand to help Cillian up. He took her slim fingers in his and stood. "You've got this," she whispered to him.

He nodded. God, he hated being a test subject. He'd much rather just punch something.

But this was for a greater purpose. For the kids out there who had no one to protect them. If this worked, they could save so many lives. Cillian's Rogue magic was special but untested. Now that he had a tangible Tracking spell to work with, he felt more confident in the outcome.

The training room had indeed been nearly destroyed by Tristan and Vivienne's fire antics. Only the wards built into the walls had kept the whole place from burning down. The entire floor had to be stripped and redone, the walls reinforced, and all the equipment replaced.

For now, officers were using the cafeteria as a temporary training facility. The tables had been folded and pushed against the wall, and the sparse equipment they had in storage had been spaced around the room. Cillian had already visited the space for a few workouts. The punching bag gave him a face full of dust, and it had a large rip that made him hold his punches for fear of severing it in half.

It certainly wasn't ideal.

But for this experiment, they wouldn't need any equipment. Once they arrived, the three of them slid equipment out of the way to clear an empty space for them to work. The last thing Cillian wanted was to accidentally fling himself—or Sofia— into a set of heavy weights.

Sofia turned to face Cillian and took his hands in hers. Her skin was soft and soothing, grounding him, and the new note he sensed when looking at her was as calming as a gentle waterfall on a hot day.

"Just like we trained, right?" she asked.

He nodded. "Piece of cake."

"I'll just be...you know, over here. A safe distance away." Quimby edged away from them, drifting toward the wall.

Probably for the best, Cillian thought. He took a steadying breath. "Ready when you are."

He felt the moment Sofia reached for the Torrent. Green light exploded around him with more force than he was accustomed to. Lights flashed, nearly blinding him. He staggered backward, but Sofia's grip on his hands kept him on his feet. Her familiar sage-and-mist scent wafted over him, mingling with the faintest hint of raspberries that was so *Sofia* that it made Cillian feel right at home.

"Help me find the spell." Sofia's voice echoed slightly in his head.

Cillian squinted, but the lights were blazing so intensely, he could see nothing but flashing green orbs dancing in front of him. "I can't see anything. It's too much."

Sofia squeezed his hands. "It's all right. I can find it on my own. Just relax. Don't panic."

Cillian nodded, even though he couldn't see her. He knew magic was tied to emotions, and if he panicked or lost his cool, it could have catastrophic consequences.

"I can feel you, Cillian," Sofia said. "You're all right. We're still linked. I swear I'll shut it down if it's too much. Are you in any pain?"

"No."

"Okay, good. Just keep me updated, all right?"

"Will do. Craic on."

Sofia was silent, but Cillian could somehow feel her consciousness drifting about like a leaf on the wind. Her presence was a brush of warmth against his skin, tickling the hairs on his arms as it inched forward, searching for the spell. He resisted the urge to shudder. He had never felt her magic so acutely before. It was a puzzling and yet oddly satisfying sensation.

"Got it," Sofia muttered. Cillian could just imagine her eyes screwed up tight with concentration, her lips twisting together in that adorable way when she was super focused on her task. "Your turn. Don't forget what we practiced."

"Right." Cillian took a deep breath. He and Sofia had trained together, trying to stretch his strange new power and see just what he was capable of. They hadn't done much, unfortunately. But with this new blood coursing through his body, Cillian was terrified he might accidentally hurt someone. Or destroy this training room, too.

Projection, Cillian told himself. *Share your memories.* He remembered that first powerful occurrence with Rebecca, when all he wanted to do was send her his thoughts and emotions to reassure her, to comfort her, to assure her everything would be okay. He would need to use the same careful gift with the Adept children they found.

He focused on that feeling and then, carefully, extended it to Sofia.

The ground quivered beneath him, and sparks of green light flashed in front of him. He froze, afraid he'd accidentally triggered some explosive spell that would kill everyone in the building.

"It's all right," Sofia said. "Easy does it. You're doing great."

Cillian's mouth went dry, and he swallowed hard. Beads of sweat formed on his forehead and trickled down the back of his neck. He conjured the first memory he could think of—when he and Sofia had sat in Xiomara's house together, and Sofia promised to help him figure out his Rogue magic. That was the first time since Jayne had dumped him when he didn't feel entirely alone.

Hands shaking in Sofia's grip, Cillian urged the memory forward, trying to stretch his magic in slow and careful increments instead of slamming it into her all at once. His breathing turned shallow and harsh as he struggled to maintain his hold on this power, afraid if he didn't keep it on a leash it might go everywhere at once.

"Let go, Cillian," Sofia whispered. "You're straining yourself, and my magic can sense the tension. Relax. You're not in any danger."

"I'm not worried about myself," Cillian said, his voice labored.

"I'm fine, too. Quimby's fine. Ease up on the reins, just a bit. Remember, you're just tapping into your Rogue magic. So far, it hasn't proven to be explosive or dangerous."

Yet, Cillian wanted to say. Who knew what he was capable of? He thought of Jayne and her massive amount of power that could probably level cities if she willed it to. He was tethered to an equal amount of power from Sofia. What if he somehow pulled that from her?

The soft stroke of Sofia's thumb across his knuckles jolted

him from his worries and fears. *You're safe,* the motion seemed to say. *There is no danger here. Trust me.*

One breath at a time, Cillian released his hold on his magic, allowing it to flow freely toward Sofia. The churning energy around him swelled, and he tensed, expecting the worst. But, to his surprise, it leveled into something calm and relaxing, where the waterfall met the sun-dappled pond.

"That's it," Sofia urged.

Cillian didn't realize he'd been clenching her fingers so tightly until he relaxed his grip. God, he must have been crushing her, and she hadn't said a word.

"Oh," Sofia said suddenly.

Cillian sensed the moment his magic touched her. A blast of power rocketed through him, but this time he wasn't afraid. With Sofia still grounding him to reality, he knew this moment was isolated to just the two of them in the Torrent. No one and nothing else mattered.

Sofia sucked in a sharp breath. "I didn't realize that moment had meant so much to you."

She'd seen the memory. Cillian's face warmed with embarrassment. "Right. Well. Let's try to project it forward, shall we?"

"Yes. I've got the spell ready."

Cillian unleashed a bit more of his magic, the energy surging around him once more. Green lights danced before him, swirling and shimmering. A low hum buzzed in his ears, growing and magnifying until it resembled a deep, melodious tune.

He didn't know if this was Sofia or the spell, but it felt right. He thought of the army of people he'd seen, all singing the same note, and realized this was the signature of the Adept. Which meant Cillian should hear the accompanying harmony if and when an Adept answered him. The spell's song echoed, drifting away as it sought out other Adepts. Cillian focused on Sofia's fingers in his as they waited. The bright lights still burned against his irises. Even with his eyes shut tight, the light still bled through. He wasn't sure how much longer he could take this.

Then, he heard it. The higher-pitched harmony flowed perfectly with their melody. An Adept was returning the call. Cillian's brow furrowed as he concentrated on it, opening his magical awareness to receive it. The harmony grew louder and louder until it swelled around him, mingling with his magic. Cillian drew it inward, trying to reverse his previous attempts. *Draw it in instead of sending it out,* he told himself, imagining a huge inhale that would bring the magic and the song into his lungs.

An image appeared in his mind: a TCO officer he knew by sight, though he couldn't remember her name. She had dark brown skin and a thick black braid that ran down her back. Her eyes were wide with surprise as Cillian's magic flowed toward her.

She stood in the hallway just outside the cafeteria, frozen mid-step as if startled by the presence of his magic.

"I see her!" Sofia exclaimed. "My God, it worked!"

Cillian found himself laughing, and then, with a *whoosh* that slammed into his chest, he lost his connection to the magic. Sofia's hands slackened in his grip, and the lights vanished, leaving everything in momentary darkness as his eyes adjusted.

"Damn, you two!" Quimby shouted from across the room. "You did it! Impressive work, even a Muggle like me could see her respond to your magic."

Cillian staggered backward with a groan, the power of his magic suddenly too much for him. Sofia's hands were on his arms, steadying him.

"Quimby, can you get him a chair?" Sofia asked. The urgency in her voice told her Cillian probably didn't look so good.

He didn't *feel* good, either. Dizziness flooded his brain, and the training room disappeared from view, leaving only blurry stars and a sickening kaleidoscope of colors.

"Hang on!" Quimby muttered, her voice much closer now, though Cillian hadn't seen her approach. He felt something cool on his forehead, just before he succumbed to the darkness.

TWENTY-ONE

ALEXANDRA THE GREAT

After sharing freshly made lasagna and crunchy garlic bread for dinner, courtesy of Tristan their unofficial chef, who could apparently make anything, the band of thieves split up for various tasks. Tristan and Ruger huddled together by the desk, looking over the research. Vivienne retired to her room, warning Jayne she'd be up at the crack of dawn for another training session.

This left Jayne and her father sitting on the sofa as Ruger and Tristan's soft murmurs echoed from the other side of the room. Jayne itched to disappear into her own room—Neil Gaiman's *Good Omens* was calling to her, and she was eager to keep reading—but she wanted to stay and soak up just hanging out with her dad. Perhaps they should be discussing something productive like strategies for the mission or developing Jayne's Guardian magic.

Instead, she found herself asking, "What happened to Alexandra?"

Henry jerked as if she'd woken him from a stupor. Perhaps he'd forgotten she was sitting next to him. He truly *was* accustomed to being alone. She understood now where her introversion came from, for sure.

"What?"

"I know you can't tell me anything about the future," Jayne said, unable to bring herself to say *my daughter*. "But you can tell me about the past, right? How did your mother get trapped inside the Torrent?"

"I already told you about this." Henry scratched the back of his neck.

"I know." Jayne shifted, turning so she fully faced him. "But I want to know the details, not just the newspaper headline. I mean, she's your *mother*, Dad. My grandmother. Were you there when it happened?"

Henry shook his head. "No, but Xiomara was."

"Xiomara? The Guardian?"

"She and my mother grew up together. Did you know that?"

Stunned, Jayne could only shake her head.

"They were like sisters. When Xiomara immigrated, Alexandra could sense her Guardian magic from miles away. Xiomara was quickly adopted into the Thorne household and cherished like any other member of the family. But when they were both called to their Guardian posts, everything changed." He paused. "Not many people know this, but for a while, we believed there were nine pockets to protect, instead of eight."

"'Believed'? So, does that mean you were wrong?"

Henry's eyes filled with sorrow. "Yes. Thirty years ago, we realized the truth. And Alexandra was a casualty of that."

"I don't understand. How could you think there was a ninth pocket? If it wasn't an access point to the Torrent, then what was it?"

"It wasn't an access point. It was the *direct entrance* to the Torrent itself."

Horror seeped into Jayne's chest. *A front door.* Which

explained why Henry was looking for a back door. The eight pockets the Guardians were protecting were more like windows into the Torrent.

But a main entrance? Jayne couldn't even fathom how much power would be generated from a magical hot spot like that.

"Where is this entrance located?" Jayne asked, her mouth turning dry with anticipation.

Henry gave her a long, steady look. For the first time, he wasn't fidgeting. He remained perfectly still on the cushion next to her, his gaze full of wariness. After a moment, he said softly, "It's in Iceland."

"Iceland? Well, damn, why aren't we going there? If there's any way to bring down the Master within the Torrent, it's by storming the front gates, right?"

"No!" Henry grabbed her arm as if Jayne were about to bolt from her seat and portal there right now. "Don't you understand? At least two people were drawn in already because they got too close. There is too much power there. Power that cannot be controlled or wielded, even by a Guardian. It's why I haven't made the journey there myself. What good would it do for me to be trapped in there as well? The entrance to the Torrent is *his* domain, and he's waiting for other victims to draw near so he can pull them in, too."

Jayne suppressed a shudder. It was like a black widow spider, spinning its web and waiting for its next meal to be ensnared. "But there has to be something you can do. Maybe you don't have to get close to it. Maybe you can study the area, the surrounding magic, the terrain..."

But Henry was shaking his head again. "A Master that powerful would have a reach for miles, Jayne. He would know as soon as I set foot on the island that a Guardian was near. Attacking from the entrance is far too risky because he'll be ready for us. But a back door? I'm not even sure he knows it exists, and that might just give us a chance. Trust me, no one is strong enough to face him head-on. The element of surprise is our only advantage."

Jayne was silent for a moment as she digested this information. "Has Ruth ever been there?" she asked quietly.

Henry's expression turned stony. "I don't know for sure. But...I speculate she has. For a while, she was hunting pockets and Guardians. She still is. With that much power emanating from such an isolated spot, she would've been drawn to it."

"Maybe that's how she got bound to him," Jayne mused. She wondered if it was intentional or if she had been forced. Knowing Ruth, she wouldn't be surprised if the woman had tried to harness the Master's power for herself, and the Master had retaliated.

A grim silence passed between them. Ruger and Tristan had retreated to the kitchen to continue their discussion, giving Jayne and Henry space to continue their solemn conversation.

"Did you love Ruth? Ever?"

"Well, of course I did. She was intoxicating. You know we went to college together, yes?"

"Oxford, right?"

"Yes. She was brilliant and fearless and had a certain way about her that drew people to her side, even then. A magnetism, a seductive—yes, Jayne. I loved her once. And she loved me. And she loved you girls, in her own way. But some women are not cut out to be mothers. The magic she sought became more important than raising a family. She traded love for a lifelong quest for unceasing power. And you know the rest."

Jayne had a hard time imagining her mother loving anything or anyone but herself. Ruth was a classic narcissist; it was all about her, and always had been.

"What was Alexandra like?" Jayne asked.

Henry smiled, his expression a mixture of sorrow and fondness. "Fierce. Smart. Loyal. Like you. Like Sofia. She wasn't afraid to question things, to dig deeper when no one else would."

"Like us? That sounds more like you."

Henry huffed a bitter chuckle. "A lot of good that did her, though. It was her curiosity that brought her too close to danger. She should never have been there."

"Wasn't that her job as Guardian?"

Henry shook his head. "A Guardian bonds to the magic of a pocket—an access point. That bond warns us when the energy becomes volatile or dangerous. She would have known—the bond would have warned her she was getting too close. Her Guardian magic was trying to save her, and she ignored it."

Jayne shook her head. "You don't know that for sure. You said it yourself, this isn't a normal access point we're talking about. This is the entrance to the Torrent itself. Maybe her bond wasn't strong enough. Maybe she couldn't forge the bond at all because she was never meant to be there."

Henry's mouth twisted with regret. It was clear he didn't believe Jayne's theories But as she scrutinized him, the guilt plain on his face, she knew it went deeper.

"You blame yourself," she whispered.

Henry's eyes snapped to hers. "Of course I do. I could have stopped her."

"How? You were so young back then. You had your own pocket to protect. Alexandra was a grown-ass woman. If she wanted to do this, nothing would have stopped her."

Henry flinched. "It isn't just that. I've made my own share of mistakes because of carelessness. Recklessness. Letting my curiosity and experiments run wild."

"The calibrator, you mean?"

"Even before that. I always threw caution to the wind. The risks were worth it to me. Until they weren't." He sighed, running a hand down his face. "It was that recklessness that originally drew me to your mother. I didn't see the risks, the warning signs. Or, if I did, I told myself it was worth it. That pursuing her and the power she was capable of were worth the dangers.

"And then we had Sofia. And you. Everything changed after that. Suddenly, there *was* a limit to what I would sacrifice. But it was too late for me to take any of it back. The damage had been done. You and Sofia were in Ruth's sights, and I couldn't undo it." Tears sparkled in his eyes. "I will never be able to atone for that."

Jayne leaned forward and pressed her hand against his. "Ruth's choices are *not* your fault. She's a grown-ass woman, too. You can't control everyone, Dad. Even if you had seen the signs and intervened earlier, she still would have inflicted damage. We each have our own free will. Your past mistakes can't take the blame for everything."

Henry sniffed, offering a watery smile. "You are wise beyond your years, Jayne."

She snorted. "I don't know about that."

He shook his head. "I know I can't forcibly alter Ruth's way of thinking. But I firmly believe in the bonds we share with others. And Ruth and I do have a bond. It's been worn over the years, on the verge of severing, but it's still there. As is the person she used to be. She was always powerful and dangerous, yes, but she wasn't always like this. When we were young, she still understood caution and wisdom. She was capable of love. It might not be my fault she became what she is, but there may still be some way I can bring her back."

Jayne's heart sank at the blatant hope in his words. She touched the hard, leathery patch of skin through her sleeve. "I don't know if there's any coming back from this, Dad."

"If it were Sofia, would you give up?" Henry's voice had sharpened.

Jayne's chest tightened with dread, horror rising inside her at the thought of Sofia becoming something dark and twisted like Ruth. "Of course not. But Sofia and Ruth are not the same."

"You're right. Sofia had *you*. She got away from Ruth. Did you know Ruth's parents were just as cruel and vile as she is now? She was raised in that environment, Jayne. Abused, neglected. It was all she knew. If Sofia had been forced to do the same, we have no idea how that would've affected her or her magic."

Jayne swallowed the foul taste rising up in her throat. She didn't want to talk about this. She didn't want to think about her sister in this way.

"If we give Ruth the same nourishment and affection that you and Sofia had, maybe things could be different," Henry said, his gaze turning distant.

Jayne was shaking her head, but she had no words. Nothing would convince her father otherwise. And could she blame him? He was right—if it were Sofia, Jayne would never give up. Ever.

And she certainly wouldn't be able to end her sister's life. Not if there was the slimmest chance she could be changed.

"But, Dad," Jayne finally said in a choked voice, "how much would you risk to bring Ruth back from the dark side? Will you watch her level cities, obliterate civilizations, destroy the world? Will you let her slaughter the TCO, murder me and Sofia, before you realize her life has to end in order for this all to stop?"

Henry's face went ashen. He tried to withdraw his hand from Jayne's, but she held it tightly, leaning forward to emphasize her words.

"Don't let this be another one of your risks, Dad. Don't let this choice of yours be something else you'll regret. Power can be a gamble that takes you too far. But so can blindness. Don't let your love for the woman Ruth *was* blind you to who, and what, she is now."

With one last squeeze of his hand, Jayne rose from the couch, heart heavy and mind plagued with fears and night-mares as she made her way to bed, knowing it would be a long while before she could relax enough to fall asleep.

TWENTY-TWO

BOUNDARIES

"Okay, here's the scenario," Jayne said, standing face-to-face with Vivienne in the safe house living room. "We're in Zagreb, in the middle of the day, canvassing the area before we steal the grimoire. The Kingdom and La Liberté are coming for us on both sides, blocking us in. The entire building has been warded to keep nonmagical people from seeing what they shouldn't."

Vivienne nodded thoughtfully. "Are we in the room with the grimoire?"

"No. We're in the museum's main entrance."

"Plenty of space," Vivienne mused. "But potential witnesses. We would need something fast and lethal. A sphinx perhaps?"

Jayne gaped at her. "Like the mythological creature that asks you a riddle and if you can't answer it, she kills you?"

"Yes. That one."

Jayne remembered how Cillian had shifted into a griffin, which was also a mythological creature. The possibilities were endless, but she hadn't considered that Rogues could just shift into any imaginary thing that popped into their heads.

Unicorns, dragons, mermaids... What were the limits? Or could Vivienne shift into literally anything they could think of?

Could Jayne *invent* a creature for her to shift into? Maybe she could pull on that dragon she'd transformed during her first week of training at Quantico. Her mind was reeling with the possibilities.

"I can feel you thinking too hard about this," Vivienne said, massaging her temples. "If a sphinx is too much for you..."

"It's not," Jayne said quickly. "Let's try it. I'd like to see what happens."

Vivienne widened her stance, her face a mask of hardened determination. Jayne reached for the Torrent, the gleaming river of green stars shining brightly. Beside her stood Vivienne, still poised and at the ready.

Jayne focused on the smell of her magic—charcoal and woodsmoke, with the faintest whiff of something feline—and said, "Sphinx." In her mind, she pictured the mythical creature —the eagle wings, human head, and lion body.

Something heavy slammed into the floor, making the walls rattle. Jayne was jerked away from the Torrent, only to find herself staring at Vivienne in sphinx form. Her face was still the same, but it was covered in fur, which was quite unsettling. Two great eagle wings were spread behind her, and she was on all fours just like her lioness form, claws out and ready to cut.

Vivienne flapped her wings, floating in the air slightly. She soared across the room until she landed on the opposite end, then slashed her claws in midair. Her fangs were bared, and she turned on her hind legs to slash again at an invisible assailant.

Catching on, Jayne entered the Torrent and retrieved her bow staff, layering an Attack spell and a Freeze spell all in one. She spun in place, then slammed the blunt end of her staff into the edge of the couch cushion. The couch quivered from the Attack spell, and then went perfectly still, though that wasn't too impressive since it was just a couch. But an ordinary opponent would have been knocked on his ass, then frozen in place by the combination of spells.

Vivienne seemed to notice Jayne's intent. "Impressive," she said.

Jayne was momentarily thrown off by the fact that Vivienne the sphinx could speak, since she had a human mouth. It was odd not hearing the voice in her head.

In a flash of white light, Vivienne shifted back to her normal human form, then ran a hand along her face. "Thank God. No fur." She shuddered, and Jayne laughed.

"I can't imagine what a strange sensation that must be."

"Normally when I shift, I feel the animal's presence and can merge with that consciousness. Everything feels right and solid, as it should be. But a sphinx? Well, that was the first time I felt a bit like myself along with the animal parts. So very different."

"Have you shifted into anything mythical before?" Jayne asked.

"A Pegasus, at Vesta's request." Vivienne offered a wry smile. "It didn't go too well. Apparently, shifting into more difficult creatures is near impossible without being bonded to a magician." Her voice was laced with bitterness.

Guilt swelled in Jayne's chest. *Well, that sucks.* She knew how it felt to be bound by limitations she couldn't control. She certainly couldn't blame Vivienne for her resentment about this. Jayne's magic was necessary for Vivienne to reach her full potential. It didn't seem quite fair.

"I don't need your pity," Vivienne snapped.

Jayne groaned. "You've *got* to get out of my head."

"I'm not in your head. Your head is linked to mine. And I can't control it. It's just part of our bond."

Jayne gritted her teeth, turning away to grab her water bottle. Her stomach rumbled. "I need lunch. We'll continue in the afternoon?"

Vivienne nodded tensely, her jaw rigid and anger rolling off her in waves. But all of Jayne's sympathy had left, leaving irritation in its place. Yes, it was unfair that Vivienne had to rely on Jayne to shift properly. But it was also unfair that Vivienne had this one-way access into Jayne's private thoughts. She knew it was because Rogues needed to be able to sense their Masters when they were called to shift. But still... It was invasive. And it needed to stop.

She enjoyed a salad niçoise, grateful that with Tristan on the team, her food choices had been elevated above elementary school cafeteria fare, then shut herself in her room and immediately reached for the Torrent. The flow of glistening stars surrounded her like a warm, comforting embrace. She sighed with contentment, enjoying this sacred space and its solitude. She didn't mind sharing power with Vivienne—most of the time. But sometimes, she missed the peace and tranquility of being in the Torrent alone.

She pictured a chain link fence, then imagined draping a white cloth over it. A spell shimmered into existence and floated before her. Jayne scrutinized it, then layered another spell on top: a kill switch, activated only by her. It appeared as a red button, merging with the blanketed fence.

Jayne collected the spell in her hands and emerged from the Torrent. The ball of glowing energy swirled in her palms.

A Boundary spell. Just what she needed.

She glanced toward the door, but it was still shut. No one was around to witness this. With a deep breath, Jayne released the spell. Something cold trickled along her forehead and temples like someone had placed an ice cube on the top of her head. She shivered as the sensation spread through her mind like a brain freeze. And she didn't even have the benefit of eating ice cream! That was just cruel. She clenched her teeth against the sharpness of it as the ice crept into her, deeper and deeper.

At long last, the sensation faded, and Jayne straightened.

She felt...nothing. Then again, this was a brand new spell, so she wasn't sure how she should feel. The true test would be when she and Vivienne were near each other, and Jayne was experiencing some embarrassing emotion. Vivienne would be sure to call her out on it.

But for now, she had to assume it was working. And the next time they trained, she would deactivate the spell and put their bond back in place. Easy peasy.

A knock sounded on the door. Jayne jerked, her face warming, though she had no reason to be embarrassed. Clearing her throat, she said, "Come in!"

It was Tristan. Jayne's stomach did an immediate backflip, but she forced herself to remain composed.

"Ruger just got word," he said, his eyes alight. "The simulation room is ready for us. Gather your things. We'll be portaling out of here in a few minutes."

CHAPTER

TWENTY-THREE

RESCUE MISSION

Cillian was out for two days straight, and Sofia was worried sick. She plotted ways to create a safe Time Catch for their impending school, followed the news reports on the paranormal occurrences religiously, and trained with Seo-Joon and Tamara, trying to harness her Master abilities without Cillian's help. Even Seo-Joon admitted Sofia's reflexes were getting faster, her magic more precise. But that didn't stop the mounting anxiety from rising inside her. What if Quimby's blood doping had permanently damaged Cillian somehow? She couldn't do this without him.

Quimby had run a few tests on the samples of his blood and assured her everything worked properly. She'd given a full briefing to Seo-Joon, plus the magnetic fail-safe, to supervise their future training sessions, as the tech expert was needed for Jayne's mission and couldn't stay.

Sofia wasn't sure if she was relieved or not. On the one hand, she felt a lot better knowing someone who wielded magic was overseeing their training; the idea of accidentally injuring Quimby was a constant plague on her mind. But on the other hand, Quimby knew the inner workings of this experiment like no one else did. If Cillian didn't recover, they would need her help. She was the only one who could fix it.

"You're fretting again," Seo-Joon teased.

Sofia blinked from her thoughts, though her fears still circulated in her mind like a nauseating tornado. "Sorry. I'm ready."

Seo-Joon wielded an Attack spell between his fingers. Tamara on his left did the same before they sent both careening toward Sofia.

Sofia accessed the Torrent, reaching for a Shield spell first and draping it over herself, then grabbing a Block spell. Before she could, the spell she'd crafted with Cillian rose up in front of her, as if knowing where her thoughts were. Momentarily caught off guard by the sight of the Call spell, which resembled a musical staff with several notes woven between it, Sofia accidentally let go of the Block spell.

Her Shield spell engaged just in time, absorbing the brunt of the attack. But with two Attack spells, the Shield could only do so much. A heavy force slammed into her chest, sending her sprawling on the hard floor. She groaned, her arm and shoulder flaring in pain.

Seo-Joon rushed over to her and helped her up. "You all right?"

Sofia groaned again and rubbed her arm. "I'm fine. Just distracted, is all."

"I think that's enough for today. Go see to your Rogue."

"He's not my Rogue," Sofia said automatically.

"Yes, he is." Seo-Joon smiled. "It's not a relationship label, Sofia. You two are bonded."

Sofia's cheeks heated. Right. Of course. She shook her head. "Yeah, okay. I'll go check on him."

As she strode down the hallway, the only thought circulating in her mind was *My fault. My fault.*

This entire plan to rescue Adept children and create a safe environment for them to learn their powers had been her idea.

And now Cillian was injured because of it. What had she been thinking? If she had been the one being dosed with a magical blood elixir and undertaking those risks, that would've been fine. But Cillian?

If he's permanently damaged by this, I'll never forgive myself, Sofia thought, her heart squeezing painfully in her chest.

Cillian was everything to her. And perhaps she hadn't realized it until this moment. Despite what she said earlier, they were becoming more than partners. More than a bonded Master and Rogue.

After the higher-ups had given the all-clear to use portals once more, the magical doorways to Sofia and Cillian's apartments had been reinstated. However, neither of them had used them yet, sleeping on the bunks in the TCO headquarters instead. Sofia got the sense that Cillian, like her, didn't enjoy being alone with his thoughts for too long, especially not after such a traumatic event. Besides, Sofia was paranoid that if she returned to her apartment, the TCO would be attacked again and she wouldn't be around to help.

But the hard truth was, it was difficult for Sofia to be alone.

During her toughest days, Jayne had always been there. Through every chemo treatment. Every anniversary of their parents' deaths. Jayne had always made time for Sofia.

Perhaps she had taken that for granted.

When Sofia reached the spare room with the extra cots, she froze in the open doorway, surprised to see Cillian already on his feet and downing a bottle of some kind of energy drink.

"You're up!" Sofia announced stupidly.

Cillian finished his gulp and winced. Upon closer inspection, she realized it was a customized green smoothie, created by Quimby to help rebuild the officer who needed a boost. She made a face.

"It's not half bad," Cillian said, raising the bottle to her. "I mean, it's no Guinness, but it's got the nutrients, you know?" He took another swig.

Sofia was prepared to wrap him in a tight embrace but faltered. He should be angry with her. He should be upset he'd nearly died because of their training. Yet, he seemed perfectly at ease.

It's not like Cillian to hold grudges, she told herself.

Somehow, it made her feel guiltier.

"I'm so sorry," she croaked. "If I'd known—I thought it was perfectly safe, I—"

Cillian shook his head and touched her shoulder, his eyes tender. "It's not your fault. We both knew there were risks. Besides, Amanda came down and talked to me. She speculates it was just a burnout. I used too much of my magic too quickly. At least I didn't set myself on fire like you Adepts tend to do."

Sofia flinched, unable to stop the image of Cillian engulfed in flames from entering her mind.

"We just need more practice in shorter segments, that's all," he went on. "It's like an exercise regimen. If you run a marathon with no training, your body's going to punish you for it. We practice one day at a time, building our endurance."

Sofia found herself nodding even though her panicked thoughts were begging her to step away, to abandon this mission. But then she remembered the news reports, the child and her family who were now being hunted by those who didn't understand magic.

Would that have been Jayne, if she hadn't been raised by Sofia?

"I'm willing to carry on despite the risks," Cillian said softly. "Are you?"

"If it means risking *you*? I don't know." Sofia sighed. "Risking myself is one thing, but you—you're too important, Cillian." Her cheeks burned from her admission, but she didn't regret it. She needed him to know.

Cillian's eyes shifted into something molten, something that made Sofia's stomach flutter. His hand moved from her shoulder to her cheek, brushing one knuckle along her jawline. Sofia suppressed a shiver of pleasure from the lightness of his touch. He had such calloused fingers, such a hardened exterior. And yet she knew better than anyone that he was one of the gentlest souls she'd ever met.

"Do you know what I thought of when I was burning from the inside out?" Cillian's voice was almost a whisper.

Dazed, Sofia shook her head slightly, afraid if she spoke she would startle him away.

"I thought of you. You're my anchor, Sofia. My safe harbor. My lighthouse guiding me home. It was you who kept me grounded when all that magic consumed me. I couldn't do this without you."

Sofia's breath caught in her lungs. She struggled to inhale, but she couldn't reach any oxygen. All she could do was stare openmouthed at Cillian, reeling from his declaration, which was so much more eloquent than hers had been.

Who *was* she right now? Sofia had always been a shameless flirt, which Jayne had often teased her for. But here and now, with this beautiful man still stroking her cheek like she was something precious, Sofia couldn't move or speak at all. She was rendered completely helpless by this Irish kickboxer and his delicious musky scent.

Perhaps it was because what she and Cillian had was so much more than flirting. So much stronger and deeper.

And that frightened her.

"If something happened to you, I don't know if I'd survive it," Sofia breathed, finally finding the will to speak.

Cillian offered a small smile, half his mouth quirking upward. He was standing close enough for her to fully enjoy the fang-shaped pattern of light freckles under his eyebrow. Every mark, every scar on his body, only made him more of a master-piece. More of a warrior. A survivor.

Just like Sofia.

"It's an occupational hazard, I'm afraid," he said. "If we both had desk jobs, this would be very different. And very boring."

Sofia laughed. She had to agree with that. She wasn't sure if she could ever go back to waiting tables or serving drinks in Nashville, not after experiencing what this world of magic had to offer.

"I'll be careful," Cillian promised. "We both will. But those kids need us."

"I know."

"So...shall we continue with the rescue mission then?"

"One step at a time, right? If it's too much, we stop. And we *aren't* working for more than two minutes at a time. Understood?"

Cillian's expression sobered, but his eyes glinted with mischief. "Yes, ma'am."

Sofia grinned but she didn't move. His hand was still resting against her cheek. She felt pulled in, drawn to him like a magnet. But her inner thoughts told her if she didn't step back right now, she'd do something she'd regret. Something they could never turn away from.

Swallowing down her yearning, she eased backward, and Cillian dropped his hand. Her skin instantly cooled from his absence. "I'll...go tell Seo-Joon we're ready for a training session. Just a quick one, though. You've only just woken up."

Cillian smiled and raised his bottle again. "I'm fortified by all these glorious nutrients. I'll be fine."

Chuckling, Sofia exited the room, still reeling from the heat of what had almost happened between them.

CHAPTER

TWENTY-FOUR

WIBBLY WOBBLY TIMEY WIMEY

W hen Jayne, Tristan, Vivienne, Henry, and Ruger stepped
through the portal, Jayne's first thought was that they
were infiltrating an illegal drug ring and the drop was
happening right here in this abandoned warehouse.

Because that's exactly what it was. An enormous, empty
warehouse large enough to hold sixty semi-trucks. Maybe
more.

"Cozy," Jayne said, rubbing her arms against the chill of the
icy interior. Clearly, there was no central heating. But that was
fine. Creature comforts were for wusses.

"This way." Ruger led them forward, their steps echoing in
the vast space.

The air smelled of dust and rot and something that
reminded Jayne suspiciously of gunpowder. "What is this
place?"

"A warehouse," Tristan said.

Jayne shot him a scathing look. He winked at her.

"An abandoned TCO training facility in the Savage River
State Forest in Maryland," Ruger supplied before Jayne could

bite Tristan's head off. "We keep it cloaked in case we need it. It'll serve our purposes well."

Jayne frowned. How was an enormous and obviously *empty* space in the middle of the woods going to help them with their simulation training? But a forest—she could use a good workout. Fresh air, sunshine. She was wilting. A hike in some trees would certainly help.

Ruger guided them to a door at the end of the room. He waved his hand over the lock, and the air shimmered with magic. A small *click*, and then the door swung open.

Jayne sucked in a breath. Judging by the size of the warehouse, she had expected this to be an exit leading them to the loading docks or something. But instead, it opened into a much smaller—and *colder*—room.

The area was almost completely dark save a single shining spotlight illuminating the center. A red panel stood on one end of the room with a wall label full of information about the Etruscans. On the opposite end was a small garniture of antique Egyptian vases. And in the middle was a large, long, vitrine that housing the mummy around whom the Liber Linteus had originally been wrapped. Even in perpetual death, Nesi-hensu was tall and regal, her corpse the color of coffee grounds.

Stretched along the wall adjacent to the mummy was the grimoire itself—thin strips of fabric, carefully spread in neat rows, all encased in glass. From a distance, they looked more like elongated wooden planks, but Jayne knew better. Even knowing they were merely a replica of the real thing, she felt her skin prickle with awareness. There was no magic here, and yet... Some innate presence within her swelled with certainty. *This is what I'm meant to do,* a voice inside her seemed to say. *This is the right path.*

Staring at the Liber Linteus, even if it was a fake, was all the confirmation Jayne needed. This was her purpose.

She stepped forward, eager to begin working, and the energy shifted around her, momentarily sucking the air from her body. Jayne staggered, her chest squeezing tight, her breaths turning sharp and ragged. Swallowing hard, she whirled to shoot an accusing look at Ruger, who lingered in the doorway. But he was frozen solid, his expression still and unresponsive.

After a moment, he stepped through the doorway, joining Jayne in the room. His solemn expression told her he wasn't surprised.

"A *Time Catch*?" Jayne hissed. "Are you insane? Do you remember the last time we trained in one of these? Amanda swore we'd never use one again."

Henry appeared behind Ruger, grinning. "Excellent. It worked perfectly."

Jayne stared at him, the way he gazed around the room with pride gleaming in his eyes. Understanding washed over her. "It's your Time Catch."

"Henry has several contained Time Catches secured around the globe," Ruger said. "He was kind enough to lend one of them to us for his training."

"And what if one of us gets stuck again?" Jayne asked.

"That won't happen," Henry said. "I've built in security measures with all my Time Catches. If something happens to this entrance"—he gestured to the doorway, through which Tristan and Vivienne now stepped—"the Time Catch will disengage until the entrance can be repaired. Time will flow normally, as it should, until the error has been resolved."

Jayne had to admit she *was* comforted knowing her father was in charge of the construction and maintenance of this Time Catch. He clearly knew more about the science behind it than she did—and quite possibly the TCO.

"*La vache!*" Vivienne murmured, rubbing her arms. She

exchanged a glance with Tristan. "This is certainly different from the Domdaniel."

A dark look crossed over his face. Jayne wondered if he was reminded of how long Vivienne had been absent, or if he simply grieved over the loss of what had once been their home. Now, it belonged to enemies who wanted them dead.

A surge of sympathy filled her chest, and she was gripped with the sudden urge to reach out and squeeze his hand. They hadn't talked about his mother being in custody, nor her upcoming trial. She should remedy that soon.

Vivienne's eyes snapped to Jayne's, and she stilled, wondering if the Rogue had sensed her spike in emotion. But Vivienne merely stepped past her to examine the rest of the room.

Does that mean the Boundary spell works? Jayne wondered, hope rising inside her.

"How is it different?" Henry asked. Jayne recognized the crazed scientist look in his eye and knew he would giggle like a schoolgirl if given the chance to properly study the Domdaniel.

"The air," Tristan said, all darkness fading from his face, replaced by his usual mask of apathy. "It feels different. Smells different. The frequency of time must be altered from what we're accustomed to."

Henry nodded. "You are correct. Unless a Time Catch is constructed with the exact time frequency, down to the last millisecond, it will not feel the same as another. I'm impressed you could infer that."

The smug look on Tristan's face made Jayne roll her eyes. She smothered a groan and turned away to study the room at large. It was quite a small space, but Jayne didn't expect much since its main purpose was to house the Liber Linteus. Once again, her eyes were drawn to those ancient strips of fabric.

"Everything is crafted with precision to replicate the room

inside the Archaeological Museum," Ruger said. "Feel free to look around and acquaint yourself with every last detail. We don't want anything overlooked during our operation. Please try not to touch anything, though, otherwise we'll have to reassemble it."

"How did you even do this?" Jayne wondered, running her finger along the cream wallpaper.

"Jayne. I literally just said don't touch anything."

She jerked her hand back and shot Ruger an incredulous look. "It's just the wallpaper. Sheesh."

"As I said, we are the CIA," Ruger said. "We have contacts all over the world. Between the photos they sent us and Henry's prior knowledge of the area, we were able to piece this together."

"That, and a powerful Tracking spell," Henry chimed in. "It allows us to momentarily see into a space without actually portaling there."

"And why *can't* we just portal there?" Vivienne asked.

"Tracking is smaller magic," Ruger said. "It doesn't require as much energy or power and is not easily detected. But portaling? That kind of magic is too strong to be overlooked. It would alert the wards, and we'd be locked in within seconds."

"Kind of like the difference between major and minor grimoires?" Jayne asked.

Tristan glanced at her and grinned, clearly remembering their training in Rome together.

Rome. Where they'd pretended to be a married couple and shared a bed and kissed in the most wild, passionate way she had ever experienced...

Jayne looked away quickly, her cheeks flaming. She waited for Vivienne to comment on the quick exchange, but the Rogue remained silent.

I love you, Boundary spell, Jayne thought.

"Yes, exactly," Ruger said, giving her a nod of approval. "Varying degrees of magic."

"So, explain to me the explosive device," Vivienne said, standing next to the case with the linen strips, her hands hovering over the glass container. The quivering of her finger-tips was the only betrayal of her emotions. Her voice and expression were perfectly composed, but the movements of her hands were delicate and careful, ever aware of the sacred relic before her. Like Jayne, Vivienne clearly knew the Liber Linteus was to be revered, even if this was merely a replica.

"It has a weight sensor," Henry explained. "If any piece of the linen strips is moved, it will detonate, blowing the shape charge outward, toward you. But if we use the Time Jumper, it will give us a few extra seconds to grab the grimoire and portal out of there before the detonator is triggered."

"Are we to remove the strips, or just take the whole vitrine?" Jayne asked, eyeing the replica of the grimoire doubtfully. Both seemed too time-consuming for the precious few seconds Henry's Time Jumper would allow. The strips were fragile and delicate, and the proper procedure for handling such an ancient relic would take far too long. But the glass case took up nearly the entire wall; it would be almost impossible to move.

When no one answered, Jayne turned to find Ruger staring at her with such intensity she knew she was missing something vital. Then, it hit her. "*Oh!* Right. The Carry spell."

Ruger nodded with a small smile. "You only need to touch the vitrine for the barest of seconds before the Carry spell will swallow it. Then, you can get out."

"But it's those seconds that present the biggest problem," Henry said. "The Time Jumper only allows for thirteen seconds. No more. So, if time resumes and you haven't left the room yet, the explosive device will still detonate."

Jayne flinched. "And I'm super fond of keeping all my limbs, so let's *not* make that happen, please."

"We think we have a solution for that," Ruger said. "With some tweaking, it might be possible to extend that to sixteen seconds."

Henry's face paled. "No. It isn't possible. It isn't safe."

"You aren't the only one with a scientific mind," Ruger said.

Henry opened his mouth to argue when a voice chimed from the doorway, "Knock, knock!"

Jayne turned, her face splitting into a wide grin. "Quimby!"

Quimby Cain was teetering slightly, her face ashen as she took in their surroundings. "Wow, that Time Catch transition is no fun." She adjusted the strap of her messenger bag over her shoulder.

"You must've come in right behind us," Tristan speculated. "We've only been in the Time Catch for a few minutes."

Quimby nodded. "I saw you walk in, but I wanted to double-check that I had everything I needed." She gestured to her bag, which clinked slightly. Jayne had no doubt there were all manner of vials tucked inside.

"Who is this?" Henry asked, his tone laced with accusation. Jayne could tell he was still upset about the whole sixteen-seconds thing.

Quimby uttered a soft gasp and raised a hand to cover her mouth. "Oh. My. God. Is that—You're *the* Henry Thorne!" She squealed and bounced on her feet. "I can't believe it! I actually get to meet you!" She surged forward, grasping Henry's hand in both of hers and shaking it vigorously.

Henry blanched, clearly taken aback by Quimby's enthusiasm. When she was done shaking his hand, he took a solid step away from her and offered a nervous smile. "Um, hello."

"Quimby Cain, tech expert." She inhaled a shuddering breath, her eyes shining. "God, this is such an honor. You are my *hero*. Your work is just absolutely stunning."

Henry frowned. "You've seen my work?"

"Of course! I'm with the team that's been analyzing your

research. Everything we find only makes me more and more in awe of you. You're a science legend. I've read everything you've done on quantum mechanics."

"She speaks as if she's known about him for years," Vivienne said incredulously. "Didn't we just find out about his existence like a week ago?"

"It doesn't take much for Quimby," said Jayne, fondly remembering her own introduction to the tech expert where a similar fangirling moment occurred, even though Jayne had only known about her magic for a few months.

"So, this is the scientist who will alter my careful calculations and add extra seconds to the Time Jumper?" Henry asked weakly, his expression wild as he looked at Ruger. "Decades of research I poured into this, and she's supposed to change everything after only studying it for a few days?"

"Oh, no, no, I wouldn't dream of changing your calculations," Quimby said quickly. "I simply want to add to them. I noticed you were utilizing certain gemstones to fuel the device. Have you considered charging those with Guardian magic ahead of time instead of waiting until the device is activated?"

Henry frowned. "That wouldn't work because of the energy of the Tesla coils. They've already been charged by so much energy that they couldn't possibly take any more."

Quimby's expression brightened. "That depends entirely on the gem you're using." She unzipped her bag and pulled out a few sheets of paper. "See, I've been studying different types of quartz stones, and with Jayne's combo-platter earth magic and Guardian blood—"

"Okay, before they both get too wibbly wobbly with their timey wimey discussion," Jayne said, turning to Ruger, "we should get started. Whether or not we have the Time Jumper, there are still the wards to get through. We should work on that."

"Easy there, Doctor," Tristan said, placing his hand on her

shoulder. Jayne looked at him in alarm, unsure if she was more surprised he understood her *Doctor Who* reference or that he was bold enough to touch her right here and now. "We just got here. And you and Vivienne still have a lot of training to do before you're ready."

"And you haven't even utilized Vesta's full powers yet," Vivienne said. "I felt Medb's earth magic when we trained, but I didn't sense Vesta at all." Her tone was accusatory, and Jayne remembered how defensive Vivienne was about the fire goddess.

"I'm just not used to it, that's all," Jayne said. "I'll get there."

"Yes, you will," Ruger said. "Tristan's right. You and Vivienne work on training until you *are* used to it. We need all the power we can get, and here in the Time Catch, we have plenty of time to harness that."

Jayne blinked. "Wait, are we going to train *here*? In this room you told us not to touch?"

Ruger sighed and approached the wall where Jayne had been inspecting the wallpaper. He waved his hand, and a door appeared. When he swung it open, it revealed a sitting room and a mini kitchen. On the opposite end of the room was a small hall that no doubt led to a set of bedrooms.

"We'll be...*living* in this Time Catch?" Jayne asked.

"Yes, living in a Time Catch," Tristan said sarcastically. "What a novel idea. Wish someone had thought of it before."

"Shut up."

"It wouldn't be the first time you've spent an inordinate amount of time in a Time Catch," Ruger pointed out.

Jayne shuddered as she remembered her time in Alarik's Time Catch. God, that had been agony. She had to admit, Henry's creation was much easier to bear than Alarik's, which had drained her magic and made it hard to breathe. Already, her lungs had acclimated to the change here, and she felt as ordinary as if they were still inside the safe house.

"You really thought of everything, didn't you, Rug?" Jayne said with a smirk.

"Just get in there, *Agnes*," Ruger said, though his mouth twitched with amusement. "We've got a lot of work to do."

CHAPTER

TWENTY-FIVE

JE VEUX ÊTRE AVEC TOI

Tristan sat at a small desk in the warehouse bunker, poring over Henry and Quimby's notes about the Time Jumper to understand as much of it as he could. He hadn't planned on getting a PhD in quantum mechanics this evening, but he had no choice. The furniture had been pushed up against the wall, just like at the safe house, but thankfully, there was more space here.

The kitchen was in a separate room along with a small dining area, providing them plenty of space to divide and conquer. Jayne and Vivienne were recovering from another training session. Ruger had portaled back to the TCO for a debriefing with Amanda. Henry and Quimby were in the dining area lost in a conversation so eye-waveringly technical he had to remove himself from their presence. He'd tried keeping up, but after the sixteenth mention of quarks and the Majorana particle, he decided to leave this part of the heist planning to the experts.

Instead, he perused the elaborate blueprints and diagrams Henry had created for his Time Jumper, which were precise and surprisingly easy to understand, once Tristan could translate some of Henry's scribblings. He identified the symbol of three triangles to represent Guardian magic, and the diagram showed exactly where that entered into the device and how it triggered the mechanism.

"Comme c'est fascinant," he muttered, turning the page to scrutinize a sketch of the interior workings of the device. Henry's handwriting might be chicken scratch, but his drawings were detailed and decipherable.

"Don't let my dad hear that, or he'll talk your ear off about wormholes and the time vortex."

Tristan looked up to find Jayne in the doorway, her hair pulled into a high ponytail. She still wore her exercise clothes— a halter tank top with sweatbands on her wrists, which Tristan knew she wore to cover up the patch of gray skin on her arm. Her tight yoga pants clung to her curves, making Tristan's mouth go dry. She raised her eyebrows as she took a long swig of water.

God, this woman has no idea how beautiful she is, Tristan thought, momentarily smitten at the sight of her.

Or perhaps she did. She was certainly confident enough.

Tristan rose to his feet, noting how Jayne's hand tightened on her water bottle, her eyes turning guarded and wary. He smirked, knowing how much his nearness unsettled her.

But she'd brought this on herself. She had approached him. "Good workout?"

Jayne lifted one shoulder. "Better than before, if that's saying much."

"It is. Last time, Vivienne the hawk nearly gouged out my eyes."

Jayne snorted loudly. "Yeah, that was a hoot. No pun intended."

"Hawks don't hoot. They chwirk."

"You're such a killjoy."

Tristan grinned. "I make it my life's mission to invalidate your puns."

Jayne rolled her eyes as she took another sip of water, but Tristan didn't miss the gleam of amusement in them.

He drew closer, leaning against the wall beside her so they stood face-to-face. He wanted to ask, *Why are you here?* But he also didn't want to startle her away. She didn't often approach him of her own volition, and he was curious to see where this would go.

So, he waited. And watched. Her eyes skirted around the room, clearly dodging his gaze. A pink flush spread along her cheeks that had nothing to do with her workout.

"I'm not done yet," Jayne said abruptly.

Tristan blinked, momentarily caught off guard. "I... What?"

"With training. My workout. Practice with Vivienne is helpful in establishing our bond, but it doesn't really do anything for me magically. Or physically." Her eyes cut to Tristan's, and heat pooled in his stomach at the stark desire burning in her gaze.

Physically. Tristan smirked, his eyebrows lifting. "Ah. I'm flattered by your proposition. Where, exactly, would you like to satisfy your physical needs? Here on the couch? Or in my bed?"

Jayne's face turned beet red, and she rolled her eyes again. "God, Tristan, you never stop."

"Only because I know you secretly love it."

Her grin betrayed her, even as she shook her head. "What I'm trying to say is, will you spar with me?"

"What about Vivienne?"

"I think the Rogue magic is more taxing for her. She usually needs to turn in after our training. I can't blame her. For as long as she was locked away with Vesta, it's probably a shock to her body, all this power and shifting."

Tristan flinched inwardly at the reminder of his sister's imprisonment, the usual guilt and regret swelling within him. *If only I'd been faster... If only I'd found her sooner... If only I'd known where to look...*

Jayne jabbed a finger into his chest, jolting him from his thoughts. "I know that face. Don't dwell on it. She's alive. She's unharmed. She's here, and safe. That's all that matters."

"Is it?" Tristan asked. "So much of her life was sucked away by her time in that grimoire."

"Yes, but she wasn't suffering! She was being trained by a freaking fire goddess. She was taken care of, Tristan. It's not like she was enduring years of torture."

"No, but I was!" Tristan's heart was racing, his thoughts frantic. He hadn't meant to burst like this, but now that he'd started, he couldn't stop. "For years, I expected the worst. A worse fate than even death. Torment, agony, being dismembered and torn apart by demons or whatever unholy creatures might be living within the grimoire. I can't just shut down those fears overnight. Yes, she's here and she's safe and I'm beyond relieved. But that won't stop the nightmares that have been plaguing me ever since I lost her." He shook his head, closing his eyes against the pain burning in his mind. "That guilt doesn't fade easily."

He felt the warmth of Jayne's body as she drew closer until her arm brushed against his. Her hand hovered close to his face as if she was unsure whether she wanted to take that leap and touch him. Something solidified in her eyes as she made her decision and pressed her warm palm against his cheek. Tristan sighed, relishing the soft, smooth feel of her skin against his. Even if, right now, he didn't feel as if he deserved it.

"You think I don't know guilt?" Jayne whispered. "My sister was kidnapped by the Kingdom. Tortured. My dad was held prisoner in exile because my mother tried to siphon my powers as a small child, and I was powerless to stop her. For years, my older sister hid us both from harm while I lived in ignorant bliss, unable to do a damn thing to help. She had a dampener on her powers that caused cancer to eat away at her body, just to keep us off the magical grid." Agony flared in her eyes, bright and potent. It called to Tristan's, beckoning him closer to share her suffering. Then her eyes focused, hardened determination gleaming in her gaze, so familiar and comforting that Tristan felt the tension in his chest ease slightly.

"But as easy as it would be to fall into that despair, to wallow in it," Jayne went on, "I can't let myself do that. Otherwise, their sacrifices will have been for nothing. All I can do is face forward and look to the future. To the things I can change. I can be better here and now. I can help. I can fight. The people I love have suffered, and I can never go back and undo that. But I can prevent other people from suffering *now*. People I love. Even strangers. Everyone is important to someone, and every effort we make matters."

A knot formed in Tristan's throat, making it hard to breathe. Her words resonated so much with him, but how often had he repeated those same ideas to himself, hoping to snap out of his bleak thoughts? How often had he tried to convince himself of the exact same thing, only for the pain to return?

"I know I can't just flip a switch and turn off your grief and guilt," Jayne said quietly. "It will take time. But if you ever find yourself sinking into that abyss again, just find me and I'll sit by your side and offer a stream of cheerful chatter until you perk up." She flashed a wide grin that made Tristan chuckle.

"Ah, how could I resist the annoying chit-chat of our glorious Master magician? To have you constantly muttering in my ear would be as pleasant as the high-pitched hum of a mosquito that won't leave you alone."

Jayne laughed. "I'll take that as a compliment. Those mosquitoes are damn persistent."

Tristan sobered and nodded. "Thank you, Jayne. I truly appreciate it."

Her eyebrows rose. "What, no smarmy reply? No quip? No insult? I'm not sure what to do with you right now."

Tristan leaned in, allowing himself to fall into those deep blue eyes, so bright with energy and humor, her face so close that he could feel her breath mingling with his. "What would you *like* to do with me?" His voice was a low, husky murmur.

Fire burned in her eyes, scorching and all-consuming. He waited for her usual protests, for her to push him away as she always did.

But she didn't.

"It's as you said," Tristan continued. "There is only here. And now. No regrets."

Jayne wet her lips, and he followed the movement of her tongue, his stomach clenching with desire.

"So, what, after one conversation now you're a seize-the-day type of guy?" Her weak attempt at humor was marred by the quiver in her voice.

"I'm a fast learner."

Their noses brushed, and Jayne's breath hitched. But still, she didn't turn away. Something was different about her. She seemed less restrained. Bolder and more curious. Tristan wasn't sure why, but he wasn't about to pass up this opportunity.

"*Mon chéri,*" Tristan whispered, raising his hand to run his fingertips down her jawline, trailing a path down her neck and throat until his hand skimmed her collarbone.

Her eyes closed and she arched into his touch with a soft gasp that made his blood boil. His other hand found her waist and drew her against him until their hips met.

"*Je veux être avec toi,*" he whispered, his mouth brushing hers. *I want to be with you.*

"*Je te veux,*" she breathed. *I want you.*

It was all the invitation he needed. His mouth captured hers, slow and sensual, his lips moving gently to give her plenty of opportunity to stop him.

A small sound escaped her, and her hands were on him, pulling him closer. She wrapped her arms around his neck, her fingers twining in his hair. Their kisses turned more urgent, more frantic, more desperate. Their tongues met, and she tasted like rose water and spice and pure heat. Tristan's insides were on fire. He needed more of this. More of her.

His mouth left hers to glide down her neck, pressing kisses along her throat. His tongue flicked along her collarbone and she moaned, her hips writhing against his. She pushed against him until his back met the wall, her body aligned with his. He could feel all of her, her curves fitting perfectly against his muscles as if they were meant to be like this, two puzzle pieces connected together.

She kissed him again, her hands fiddling with the edges of his shirt until her fingertips met his bare skin. He groaned against her mouth as her hands splayed along his chest and abdomen, exploring the ridges and planes of his body. Jayne tugged at his shirt, undoing one button at a time with agonizing slowness. He nearly growled at her to simply rip the shirt off, but in seconds, she was done, and the shirt floated to the floor.

He hooked a thumb under the waistband of her pants, his skin brushing the tender skin there, and she closed her eyes and made a strangled sound that only inflamed him further.

He tugged gently, guiding her forward. With a few drunken steps, they made their way into his bedroom. He kicked the door shut just as Jayne shoved him onto the bed before climbing atop him, her legs straddling him. She was a goddess, this woman. And the glint in her eyes meant she knew exactly how much she was torturing him.

Her lips were on his, her teeth grazing his tongue. She was fumbling with his belt, even as he thrust upward, straining against the fabric of his jeans. When her hands brushed against his hardness, he nearly cried out. God, he needed her...

"Mon amour," he murmured.

Jayne went suddenly still and sat straight up.

Startled, Tristan looked up, unsettled by the look of fear and uncertainty that crossed her face. She was panting, her lips smeared from their kisses, her eyes wild with desire. But something else crept into her expression.

"What—what's wrong?" he asked breathlessly, his insides still a volcano of desire and longing. He could almost scream with the agony of it, of resisting her, of waiting.

"Do you love me?" she asked.

Shock speared through him. "What?"

"Tristan, do you love me?" Her voice was clear, now, and something like panic crept into her tone.

Merde. "I— Why would you ask that?" He wasn't sure if he could answer. And even if he could, what was she afraid of—that he did? Or he didn't?

Jayne was climbing off him, and a protest died in his throat at the look of pure torture on her face. What had happened? He wasn't sure how, but it was clear he had catastrophically ruined this moment.

"I can't do this," Jayne said, her hand on her forehead. She looked so distressed she might cry.

Tristan drew closer to her, but she lifted a hand. "Please don't. I just—" She broke off, pressing her lips together.

"What did I do?" Tristan asked gently. "Please tell me. I didn't mean to hurt you, Jayne."

"I know. I *know.* God, I know how you feel, Tristan. The problem is, I don't know how *I* feel." She bit her lip, shaking her head. "This means more to you than it does to me."

"You can't possibly know that."

"But I do! You've been hitting on me for weeks now, always pressing my concerns and doubts and objections. And now, what? I just cave in and sleep with you? What happens after that? It might just be a night of pleasure for me, but it would solidify something for you. It would mean more to you because..."

Because I love you, he thought. And it was true. Oh, how he knew it.

But she didn't love him.

He shouldn't have been surprised by this. But even so, the knowledge crashed down on him, dousing his desire like a bucket of icy water.

"I can't give you what you want," Jayne said. "And it's not fair of me to give in just because I find you attractive. It's not fair to you."

"I'll be the judge of what's fair to me," Tristan snapped. "I know exactly where we both stand, Jayne, and I fully consent to this."

"Fine. But I don't. You spoke to me of guilt, how that pain doesn't just disappear overnight. That's what this will do to me, Tristan. I'm not one hundred percent on board with the idea of being with you. If we do this here and now, when I can't promise to commit to anything—despite how much I know you want me to—it will wreck me." Her eyes shimmered with tears, and suddenly Tristan understood.

"This is about Cillian, isn't it?"

Jayne groaned and covered her face with her hands. "I am not in love with Cillian."

"I know you aren't. But he was, wasn't he? He had feelings you couldn't reciprocate. You don't want to repeat that heartbreak."

Jayne dropped her hands to stare at him, her face a mixture of shock and anger. "You don't know anything about that."

"Here's what I know." Tristan drew closer, but all arousal was gone from him. He felt only rage. How dare she presume to make decisions for him? To know his mind? "I know you're afraid to take a leap. And it's childish of you to pin this on me and my feelings when it's always been you holding us back.

Make all the excuses you want, Jayne. But I can assure you, if we make love and you decide you want no more after tomorrow, I'll survive. I won't crumble. I won't shatter into a million pieces. I'm much less fragile than you think. And as hard as this is to hear, the world doesn't revolve around you. We aren't all smitten with you, just waiting around for you to break our hearts. So get over yourself and face the truth: you're a coward, Jayne Thorne."

Ignoring the look of utter betrayal and hurt on her face, Tristan stormed from the room, too angry to see straight.

CHAPTER
TWENTY-SIX
IT'S GO TIME

Sofia and Cillian trained for several days with Seo-Joon, using his new powers in short spurts, just like they'd planned. Seo-Joon recommended they take baby steps to help Cillian and his magic acclimate to the power now running through his veins, like stretching a muscle.

Sofia could tell Cillian deeply approved of this metaphor. He smirked and raised his eyebrows at Sofia as if to say, *See? I told you.*

Sofia could only blush and avert her gaze from him. God, when had she become such a schoolgirl? They were partners, and this mission was important. She needed to set aside her feelings and get a grip.

They started with Cillian meditating for a moment to access the particular note that indicated the presence of another Adept, then they bonded through the Torrent. For Sofia, this was easy as pie. She felt nothing very different, only a sense of extra weight to her magic, as if she were holding dumbbells. But it was manageable.

Cillian, however, had a much different experience.

"Bright lights," he said, eyes screwed shut, once they had

pulled him back from the Torrent. He winced. "It's still over-whelming. I can't see anything. Something's wrong with me."

"That's all right," Seo-Joon reassured him. "Your body and your senses are still adjusting. Let's take a lunch break and then go again."

They went to the cafeteria, and Sofia was happy to see the day's special was a cold smoked salmon and asparagus salad. It was delicious, but she stopped to brush her teeth in their temporary quarters on the way back. Salmon breath in Cillian's face was definitely not going to help his concentration. Then again, she could just have him shift into a big cat.

They returned to the training room to try again. This time, when they reached for the Torrent and Sofia summoned the Call spell, its shimmering music notes beckoned to her, too.

"Oh. I hear it! It's working, Cillian!"

She used her free hand to grasp the spell. As soon as she connected with it, Cillian went taut beside her, his muscles straining.

"Stop!" Sofia cried out, letting go of the spell. Cillian relaxed again.

Seo-Joon, who had been watching from a safe distance, glanced at them both, brow furrowed. "What happened?"

"A bit of pain," Cillian muttered, pinching the bridge of his nose. "Only when we connected with the spell. It was like sensory overload."

"Okay," Seo-Joon said. "Let's go again, then we'll take a break."

This pattern continued for several hours. Sometimes they took an actual break, with snacks and rest and relaxation. But most of the time, Seo-Joon encouraged more "productive" breaks such as Rogue training and sparring.

"It's important to keep those other muscles active, too," he pointed out.

By the end of the first day, Sofia's entire body felt like Jell-O.

Between the practice with Cillian's new senses, followed by a particularly rough kickboxing session, then some magical sparring with Seo-Joon, she was exhausted and bone-weary.

She couldn't imagine how Cillian was feeling, though. They'd done six rounds of sensory adaptation, and though he remained optimistic, she could see the way it wore on him. After each practice, his eyes looked a bit more strained, the lines on his face more pronounced, his complexion a bit paler. It was like his own body was draining him one drop at a time.

Was this even healthy? If he used this enhancement too much, would it have permanent effects?

"I know that look." Cillian sank onto the cot opposite Sofia's, where she was perched on the edge. "You don't need to worry about me."

"Well, I can't exactly help it. Years with Jayne have molded me into the perfect embodiment of anxiety."

Cillian snorted, closing his eyes as he leaned back and rested his head on his arms. "That woman gives everyone high blood pressure."

Sofia laughed, her stomach twisting at the thought of Jayne. God, she missed her. The work they were both doing for the TCO was so important, but their separate missions drove them farther and farther apart.

She needed her sister. She needed to talk to her. And not just about everything going on with her new assignment, but about...Cillian.

Sofia couldn't deny that something was changing between them. Something that frightened and thrilled her at the same time. But she couldn't allow anything to happen without talking to Jayne first. Sofia had sworn she wouldn't pursue Cillian, and every heated moment she shared with him only made her feel guiltier.

She didn't know if she wanted to pursue Cillian. But there

was definitely something there. Something she couldn't resist much longer.

And she wasn't sure if she wanted to.

Three days of training and sparring later, Seo-Joon announced they were ready. It was all coming easier, more naturally, summoning the Call spell and casting it. Like the first time, Sofia had experienced a vision of their spell reaching the nearest Adept—Tamara, who was in the next room. Sofia heard the note Cillian broadcast, and the responding harmony as Tamara answered.

And as an added bonus, Cillian was looking healthier and stronger. His body was finally adapting to the enhanced blood.

After they'd successfully cast the spell three times, Seo-Joon clapped his hands together with a wide grin. "I think you two are fully prepared. It's go time!"

Amanda was ready for them when they sought her out. As Cillian and Sofia stood expectantly in front of her desk, she slid a file folder toward them.

"I've already compiled a list for you," she said. "These are the reports of magical activity in children all along the East Coast. I've highlighted the three most flamboyant cases, ones that are making news. I would recommend you start with those, but go carefully. We don't need the media catching wind of the TCO's involvement before we're ready to announce our intentions."

Sofia took the folder and flipped through it, recognizing the news report of the New York family that had triggered this entire operation. "And the Time Catch? Is it ready?"

"Yes. Henry has given coordinates and explicit instructions for maintenance and safety. Hector, Tamara, and Seo-Joon will be on site to receive any students who agree to join you." Amanda slid another folder toward them, which Cillian took. "This brings me to my next order of business. We cannot risk the appearance of the U.S. government abducting children against their will. You *must* receive permission before you take the children. I've made several copies of these documents. It's full of information as well as a legally binding contract that a parent or guardian must sign. Of course, they are welcome to come and supervise their children's magical education if they wish."

"And what if the parents are...less than understanding about their child's magical abilities?" Sofia asked uncertainly, peering over Cillian's shoulder to inspect the documents.

Amanda sighed heavily. "Then, I'm afraid our hands are tied. For now. I'm in discussions with the director about this, and he does see the benefits of spreading awareness and education to the nonmagical community. But, for now, while things are still hot and controversial, we can't afford the risk."

Cillian's face was stormy. "And if the child is in mortal peril?"

Amanda's steely gaze cut to him, unperturbed by the fierce glare he was giving her. "As with all assignments, you are to protect civilian lives to the best of your ability. If a child is in peril, you should intervene. But we are doing this by the book, Cillian. Protect the child as best you can, but you cannot simply abduct them if their parents are hostile. We will inform the local authorities of the child's unsafe situation, and they will take it from there."

"You think the local authorities will protect a child with magic?" Sofia said. "The second they show signs of being different, they'll be locked up—not for their safety, but for everyone else's. They'll be imprisoned and experimented on for the rest of their lives."

"Neither of you are using your heads right now," Amanda snapped. "How do you think this will play out if you just take kids whenever you want? People will revolt. This mission will no longer be covert. The masses will know the U.S. government is behind it, and the magical community will be hunted. We have suffered too much to see things come apart now. This is a precarious situation and we must tread carefully. I know it isn't ideal, but it's temporary. One step at a time. We'll do it this way, and once the first assignment is complete, we'll reconvene and make plans for the future. All right?"

Sofia ground her teeth together, unable to shake the memory of Ruth and Jayne from her mind. *What if the child is in the custody of a monster like Ruth?*

But Amanda was right. Despite their spells and capabilities, they were still employees of the U.S. government. There was still plenty of red tape and rules to follow.

"We understand," Sofia said at last. Cillian was still tense beside her, and she knew he had the same concerns she did. Gripped by a sudden boldness, she reached out and took his large, calloused hand in hers, squeezing it reassuringly. His stance slowly relaxed as he squeezed once in response as a silent thank-you.

Amanda nodded once and clasped her hands together on the desk. "Be careful out there. Remember, we aren't the only people with this information. This is all over the news. I have no doubt other Adepts will be searching for hidden talent as well, and they may not have good intentions like we do."

Sofia exchanged a glance with Cillian. His eyes were still hard, razor-sharp like shards of glass, but the pinch of his eyebrows and the downward curve of his lips betrayed his unease.

She understood that fear completely. Neither of them were worried for themselves—but they were worried for the children. What if they got there too late? What if the Kingdom, or some other nefarious Adept, got to them first? They'd seen it happen once already with Hans and the Guardian children he'd kidnapped. If it started en masse, they'd have bigger problems.

"We'll be careful," Sofia said at last.

This was too important. The burning intensity of her chest

pushed her onward, melting away her fears and anxiety. Never before had she felt so determined, so full of purpose and certainty and assurance that this was her calling. Her mission. Her task.

This was what she was meant to do. And she would not fail.

TWENTY-SEVEN
PLANS IN MOTION

A tendril of guilt worked its way into Amanda's chest as she watched Cillian and Sofia leave her office. But deep down, she knew she'd done the right thing.

She hadn't been lying when she'd warned them they weren't the only ones with this information. Thanks to her surveillance of Pierce's correspondence, she knew for a fact that the Kingdom was aware of three names on the list of magical children—the same three she had highlighted and urged Cillian and Sofia to get to first.

Amanda had done what she could. She'd sent messages to Pierce about other Adept children, giving false locations, hoping to lure the Kingdom away from Cillian and Sofia's efforts. She'd even stationed a few teams near the fake spots to be on the lookout for Kingdom activity in the hopes of bringing them into custody.

But if Ruth herself were to show up? Amanda wasn't sure her tactical team could handle that amount of power. Even Sofia and Jayne together hadn't been able to defeat the Kingdom Head.

Amanda could only hope that Ruth would send in some of

her henchmen for the grunt work instead of doing the deed herself. Best-case scenario, the TCO would apprehend a couple of Kingdom goons and interrogate them for critical intel.

Worst-case scenario? Ruth—or even Hans Kaufmann— would ambush Cillian and Sofia and capture them. Or worse...

Amanda shook these despairing thoughts from her head. They would do her no good. Cillian and Sofia could handle themselves. She'd been so close to warning them—to revealing her source, to exposing what the Kingdom already knew. It had been on the tip of her tongue, but then she'd seen the fire in Cillian's eyes, the blazing determination on Sofia's face. They both had seemed so fierce. So unafraid. They were warriors. Soldiers unafraid of the risks of the mission.

She knew them well enough to know that nothing would stand in their way. This task was too important to both of them. And when Amanda had mentioned the foes they might encounter? That determination had only burned hotter.

Cillian and Sofia would not be deterred. He was a powerful Rogue, and she was a capable Master magician. Amanda knew they would be fine.

Besides, she had to maintain her cover. If it became obvious that Cillian and Sofia knew about the Kingdom's movements, Amanda would lose her advantage on Pierce's information.

Her thoughts turned to her traitorous assistant as she pulled up the video and audio feeds of her surveillance. Pierce was currently on the phone with a government official, which Amanda did not need to hear. But she scanned through the emails recently sent from his personal account, pausing when she found something interesting. It was from an email address she didn't recognize. Whoever it was hadn't sent Pierce an email before. Another Kingdom operative perhaps?

With bated breath, she read the message:

Mother has caught the flu. Will send for medication to eradicate it.

Amanda frowned and pulled out her extensive notes, hoping to decipher more of the code. From what she could interpret, *Mother* referred to Ruth. *Caught the flu* meant she was in peril. *Medication* referred to a team of reinforcements.

But *eradicate*? Amanda had to reread her notes several times to make sense of it all. At first glance, it seemed that Ruth was dying—which wasn't hard to believe, given what Amanda knew of her Wraith business—and that the Kingdom would do everything they could to heal her.

But the word *eradicate*, based on Amanda's cipher, didn't mean to heal or cleanse. It meant eliminate. Execute. Assassinate.

She felt a spark of wild hope.

The Kingdom was going to turn on Ruth.

CHAPTER
TWENTY-EIGHT
TIMES LIKE THESE

J ayne had really mucked things up.

But the damage was done. All she could do was move forward and let that bridge burn instead of waste time trying to repair it.

She wasn't sure why her restraint had snapped so easily. Perhaps the success of the Boundary spell had made her bolder. Knowing Vivienne wouldn't burst in on her and Tristan had ignited a flame inside her, urging her onward.

She was tired of resisting him. Resisting what they both wanted.

But Tristan was right. This *was* about Cillian. She couldn't break someone else's heart. If Tristan was in love with her, then he deserved better than some cheap moment of carnal weakness.

He could hate her if he wanted to. It was better than both of them diving headfirst into something that could crush them both.

At least, that's what Jayne told herself.

The morning after her almost-dalliance with Tristan, the

team got to work. Henry had flat-out refused to let Quimby alter his Time Jumper, but he did allow her to stay and watch.

Progress, Jayne thought. *At least that's something.* Her father, she was coming to realize, was just as stubborn as she and Sofia. She'd always thought they'd gotten their fierce determination from Ruth, but Henry had his own type of fire. Oddly enough, it made her proud—not just that her father had a backbone, but that she and Sofia were so like him. They were Thornes, through and through.

"The trick is to balance your Guardian magic and the Carry spell at the same time," Henry was saying, gesturing from Jayne to the replica of the Liber Linteus. The team stood in the cold room, preparing for their first simulation.

"I've never fully tapped into my Guardian magic before," Jayne said. "This may take some practice."

"Of course you have," Henry said incredulously. "What do you think fuels those totems on your forehead?"

Jayne faltered, her heart jolting. She exchanged a confused glance with Ruger.

"Are you saying these deities are powered by Guardian magic?" Ruger asked slowly.

"Not exactly," Henry hedged. "But it comes from the same source. At least, that's my theory. Whatever Master abducted my mother and Jayne's daughter was drawn to their Guardian magic. We know Guardian magic bonds to the access points of the Torrent. Ergo, it makes sense that this Master—this god—is also connected to that magic. The Torrent is his cage, after all. It is fueled by his power. And Guardian magic is a direct link to the Torrent."

"That would explain why the deities are seeking out Jayne to house their powers," Vivienne said. "She's not only a powerful Master, but she's a Guardian, too. She has the right combination of DNA and natural power."

Jayne sniffed. "And here I was, thinking they chose me because I was a badass."

Tristan snorted, but when Jayne met his gaze, he had already smoothed his expression into something bland, his attention on Henry.

Something heavy sank into Jayne's chest, but she ignored it and asked, "Okay, so do I pull on Medb and Vesta's power then? Would that work?"

"That's what we'll have to find out. In order for you to be mobile while the Time Jumper is active, a certain amount of Guardian magic must be present. I'm curious to know if the totems will be enough."

"Great." Jayne clapped her hands together. "Let's do this. So, Tristan and Ruger are in their positions. Vivienne and I approach the room and disassemble the locks. We have how long? Five minutes?"

Henry gave a brisk nod. "Five minutes, if we're lucky, until the local authorities are notified. But that will be plenty of time. The trick is getting the task done before the Time Jumper shuts off."

"Which is thirteen seconds."

"Um, Dr. Thorne, excuse me?" Quimby piped up, adjusting her glasses, her eyes wide with excitement. She held out a small device. To the naked eye, it looked like an Apple watch. "If you would allow me to test this out," she said shakily, "I've made something that might help. This has a quasi-Cauchy surface with a functional mechanical mainspring that divides the past from the future. The idea being, it will dilate the curve of time in the space time continuum, hence increasing the Time Jumper's abilities for a few more seconds."

She grinned fondly at her Apple watch time travel machine. "I also infused it with Guardian magic. Even if the mechanical portion doesn't work, it should serve as a battery to keep the Time Jumper charged for longer."

Henry's eyes narrowed. "How much longer?"

"If everything works perfectly? By my calculations, five seconds. But to be safe, let's assume it's three."

Henry was already shaking his head, stubborn as ever. "No. I've told you, it's not just a matter of having enough power. It's the threshold between small magic and greater magic. The Time Jumper acts within that threshold, but playing around by adding any more time will cause a ripple effect on the time vortex. I've researched and calculated this thoroughly."

"So have I. That's what the curve fixes for you. I really think it will work."

"Let's try it," Ruger said.

Henry shot him a scandalized look as if Ruger had just suggested everyone dance naked under the full moon.

Ruger shrugged. "We *are* in a Time Catch. You told me yourself this atmosphere negates the effects of the Time Jumper. It's a controlled experiment."

Henry sputtered something incoherent, then ran a hand through his already messy curls. "I—well, yes, I did say that—"

"Time to let the others play, too, Dad." Jayne patted him affectionately on the shoulder. "We're a team, after all." She wasn't sure why, but she looked at Tristan when she said it.

He still wouldn't meet her eyes.

A surge of annoyance flared in her mind. Fine. They'd hated each other in the past and performed their missions perfectly. They could do it again.

Besides, Vivienne and Jayne were partners in this simulation. Tristan would be on lookout. If anything, this would be a bit of a relief to be separated from him.

At least, that's what Jayne told herself.

"All right. All right." Henry lifted his hands and waved them slightly, his eyes closed with exasperation. "We'll do it your way. But if my Jumper short-circuits at all, I'm calling it off. This is the only prototype I have, and we don't have the time for me to develop a new one."

"Actually, we do," Tristan said with a smirk. "We're in a Time Catch."

Henry gave him a deadpan expression that made Jayne laugh with pride. "There are limits to this environment. Even the most perfectly constructed Time Catches will cause ill effects after too long. By tomorrow, we'll need to resurface so our magic and our minds can recharge."

Jayne shuddered as she remembered her fellow operative Deirdre's haggard and terrified expression when she was rescued from the Time Catch she'd been stuck in. "But you've been in Time Catches for years, Dad."

"And look how I turned out." Henry offered a wry grin, gesturing to his wild hair with a shaky hand.

Ah. He does *know how kooky he is.* The thought made Jayne strangely sad. Had he locked himself in Time Catches out of necessity, or ignorance? Perhaps he hadn't known all the dangers when he'd first gone into hiding.

Whatever the reason, Jayne couldn't help but feel guilty. If only she and Sofia had been able to help him, he wouldn't have had to do all this alone.

Vivienne shot her an odd look, but Jayne ignored her.

"What do we need to do to activate this?" Ruger asked, gesturing to Quimby's battery pack.

"Just keep it within five feet of the Time Jumper." Quimby turned the battery over and gestured to a tiny green button. "Push this button for an extra boost. I recommend doing this right before engaging the Time Jumper. The battery will beep loudly when it's drained." She gave Jayne a solemn look. "And it will go fast. Based on your father's notes, the Time Jumper requires a massive amount of power."

"So Quimby's tech should be a big help, then," Jayne said, trying not to feel nervous at the thought of producing so much

Guardian power—power she still felt unfamiliar with. Sofia would be much better suited to the task. She'd tapped into her Guardian magic seamlessly and wielded it like a freaking goddess.

"Let's get into position," Ruger said. "Tristan and I will step outside and cast our Tracking spells to ensure we can sense everything happening in the vicinity. Vivienne, you position yourself on the outside of the door."

"I think a hawk would be best for this." Vivienne wiggled her eyebrows at Tristan, who laughed.

A flare of jealousy climbed up Jayne's throat. The easy way the two of them bantered together, she'd never had that with him. The crinkling of Tristan's eyes, the way it made him look years younger, so different from the solemn, brooding mask he habitually wore.

Focus, idiot. It's not like you've broken up. You weren't anything to begin with.

A breakup. Exactly what she'd been trying to avoid. But better to rip off the Band-Aid now as opposed to gouging it off with a rusty knife, after they'd fallen too hard for one another. It would be much more painful if they'd let this continue.

Right?

"Why a hawk?" Quimby asked, cocking her head in curiosity.

"A small but vicious creature," Vivienne said with a smug smile. "I can perch out of sight but effectively maim any enemies who get too close."

"I feel like a yellow jacket or a wasp might do the trick just fine," Ruger said, rubbing his chin. "That could keep out of sight much better than a hawk."

"Yes, and I could be squashed just as easily," Vivienne said sharply. "Besides, shifting into an insect is insanely difficult. I've only managed to do it once or twice. Their shortened life-span makes the connection much weaker."

Jayne's eyebrows lifted with interest. She hadn't known this. She made a mental note to ask Vivienne all kinds of questions about shifting later. Most of what she knew was from what Cillian had experienced, and he'd only just discovered his Rogue powers. But Vivienne had almost a lifetime of knowledge, and Jayne itched to learn more. Imagine all the books they could fill with her knowledge... They could keep them in the TCO library alongside the few texts about Rogues. The entire TCO could be trained properly on Rogues. And then—

"Agnes."

Jayne snapped out of her bookish reverie and scowled at Ruger.

"Stay with us," he said. "We have a mission to prepare for, remember?"

"Right." Jayne smoothed her palms along her jeans and took a deep breath. "I'm ready. And don't call me Agnes again, or I'll sic the hawk on you."

Quimby handed her the battery pack, which was so warm it almost burned Jayne's fingers. Quimby, Tristan, and Ruger stepped out of the room. Tristan didn't look back, but Ruger gave her an encouraging nod and Quimby offered a thumbs-up before departing.

Vivienne lingered, looking at Jayne expectantly, a small frown creating a divot between her brows.

Jayne slowly dropped her Boundary spell, and the connection between them intensified. Vivienne sighed as Jayne reached for the Torrent. The gleaming river of stars surrounded them both, and she focused on Vivienne's familiar presence and power before murmuring, "Shift into a hawk."

With a loud screech, Vivienne obeyed, her body shrinking as great wings spread from her sides. Her talons extended as she hovered in the air, her predatory eyes fixed on Jayne as if to say, *Don't screw this up.*

Henry held the door open for her, and the hawk glided out.

When the door shut behind Vivienne, Jayne exchanged awkward smiles with her father.

"Well, here we are."

"Clock is ticking, Jayne," Henry said.

"In more ways than one." She approached the vitrine with the linen strips inside and sensed Henry following close behind her. *Okay, Jayne. One step at a time.*

Step one: Activate the battery and the Time Jumper.

Jayne pushed the green button on the battery pack. It grew even hotter in her hands, and she hissed in pain before shoving it into her pocket. It still scorched her, but at least the thickness of the denim dulled the pain. Energy swirled around her, lighting up a presence within Jayne that she yearned to explore. But now was not the time.

She flexed her fingers, stretching her hands toward the glass case, hovering just a few inches away. "Now."

A tiny beep sounded behind her, then the air shifted. Jayne reached for Medb's ice-cold power, trying to gather it around herself. But the searing heat of the battery burned her flesh, and the thick sludge of the Time Jumper smothered her senses. In the TCO atrium, she hadn't been aware of the time freeze when it happened. But now that she was right here next to it, ready for the change, it was much more suffocating than she remembered. Like a thick, invisible blanket tightening around her, cutting off her circulation. She choked, trying to breathe, trying to focus on the goddess magic within her, but the air was so damn stifling that she couldn't focus on a thing...

"Jayne?"

She tried to move, but her body was locked in place by the Time Jumper. She couldn't summon her magic at all. She was as useless as a statue.

Another beep and the Time Jumper disengaged. The air flowed more smoothly, and Jayne gasped, her heart thundering inside her.

She wiped the sweat from her forehead. "Damn. That was tougher than I thought."

Henry offered an apologetic grimace. "Yes, it can be difficult to maintain your magic while the device is active. But I could feel that battery pack working." He gestured to Jayne's pocket. "I think your friend is right. It's a massive powerhouse of energy. I'm excited to see what I can do with it."

The door opened, and in a flash of white, Vivienne appeared in human form, her face red with exertion. "*Ouf!* I wasn't expecting that. Whatever affected your magic affected mine as well." She gathered the sweaty strands of her hair into a messy bun and fanned her face, despite the chill of the room. "If I come across an opponent, I'm not sure how I'll fare when my energy is depleted like that."

Unease churned in Jayne's mind. So, not only had she failed spectacularly, but Vivienne was also handicapped. What if something happened to her Rogue because of it?

"It will only be for a few seconds," Henry reminded her. "Remember, you and any enemies you come across will be completely frozen. They'll be caught off guard, too."

"Not like me, though," Vivienne said. "My strength is linked to Jayne, and she'll be quite busy for those few seconds when the Time Jumper is engaged. If she's depleted, then so am I."

Jayne bit her lip. "Is there anything we can do?"

"We can train." Ruger entered the room next, followed by Tristan and Quimby. "Tristan, you spar with Vivienne during our next simulation to see how she fares when faced with an opponent."

Tristan nodded once, giving his sister a wicked grin. She stuck out her tongue in response.

"Did the battery work?" Quimby asked eagerly, her hands clasped together.

"Dad thinks so." Jayne fished the device from her pocket,

wincing from the heat. "I'm not so sure, though. Why is it so *hot*?"

"It must be reacting to the magic in your blood." Quimby took it from Jayne and inspected it curiously. "It doesn't feel hot to me."

"Now that we know what to expect," Ruger said, "let's try again. We've still got a lot of work ahead of us."

TWENTY-NINE

THE TIME TO STRIKE

L ars sat at a desk nestled in the corner of his office in the Kingdom's Time Catch, poring over maps marked with tiny red dots to indicate the movement of their enemies. Too far to track. Too spread out to target. But they were certainly on the move.

Someone knocked on the door, and Lars muttered, "Enter," without looking up.

He could smell the rippling fury and magic emanating from Blaine even before he looked up. The scent was tinged with the foul Rogue magic he'd been experimenting with.

"Still no word from the Head," Blaine said without preamble. "She's gone dark. Kaufmann, too."

Lars was unsurprised by this. The Head had been teetering over the edge for months now. It was only a matter of time. Like a good second-in-command, he had assured her the Kingdom still stood behind her, supporting her every decision.

He'd been lying.

And the moment she squandered the Kingdom's funds to hire mercenaries to invade the TCO, she'd sealed her fate. Her actions had been reckless, and the other commanders within the Kingdom were furious with her. It wouldn't take much to push them over the edge, to urge them to oust Ruth completely.

"How long?" Lars asked.

"A week. Last we heard, she was seeking out a dark and deadly artifact that could help us defeat our enemies."

Lars snorted. He'd heard that one before. He knew Ruth well enough to taste her deception from a mile away. She kept everyone at a distance because of her thirst for power, and her desperate need to keep secrets.

This was definitely the latter.

If Ruth was truly in pursuit of some powerful weapon, she would have contacted him by now. She would have sent for reinforcements to acquire it. Ruth never went after something herself—at least, not without a powerful team behind her. She'd always relied on Lars to do the dirty work.

No, this was something else. Something personal.

Which gave him the perfect opportunity to strike.

"Any word on the daughters?" Lars asked, rolling up the maps on the desk.

"Both on the move. The older one is with her Rogue, heading fast toward Pennsylvania. Our intel shows a sharp spike of Adept activity in the vicinity."

Lars frowned. Adept activity? That certainly wasn't anything to sneeze at. Perhaps the TCO had intelligence that they didn't. "And the younger one?"

"Off-grid. But our trackers have caught wind of an unusual combination of energy swirling near the western edge of Maryland."

Lars rubbed his chin. Now, *that* was interesting. "'Combination of energy'?"

"A mixture of her usual Adept powers and something...else. Something we've never encountered before."

"Guardian magic?"

"Not exactly. But whatever it is, our Tracking spells are coming up empty. It's heavily cloaked."

Lars's brow furrowed as he stared intently at the chipped surface of his desk. So, Jayne Thorne was dabbling in something new. But why? Her team had to be planning something. And based on their previous tactics, it likely involved another necromantic grimoire.

"Alert all the resources we have on the totems and grimoires," Lars said, a plan formulating in his mind. "We need to be ready for them when they make their move."

"Should I send a team to Maryland?"

Lars considered this. It was what Ruth would have done. But it, like all her other plans, would inevitably fail. "No. We have to remain a step ahead. Feed the intel anonymously to La Liberté. Let them do what they will with it."

"La Liberté?" Blaine frowned. "But Labelle—"

"Yes, I know she's being held for trial at the Hague. But I've heard her temporary replacement is hotheaded and impulsive. Perhaps with the right incentive, he'll strike hard and fast, and the little Thorne witch won't know what hit her."

A slow, wicked smile spread along Blaine's face as he caught on. "Keep them busy while we intercept the next grimoire."

"Exactly. Check with our source within the TCO and cross-reference his intel with our research. There has to be a match somewhere that will lead us to the grimoire. And, with any luck, the dream team will be too preoccupied to stop us."

Blaine was practically giddy with excitement, the vengeful lust burning bright in his eyes. He was thirsty for blood. They all were. "And the Head?"

"She's made her choice." Lars rose from his desk. "Her reign has come to an end. The time to strike is now. Let's lead our people to victory once and for all."

THIRTY

SEARCH AND RESCUE

S ofia was surprised and a bit impressed by how simple it was to conjure her own portal to Pennsylvania. She and Cillian stepped through, emerging in a thick, wooded area secluded from prying eyes. After making their way to downtown Pittsburgh, where the Adept child was last spotted, she and Cillian booked a cheap motel room purely for the privacy to cast the Call spell without worrying about witnesses. If they cast spells out in the open, that was just asking for trouble. At least the motel room provided four walls and a door as a barrier.

"What's stopping this from attracting random Adepts in the area?" Cillian asked.

"I think we have some level of control over the visions we get and who the song seeks out. The Adepts will still hear it, but we can steer it away from them if needed." She bit her lip, watching him. "But just in case, we probably shouldn't stay here too long. More experienced Adepts may be able to use the spell to track us here."

Cillian shot her a crooked grin that made her insides flip. "Let them come. We can handle it."

Sofia snorted. "Don't get cocky. We aren't invincible, and we don't have any backup."

"I know. But you're a badass, Thorne. With you, no one can touch us."

Sofia's cheeks heated from the compliment. "You're pretty tough too, Pine. Don't sell yourself short. Are you ready?"

"Fire away."

Sofia took his hand in hers, which was as easy as breathing. His palm seemed to mold against her skin, fitting their fingers perfectly together. With a deep breath, she closed her eyes and reached for the Torrent. Cillian's hand tightened in her grip before relaxing slightly, no doubt experiencing the intense bright lights he mentioned before. After giving his fingers a reassuring squeeze, Sofia sifted through the gleaming river of stars, searching for their spell.

It was ready for them, hovering nearby expectantly. Sofia clasped it in her free hand before turning to Cillian and releasing it. A beautiful melody swelled around them, twisting and turning, the notes flowing over Sofia like gently lapping waves. As the song intensified, Cillian tensed next to her once more, his grip tightening on her fingers.

"Easy now," she coaxed him.

"I'm all right." His fingers loosened, but not by much. He was still full of tension and strain, and she could feel every inch of it.

Sofia felt the exact moment when Cillian's magic started to spread. His familiar mossy scent wafted around her, and she followed it. The magic pulled, tugging her forward until her surroundings changed. She was no longer among the green river of stars but at a park alongside a pond. In front of her was a golden retriever attached to a leash, being led by a man with graying hair. The man froze suddenly, head whipping around as he sensed the presence of their spell.

"Not him," Sofia said quickly. "Next."

Cillian moved slightly beside her, and the vision changed again. Now they were inside a spacious living room filled with plush furniture and elegant throw rugs. On the wall was a massive television unit showing the news. A woman in her forties was washing dishes from the kitchen sink, eyes on the screen as she worked. When she heard the melody of their spell, she straightened, eyes wide, and glanced around the house.

"Hello?" she called.

"Next," Sofia said.

It took them four more tries before they finally found something promising. A child sat on the edge of a lumpy bed watching TV. But unlike the middle-aged woman from before, he was watching cartoons, and the TV was much smaller. An identical bed rested opposite him on the other side of the room, along with a microwave and mini fridge.

"A motel room," Sofia whispered.

The song surged toward the child, who jerked upright with a soft gasp. His head turned, and Sofia recognized ten-year-old Gregory Hitchins, one of the children they'd been looking for. His wide brown eyes scanned the empty motel room, fear stark on his expression.

Then, he burst into flames.

"Oh my God!" Sofia shrieked, reaching forward, desperate to save him, but Cillian wrenched her hand so forcefully he nearly pulled a muscle.

"It's not real," Cillian said through gritted teeth.

"Wh-what?" Sofia's eyes were still glued to the child, but as she watched, she realized the flames weren't quite right. Unlike the usual reddish orange, these flames were bright white, surrounding the child almost like an aura or a glow.

"It's—it's my blood." Cillian's voice sounded so strained that Sofia finally turned to look at him. He was covered in sweat, his face red with exertion. "It's enhancing the energy around him. Like a sort of...ether."

Ether. Of course this child would be projecting so much energy, with his magic only recently discovered and still volatile.

Cillian grunted in pain, and Sofia clutched his hand tightly, knowing he didn't have much time left. "We have to find out where he is. Can we, like, I don't know, zoom out or something?"

"He has to respond to our call," Cillian said. "It's the only way."

"Right." Sofia urged the spell forward, and the melody swelled. The child gasped again, his white ether pulsing as if it had its own heartbeat. Gradually, Gregory's expression shifted from fear to curiosity. He extended a hand toward them, and though Sofia knew he couldn't see them, she found herself reaching back as if their fingers could touch.

And then she heard it. The answering harmony echoed in the air, though it was faint. Cillian made a noise beside her, though she couldn't tell if it was in pain or recognition of the tune.

"You got it?" she asked, her gaze still glued to Gregory, who was now grinning at the spirals of white magic flowing around his fingers.

"Yes. Got it. A town called Ohiopyle. About sixty miles south of us."

"It looks like he's alone," Sofia said, scanning the motel room for an adult or a sibling. "Didn't the reports say he had a mother and sister with him?"

"Sofia... I can't..."

"Right, sorry."

Sofia released the spell, and the vision dissipated, leaving them back in their own motel room. Cillian slumped forward, and she caught him with an "oof," straining under his weight.

"I've got you," she grunted. "Easy does it." Carefully, she guided him to one of the twin beds and let him collapse on the mattress. Cillian exhaled deeply, his eyes closing and his breathing raspy.

"I think we took it too far," Sofia said, her heart twisting at the sight of him so weakened. "But you were sixty miles away, Cillian. That's incredible!"

"It's fine," he mumbled against the pillows. "We found the kid, didn't we?"

"Yes, but now you need to recover. If we'd held on too long, who knows what might've happened to you?"

"Good news is, it doesn't look like any other Adept is after him."

"Yet," Sofia warned. "But someone might have heard our Call spell. We need to get to him before anyone else does." She gazed mournfully at Cillian, who looked seconds away from passing out. She wished she could just let him rest, to sleep off the effects of his magic.

As if reading her mind, Cillian cracked open one eye, giving her a silly, sleepy grin. "I can feel you worrying about me, Sofia. Really, I'm grand. Just get the portal ready."

Sofia shook her head. "I think we should drive. It'll give you time to rest up, and a portal might draw more Adepts to the area. We want to be as covert as possible."

"But the kid—"

"You'll be no help to him like this." Sofia gestured to Cillian's large body sprawled on the tiny bed. "You can nap in the car."

With a heavy groan, Cillian pushed himself up and gazed wearily at Sofia. "All right. You drive. But I'm in charge of the music. None of that alternative pop shite you Americans like so much."

CHAPTER
THIRTY-ONE
DESPERATE TIMES

"It's that one."

Ruth followed Hans's gaze to the motel room door, number 45. The building was nestled in a small city in Pennsylvania, unassuming and unimportant. The perfect hideaway.

If not for Hans's powerful Tracking spell, the boy might not have been discovered at all. A shame this child was so clueless about Adept magic and its possibilities. Any other day, Ruth might have lamented the waste of potential.

But not today. Already, the beast within her was growling, clawing at her insides, demanding to be set free. To feed.

Desperate times called for desperate measures. Ruth would do what was necessary to survive, even if it meant sacrificing innocent Adepts.

"For the greater good," she muttered, the Kingdom's motto —her motto—though she wasn't quite sure she believed it anymore. After feeding her Master tonight, he would only grow hungrier. She was only making him stronger. More demanding.

But what could she do? To give up would mean a fate worse than death. Worse than this enslavement.

"We aren't alone," Hans said suddenly.

Ruth shrank away from the staircase leading to the second floor, shrouding herself in the shadows of an SUV parked nearby. "Who? Where?"

Hans sniffed the air. "I smell a Rogue." He arched an eyebrow at her.

Ruth swore under her breath. That damned Irishman, no doubt. He was still new to the game, didn't have control of his Rogue powers yet. It would be easy to dispose of him, if he were alone. But she doubted that was the case. Her heart thudded in anticipation.

"He's got company," Ruth reminded Hans. Jayne would be nearby. Or perhaps Sofia.

But Ruth had bested both of them before. She could do it again. With the beast inside her, and this ravenous, nothing could stop her. If anything, it made her more dangerous. More lethal.

She wouldn't be able to hold it back. It could quite easily tear her daughters apart.

But she had no room for sorrow or remorse today. Jayne and Sofia had made their bed, and now it was time to lie in it. They'd only brought this on themselves.

Survival, Ruth reminded herself. *It's me...or them.*

She'd once had dreams of drawing her daughters over to her side. That much power? That much strength? The Kingdom could achieve its goals so much faster with the Thorne sisters fighting for their cause.

But that ship had sailed.

Whoever got in her way would die a painful death today. And if it was Jayne? Well, all the better. Ruth could take those totems for herself and buy more time for her Master.

Someday, she would be free.

"They're getting closer," Hans muttered, glancing nervously at Ruth. "It's your call."

"We move," Ruth growled, her voice deep and rumbling

with the power of the Master flowing through her. Without waiting for a reply, she emerged from the shadows, claws extending from her fingertips.

THIRTY-TWO

LIFE COULD BE A DREAM

Jayne dreamed of firestorms and dark magic. She recognized the intoxicating pull of the goddess magic within her and beckoned it closer, embracing it, accepting the call.

The fire swirled around her, but she wasn't afraid. She stood expectantly on the cliff, waiting for the warrior goddess to return to her.

But no one came. Jayne stood there, alone, swept up in this storm, for several minutes.

"Do I need to call you or something?" Jayne shouted into the maelstrom. "Is there a secret password?"

No answer. Damn. Well, Jayne had promised to practice summoning these dreamscapes at will, so now was as good a time as any. She closed her eyes and focused on the ice-cold magic within her, igniting it. She suppressed a shiver but let it course through her, swift and merciless, chilling her to the bone.

Warrior goddess, she thought. *Speak to me.*

A new energy flowed through her veins, a jolting combination of hot and cold, steam and ice. Gold light flashed in her mind, and she remembered what Henry had said about Guardian magic and deity magic stemming from the same source.

Jayne's eyes flew open, and her palms burned with gold light. She sent it straight into the firestorm, and jets of gleaming magic poured from her fingertips, spiraling toward the rippling flames, tearing a hole through the funnel cloud.

The flames separated and dispersed in the air, leaving a billowing cloud of smoke in their absence. Panting, Jayne lowered her hands, waiting for the smoke to clear. On the opposite side of the smoke was a cliff identical to the one she stood on.

Her chest tightened with unease as she remembered seeing Ruth Thorne atop this same cliff. Was her mother there, waiting for her? Could she kill her in her dreams?

Sure enough, there was a figure crouched on the bluff. No... Jayne squinted and made out *two* figures sitting together on the cliff's edge, side by side, their feet dangling like two children lazily dipping their toes in the water.

What the actual hell?

Jayne summoned her gold magic again and weaved a portal in the air before stepping through. She appeared on the opposite cliff, standing before the pair of figures.

One of them wore a brilliant copper toga, her white hair in a long braid down her back. Vesta, the fire goddess.

And sitting next to her was Vivienne. She turned and looked Jayne over with smug amusement. "Ah. So nice of you to join us, Jayne."

Jayne sputtered a string of incoherent swear words, but Vivienne got the gist and tsked in disapproval.

"Have some respect," she said mildly. "You are in the presence of a goddess, after all."

"How the hell are you *here*?" Jayne demanded. "I thought you had to have a totem to use the dreamscape."

"And I do. Through *you*."

When Jayne only stared in a mixture of horror and confusion, Vivienne laughed. "What, you thought you were the only one with these special visions? We are bonded, remember?"

Jayne gritted her teeth. Ah, yes, this bond that allowed her to share literally everything with Vivienne, whether she wanted to or not. She'd forgotten to put the Boundary spell back into place.

Making a mental note to do that as soon as she was conscious, Jayne plopped down on the ground on Vivienne's other side, swinging her legs over the edge like the other two.

"So, what, you guys come here for some girl talk?" Jayne asked, leaning back on her palms. "Some goddess gossip?"

"War is brewing, Jayne Thorne," Vesta said solemnly. "We have more important things to discuss."

"Right." Jayne sat up straighter. "Sorry, you two just looked so relaxed up here."

"We've been here for hours," Vivienne said. "My legs were tired."

Jayne laughed. "Makes sense." She looked at Vesta. "What information do you have for us?"

"As I have told *ma fille*, I am limited by what I can say. But you and your comrades are on the right path. You must continue this course."

"Keep doing what we're doing." Jayne nodded. "Okay, cool. But you two have been talking for hours, right. I have a feeling there's more."

Vesta hesitated, exchanging a glance with Vivienne. "It is not Minerva who awaits you in the next grimoire."

Jayne raised her eyebrows at Vivienne's sour expression, trying not to look too smug. *Told ya.* "Ah. Then, who is it?"

"That's what I'm trying to figure out," Vivienne said. "She can't utter the goddess's name, so I've been asking her questions, trying to narrow it down."

"Oh, neat. I'm a beast at twenty questions. I can help."

But Vesta shook her head. "Her identity is not important. It will not help your journey. What is important is that the Master is rising. He grows in strength, fueled by those he has abducted."

Jayne's blood ran cold. Alexandra, and...her daughter. This psychotic Master was feeding off them like a vampire. How long did they have left before they were nothing more than corpses?

"His reach is extending far beyond what we once knew," Vesta went on. "He can see everywhere now. Tread carefully. The magic you use to summon me can also summon him."

In a flash, Jayne's mind returned to that moment in Paris when she'd opened the Book of Shadows, and that other-worldly presence had called to her.

"Can he come here?" Vivienne glanced around as if expecting the Master in question to arrive any moment.

"Before? No. This was a sanctuary just for us V—" Vesta's lips clamped shut, her expression turning strained. Red bloomed across her cheeks, and she exhaled deeply as if she'd held her breath for a full minute. Slowly, she shook her head. "I'm sorry. I cannot say."

Jayne was torn between frustration and genuine concern for the goddess. She looked at Vivienne. "Is it always like that?"

Vivienne offered a long-suffering sigh. "Yes. I'm quite used to it by now."

Vesta ignored them. "For now, no, I do not think he can come here. But he is growing stronger by the minute. It is only a matter of time before he carves a path here. Be careful."

"How can we protect ourselves?" Jayne asked. "We need to communicate with you, and Medb, and any other goddesses on our side. But how do we do that without opening ourselves up to him?"

Vesta's eyes turned grim. "There is no way. The path to communicate with deities is all the same. He is connected to that path, so there will always be a risk." She leaned forward, taking Jayne's hand in hers. Her skin was warm and smooth. "Take care, Jayne Thorne. Only summon us in dire need. As I said before, you are on the right path. Continue what you are doing, and you will reach the grimoire and receive the message that is waiting for you there."

Jayne was rendered speechless by the tender emotion glowing in Vesta's eyes, the earnest plea and sorrow plain on her face. Jayne glanced at Vivienne, who watched the goddess with equal parts sadness and solemnity.

Then, Jayne understood. Vivienne wasn't just sitting and chatting with her mentor for old times' sake. She was saying goodbye.

Because the dreamscape wasn't safe anymore. It wasn't a sanctuary. At any moment, the dark Master could appear and attack.

Jayne wasn't sure what would happen if she was attacked in a dream, but she had a hunch it wouldn't be pleasant. What if he could somehow trap her here? What if he could take her totems from her?

She couldn't risk it. And she understood why Vivienne was so reluctant to leave. Once she did, there was no telling when she could come back.

Jayne swallowed down the knot in her throat and squeezed Vesta's hand. "I understand. Thank you for the warning." She paused. "Can I still use your magic?"

"Yes. Your body is infused directly with my power and Medb's. The Master cannot access your magic unless he does the same."

Jayne shivered at the thought of this evil entity infusing a part of himself into her. She didn't even want to know what that magic would feel like.

"You are our vessel, Jayne Thorne," Vesta said. "Do not

forget that. We are all counting on you to restore the balance and stop the Master from achieving his goal."

"What *is* his goal?" Jayne asked.

Vivienne made an exasperated sound, and Jayne gathered this question had been asked before.

Sure enough, Vesta shook her head sadly. "I cannot say. But it isn't hard to guess. Seek your histories. The legends are there. You only have to look for them."

Jayne frowned. Histories? But how could she research the history of an unknown time period where an unidentifiable god sought out some dark and unknown purpose? The details were so vague she wouldn't even know where to start.

"It is time." Vesta stood abruptly, brushing dust and dirt from her toga. "I trust you both to do what needs to be done. Our fate is in your hands, but I have faith you will succeed." She offered them a very motherly smile, and Jayne's heart warmed at the sight. She knew Vesta and Vivienne shared a special bond, but there was still that mushy, fuzzy feeling inside her to see this great goddess beaming at her like that.

Medb hadn't been as nurturing. The earth goddess was a bit more hands-off with her mentoring.

Vivienne stepped forward, embracing Vesta tightly. Vesta affectionately rubbed her back and whispered something in her ear, which made Vivienne's face tighten with anguish.

Then, to Jayne's surprise, the fire goddess hugged her next. Jayne fell into the warmth of her, the solid encouragement of Vesta's arms around her. Jayne had never truly known the affections of a mother before. Sofia had been the only mother figure she'd ever known, and though she'd been wonderful, this, here and now, made tears sting her eyes at what could have been. Perhaps in another life, she could have had a love like this. A family like this.

Eyes brimming with tears, Jayne met Vivienne's gaze over

Vesta's shoulder. The Rogue's eyes were also moist, and she nodded in solidarity.

They were so similar. Both with cruel, distant mothers. Both forced to grow up away from that familial warmth and love. It was no wonder Vivienne had such a kinship with Vesta.

"We aren't alone," Jayne said as she withdrew from Vesta's embrace. "We have allies. Friends. Family. We have a team."

Vivienne nodded again. "We will fight for you, Vesta. And we will win."

Vesta's face glowed with pride as she took both their hands in hers. "I know you will, my daughters."

Jayne had to suppress a fangirl-esque squeal at the word *daughters*. What an honor! To be called Vesta's daughter? God, no wonder Vivienne was constantly gushing about Vesta. It made Jayne want to shout from the rooftops, to share this news with everyone. *Daughter of the fire goddess! That's right, bitches!*

Jayne felt something tug just behind her stomach. She jerked, her body twitching from the movement.

"The real world calls," Vivienne said glumly, sharing a knowing look with Jayne. "Time to get back to work."

Jayne opened her mouth to respond, but in an instant, the cliff and smoky sky vanished, and she sat upright in bed, gasping for breath. The room was dark, and it took her eyes a moment to adjust. Her heart thundered chaotically in her chest, her head reeling from her conversation with Vesta.

When her pulse settled and her breathing slowed, she shot up from bed and dressed in her workout clothes.

Vivienne was right. It was time to get back to work.

THIRTY-THREE

A COMPLICATION

Despite how often Henry insisted Jayne would adjust to the sluggish nature of the Time Jumper, she still couldn't quite get the hang of it. Days passed, one training session after another. Jayne wasn't sure exactly how much time went by, seeing as they were in a Time Catch and the world was actually frozen right now. She woke, sparred with Vivienne to warm up, then spent the next several hours in the simulation room, breaking only for a quick lunch and powder room break before returning to their training. Every now and then, they alternated stepping out of the Time Catch for a solid minute just to reacclimate their bodies to the normal flow of time and reality. This routine continued, repeating four times before Jayne was ready to throw in the towel.

And then, miraculously, she started making progress.

Henry activated the Jumper just as Jayne connected with the totems' magic. She had Medb's staff in hand, hoping that the familiar shape and feel of the wood would help connect her to the goddess. The ripple of ice-cold deity magic flowed through her, chilling her to the core, but she was used to it by now. She kept her breathing steady, allowing it to sweep over her without any restraint.

Come to me, she beckoned, willing the magic to draw closer.

The air shifted, squeezing the breath out of Jayne's chest. Though her instinct was to tense up, to resist the change, she forced herself to relax and allow this feeling to wash over her, just like Medb's magic.

Vesta, your turn, Jayne urged, picturing the goddess of fire. She remembered how the fireball had appeared in her fingertips in the TCO atrium. Her skin warmed from the memory, the fire within her warring with Medb's icy presence. Burn and freeze, hot and cold. The energies churned inside her, almost making her feel nauseous. At last, the two powers found a sort of equilibrium, one balancing out the other. The left side of Jayne's body was numb with cold while the right side burned as if she'd been sunbathing for too long.

Wow, this is damn uncomfortable, Jayne thought with a wince, *but if that's what it takes for you two to get along, then fine.*

Still struggling to breathe properly, Jayne shifted her limbs, trying to move one foot forward. So far, every time she'd tried moving, the Time Jumper had kept her frozen in place.

But not this time. Jayne's foot inched forward, and she almost whooped in triumph.

Easy there, Jayne. Don't screw this up.

"You've got this, Jayne," came Henry's voice behind her. She'd almost forgotten he was there. "Stay calm. Stay focused."

She would have nodded, but she didn't want to break her concentration. Her attention was fully on her legs and getting them to move. Her other foot shifted, sending a spiral of hot-and-cold agony slicing through her. Each movement was like walking on needles, as if the Time Jumper had wounded the goddesses' magic somehow and it was lashing out in response.

Carry spell, Jayne reminded herself, thinking of the next step. She faltered, caught between maintaining balance with

Medb and Vesta's magic and trying to summon the Torrent. She felt like she was juggling too many things, and if she added another, the balls would all drop.

"Their magic won't leave you," Henry said. "I can sense it. The Guardian signature is strong within you. It will hold. You can do this."

Jayne hissed a breath through her teeth, closed her eyes, and reached for the Torrent.

It was like nothing she'd ever seen before. What had once been a glistening, flowing river of green stars and shimmering light was now something still and silent. The stars were frozen, the light suspended in the air, unmoving. It was eerie. Jayne imagined herself hovering in outer space, in that utter quiet and massive void, surrounded by stars and wonder. Nothing moving. The emptiness sucking her in.

Terrifying. And awe-inspiring.

How do I find the spell if everything is frozen? Jayne wondered, glancing around at the immobilized Torrent. But as she squinted into the river of stars, she realized it wasn't completely frozen. There were still faint, rippling movements within its current.

The Torrent was still active—just at a fraction of the usual pace.

Cold and warmth flooded Jayne's veins, urging her onward, the strength of the goddesses' magic intensifying as if they were growing impatient. It was like her body was covered in icy-hot patches from Hell.

Okay, okay, Jayne thought, trying to ignore the sweat trickling down her neck. *Carry spell. Where is it?* She envisioned the basket-shaped spell she was all too familiar with.

To her surprise, the spell appeared before her, the image flickering as if it might vanish at any moment. Desperate to grab it before she lost her grip on all the magic coursing through her, Jayne took it in her hands and brought herself back to the simulation room.

A sharp *beep* made her jump, and reality slammed back into her with an exhausting *whoosh*. Jayne stumbled backward, her chest heaving, her breathing strained. She coughed, choking on the sharpness of the oxygen in her lungs. The spell dropped from her fingertips, and the icy heat of deity magic fled from her, leaving her empty and clammy.

The world shifted, and she was falling backward, but her father was there, his arms catching her.

"I've got you," he said quietly, keeping her on her feet. "You went through a lot. It's all right to take a beat."

Still covered in sweat, her body shivering, Jayne shook her head. "Not enough."

"For now, it is. We have time, remember? It's why we're in this construct."

Jayne swallowed hard, knowing he was right, but she couldn't shake the growing sense of urgency and dread thrumming through her blood. It was easy to tell herself she had all the time in the world while inside this Time Catch, but what if she didn't? What if something was happening out there in the real world that was endangering everything, and she was hiding away in here, oblivious to it all? A heavy shadow of foreboding hovered over her like a dark rain cloud eager to dump its contents on all of them.

The door opened, and Ruger, Vivienne, Quimby, and Tristan entered. Vivienne was out of breath, her face red, and her hair a frizzy mess around her head. Tristan had several minor cuts on his face, no doubt from Vivienne's evil hawk form.

Ruger approached Jayne at once, his dark eyes concerned. "What happened?"

"I got closer," Jayne said, straightening as her legs felt more solid. "But I took too long. Balancing the deity magic and the spell from the Torrent, it's..." She shook her head again, frustrated with herself. She was a Master magician. Why couldn't she do this? "I ran out of time."

"Remember, there's a cushion," Quimby said, taking the small battery pack in her hands and inspecting it. "If you're a second or two late, this will compensate for it."

"Don't be too hard on yourself, Jayne," Ruger said. "This is quite the challenge. Even a normal Adept wouldn't be able to master it."

"But I'm not a normal Adept! *I* should be able to do this."

"We've talked about this," Vivienne said. "You still have weaknesses. You aren't invincible. Remember, you've only had your powers for a short time. You act as if you've been training your whole life. Give your body some time to adjust and stretch and access these new abilities."

Jayne wiped sweat from her forehead. "I know, I know. You're all right. I just feel like we're wasting time."

"I told you, this construct gives us time," Henry said. "It's —"

The ground shook, and a series of blaring alarms rang out in the small space. Jayne stiffened, her eyes finding Henry, whose face had gone paper white.

"No," he whispered. He hurried to the wall adjacent to the mummy replica and waved his hands. Gold light shimmered in the air, revealing a small keypad built into the wall. Henry pushed a few buttons, read the screen, and swore under his breath.

"What is it?" Jayne demanded.

"I don't know how, but someone has found us," Henry said.

Quimby uttered a soft gasp, her hands fluttering as if looking for something to do, some scientific way to get them out of this mess.

"How?" Tristan asked. "Anyone outside of this construct should be frozen. Or, at the very least, severely slowed down."

Henry shook his head. "They're wielding some kind of magic that's immune to my time barriers."

Jayne's jaw dropped. "They have tech that rivals *yours*? How?"

"There's only one person who figured out how to penetrate a time barrier." Henry's eyes had grown solemn, his expression hard. "Valeri Rudik. And last I heard, he was captured."

"By La Liberté," Tristan said, his jaw tense and his eyes blazing. *"Putain."*

"It's Pierre, isn't it?" Vivienne asked him, and he nodded.

"Pierre?" Jayne asked. "Your old-friend-from-the-past-who-hates-you Pierre? The one who took command of La Liberté when your mother was arrested?"

Tristan shot her a flat look. "Yes, I think that about covers it."

"Putain indeed," Jayne muttered.

Ruger was already gathering supplies into a black duffel bag, his movements quick and practiced. He no doubt had vast experience with fleeing on short notice. "Henry, can you collapse the simulation room? We can't leave this for them to find."

Henry nodded and started punching more buttons on the keypad. An eerie green smoke started to fill the room.

"What the hell is this?" Jayne asked, panic rising inside her. "You aren't poisoning us, are you, Dad?"

"Of course not," Henry said impatiently, still pushing buttons faster than a teenager texting on a cell phone. "It's a variation of my formula. It destroys only magical constructs. As long as you have blood flowing through your veins, you're fine."

"Tough luck, Nesi." Jayne affectionately patted the vitrine holding the mummy before turning to Ruger. "Can we portal out of here before they find us?"

"We can't portal within a Time Catch," Ruger said. "We have to exit first. And they will likely be waiting for us."

"I'll cause a diversion," Tristan said. "It's me Pierre wants. We've been feuding for years, and this is the confrontation he's been waiting for."

"No!" Jayne and Vivienne said at once. Vivienne and Tristan stared at Jayne like she'd grown a second head.

"If I don't, he could capture all of you," Tristan argued.

"Let me stay, too," Vivienne urged. "I know him. I can talk some sense into him."

Tristan scoffed, his expression full of doubt.

"No," Ruger said, his shrewd eyes darting between the siblings. "Jayne needs Vivienne. We can't do this mission without her. I'll stay behind with Tristan, and we'll meet up with you in Croatia."

"Ruger—" Jayne protested, stepping toward him.

He pulled a business card from his pocket and pressed it into her palm. "This is the safe house. Memorize the address, and I'll meet you there."

"This is ridiculous!" Jayne cried. "We can fight them!"

"We can't always fight our way out," Ruger said sharply. "The attack on the TCO proved that. There is a time to take a stand, and a time to run. This is the latter."

"But with my magic—"

"Your magic is spent," Tristan said. "Even at full power, if Pierre has brought his La Liberté soldiers with him, you won't have a chance."

His eyes bore into hers, pleading. Willing her to accept this. Concern shone in his gaze. God, there was so much left unsaid between them...

"Tristan." She stepped toward him.

The green smoke thickened around them. A sharp hissing sound made them turn to find the mummy melting through the glass case toward the floor. The linen strips suffered the same fate, and Jayne's chest squeezed with panic at the sight. Even

THE PROPHECY OF WIND

though she knew they were fakes, it still hurt her heart to see them destroyed.

"We have only a minute left," Henry said, closing the keypad and stepping back. "I need to grab my notes." He hurried into the other room.

Quimby uttered a soft squeal. "Oh! Me too." She disappeared after Henry.

"Vivienne, will you get my bag?" Tristan asked. "I can't risk Pierre getting his hands on it."

Vivienne nodded once and exited the room. Ruger went back to shoving items into the duffel bag.

Jayne took a deep breath before facing Tristan again. She closed her eyes, finding the Boundary spell before locking it into place. She wanted to speak with him without worrying about his sister eavesdropping.

"Tristan, about what happened," Jayne began, but Tristan took her hands in his, silencing her. His eyes were soft and gentle. No sign of anger or spite or resentment.

"*Mon amour,*" he whispered, brushing a strand of hair behind her ear. "I will fight any fiend that comes for you. A thousand times over."

Emotion filled her throat. She had to speak *now* before she lost her nerve. "I'm sorry. You were right. It's all been me and my misgivings, my insecurities, my fears." She said the words in a rush, afraid she wouldn't be able to say everything she needed to say.

"I should never have called you a coward," he said softly, his eyes full of regret. "I was angry and didn't mean it. I'm so sorry, Jayne."

"No, I'm sorry. Everything you said was right, and I shouldn't have pushed you away. I just wasn't ready for things to get serious. And I don't know if I ever will be. It isn't your fault, and I'm so sorry I made you think it was."

Tristan exhaled with a smile, leaning in and pressing his

forehead against hers. "Our hearts are different and they want different things. But I do love you, Jayne Thorne, and that will not change, even if you hurl the nastiest of insults at me."

Jayne wanted to laugh, but she feared it would come out as more of a sob. What if she never saw him again? What if La Liberté captured him? What if Pierre killed him on the spot?

Before she could overthink it, she pulled Tristan's face down to hers and kissed him fiercely. He snatched her waist, molding her body to his, crushing her with urgency and demand. Her mouth claimed his, her tongue ravishing him as if she could keep him with her by sheer force of will. He groaned into her mouth as her teeth scraped his lower lip. When they broke apart, they were both panting, foreheads pressed together once more. At some point, Ruger had left the room. The blessed man had given them the privacy they needed.

"Come back to me, Tristan Lowell," Jayne breathed.

"I swear it." Tristan's eyes darkened with heat and amusement as he brushed one last kiss against her mouth.

The door opened, and Jayne stepped back, turning away before anyone could see her tearful eyes or smeared lips.

"Ready," said Vivienne.

"Tristan and I will exit first," Ruger said, handing the duffel bag to Jayne. "The rest of you follow right after. They won't be expecting two waves of us." His gaze cut to Tristan. "You ready to wield some power?"

Tristan spread his hands, summoning red sparks, and flashed a lethal grin. "Always."

Jayne's heart fluttered. Damn this man. Why did he have to be so sexy?

"Let's go." Ruger turned to leave.

"Be careful, Rug," Jayne said in her fiercest voice.

Ruger shot a knowing look over his shoulder before he and Tristan stepped through the doorway and vanished from sight.

"Get ready, Jayne." Vivienne took her hand, her eyes burning with intensity.

Jayne nodded, using her free hand to grasp Henry's. In turn, he took Quimby's hand. After a few moments, they followed, exiting the Time Catch and emerging into the real world once more.

THIRTY-FOUR

OLD FOES

Tristan could still taste Jayne's kiss on his lips as he and Ruger emerged from the Time Catch, see that desperate fire burning in her eyes, and he used the image to fuel him, to urge him forward.

I will survive this. I will triumph. For her.

The red sparks danced along his fingertips even as the rush of time swarmed around him, crowding his lungs and his breath. He unleashed a Block spell, knowing Pierre would take advantage of their momentary stupor exiting the Catch. Though Tristan and the others had been holed up for a few weeks training, if all had worked properly, barely a moment would have passed in the real world. But he couldn't know that for certain, and the fact Pierre and his men had tracked them... something wasn't right. His team would be fresh and unaffected, so Tristan put extra power into the spell, throwing it wide as they stepped back into the real world.

A grunt told Tristan his spell had hit someone, so he flung another. He sensed Ruger casting spells beside him, following his lead. Tristan's vision was blurry, his steps sluggish. *Come on,* he thought impatiently. *Get past it. Fight!* He shook his head, trying to ward off the dizziness, trying to breathe.

A pair of hands grabbed him, and he ducked down, his elbow connecting with someone's shin. He slammed his fist upward, and his assailant groaned and crumpled.

Gradually, his surroundings came into focus. He could make out the steep walls of the warehouse. A crowd surrounded him and Ruger—probably twenty figures, maybe more.

So many... He couldn't hesitate a moment longer, someone might spot Jayne. Tristan wouldn't let them find her.

"Come face me yourself, you coward!" Tristan roared, spreading his arms. Green light burned from his palms, growing in intensity until the closest soldiers had to shield their eyes. Beside him, Ruger wielded a complex spell and slammed his fist into the ground. The earth rumbled, and cracks split beneath them. From within, red lightning flashed, taking down the three enemies closest to them.

"Enough!" roared a familiar voice—a voice Tristan hadn't heard in years. It brought back memories of blood and resentment, betrayal, and fury.

Tristan dropped his arms, but his fists remained tight by his side. Rage pulsed through him as the crowd parted to reveal the man he had hoped he'd never see again. He had short brown hair, buzzed nearly to his scalp. A long scar ran along the left side of his face, an injury Tristan knew had left one eye blinded, the iris a whitish blue in contrast to the dark brown of the other.

Despite the anger this man inspired, Tristan forced an easy smile on his face. "Ah, Pierre. How lovely to see you again. It's been too long. Tell me, how fares your mother?"

Pierre flashed his teeth in a smile that looked more like a sneer. "I'm surprised you care, after you turned us over to our enemies and left us for dead."

Tristan frowned in mock confusion. "I distinctly remember

offering every single one of you an opportunity to join me. To take the TCO's offer of protection."

Pierre scoffed, his one eye darkening with hatred. "You wanted us to roll over for those Americans! To be enslaved to them. We would rather die than give up our independence. Or have you forgotten our entire mission? The mission *you* grew up with?"

Tristan shook his head. "I was never given a choice, Pierre. That mantra was shoved down my throat from birth. I always wanted more than this, and you knew that."

Pierre's expression hardened, and he pointed a finger at Tristan. "Show me the magic you've found. I know it's here. My people have been tracking it."

Tristan's mind worked furiously to keep up. Were they referring to the magic of the Time Catch? Or Jayne's goddess powers? "Why would I share this with you?"

Pierre offered a cruel smile. "Simple. If you don't, I'll kill your entire team."

Ruger summoned a ball of red light and growled, "Go ahead and try."

Pierre's eyes narrowed as he sized up Ruger for the first time. Tristan was pleased to see the barest sign of unease, and he was grateful for Ruger's intimidating presence. Even if they were still outnumbered.

Pierre turned to the man next to him, a tall and wiry fellow named Jean who worked in the tech department. "Anything?"

Jean held a small device in his hand. He squinted at the screen, then shook his head. "There are traces on them, but whatever it was, it's gone."

Tristan loosed a breath of relief. Jayne was safe. She had to be; otherwise, that device would show her power was still close by.

"I see you're making good use of your hostages," Ruger said with an edge to his voice. "Does this mean Rudik is still alive?"

Tristan had to fight to keep his composure at the fury in Ruger's voice. He'd been captured and interrogated by La Liberté—which Tristan was technically responsible for because he was working undercover at the time. Even though there was nothing he could have done without blowing his cover, he regretted it bitterly.

So many lines crossed. So many evil deeds. It's no wonder Jayne has reservations about being with me.

Tristan shoved these thoughts away. They weren't helping.

Pierre cocked his head at Ruger. "Yes. He still lives. For now." His eyes cut to Tristan. "But that's not why we're here. Tell me where the magic is, Lowell. Or I'll cut the information from your mind." He raised one hand and summoned silver sparks.

This time, Tristan couldn't help flinching. He remembered all too well how talented Pierre was with Mind spells. He could, quite literally, slice his way into someone's thoughts with careful precision.

And it was extraordinarily painful. Tristan knew that firsthand.

But he also knew how to shield his mind from revealing certain truths. He had to—his undercover operation reporting to the TCO had depended on it.

He could withstand Pierre's torture, as unpleasant as it might be. He was unafraid. He lifted his chin in defiance, determined to say as much, but what Pierre said next shocked him into silence.

"Don't you think this magic is worth sharing with us?" he said angrily. "Your own mother... Think of what it could do for her!"

Tristan faltered. What the hell was he talking about? Yes, Gina Labelle would kill for Jayne's power. But the look in Pierre's eyes was deeper than that... As if Gina could personally benefit when others could not.

I need more information, Tristan thought. Choosing his words carefully, he said, "In *Maman's* hands, this power is dangerous. Surely you must see that."

"And you think it would be better in someone else's hands? The Kingdom? Do you know what they do to Rogues?"

Surprise rippled over Tristan. Rogue magic.

La Liberté wasn't here for Jayne's magic. They were here for Vivienne's.

They must have sensed Vesta's power fueling Vivienne's spells, mingling to create something foreign and new. Something Gina would want desperately.

A hard lump of anxiety formed in Tristan's throat. What did La Liberté know of Vivienne? Did they know she'd returned? Surely, Gina had pieced it together, but had she shared the information with her comrades before her arrest?

"This isn't a magic I can simply give to you," Tristan said, shaking his head. "It must be discovered. Unlocked. It's a personal matter, and not all Rogues have access to it. *Je suis très désolé.*"

He felt Ruger's eyes on him as he, too, caught the sarcasm and slowly worked out what they were talking about.

Pierre's gaze hardened. "Wrong answer." Still holding the sparks in his palm, he edged closer to Ruger. "Why don't I start with your friend here? I know your mind all too well, Lowell, but this one? I'm aching for a new test subject."

Tristan clapped his hands together, summoning a powerful Shield spell to surround himself and Ruger. He offered a smug smile at the look of alarm on Pierre's face as the glistening green dome prevented his approach. "I believe I was quite clear with my answer, Pierre. No matter how much pain you inflict on us, we cannot simply give you Rogue magic."

"No, but you can provide the means to unlock it!" Pierre shouted. "This was always your problem, Lowell. You never shared information. You never saw the benefit of helping out your colleagues. Your family. We were a team, and you could never understand that."

Tristan chuckled. "Oh, you poor, ignorant fool. You really don't know anything, do you? La Liberté was never my family. It was my cage."

As Pierre's expression morphed from confusion to fury, Tristan took advantage of his lapse in concentration. He spread his hands, dissolving the Shield surrounding him and Ruger. The green dome dissipated, and flames took their place. With a grunt, Tristan pushed his palms outward, and the wall of fire glided toward his enemies.

Shouts of alarm echoed in the warehouse as the Adepts dove out of the way, desperate to avoid getting scorched.

Ruger, catching on quickly, was already spinning his hands together and summoning a portal for them to escape through.

But Pierre wasn't having it. He roared in fury and lunged, tackling Tristan to the ground. The back of his head collided with the hard floor, and stars burst in his vision. Groaning, he jerked his knee upward, and Pierre tumbled off him, clutching his crotch and moaning in pain.

Rolling quickly, Tristan edged away from Pierre, trying to clear his head, which was still spinning. Pierre's hands were on him, pressing him down, holding him there. A fist collided with his jaw, once. Twice. Three times. Tristan tasted blood in his mouth. Felt it trickling down his face. Dizzy and incoherent from agony, all he could do was reach for the Torrent and grab the first spell he saw: the Boomerang.

Tristan unleashed it. With a loud *crack,* Pierre was flung off him by the slice of his magical boomerang. Enraged, he surged forward, but the boomerang came flying back, slamming at Pierre from behind, right between his shoulder blades.

Pierre collapsed, but he wasn't quite unconscious. With a low, choked sound, his arms pushed himself upward as if he was determined to climb to his feet again. But his back was broken. It would take a healer, and time.

One down.

Around them, the rest of La Liberté had closed in now that Tristan was too weak to keep up the wall of flames.

Ruger battled three Adepts at once. A spell caught him in the arm, slicing through fabric and flesh, but Ruger was undeterred. He shot an Attack spell at the fighter closest to them, followed quickly by a Fog spell. Dark gray plumes of smoke poured from his fingers, surrounding the crowd and obscuring them from view.

"No!" Pierre groaned. "Do not let them escape!"

Bodies crowded around Tristan. He felt a blow to the stomach, and another to his throat. He couldn't breathe. His entire body was on fire. He fought blindly, his fist connecting with something soft and fleshy.

A rough pair of hands seized him. He fought to escape, thrashing against the grip, when a low voice muttered, "Easy. It's me."

"Ruger." Tristan spat a mouthful of his own blood.

"Let's get the hell out of here."

Ruger had summoned a portal, and the gleaming golden doorway appeared before them. Just as the fog started to disperse, Ruger shoved Tristan through before jumping in after him, Pierre's scream of anger echoing behind them.

CHAPTER

THIRTY-FIVE

PETER PAN

As she approached the dark motel with Cillian, apprehension and determination coursed through Sofia's veins. Her fear warred with her anger, but both provided fuel for her magic. She felt it warming her blood, eager to be unleashed.

"Ruth is here," Cillian murmured.

Sofia stiffened, pausing for only the briefest of seconds before hurrying onward. Why was she here? Why wouldn't she send one of her thugs to do her dirty work?

The idea of facing Ruth Thorne should have frightened Sofia. But instead, it only made her more motivated to get to Gregory first.

If Ruth was here, then the boy's life was in very grave danger.

"I feel like Peter Pan, about to lure an innocent child from his bed with promises of a magical world," Cillian said under his breath.

Sofia knew he was trying to diffuse the tension, to put her mind at ease. But she was too tightly coiled to muster a laugh, though she did manage a small smile at the attempt.

"Two Peter Pans. I refuse to be called Tinkerbell," she teased, though her tone was grim. "Besides, Captain Hook lurks nearby, ready to skewer the poor boy if we don't get to him first."

They silently climbed the stairs to the second floor of motel rooms. The chilly northern air whipped around them, even more eerie given how dark and quiet their surroundings were. This motel was in the middle of nowhere, and the empty void of darkness beyond the parking lot seemed like it was waiting to swallow them whole. During the daytime, Sofia was certain she would see trees or fields or something pleasant. But out here, without the lights of a bustling city, the darkness was so ambiguous and uncertain that anything could be lurking within.

Like Ruth.

"She's not alone." Cillian inhaled deeply, his expression hardening as he shared a solemn glance with Sofia. "It's Hans. I can smell his Guardian magic."

Sofia stopped in her tracks. "Hans Kaufmann?" she hissed. "They're both here to abduct one innocent child? What the actual hell?" She shook her head. "Something's not right. This is either an elaborate trap, or there's more about this kid that we don't know. Could he be a Guardian?"

"You saw the vision. You would have felt it if he were."

Sofia gnawed on her lower lip, suddenly unsure. Cillian was right—ordinarily, her Guardian magic would sense another Guardian. But what if she'd been mistaken? What if there was something unique about this boy that they had overlooked?

Or what if it was a trap? What if the Kingdom had sent an entire army to apprehend them, and they were shielded from Cillian's keen sense of smell?

Sofia reached for the Torrent, wrapping her own Shield spell around them both. It didn't feel like much, but it made her feel a bit better as they drew closer.

When they reached room number 45, a tendril of icy dread trickled down Sofia's spine.

The door was already open.

In a flash, Cillian shifted to his wolf form and prowled inside, a low growl building up his throat. Sofia followed behind, wielding an Attack spell on her fingers. The air reeked of rotting roses and something else. Something foul and decaying, like the stink of a corpse. It overwhelmed the floral fragrance so all Sofia smelled was death itself.

A small whimper echoed from within the dark room. Sofia surged forward, gathering light in her palms to guide the way. Cillian's enraged roar filled her ears, but a calm voice said, "Not a step closer, dog."

When Sofia was close enough to see, she stiffened, her blood running cold. The boy was sitting cross-legged on the floor, surrounded by a circle of gemstones. A strange red light emanated from Gregory's body. His eyes were closed, and he swayed slightly, clearly in some sort of magical trance.

Standing above him, outside of the gemstone circle, was Ruth Thorne. Red light gleamed from her palms, tugging at the energy rippling off the child. Her eyes were all black, and leathery black wings extended from her shoulder blades.

"Oh my God," Sofia whispered in horror. She'd heard Jayne's description of Ruth when she transformed into this dark creature, but it was so much more horrifying than she could have imagined. And it seemed Ruth had only transitioned halfway—her graying blond hair remained, as did her arms and legs. But patches of her skin were dark gray and toughened like the hide of an alligator. Claws protruded from her fingers, and long fangs gleamed along her teeth.

Cillian growled again, and only then did Sofia see Hans poised with a dagger aimed straight at Cillian's snout. The dagger also glowed red, and Sofia didn't want to know what kind of magic was infused in it.

"One step closer, and I'll mangle your pet," Hans warned Sofia. "You both are too late to stop this."

"What the hell are you doing to him?" Sofia shrieked, her heart seizing in her chest.

"He'll be fine," Hans said in a bored voice. "We won't kill him."

Sofia only shook her head, numb. Even if she did believe Hans, she couldn't just stand and watch while Ruth siphoned the magic off the poor boy.

Just like she'd tried to do with Jayne.

Fury burned through her, bleeding out all other emotions. Her hesitation melted away, and Sofia dropped to the floor, slamming her hands against the carpet as she sent the Attack spell straight down. The walls and floor rattled from the impact. Hans staggered, and Cillian took the opportunity to lunge, knocking the dagger from his grasp. Hans screamed as wolf fangs clamped down on his wrist.

Sofia sprinted toward Ruth, whose arms flew up a second too late. Sofia collided with her, dragging them both to the ground. The red light from Ruth's hands vanished, as did the red aura surrounding the boy. Gregory crumpled to a heap in the center of the gemstone circle.

A loud, feral roar erupted from Ruth as she shoved Sofia off and climbed to her feet. Her skin was now entirely gray, her eyes blood-red. She was completely unrecognizable. Horns protruded from her head and the tips of her wings. She let out another screech and lunged at Sofia.

Sofia cried out, slamming her foot into the creature's face. She remembered what Jayne had said: magic was useless against it. She drew back and kicked again, harder this time. Something crunched, and inky blood poured from the creature's snout.

Ruth howled and cringed away from Sofia, but a long swipe

of her claws caught Sofia's leg in a tight grip. Pain radiated along her calf as the claws tore through her pants, digging into her flesh.

A mass of white fur overtook Ruth as Cillian pounced, claws tearing at Ruth's leathery skin. Ruth released Sofia, who wriggled away, panting and gritting her teeth against the throbbing wounds in her leg. Blood poured from the rips in her pants, but she didn't have time to focus on it. She needed to get to the boy. She shot a glance toward Hans, who was unconscious in a bloody heap next to the gemstone circle.

While Cillian distracted Ruth, Sofia crawled toward the boy's limp figure. "Gregory?" she hissed. "Gregory, can you hear me?"

The boy shifted, stirring slightly. His face was far too pale.

Afraid the enchantment surrounding the gemstones was still in place, Sofia used her good leg to knock one out of the way. Sure enough, the air rippled, and a sheen of pale light Sofia hadn't noticed before disappeared, leaving the space open. She crawled closer and gently shook Gregory's shoulders.

"Wake up," she urged. "You have to wake up. I can't carry you." She shoved him more forcefully. *"Gregory."*

The boy blinked hazily, his eyes haggard and droopy. As he looked at Sofia, alarm crossed his features. He inhaled a sharp gasp and scurried away from her, eyes wide as he took in the wolf and Ruth's creature still fighting. "What—*what*—" His lower lip trembled, and tears filled her eyes.

"Gregory, your mother," Sofia said, her heart breaking for this poor boy. "Where is she? And your sister?"

Gregory's face crumpled, and he shook his head, pointing toward the motel room door.

Oh, God. That either meant they had left him here, or Ruth and Hans had killed them. Both options were devastating.

"Okay. Okay." With a sharp moan of pain, Sofia pushed

herself into a sitting position and looked the boy in the eye. "My name is Sofia. I have magic, like you." She focused on the rendezvous point at the TCO and waved her hand, summoning a golden portal into existence. It shimmered to life between the two twin beds.

Gregory gasped again, but his eyes were filled with awe as he gazed at the portal. "How did you do that?"

"I can show you. But you have to come with me. I'm going to take you away from the people who tried to hurt you, but I won't do it without your permission." She paused. "Will you come with me?"

Gregory bit his lip, flinching as Ruth unleashed another roar, her lethal eyes turned toward them. She'd seen the portal.

"Please," Sofia begged, knowing they were out of time. Cillian's white fur was matted with blood, and his movements were slowing.

Gregory nodded fervently, and Sofia released a breath before helping him to his feet. Pain lanced through her as she leaned on the bed for support.

"You first," she said.

Gregory looked up at her in shock and terror.

"It's you she wants," Sofia said. "I'll be right behind you, I swear it. There are friends on the other side waiting for you."

Gregory gulped, his lip trembling again, but a determined glint filled his eyes as he stepped through the portal.

Ruth screeched, and one of her wings swiped at Sofia, knocking her down. She grunted, barely catching herself on the edge of the mattress. Cillian launched into Ruth once more, pinning her to the floor.

Thinking fast, Sofia gathered her hands together and summoned a Light spell. It gleamed in her palms, and she sent it flying toward Ruth.

Cillian rolled out of the way just in time. The light burst in

Ruth's face, making her roar, her eyes cramming shut against the intensity of it.

"Now!" Sofia cried.

Cillian lunged forward, and together they tumbled through the portal, leaving Ruth's enraged screams behind them.

CHAPTER

THIRTY-SIX

UNHINGED

The beast unleashed a terrible roar as the Adepts and the child vanished in the portal. The blinding glow of the woman's spell faded, but it still burned against the creature's eyeballs, singeing them.

A groan from across the room, and then a quiet "Ruth?"

The creature shook its head, identifying the voice. Clarity broke through the cloudy haze of its mind, and Ruth remembered. She scrambled to hold on to her awareness, clawing to the surface of the beast's thoughts.

Mine, she claimed. *This body is mine. Give it back.*

The beast's wings receded. The gray skin faded to her usual pallor.

Just before she returned to herself, the door burst open. Several men clad in all black, wearing helmets and wielding guns, surged into the room.

The beast returned in full force. Another piercing screech and its wings were back. It lunged for the intruders, but a Shield spell blocked it. Growling, the creature pushed again, swiping wings and claws, burying its fangs into the force field of magic. It didn't take long for the Shield to crumble.

In the recesses of the beast's mind, Ruth recognized the gear. This was a tactical team from the TCO. Sofia and Cillian had not come alone.

Well, then. She would have to send them a very clear message.

This time, she willingly succumbed all control to the monster within her. It didn't matter anyway. She hadn't siphoned the child's magic. Her Master still needed to be fed. Even if she held on to her awareness, he would merely take it from her once more.

The beast salivated as it approached the men, thirsty for blood.

"Ruth," Hans said slowly, staggering to his feet.

But the creature ignored him. With a feral howl, it pounced, claws and fangs slashing, blood spraying, and the officers' screams echoing in the beast's mind.

And oh, how the monster enjoyed it.

CHAPTER
THIRTY-SEVEN
A GRIEVOUS ERROR

Jayne was immensely grateful Ruger had already prepared the portal spell that would take them to Croatia. Her insides jumbled at the thought of him and Tristan facing La Liberté alone. But there were no other options. If she remained, it would be so much worse. She understood that now.

While Tristan and Ruger had Pierre and his comrades distracted, Jayne, Vivienne, Henry, and Quimby snuck out the back exit. Jayne suppressed every instinct that called to her to kick La Liberté asses. She clenched her hands into tight fists and followed the others out the door.

The brightly burning sun of midday scorched them all, blazing high from above. Vaguely, Jayne wondered what day it was, then realized it was probably the same day they'd entered the Time Catch. *Wild,* she thought. *I'll never get used to that.*

"Everyone ready?" Jayne asked. She didn't wait for their response before she reached for the Torrent and conjured the portal Ruger had prepared. It was heavier than normal, and she knew this was because it covered a farther distance than she normally traveled.

When she had the gold light in her hands, she unleashed it, and a gleaming doorway appeared before them. With a quick glance at the warehouse behind them, Jayne stepped through, sensing her father, Vivienne, and Quimby falling in after her.

They tumbled into a narrow street lined with cars on either side. Buildings were sandwiched together up and down the road in such a European fashion that Jayne ached to return to Paris. She straightened, turning just in time to catch Quimby before she face-planted onto the concrete.

"Thanks." Quimby adjusted her glasses, her mouth falling open wide as she took in her surroundings. "It's...*amazing*!"

Jayne wasn't so sure about that. The walls were stained with graffiti, and the buildings weren't much to look at. But, she supposed, that was the point of a safe house—to blend in. Not draw too much attention.

She recalled the address from the card Ruger had provided, then glanced up at the street sign. "It's on this road. Come on, let's go."

After ensuring Vivienne and Henry had made it safely, Jayne led them down the sidewalk, glancing up at the buildings now and then to make sure she hadn't passed it.

Before they reached their destination, however, Jayne caught a whiff of something familiar. Something magical. Frowning, she stopped, glancing over her shoulder.

Vivienne stiffened beside her. "I sense it, too. We aren't alone."

The hairs on Jayne's arms stood on end, her flesh prickling with the awareness of being watched. Her body thrummed with anticipation, warring with the idea of running or staying to fight.

But she couldn't lead their enemies to the safe house. They had to end this here and now.

Thank goodness this street isn't too populated, Jayne thought, casually draping a Shield spell over them. Quimby's face was pale, but her mouth was set in a determined line. She had one hand in her messenger bag, no doubt grasping her latest devious piece of technology that would likely serve them well in a fight. Jayne had to admire her courage; she wasn't field-trained, and she didn't have magic. But she certainly wasn't helpless.

"Come out, come out, wherever you are," Jayne muttered, her eyes roving up and down the street. There wasn't a soul in sight. It was completely empty and far too quiet for her liking. She tightened her grip on the strap of her duffel bag.

Right. Bags. Probably not the greatest thing if a fight breaks out. Summoning a hasty Carry spell, Jayne threw her their bags into the net and closed the spell. The weight of the now hidden gear sank onto her, dragging her down, but it wasn't painful. Hell, she'd carried Rogues before. This was nothing.

Closing her eyes, she reached for Medb and Vesta, and that icy-hot sensation rippled over her, making her shiver from the intensity of it.

Vivienne whirled to her with an alarmed look. "Jayne. You—"

A blast of red magic exploded on the sidewalk, ricocheting off their shield. The explosion was so violent that the shield cracked, sending Jayne and the others stumbling backward. Jayne held up her hands, reinforcing the shield and scanning the street for their attackers.

But whoever it was remained in the shadows, unseen.

"Come out, you coward!" Jayne called. "You call this a fight? It's pitiful. I know you can do better than this."

After a moment, a figure stepped into view, wearing a smirk Jayne knew too well. Her shoulders sagged, her expression twisting with disgust.

"Blaine," she greeted, spitting his name like a curse. "If it isn't the sword-wielding Rogue torturer himself." She'd once fought him while he brandished a sentient Rogue blade—an actual magical being who'd been tortured into shifting into Blaine's very own weapon. Thankfully, Jayne had rescued the Rogue and seen him safely into TCO custody.

But he couldn't have been the only Rogue Blaine had experimented on. What if the Kingdom had more of them imprisoned? What if he was about to whip out a sentient pistol?

Blaine clasped his hands together, his smirk widening. He looked completely at ease, as if going for a stroll in the streets of Zagreb was an ordinary occurrence for him.

"A pleasure to see you again, Jayne Thorne," he said, his tone dripping with smugness. "I can't wait for you to see what we've got planned."

Panic roared in Jayne's chest, screaming at her that something was wrong. Once more, she scanned the street, but it was only Blaine, and he had no weapons.

Trap, trap, trap, her brain sang. Of course it was a trap. One faction had stayed to battle Tristan and Ruger while the other waited for them on the other end of the portal. They were compromised.

The question was: Where were the others? How could she stop a threat she couldn't see?

The ground rumbled, and Jayne teetered, colliding with Henry. She grasped his arms, determined not to fall. Beside them, the buildings shook, the windows rattling. A car alarm went off, the sound blaring along the street.

A flash of lime green, and then dozens of figures appeared out of nowhere, surging toward them with shouts and battle cries. Jayne barely had time to collect herself before one of them was on her with...a *spear*? What the hell? She blocked a strike and aimed a kick, sending the attacker stumbling backward. She struck his jaw, then his shoulder, finally connecting her elbow with his gut. He crumpled, and Jayne straightened, taking in their new foes.

They were dressed like medieval cosplayers. There was no

other way to describe them. Animal skins, crude homemade leather, mud painted on their flesh for camouflage. Had Blaine gone back in time several thousand years and grabbed an ancient tribe of some sort to take them out?

Vivienne shrieked, her hands up in defense as one of the medieval attackers summoned thick vines like ropes, twirling them in his fingers as he tried to wrap them around her neck.

Magic. These newcomers were wielding magic, but it was unlike anything Jayne had ever seen. One of them clapped their hands together, and a shower of rocks and pebbles rained from the sky. Jayne dove out of the way and shot a Block spell straight at the rocks, deflecting them before they crushed Quimby.

"Have you ever seen this before?" Jayne asked.

"No!" Quimby's hands were covering her head. "But the signature has traces of something familiar. It's like a diluted version of the magic I've encountered. Something altered."

Altered.

Jayne searched the crowd, her heart dropping like a stone when she realized she couldn't find Henry.

"Shit." She whirled, hurrying up the sidewalk, dodging a pitchfork and a wooden sword in the process. Then—

"No!" she screamed, racing forward.

Blaine had somehow dragged her father away from the fray and was summoning a golden portal. Jayne accessed the Torrent and grabbed Medb's staff, layering a Freeze spell with an Attack spell before launching it toward Blaine like a javelin. The staff struck the ground at his feet, exploding in a shower of white sparks.

Blaine cried out, his feet suddenly frozen in place by thick blocks of ice. The Attack spell worked up his legs, making his body jerk uncontrollably. He released Henry, who darted toward Jayne, wiping blood from an injury on his lip.

"We can't fight them all," Jayne said, tugging Henry further away from Blaine and searching for Vivienne and Quimby. "Dad, we have to get out of here. The Jumper... Can you—"

She didn't finish her sentence before Vivienne's cry rang out. "Jayne, you must let me shift!" Her voice was ragged and desperate, and Jayne finally spotted her fighting off three men at once.

Reaching for the Torrent, Jayne murmured, "Shift, Vivienne. It's Lioness Time."

But nothing happened.

Come on, she urged, sending the order again. *Shift, Vivienne!*

Still nothing.

Horror pooled in Jayne's stomach as she realized she'd never deactivated the Boundary spell. They were still disconnected.

"Jayne!" Vivienne broke off with a strangled cry as one man's spear sliced into her arm. She went down on one knee, and another attacker swung his dagger.

Jayne grabbed the first thing she could find from the Torrent: a glowing rope that reminded her of Wonder Woman's lasso. Thinking of the thug she'd taken out in Rome alongside Tristan, she twirled the rope in her hands before whipping it toward the assailant with the dagger. The rope twined around his ankle, and with a sharp tug, Jayne pulled him to the ground. The magic sliced him in half. She turned away before she gagged, she hadn't Spelled to Kill.

"Quimby!" Jayne shouted. "Tell me you have something we can use!"

Quimby ducked to avoid a blow to the head and withdrew what looked like a small grenade from her bag. "It'll take out everyone's magic—but that includes yours, Jayne!"

"I don't care—do it!"

Quimby nodded and hurled the device toward the ground. It exploded in a plume of murky gray smoke.

As soon as Jayne inhaled it, a sour taste filled her mouth,

making her choke. A cold emptiness took hold of her, clenching her lungs tightly and making it hard to breathe.

Around her, the attackers fell to their knees, gasping and clawing at their throats. Weapons clanged to the ground with a loud clatter.

Jayne didn't waste any time. She sprinted toward Vivienne and helped her to her feet. The Rogue winced in pain, but the wound didn't look too deep. After gathering Quimby and Henry to her side, Jayne tugged on their arms, urging them down the street as they used the fog for cover.

Before they could fully escape, another figure blocked their path. Jayne frowned as she recognized him: Lars. The Kingdom's second-in-command.

"I'm afraid I can't just let you walk away," he said smoothly.

Jayne bared her teeth at him. "Just try and stop us." It was an empty threat, of course, and Lars knew it. But Jayne was fed up. If he didn't get out of their way, she would open a can of whoop-ass on him with no regrets.

Beside her, Henry shifted, his hand reaching into his pocket. He had something planned, Jayne was certain.

Determined to keep Lars's attention on her, Jayne lifted her chin. "Where's Ruth? She's gotta be around here somewhere, pulling your strings." She glanced around, pretending to search. The gray smoke was slowly fading, and some of the medieval attackers were rising to their feet.

They were running out of time.

"You know as well as I do that Ruth Thorne has not been herself lately," Lars said coldly. "She no longer values the Kingdom's success above all else."

Jayne stilled. Was Lars implying that Ruth was out? Did that mean he was in charge of the Kingdom now?

She wasn't sure if this was good or bad news. Lars was much less terrifying than Ruth, but if Ruth was so unhinged that her own people would turn on her, then things with her Wraith must have taken a turn for the worse.

A flood of awareness filled Jayne's chest, and she inhaled deeply. The goddesses' swell of magic burned within her, and she offered Lars a lethal grin. "Well, how about that?" She extended a hand, and Medb's wooden staff soared into her palm. She slammed the flat end into Lars's chest, and he staggered, eyes wide. With a smooth arc, Jayne swept the staff under his legs, knocking him over, then smashed it into his skull, rendering him unconscious.

Panting, Jayne turned to Henry, who held Quimby's battery pack in his hand. "Still a bit of juice left, it seems." He shot her a satisfied smile, and Quimby beamed with pride.

Jayne offered an exhausted chuckle. The battery had amplified her Guardian magic. Perfect for their situation, as she and Henry were the only ones present who could utilize that kind of power.

She shot a glance behind her. A few attackers pointed to her, shouting amongst one another.

"Let's get the hell out of here," Jayne said, and the four of them took off running down the street.

CHAPTER
THIRTY-EIGHT
PARTNERS

When they reached the TCO safe house, Jayne and Henry immediately worked on warding the building, layering Shield spells and other various protection enchantments just in case. It made Jayne nervous that their enemies were still close by. If they had a powerful Tracking spell, could they still find them?

From the corner of her eye, Jayne watched Quimby tend to Vivienne's wounds. The Rogue had sustained many injuries, the worst of which was still bleeding freely on her arm. Guilt and agony wrestled within Jayne, but she focused on finishing up the wards. She could clear the air with Vivienne once they were safe, heal her Rogue's wounds.

The apartment itself was small but elegant. A dark blue sofa stretched across the room, with matching navy drapes accenting the windows. Jayne caught a glimpse of the narrow street and its long stretch of buildings before she drew the curtains. A small kitchen was on the opposite side of the living room, and Jayne was relieved to find it fully stocked—even with frozen pie. She fixed everyone a cup of chamomile tea, hoping it would produce the soothing vibes they all needed after the surprise attack.

When Vivienne was bandaged and sitting at the table, she took a sip of her tea and looked at Jayne. "What happened out there? Why couldn't I shift?"

Jayne sighed. God, she'd really screwed up. "It's my fault. I created a spell and forgot to deactivate it before the attack."

Three pairs of eyes fixed on her with a mixture of confusion and concern.

"You created a spell?" Henry repeated slowly. "What kind of spell?" His eyes lit up, bringing out his inner scientist.

"Yes, what exactly was this spell?" Vivienne's tone was cutting, her accent more and more pronounced with each word. "And why did it impact my abilities when my life was in peril?"

Damn, damn, damn. Jayne rubbed her forehead. "Look, I'm so sorry. This wasn't meant to happen. It's all my fault, and I feel terrible, I just—"

"Get to the point, Jayne!" Vivienne snapped, her eyes full of rage and the slightest edge of panic. Jayne couldn't blame her. Vivienne had almost died because of Jayne's carelessness.

"It was a very specific Boundary spell," Jayne said quickly. "To keep you out of my head. To keep my thoughts and emotions private when I needed to be alone." Her words trailed off as she felt like a total and complete ass. In her mind, the reasons behind the Boundary spell were perfectly valid. But uttering them aloud made her realize what a foolish decision not mastering its use had been.

Vivienne's eyes narrowed. Her nostrils flared, and pink splotches appeared on her cheeks. She slowly rose to her feet, fury rippling off her in brutal waves that Jayne could feel, even with the Boundary spell still in place.

"You separated our bond—intentionally—just so you could flirt with my brother without my interference?" Vivienne's voice was lethally quiet. Jayne would've preferred if she'd yelled. "You almost got me killed because of your petty romantic fantasies? Are you serious?" Her voice rose with each word. "How could you be so careless?"

"You had open access to my brain at all times!" Jayne cried. "It's invasive, Vivienne, and you don't have the decency to just let things go. You call me out on my private thoughts and emotions, airing them out for everyone to see."

"I'm a blunt person," Vivienne said. "If I'm doing something you don't like, just tell me. That's what partners do—they communicate. They don't go behind each other's back and make life-changing decisions that could put the other one in danger. *Merde*, Jayne. All this time, our bond was clouded, and I simply thought it was because we weren't compatible. Now I see you were being reckless with our powers. How can I trust you now?"

"I know. God, I know. I seriously messed up. But Vivienne, I need some space. I need some privacy. We have to have some boundaries. You don't know what it's like, to have someone constantly picking around your brain! This is a one-way street, so it's not like you have this problem! And even if I could see into your brain, at least I would be respectful about it and back off when it made you uncomfortable."

Vivienne's hands were shaking as she curled them into fists at her side. "I don't know what it's like? You don't know what I've been through. The world isn't all about you, Jayne Thorne. I was trapped inside a grimoire for years, unable to get out, to see my family, to know if they were okay. And then, when I do finally escape, I taste freedom for one second before this damn bond snaps into place." She snapped her fingers, eyes ablaze. "Just like that, my freedom is stolen from me once more. I'm chained. To *you*."

"That's not what this is!" Jayne argued.

"Isn't it? Adepts are always taught that Rogues are nothing more than tools to be utilized by someone stronger. A weapon to wield. This is what my mother fought so hard against. I may be able to keep my thoughts to myself, but my magic isn't my own anymore. It's *yours* to do whatever the hell you want to with it because you're a *Master magician.*" She spat the words, her face twisting with disgust. "You get Vesta's power and mine added to your arsenal, but no, it's not fair for poor Jayne Thorne because her Rogue can sometimes read her thoughts."

Jayne could only stare at Vivienne, stunned by her words. Her chest hollowed as the truth rang in her mind. Vivienne was right. And Jayne was a class A asshole.

But Vivienne wasn't finished. She took a threatening step toward Jayne, waving her finger in her face. "If you have something to say about me and my magic, you tell me. You think I like this bond any more than you do? I don't. I'd trade anything for my freedom, to use my magic the way I want to. But I don't have that choice. We aren't all as lucky as you, Jayne. Maybe you'll remember that the next time you risk someone else's life for your own careless whims."

With an angry huff, Vivienne stormed from the room, slamming the bedroom door behind her. An awkward silence filled the small space, and Jayne could keenly feel Quimby and her father watching her. Her cheeks were hot, her breathing labored, and she couldn't stop shaking.

She didn't know how to fix this. But she needed to. They were here, in Croatia, ready to execute their plans, get the grimoire, and finally meet this mystery warrior goddess.

But now, because of Jayne, a wedge had come between her and Vivienne. Something much more damaging than a simple Boundary spell.

Gritting her teeth, Jayne summoned the Torrent and activated the kill switch on her Boundary spell. Immediately, a flood of awareness and anger filled her body, swelling until she felt like a balloon ready to burst.

Vivienne. She was so livid that Jayne could feel her fury in her bones.

Groaning, Jayne sank onto the couch and buried her face in her hands. Her insides were a jumbled mess. Regret, agony, self-loathing, all wrapped up in the confusion and turmoil of facing a new enemy, and the worry and fear for Tristan and Ruger. It was all too much. She wanted to run and hide. She wanted to immerse herself in a good book. But even her most treasured copy of *The Hobbit* wouldn't be enough to pull her out of this gigantic mess she'd created.

She felt a weight press in next to her, and her father's hand on her shoulder, patting awkwardly. She almost laughed. Henry was never particularly affectionate, so this gesture meant a lot to her—she knew how uncomfortable it made him. But she couldn't bring herself to tell him she was fine because, well, she wasn't. And right now, she needed her dad.

Jayne leaned in to Henry's touch, resting her head on his shoulder. He reclined slightly, his body awkwardly angled toward her. As if he didn't mind curling up against her, but it was still a new experience for him.

For a long moment, the two sat there like that on the couch, just breathing next to each other. Quimby busied herself in the kitchen, and the smells of toasted bread and hot cheese filled the air. Jayne knew she needed to get up, to fix things with Vivienne, to work on their plan for getting to the Archaeological Museum. But she was spent—physically and emotionally. For now, she just needed someone next to her, and Henry seemed to understand that.

A shrill beeping sound blared in the living room, and Jayne bolted to her feet, her head spinning. Green lights flashed from the ceiling, and she whirled, panicked, to meet Henry's gaze.

"The wards," he said, hurrying to the front door. He peered through the curtains, then exhaled loudly. "It's Ruger."

Jayne's heart lurched. "Just Ruger?"

But Henry was busy disabling the wards, muttering to himself in another language. He swung open the door, and Ruger stumbled in, dragging a half-conscious man with him.

"Tristan!" Jayne surged forward, helping Ruger lay Tristan along the sofa. Bloody welts covered his face, and his breathing was labored and wet.

Jayne glanced up at Ruger, who was better off, but not by much. He was cradling one arm against his chest. A long cut ran down his shoulder, his shirt torn from the wound, and several scrapes and fresh wounds lined his face.

"What happened?" Jayne breathed, turning back to Tristan to peel his sweaty and blood-crusted hair from his face.

"La Liberté," Ruger grunted before sinking into the armchair, wincing from the movement. "Pierre brought a whole army with him." He looked from Henry by the front door to Quimby, who hovered in the kitchen doorway. "Where's Vivienne?"

On cue, the bedroom door opened, and Vivienne stood on the threshold, still vibrating with anger. But when her gaze fell on Tristan, her fury melted away. *"Oh, mon dieu!"* She rushed into the room, kneeling next to the couch, her hands hovering over Tristan as she inspected his wounds. *"Frère, que s'est-il passé?"*

"La Liberté cornered us," Ruger said. "We thought they were after Jayne's magic or the totems. But they weren't. They were after you, Vivienne."

Everyone in the room went perfectly still as they registered his words. Vivienne looked from Tristan to Ruger, her face pale with shock. "Me? Why?"

Tristan coughed, and a trickle of blood dribbled from his mouth. He tried to sit up, but Vivienne urged him back down, whispering to him in French.

"Your Rogue magic," Tristan said hoarsely. "They could sense it was...different. Pierre wants it to help *Maman*."

251

Vivienne's lips thinned. "Well, she can't have it. Part of it comes from Vesta. The other, from...Jayne." She cut a quick glance at Jayne, her eyes hardening.

"I know that," Tristan said. "But Pierre doesn't. And I couldn't exactly tell him about you and Vesta. I don't even know if he realizes you've returned. But they had technology from Valeri Rudik that can track your powers."

"Val?" Henry drew closer. "He's alive?"

"He is," Ruger said. "But if he's revealing his research and technology, he can't be in good shape. I'll be sending a report to Amanda and a request to extract him as soon as possible."

Henry ran a hand down his face, his eyes full of torment. Jayne knew it must be tearing him apart to know his friend was being tortured.

"If they can track my powers, then what can we do?" Vivienne asked. "They could be on our doorstep at any moment."

"They wouldn't be the only ones," Jayne muttered darkly.

Ruger's steely gaze shot to hers. "What does that mean?"

Jayne quickly filled them in on the Kingdom, Lars, and the strange historical cosplayers who wielded a foreign magic.

"It was earth magic," Vivienne said. "I thought I recognized its scent from you, Jayne, but I couldn't be sure."

Quimby slapped her forehead. "Of course! I recognized it, too, from the tests we ran on your totems. It's a form of deity magic, but it was very watered down. Nothing near as potent as Medb or Vesta's power."

"They have earth magic?" Jayne asked. "How?"

"Vesta told me there are factions of magic-users who believe that true magic has been tainted over the years," Vivienne said. "They want the world to go back to what it was before the Torrent was ever created."

"Another group of archaic terrorists," Jayne mumbled. "Great."

"These are different, though," Vivienne said. "You saw

them. They don't use technology or modern spells. But they are still powerful."

"The Disciples of Gaia," Ruger said slowly.

Vivienne looked at him curiously. "You've heard of them?"

He nodded. "We've been getting reports of activity across Eastern Europe. We've only learned of their existence recently, but with magic exploding everywhere, it stands to reason some of the older shamanistic cultures could start revealing themselves."

"Or be revealed," Jayne said. "Do you think they're the ones who set up the protective wards around the Liber Linteus? Could they be in charge of guarding it?"

"It's very possible. Keeping Adepts from accessing the old texts because they believe it should never be tampered with in the first place. It should remain in its final resting place."

Jayne shook her head. "I don't understand. Do they think that powerful magic can just sit there for all eternity?"

"From what we've heard, it seems as though they want to destroy the Torrent completely."

Henry's face paled. "But that would destroy the world. The Torrent is too vast, too all-consuming to simply destroy. Centuries ago, maybe, but it's only grown since then."

"It's not just that," Vivienne said in a low voice. "The Disciples believe a powerful and malicious god created the Torrent as a dwelling for himself and his power."

A grim silence fell among them as they processed this.

"They aren't far off," Henry said quietly.

"If they believe that, can we bring them to our side?" Jayne asked. "I mean, we want to take out this Master god dude as well, right?"

"They believe it's a grievous sin to practice the kind of magic we do," Vivienne said. "They would never join us."

"And yet they would join the Kingdom?" Jayne asked. "How are they any better?"

"I have a feeling Lars fed your location to them," Ruger said. "He was relying on the chaos of you fighting a battle on two fronts. I don't think the Disciples knew the Kingdom would be there at all."

"But if this new organization is active here in Croatia, then they will likely be an obstacle in getting this grimoire," Jayne said. "We'll need to alter our plans."

Ruger shook his head. "No, proceed as normal. We factored outside threats into our plan when we organized this mission. If we take too long to act, the Kingdom or the Disciples will get there first."

"We can't do anything with my brother like this," Vivienne said, gesturing to Tristan's limp form. "Or you, for that matter." She waved a hand at Ruger's wounded arm.

"I can fix that." Jayne scooted closer to Tristan, kneeling beside Vivienne. As she pressed her hands against him, he suddenly lifted his head, eyes wide with a warning.

"Jayne," he croaked. "Don't." With trembling fingers, he clutched at the sleeve of her shirt—the precise spot where the leathery gray patch of skin rested.

Jayne squeezed his hand. "I don't care. I'm not just letting you bleed out all over this beautiful upholstery."

Tristan's mouth quirked up, and he leaned his head back, releasing something between a cough and a chuckle.

Jayne summoned the deities' power, and the heat and ice flooded her veins, sharp and piercing. A shiver rippled over her, but she embraced the power before pressing her hands against Tristan's chest. "Heal," she whispered.

She mentally transported herself to the Luxembourg Gardens in Paris, when she first tapped into Medb's healing earth magic—bringing roots to the earth, fresh blossoms and seedlings sprouting, vines and lush green leaves gleaming in the sunlight...

Tristan unleashed a low groan, his chest rising slightly from the power flooding into him. A sharp pain sliced into Jayne's arm, and she flinched. But she pushed onward, ignoring the pain, even as fire burned in her chest, scorching a path along her blood. Her vision darkened, her flesh sizzling from the usage of too much power, too much, too much...

A pair of hands seized her shoulders, jerking her backward. Her hands left Tristan, and a zap of electricity brought a shock of awareness. Her vision cleared, and she found herself gasping for breath. Ruger held her back, his dark eyes scrutinizing her.

"Jayne... What was that?"

Jayne rubbed her chest, struggling to breathe. Her skin still felt like it was on fire. On the sofa, Tristan was sitting up, his clothes and skin still stained with blood, but his injuries fully healed. A wave of relief washed over her as she sagged against Ruger's grasp. Her arm itched something fierce, and as she pulled back her sleeve, a collective gasp echoed around her.

The dark and leathery patch of skin had spread. It now covered almost her entire forearm.

Jayne swallowed down her horror and looked up to find every pair of eyes fixed on her. She forced a nervous chuckle. "Yeah. Uh. It's kind of a long story."

THIRTY-NINE
THE TRAP

Amanda stared at the photographs on her desk, her hands shaking with rage. The images depicted her entire tactical team slaughtered, limbs torn apart.

Ruth fucking Thorne. The Head herself had shown up to abduct the same child Sofia and Cillian had been after.

Amanda had sent her people directly into the path of a feral, bloodthirsty beast.

The photo in her hands crumpled, her fingers unable to hold it steady any longer.

How had it come to this? Amanda had been so careful. And Ruth rarely did her own dirty work, relying on her disciples for almost everything.

But with her own people in the Kingdom turning on her, she must have very few loyalists left, and a Wraith possessing her.

It was time to pull the plug on this operation. Amanda had more than enough evidence against Pierce. She had laid false trails for him, which had led directly to the Kingdom. Pierce's contacts had been buzzing for days about the location of the

Tiriosis and who in their organization was hiding it. Someone even accused Pierce of keeping it for himself.

It was an advantage, tracking his correspondence and gaining intelligence on the Kingdom. But it wasn't worth the risk. Not anymore.

The TCO was crippled. And Pierce needed to be held accountable for that. It was time to bring him in.

Amanda scrubbed a hand along her face and took several deep breaths. *Focus. You can't change the past. But you can put plans in motion for the future.*

She pulled up the dummy email she had created that mimicked the same IP address that she suspected came from Ruth's emails, based on the messages she'd intercepted. After consulting her notes thoroughly to ensure she was using the code properly, Amanda wrote:

> *Mother needs to meet with Doc's assistant urgently. Be at the super-market at noon.*

She read through it twice and nodded. It looked perfect. *Doc's assistant* was Pierce. *The supermarket* was a previous rendezvous point for Pierce and his contacts—a parking garage on Dolley Madison Boulevard Amanda herself used sometimes when she was running errands in downtown McLean.

After sending the message, Amanda dialed Joshua's number. When he picked up, she said, "The trap is set. We're taking the mole down today. And I need to brief you on another mission. We have a team in Zagreb, and I'm authorizing them to activate."

CHAPTER
FORTY
A SAFE HAVEN

Much to Cillian's relief, Sofia's injuries were minor. Based on the amount of pain she was in, he thought for sure she'd torn a ligament or fractured a bone. But since it appeared to only be a sprain, Sofia was eager to go into the field again.

"Easy there," Cillian said when Sofia looked like she would jump out of bed and dive headfirst into another dangerous situation. "Take a beat to rest and recover. Besides, we need to make sure Gregory is settling in well."

Sofia bit her lip and nodded, but she didn't relax. Instead, she swung her legs over the edge of the bed and tried to rise.

Cillian placed his hands on her shoulders to keep her in place. "Sofia."

"There's still so much to do. What if Ruth and Hans go after another one? What if we aren't there to stop it?"

"And what if you jump into battle with an injury and get yourself killed?" Cillian said sharply. "Be smart, Sofia. You can't do anything while you're healing. What would you say to me if our roles were reversed?"

Sofia's blue eyes appraised him as if just taking in his

injuries. Thankfully, his wolf form healed rather quickly, but he was still covered in cuts and bruises. She deflated slightly, her shoulders sagging. "You're right. I'm sorry. It's just, seeing her there, like *that*—" She broke off with a shudder.

Cillian nodded, his blood chilling from the memory. He'd never seen anything like that creature before. And to watch, before his eyes, an actual human being morph into that *thing*? It was wilder than him turning into mythical creatures.

He took in Sofia's pale and haunted expression. She was still traumatized from the events in the motel room, and he couldn't blame her. He extended his hand and attempted a gentle smile. "Come on. Let's go talk to Gregory."

Sofia's face lit up. She reached for the crutches by her bedside, but Cillian shook his head. "Just lean on me. If it gets to be too much, I'll carry you."

Her cheeks reddened, sending warm satisfaction coiling through Cillian's chest. He loved making her blush.

He helped her rise to her feet, and she looped her arm through his. He had to admit, there was something strangely comforting about her body leaning into his, her warmth surrounding him.

She stumbled forward, her leg hovering in the air, and winced. "Sorry."

"What for?"

"I'm going to have to lean heavily on you for this to work."

Cillian laughed. "Go on, then. I'm stronger than you think."

Sofia huffed a laugh, but it sounded more like a scoff. She hobbled forward, tugging sharply on his arm. But Cillian kept his arm taut, easily maintaining a rigid stature. When Sofia looked at him in surprise, he offered a lopsided grin.

"I'm a statue. I won't be moved. Promise."

Sofia smiled, and this time it reached her eyes. Together, they moved toward the door, finding a rhythm with each step.

It took them much longer than usual to get to the set of offices on the second floor. Amanda had hidden a portal in Ruger's office that led to Henry's Time Catch, claiming it was safer if fewer people knew about it. Cillian couldn't blame her.

When they reached the office, Cillian swiped his key card to gain access. They stepped into the room, and a blast of churning energy washed over him like a rippling wave of heat. The gleaming golden portal awaited them on the other side of the room.

"Ready?" Cillian asked.

Sofia tightened her grip on his arm but nodded.

After ensuring the door was closed and locked behind them, Cillian helped Sofia through the portal. Magic rippled over him, making every inch of his flesh tingle in response. The air was sucked from his lungs, a squeezing pressure pushing on his chest.

In seconds, they appeared in what looked like a classroom. A chalkboard covered one wall, opposite a small row of desks. Sitting in a swiveling desk chair was Seo-Joon, spinning in place with a lazy smile on his face. And in front of him, at one of the desks, was Gregory.

Cillian cocked his head at the strange sight before them. "Having fun?" he asked Seo-Joon.

Seo-Joon paused mid-spin and grinned. "Oh, the best. We're just getting to know each other."

"And how's that going?" Sofia's eyes were on Gregory, who looked scared out of his mind.

Seo-Joon half-shrugged. "He'll only answer one question at a time, so we're alternating. He just asked me where I'm from, and I'm waiting on him to answer the same question."

"Mind if I give it a shot?" Sofia asked.

Seo-Joon gestured toward the row of desks. Sofia sank into the one next to Gregory. He raised his eyebrows at her but otherwise seemed unaffected by her presence.

"Hi," Sofia said warmly. "Remember me? My name's Sofia."

Gregory nodded. "I remember. You saved me."

"Yes, that's right." Sofia's expression brightened. "How are you doing? I know you've been through a lot."

Gregory sat up, clearly comforted by the presence of someone he recognized and trusted. Cillian crossed his arms, watching the exchange with a mixture of pride and affection.

"I'm scared," Gregory admitted.

"It's okay to be scared," Sofia said. "I know you may not believe this, but you're safe here. No one will try to capture or hurt you while you're here with us. This is a safe haven for you —and for anyone else who needs help with their magic."

Gregory bit his lip, dropping his gaze to the wooden surface of his desk. "I miss my mom."

Sofia's smile faded. "I'm so sorry. Will you— Is it all right if I ask what happened to her?"

"There were people after us," Gregory said, wringing his hands together in his lap. "We were running. And this...this..." He gestured around himself, his expression helpless.

"Magic?" Sofia offered.

Gregory nodded. "This magic thing happened. I couldn't control it. It stopped the men from chasing us, but it hit Mom, too." His lower lip trembled, and his eyes filled with tears. "They—they took her. She tried to fight, but they—they—hit her with some kind of magic, and she fell down and—"

Oh, God. Cillian closed his eyes. The bastards actually killed the boy's mother in front of him? His heart raged with a mixture of anger and sorrow. This poor kid.

Sofia reached forward and took the boy's hand. "I can't imagine how horrible that was. I'm so sorry you went through that, Gregory. But it is not your fault. Your magic was just trying to protect you, and without the proper training, it's impossible to predict or control."

261

Gregory blinked rapidly, and a single tear raced down his cheek. "My sister got away."

Sofia straightened, exchanging a shocked glance with Cillian. "She did? What's her name?"

"Hazel. When my magic attacked, she hid. The men weren't looking for her. I—I ran, because I knew it was me they were after. I thought if they were busy chasing me, they wouldn't be looking for her. We got separated, and I have no idea where she went."

"How old is she?" Cillian asked.

"She's twelve."

"Where did you last see her?" Sofia asked.

"We were in that motel together," Gregory said. "We were about to move to another place when the men found us. I thought it would be safe to go back to the motel room, since the bad guys would think we'd already left."

Sofia looked at Cillian with hope in her eyes. "Maybe we can cast the spell again, see if it lead us to her?"

He shook his head. "It won't work if she's not an Adept, Sofia. We don't know if she has magic."

Gregory tensed, panic flaring in his eyes. "What spell? Don't —don't hurt her, please."

Sofia squeezed his hand. "It's not painful. Do you remember hearing a magical song that called to you while you were in that motel room? Before we arrived?"

Gregory's eyes grew wide. "That was *you*?"

Sofia smiled and nodded. "We invented a spell that can call out to other people with magic. We'll use the same spell to try to find Hazel. Would that be okay?"

Gregory hesitated before nodding.

"Good." Sofia patted his hand. "In the meantime, it would really help if you worked with my friend Seo-Joon here. He has magic, too, and he can teach you how to control yours so you don't hurt anyone again. How does that sound?"

Gregory swallowed, his face still pale, but he seemed more certain as he said, "That sounds good."

~

"You can't go anywhere until you've healed," Amanda said briskly when Sofia proposed an excursion to find Hazel.

"Ruth and Hans probably already know about Hazel," Sofia insisted. "It's only a matter of time before they find her. Amanda, if we don't act now, that girl will be taken."

"I agree with Sofia," Cillian said.

Sofia looked at him in surprise, and he winked at her.

"You think it's wise to put an injured soldier in the field?" Amanda asked incredulously.

"With painkillers and the Ice spell we discovered, she should be able to move around easily," Cillian said. "Plus, I've been practicing my projection powers. I think I might be able to send magic to her leg to ease the pain."

Amanda's eyebrows lifted. "Well, that would certainly be something." She waved a hand. "Show me."

Cillian faltered. "What?"

"Show me how you would do it. You have to practice it first. Besides, I wouldn't dream of sending you into the field unless we're sure this works. So, go on."

Suddenly nervous, Cillian shifted on his feet. He cleared his throat and muttered, "Okay. Aye. Sure." With a deep breath, he closed his eyes, focusing on the memory of when Jayne healed him at Medb's tomb. He remembered the excruciating pain, the bright light of her magic, the heat of that power encompassing him...and the pain ebbing away, leaving nothing but warmth and clarity in its wake.

Sofia took his hand in hers, and Cillian's brow furrowed with concentration as he sent this memory into her, feeding it to her injury.

She gasped, but he kept pushing, urging the feeling forward. He felt her straighten beside him.

"Oh my God," Sofia whispered with a breathless chuckle. "That's *incredible*."

Cillian opened his eyes and wiped sweat from his brow. When he looked at Sofia, she was standing solidly on both feet, gazing down at her injured leg in amazement.

"You healed it!" she said, beaming up at him.

Cillian shook his head. "It's only an illusion. I sent you a memory of being healed, and that magic is surrounding your wound right now. It's only temporary—as long as I can hold the spell."

Amanda was on her feet, peering down at Sofia's legs in curiosity. "Remarkable," she said. Her eyes darted to Cillian, drilling into him as if she was about to question him tirelessly about the process. Instead, she said, "I'm impressed, Pine. You've managed to trick Sofia's body into thinking it's been healed. That could certainly come in handy in the future."

Cillian's surprise lodged itself in his throat, preventing him from speaking. He wasn't sure if Amanda had ever complimented him so thoroughly before.

She chuckled lightly at his stupefied reaction. "You two gather what you need. I'll arrange a portal to transport you to the motel." Her face darkened. "Our cleanup crew might not be quite finished."

Cillian felt a chill at her words. He'd heard about the TCO tactical team that had been disemboweled by Ruth's monster. If he and Sofia had only remained for a moment longer, they could have done something, could have stopped the carnage...

"We can't change what's happened," Amanda said sharply as if reading his thoughts. "But we *can* prevent this from happening again. Now that we know that Ruth is hunting Adept children, we can be more prepared. I want Seo-Joon and

Tamara going with you. We'll leave Gregory in Hector's care in the meantime."

Cillian nodded, relieved that they wouldn't be facing Ruth on their own again. Especially with Sofia still injured.

Amanda waved her hand toward the door. "You're excused. The portal will be ready in two hours. Be careful."

FORTY-ONE
RUNAWAYS

B lood. So much blood.

Sofia's stomach roiled as she walked into the motel room. Mere days ago, it had been an unassuming room, quaint and plain and completely ordinary.

Now, it was a bloodied battlefield. The bodies had been removed, but the blood covering the carpets was so horrifying that even Seo-Joon didn't have anything to say to lighten the mood. Sofia, Cillian, Tamara, and Seo-Joon wordlessly ducked under the caution tape, ensuring the door shut tightly behind them as they entered the crime scene.

"Amanda said the team arrived just minutes after we'd left," Sofia whispered. "If we'd known..."

"If you'd known—if you'd stayed—that kid might not have escaped," Tamara said. "I think that's why Amanda didn't tell you the team was nearby. You might have waited for backup instead of acting immediately. You saved that boy's life, Sofia."

Sofia nodded, though this didn't reassure her at all.

"Let's cast this spell so we can get out of here," Seo-Joon muttered, his expression uncharacteristically grim.

"I agree, mate. This mank is minus craic," Cillian said.

Sofia raised a brow. "That's a new one."

"New what?"

"Irish idiom."

"I don't speak in idioms."

"Ah, but you do, *mate*," Seo-Joon said. "When we get back, we'll make you a list."

Cillian huffed a laugh and poured on the brogue. "Come on then, lass. Let's have a go."

Sofia and Cillian faced one another, grasped hands, and reached for the Torrent.

It was almost effortless this time. Perhaps it was because of all their practice; or perhaps their grave surroundings made Cillian more determined, more focused on the task at hand. Sofia grabbed the spell, and she didn't even have to guide him through the process. His hand remained firm in her grip as they cast the spell together, the comforting song washing over them and spreading beyond the room, beyond the motel grounds.

Images flashed in Sofia's mind, and she thumbed through them as if flipping through the pages of a magazine. An older gentleman sat at his desk and looked up when he sensed the spell. They quickly moved on to a young woman doing yoga in her studio apartment. From there, they reached a girl with short, jet-black hair, sitting cross-legged in front of a fire. Beside her were several other children.

Every single one of them looked up in alarm when the spell drew closer.

Sofia gasped. "Do you see—" But Cillian was already reaching out, sending tendrils of song sweeping over all of them. A gleaming white aura shimmered to life, surrounding each and every child.

There were seven of them. And all of them were Adepts.

The closest figure, a girl with blond pigtails, reached out a hand to touch the spell. As she did, the answering harmony poured from her magic, soothing and inviting.

She had answered the call.

"Do you have the location?" Sofia whispered, afraid of breaking the spell. This was too important—too monumental for them to screw up.

"Almost." Cillian's hand tensed, his palm sweaty against hers. For the briefest of moments, the magic surrounding her wounded leg faded, and she hissed from the sudden sharpness of the pain. "Ah, there it is. They're in Wilmington. Near Banning Regional Park."

Relief filled Sofia's chest. That wasn't too far. She released Cillian's hand, and he groaned, his big frame sagging. Her leg still throbbed in pain, but given what Cillian had just endured, she could handle it for a few minutes. She hovered by the bed, her leg raised as she rested her weight against the edge of the mattress.

"That was different," Seo-Joon noted, concerned. "What happened?"

"It's a whole crowd of Adept kids," Sofia said. "Judging by Gregory's description of her, we found Hazel. And she's joined a little club of Adept runaways."

Seo-Joon's eyebrows lifted. "That's kind of awesome. Like a little team of superheroes."

"Superheroes who can't control their powers and who are probably sending off a major magical hot-spot signal to attract all kinds of unsavory people," Sofia said.

Seo-Joon winced. "Yeah. Good point."

Sofia turned to Cillian, who was still panting. "Do you need time to recover?"

He shook his head, his eyes clear as he looked at her. She felt the magic flowing from him, seeping into her leg and sending warmth and healing to her injury. He grinned. "I'm knackered, but let's go get the nippers. Portal away."

"Mangling the King's English," she sighed. She straightened, putting weight on her leg with ease, and weaved her hands in the air, focusing on the location Cillian had provided. A portal spun into view, creating a glowing doorway in front of them. After ensuring the other three were behind her, Sofia stepped through.

There was no point in being subtle; it was late evening, and the kids were crowded around a fire in an abandoned alley near the park. There were no witnesses, the area was secure for the moment, so this was one of the few times when Sofia saw the benefit of exposing her magic to these kids. They needed to believe they weren't crazy; that there were more people out there like them.

When she, Cillian, Seo-Joon, and Tamara appeared, the kids all shot to their feet. One of them gathered sparks in his hands, his eyes full of terror.

Sofia raised her hands, palms out. "Easy now. We aren't here to hurt you."

"That's what the other guys said," said the black-haired girl.

"Are you Hazel?" Sofia asked her.

The girl's eyes narrowed, and she took a step away from Sofia.

"It's okay," Sofia said quickly. "Gregory sent us. He's worried about you. Here, he told me to give you this." She slowly reached into her pocket, ensuring her movements were careful and obvious so as not to frighten the children any further. After several tense seconds, she pulled out a folded piece of paper and extended it to Hazel. It was a drawing of a dragon. Gregory had claimed Hazel would know what it meant. Apparently, they had been working on a series of comic strips about a dragon named Gorgon.

Hazel hesitated, her eyes shifting around nervously, before she snatched the paper and backed away from Sofia. She unfolded the picture and stared at it for several long moments. Her eyes filled with tears as she looked up at Sofia. "Is he all right?"

Sofia nodded. "He's safe. He's with our people."

"Who are *your* people?" asked a boy with short, spiky hair.

"We work for the US government," Cillian said. "We're part of a team of magic-users like you. We'd like to teach you how to control your powers. But we won't force any of you if you don't want to. We're not here to hurt or kidnap you. I know that's hard to believe, but I also know you all have been through a lot. I need to warn you, though, if you stay, your magic will serve as a beacon alerting all kinds of people to your location. Not all of them will be friendly. If you come with us, we can show you around and help you access your magic safely. Then you decide from there where you want to go."

The kids all exchanged uncertain glances.

"Take a minute to discuss it," Seo-Joon said. "We know this isn't an easy decision. If you have questions, please ask."

"What do you mean, you work for the government?" asked a girl with blond pigtails. "Like the FBI? The CIA?"

"Unfortunately, we can't explicitly tell you which organization," Tamara said. "That's classified info. But it's a magical division of a US government agency."

"The people who are after us," Hazel said. "Who are they? Why do they want us?"

"There are other magical organizations out there," Sofia said. "Organizations hungry for more power and magical fuel. Some of them are drawn to your volatile magic and want to steal it for themselves."

"What do *you* want with our magic?" asked the boy with spiky hair, his eyes narrowed with suspicion.

"We want to train you," Cillian said. "We know what it feels like to discover you have magical powers. We know how terrifying it is. We're hoping to teach you so you can wield it safely —so you don't hurt anyone. Our goal is to train you well enough to help you adjust into society without drawing unwanted attention. You'll be able to live your lives again without fear of being hunted."

"It's too late for that," said a girl with dark brown skin and wide, haunted eyes. "They killed my parents."

Several other children murmured their agreement, some claiming their siblings were murdered, others stating their parents tried to turn them over to the authorities.

Sofia's heart twisted. God, these kids were so young. Too young to have to endure all this. She swallowed down the knot of emotion in her throat and stepped closer to them, grateful none of them cringed away from her. "You're right. It's too late to change what's happened. And I'm so sorry for what you've been through. But we're here to stop anything like that from happening again. Magic is changing. It's growing stronger every day. It's why people like you are discovering their powers. It's going to keep happening, and more and more kids—adults, too—are going to realize they have magic. It's a dangerous world right now, and we're just trying to make it safer. For you, and for everyone."

Hazel, who was clutching Gregory's drawing to her chest, said, "If my brother is with you, I want to see him. I'll go with you."

"Hazel," hissed the spiky-haired boy.

She shot him a sharp look. "He's my brother. Even if these are the bad guys, I'm not leaving him on his own."

The boy scowled as Hazel strode over to where Sofia stood and looked her in the eye, expression unflinching. "Do you swear to take me to him?"

Sofia nodded. "I swear on my life."

Hazel nodded once as if that settled everything.

"I'll go, too," said the dark-skinned girl.

A few other children voiced their assent, but the spiky-haired boy remained silent and stony. Soon, all but three of them had crossed over to stand next to Sofia and Cillian. Those remaining huddled together, whispering amongst themselves. Sofia clasped her hands in front of her, trying not to eavesdrop, though she heard words like *dangerous* and *lies*.

"Can we see your magic?" asked the girl with pigtails.

"Sure." Seo-Joon beamed as if he'd been waiting for this question. He pressed his palms together, and a faint light glowed between them. When he spread his palms, several glowing butterflies burst from his hands and flew high into the sky.

Some of the kids gasped, and a few of them murmured, "Ooh!" Even the spiky-haired boy gazed up at the glowing butterflies with awe on his face.

"Can you teach us how to do that?" Hazel asked.

Seo-Joon shrugged one shoulder. "Maybe. It's a bit complex, but we can work our way up to it."

"If we go with you," said the spiky-haired boy, "will you be our teacher?" He pointed to Seo-Joon.

"I'll be one of them," Seo-Joon said. "But there will be others to instruct you, too. We all specialize in different forms of magic."

"I hate to rush you all," Sofia said, her skin itching with anxiety, "but the longer we stay here, the more attention we'll draw to ourselves and our magic. This much energy in one location is bound to lure someone here." *Someone like Ruth.* She couldn't help but glance toward the darkened street, expecting that horrifying gargoyle to rear its ugly head.

The remaining three kids bent their heads together and whispered hurriedly for another moment before breaking apart, their expressions resolute.

"We'll come with you," said the spiky-haired boy.

Relief filled Sofia's chest as she gestured for them to come closer. The children gathered around her as she summoned a portal back to the TCO. The golden doorway gleamed to life before them, and the kids gasped and burst into excited murmurs at the sight of it.

As Sofia helped shepherd the kids through the portal, she heard a sickeningly familiar roar in the distance. Urgency pulsed in her veins, her instincts quivering in alarm. *Something is out there.*

She shared a glance with Cillian and knew from the grimness of his expression that he'd heard it, too.

"Quickly now," she urged as the last of the kids stepped through. She insisted on going in last, just to make sure everyone got in safely.

When Sofia was the only one remaining, she squinted into the darkness. Just before she dove into the portal, she saw a winged creature soaring toward her. But in a flash of gold light, she was through, and the portal collapsed on itself, leaving behind the darkness and whatever was lurking out there.

CHAPTER
FORTY-TWO
DRAGO MI JE

After Jayne filled everyone in on the history behind her weird skin condition, and the fear that she might end up with her own Wraith-sized problem, it took a while for the rest of the team to digest this information. Henry, of course, wanted to gather some skin samples for study, which Quimby eagerly supported. Ruger wanted to report this to Amanda immediately to see what their next course of action should be. And Vivienne... Well, Jayne wasn't sure if Vivienne was still pissed at her, or if she was actually rendered speechless. She only gazed at Jayne's arm with a furrowed brow, expression unreadable, before silently leaving the room.

After an exhaustingly long debate, Jayne finally convinced everyone to table this conversation for later and focus on the mission. There wasn't time for them to sit down with Amanda or run tests on her skin. With enemies breathing down their necks, they didn't have a minute to spare.

"We'll discuss this more in depth later," she said. "I promise."

"But in the meantime," Tristan said sternly, "no more healing people."

"Agreed." Ruger leveled a hard look at her.

Jayne raised her palms in surrender. "All right, fine. But you two better not get mortally wounded or anything, or else you'll be screwed."

Putting an end to their argument, Ruger took a call on his encrypted line. "Yes, ma'am. Understood." He hung up, now brimming with excitement.

"That was Amanda. We are a go for Zagreb. Mission approved by the director himself."

There were still a few last-minute details to iron out before putting their plan into action. Unfortunately, some corners couldn't be cut, and Jayne put her foot down on the idea of pretending to be an American tourist who didn't speak Croatian.

"No way," she said. "I need the Fluency spell. What if the staff suspects something and are whispering amongst themselves? I need to be able to eavesdrop effectively for this to work. Unless you want me to try and yank one from the Torrent?"

"That won't happen," Ruger said. "They all live in the library. Katie spent years collecting them."

"Good to know. Pretty please set me up a portal, so I don't waste energy that we need for the battle ahead? I'll only be five minutes, tops. Swear."

He rolled his eyes and waved a hand, conjuring a portal.

She wasn't sure why no one believed her. She did have *some* level of restraint, even when it came to libraries.

When Jayne arrived outside the TCO library, she took a steadying breath to prepare herself. "In and out, Jayne. No dilly-dallying." After nodding once, resolutely, she swiped her key card and opened the door.

As usual, the room resembled a boringly cluttered storage closet, with a few old books and some three-ring binders stacked haphazardly against one another, covered in dust. Even though it was an illusion, Jayne couldn't help but cringe at the sight. It was a very convincing display. So convincing, in fact, it made her librarian heart hurt.

She headed deeper into the space, and the scene shifted, the shelves elongating and widening, the books righting themselves, dust disappearing, and the space opening up row by row, shelf by shelf, into the vast expansive library Jayne knew and loved. She loved it even more than the Library at Trinity College in Dublin and the Bodleian at Oxford combined, and that was saying something.

Breathing in the fresh scent of vellum and parchment, Jayne gave a happy sigh and bounced forward, eager to find Katie Bell and access the spell.

The older woman was bustling around, rearranging books on a shelf near her desk. She looked up at Jayne's approach and beamed. "Jayne, dear! It's been too long."

"Yes, it has. I wish I could live here." Jayne gazed longingly at the shelves that stretched toward the ceiling.

"I was so thrilled to hear that your father was brought in safely." Katie paused with her work, her lips thinning and her eyes shining with uncertainty. She looked almost nervous. "Is he all right?"

Jayne scrutinized Katie, who was definitely acting odd. "You know my father?"

Katie blushed. "We went to school together a lifetime ago. But yes, we were close, once upon a time."

Close. Jayne homed in on that word, every instinct of hers buzzing. A sudden memory came to her mind: Katie, hiding a stack of books about time travel and wormholes when Jayne caught sight of them. "You were at Oxford with my dad... Katie Bell, you've been helping him all along, haven't you?" *And you liiiiiike him,* she wanted to add, but she wasn't in middle school, so she bit her tongue.

Katie's blush deepened. "I—I couldn't say anything, Jayne dear. I hope you understand."

"Sure." Even as she said the words, she couldn't stop the hurt from spreading through her chest. Henry had reached out to Katie—*trusted* Katie—but not Jayne. How long had Katie known Henry was alive? How long had she kept this secret?

Jayne shook her head. It wasn't important right now. "He's doing well. Thank you for asking. And I appreciate all you did for him. I'm sure it helped him stay alive. Unfortunately, I can't stay long. Can I get a Fluency spell for the Croatian language?"

Katie's mouth puckered as she thought this over. "Ah, Croatian. I'm sure we have an edition somewhere, but it may take me a minute to unearth it from our archives." She raised one finger before hurrying off. "Just a second, sweetie."

"Take your time." Jayne paced up and down the length of the nearest shelf, eagerly glancing at the spines. *Fifteenth-Century Adept History. A Comprehensive Guide to Attack Spells. What Is the Torrent? An In-Depth Analysis of the World's Source of Magic.*

She was about to pick up a history textbook, eager to uncover some clues about the mysterious Master lurking in the Torrent, when a familiar voice made her freeze.

"Jayne?"

She spun around and saw her sister, arms full of books, rounding the corner.

"Sofia!" Jayne rushed forward, giving her sister an awkward side-hug to avoid knocking over the massive pile of books. "What are you doing here? Why so many books?" She craned her neck to read the titles. "*Spells for Beginners, How to Train Your Adept Child.*" She arched an eyebrow. "Is there something you want to tell me, Sofia?"

"Oh, uh." Sofia laughed, her cheeks slightly pink. "We've been rescuing Adept children on the run so we can teach and train them. Help them access their magic safely."

Jayne's chest warmed at the thought. "That's amazing! What a brilliant idea."

Sofia nodded, slightly breathless. Her gaze darted to the exit behind Jayne. "Right. Um..."

Jayne cocked her head. "What's up? Something on your mind?"

Sofia sighed and set the stack of books down on the nearest table. Strands of blond hair had come loose from her ponytail, and she nervously tucked them behind her ears. "I actually need to talk to you about something. It might...be a little awkward."

Jayne snorted. "Well, I already know about the birds and the bees, so you're a few years late to that one."

Sofia shook her head, wringing her hands together in front of her. "It's about Cillian."

Jayne stilled. "What about Cillian? Is he all right? Is he hurt?"

"Oh, nothing like that. It's just— Okay, I'll just say it. I think I'm developing feelings for him. And I think he feels something for me, too. Nothing's happened, per se, but we've had some... moments." She grimaced, glancing up at Jayne with apologetic eyes.

Jayne frowned. "I fail to see the problem. I mean, that's good, right? If you two like each other, have at it."

"Oh, Jayne, I couldn't do that to you! I came between you when he and I bonded, and I swore I wouldn't pursue him, and now I'm going back on my word, and I just feel terrible—"

Jayne laughed and clutched Sofia's hands in hers, silencing her. "Sofia, it's fine. Do you really think I'm that petty? I have zero romantic feelings for Cillian anymore. He and I were destined to be friends. All the Rogue/Master stuff created such weirdness between us because we weren't supposed to be matched. Listen to me. I would never presume to hold some messed-up sense of ownership over him just because we dated for a little while. If you two have serious feelings for each other, then I am all for it. You have my blessing." She waved an invisible wand and tapped it on Sofia's forehead.

Sofia chuckled nervously. "You're serious?"

"Of course! God, who do you think I am, Regina George?"

Sofia squinted. "Is she from *Mean Girls*?"

"So fetch," Jayne said with a nod.

Sofia's smile warmed, and she squeezed Jayne's arm. "So... you're sure?"

"Absolutely. If this is what you want, then I'm really happy for you. For both of you. Cillian deserves to be with someone who sees him and understands him perfectly."

Sofia wrapped her arms around Jayne, hugging her tightly. "You're the best."

"This is uncharted territory for us. When's the last time we had feelings for the same guy?"

Sofia snorted. "Um, never? You always liked the nerds, and I always went for—"

"The tattooed meatheads?"

"I was going to say the bad boys, but sure."

"Cillian is an exception, I suppose."

Sofia withdrew, her voice laced with affection. "He certainly is." She hoisted the stack of books back into her arms, adjusting her grip before the top one fell over. "I'd love to stay and catch up, but we've got a lot of work to do."

"Same, girl. But we'll chat soon, okay?"

Sofia nodded, her expression much more relaxed than when they'd first bumped into each other. Jayne watched her exit the library, her heart twisting and filling at the same time. She already missed her sister, but it had been so nice to catch the briefest glimpse of her, even if only for a moment.

And Sofia and Cillian. Wow, what a development. Jayne searched within herself, looking for any bitter feelings or resentment or anything, really. But no. All she felt was relief that Cillian and Sofia had found solace in each other. They both needed someone steady and solid to rely on.

"Got it!" said a chipper voice from behind Jayne. She turned and found Katie waving a thick red book in her hand. "Andrija Kačić Miošić's most important work, *Razgovor ugodni naroda slovinskog*, originally published in 1756. That's a very rare early 1900s reprint, so please, be careful. It has the spell you need."

"You're a doll, Katie." Jayne accepted the book, which buzzed against her palm. When she flipped it open, a surge of energy pulsed through her, quivering through her bones. Letters and phrases swarmed her mind, and whispers filled her ears. When the spell faded, she closed the book, eyes wide, processing the magic now imprinted in her brain.

Katie raised an eyebrow. *"Kako si?"* How are you?

The translation was crystal clear in Jayne's mind. She eagerly replied, *"Ja sam dobro, hvala. Drago mi je!"* I am well. Glad to meet you!

"Ordinarily, to be safe, I'd prefer to make our way separately to the museum," Ruger said as Jayne and the team triple-checked they had all the supplies they needed. Jayne pocketed the Time Jumper and gave Quimby's battery pack to Henry. Quimby, who had already portaled back to the TCO for her own safety, had packed bags for Tristan and Ruger full of fun tech and goodies to spring on whoever might attack while they guarded the perimeter. "But in this case, our enemies already know we're here. There's no reason to delay, so we will just portal there and face whatever is waiting for us."

Jayne nodded briskly. "Sounds like a solid plan."

"Remember, we're only canvassing and collecting information," Ruger reminded them. "Scope out the area. Note any security measures we might not know about, anything new that might interfere with the mission. Keep your heads down and blend in with the other tourists. Come closing time, we'll put our plan in motion."

Vivienne emerged from her room, wearing a crossbody bag and a casual but elegant silk plum shirt and matching wide-legged pants that made her look tall and slender. And very French. It made Jayne's crisp white shirt and black cropped pants look stiff and cranky by comparison.

"You look great," Jayne said with a small smile. Vivienne responded with a haughty look.

Suppressing a groan, Jayne caught Vivienne's arm before she turned away. "Look," Jayne said in an undertone, "I know you're still upset with me, and for good reason. I'm truly sorry. I made a terrible mistake, and I swear it won't happen again. I haven't touched the spell since then, and I never will. Because you're absolutely right. Our bond is more important, and if something isn't working, we need to communicate. I'm new at this too, okay? I swear I'll do whatever it takes to protect you and get you out in one piece."

Vivienne stared at her, expression firm and unyielding. After a moment, she said, "I know you meant well, Jayne. I do think we work well as a team. But it will take me a while to learn to trust you again."

Jayne nodded. "That's fair."

"For what it's worth, I know I didn't make things easy for you. Or my brother." Her eyes flicked to Tristan, who was slipping into a black leather jacket. His white shirt was unbuttoned at the collarbone, hinting at the planes of muscle underneath.

Jayne tore her eyes away and cleared her throat. "When all this is over, I'd really like to have a chat with you about how our bond works and any boundaries we might want in place, for both of us. You're right, you shouldn't be just a weapon to be wielded, and I never want you to feel like I'm using or abusing your magic against your wishes."

Vivienne's severe frown softened slightly. "I appreciate that, Jayne."

"Everyone ready?" Ruger called, standing by the front door. He was wearing a slick black suit that was perfectly tailored for his massive shoulders and long legs, with dark purple suede loafers. Henry had managed to knot his own tie, though it was already a bit rumpled, classic professor taking the kids on a field trip. And Tristan was, as always, perfection in a gray cashmere sweater, dark wash jeans, and broken-in Chelsea boots. He might as well be strutting the catwalk in Paris, ignoring all the patrons there to swoon over him.

They cleaned up well.

"Aye aye, Cap'n." Jayne saluted as she and Vivienne drew closer. She felt Tristan's eyes on her, and this time, she didn't resist the pull. Her gaze locked with his, and heat coiled in her stomach, climbing up her chest and lodging in her throat. Half his mouth quirked upward in a smile, his brown eyes molten. God, he was beautiful. Almost too beautiful to look at.

But for once, that didn't frighten her. Not anymore. Not when she'd seen him being dragged in by Ruger, bloodied and half-dead.

For one horrifying moment, Jayne had feared she'd lost Tristan. And that moment changed everything for her. She didn't want to hold back. She didn't want to be afraid. She didn't want to wait for a tomorrow that might never come.

As their gazes held, Jayne tried to convey all of this with her eyes, hoping he understood. The scorching desire only burned hotter in his gaze, and her toes curled in response. She would really like to get him out of that sweater.

Vivienne cleared her throat, elbowing Jayne. Snapping out of her naughty fantasy of herself and Tristan tangled up in bed together, Jayne looked up to find Ruger summoning the portal to the plaza just outside the Archaeological Museum.

When the gold doorway appeared, Ruger said, "Tristan and

I will enter first and take our positions. Wait a moment before following."

Jayne nodded, her chest tightening with unease. Just before Ruger and Tristan stepped through the portal, she blurted, "Wait!"

They both turned, and Jayne strode forward before she lost her nerve, gripping the lapels of Tristan's jacket and pulling him to her. Her mouth crashed against his with a bruising kiss, fierce and intense, her tongue twining with his. He made a startled sound but returned the kiss with equal enthusiasm, one hand cradling the back of her head while the other pressed into her waist.

When she broke away from him, his eyes burned with the same desire and yearning she felt coursing mercilessly through her veins.

With a brisk nod as if they'd just exchanged pleasantries, Jayne stepped back, breathless. "Okay. Carry on."

Tristan blinked at her, and she reveled in the satisfaction of catching him off guard. For once, he didn't have some clever quip ready to fling her way. Vivienne snorted, then disguised it as a cough. Ruger rubbed his forehead, looking exasperated. Henry averted his gaze, his cheeks turning pink.

"Right." Tristan's voice was a bit strangled. He straightened his jacket and squared his shoulders. "Okay then."

Jayne watched, unable to stifle the knot of nerves twisting in her stomach, as the two of them vanished through the portal.

"Way to go, Jayne," Vivienne said with a chuckle. "You successfully messed with his head right before a critical mission."

Jayne waved a hand. "He'll be fine. This is Tristan we're talking about." She drew closer to the portal, but Henry stopped her.

"Remember," he said. "Thirteen seconds on the Time Jumper. No more than sixteen. Otherwise—"

"Yes, catastrophic consequences to the time vortex," Jayne said. "I know, Dad. We've got this."

Henry nodded, rubbing his hands together, then running them through his already messy curls. Jayne wanted to tell him to relax, but she knew it wouldn't do any good. He wasn't field-trained, and they were testing his technology on something huge. She couldn't blame him for being a bit nervous.

"Ready?" Vivienne asked.

"I was born ready." Jayne took her father's hand, then Vivienne's. Together, they stepped through the portal.

Only to find the Disciples of Gaia waiting for them on the other side.

CHAPTER

FORTY-THREE

THE KIDS ARE ALL RIGHT

S ofia had never felt more emotionally drained, but the sense of purpose and rightness flowing through her made it all worth it.

She was way outside her comfort zone with this whole school-for-Adepts thing. As she, Seo-Joon, Tamara, Cillian, and Hector collaborated, trying to come up with a plan to introduce safe magic one step at a time to these kids, the burden of the work they were doing weighed heavily on her.

These kids needed rescuing. But more than that, they needed training. Whatever Sofia and the others decided to teach would be ingrained in them for years. Possibly the rest of their lives.

No pressure.

True to their word, Sofia and Cillian did everything by the book. They questioned the kids whose parents were still alive about their whereabouts so their legal guardians could be tracked down. Unfortunately, two of the kids were forced to leave the TCO because their parents vehemently refused to cooperate. But Kendra, the girl with blond pigtails, had a mother who was very interested in overseeing the magical training of her child. In no time at all, Amanda arranged a secure transport to the TCO, and Kendra's mother was there, sitting at a desk alongside the other children.

It took several long hours of arguing and discussing, dozens of pots of coffee, and ample servings of snacks and one lovely pilfered pie—blueberry, her sister's favorite—before Sofia and her colleagues came up with a training regimen appropriate for the children. It was difficult, teetering between arming the kids to defend themselves, and also teaching them that magic wasn't to be feared. Sofia didn't want to immediately start training them as soldiers, but she didn't want them to be helpless, either.

Hector, an older Adept Sofia knew only from Jayne's stories about him, was unrelenting in his desire to follow TCO rules and protocol. It took a lot of passionate arguing from Sofia and Cillian to finally get him to shift his view and think outside the box.

When the plan was set, and the next week of training and lessons had been outlined, Sofia left the Time Catch and collapsed on her bed in the TCO headquarters, exhausted and bone-weary. She closed her eyes, but as much as she willed sleep to come, her mind was still buzzing with anxiety and energy.

She sat up, peeling her hair off her face. She needed a shower. And about a week's worth of sleep.

But her brain wouldn't shut off. All she could think about was those kids out there they hadn't saved yet. Kids who needed them.

"Can't sleep?"

Sofia looked up to find Cillian leaning against the doorway. His eyes were shadowed with drowsiness, but, like her, he seemed fully alert.

Sofia rubbed her temples. "No. There's still so much work to be done."

"You're only human, Sofia. There's only so much you can do in one day."

Sofia offered a wry grin. "Not true, when you're in a Time Catch."

Cillian chuckled and strode into the room before sinking onto the cot next to her. His leg brushed against hers, sending warmth shooting through her body.

"I want to go back out there," he murmured, his eyes fixed straight ahead at something unseen. "To save as many more as we can."

Sofia's heart swelled from his words. "Me, too. But like you said, we're only human. We can't do everything, Cillian."

He sighed, his broad shoulders drooping. "I know."

Sofia wasn't sure if it was her sleep-deprived brain or the boldness of the moment that gripped her, but she found herself leaning her head on Cillian's shoulder. He went still, and for one wild moment, she thought she'd gone too far, that he would pull away from her. But then he relaxed, his head leaning against hers in return. With a sigh, Sofia closed her eyes.

Moments later, she woke, confused and disoriented. Her head was against Cillian's muscular chest, his inviting scent surrounding her. Sunlight streamed in through the window, though it was the middle of the night when she'd been talking with Cillian earlier.

Beside her, Cillian's eyes were closed as he breathed heavily and slowly, his head propped against the wall behind him, one arm draped around Sofia's body, holding her against him. Sofia's back ached from the awkward position she'd slept in, but she'd never felt more comfortable in her life. The warmth of being next to Cillian, the feeling of safety and home... She couldn't shake that. She supposed she should feel embarrassed or awkward to find herself in this position, but she didn't. Maybe if she hadn't spoken with Jayne already, she would feel those things.

But in this moment, all she felt was certainty.

She reached forward and tucked one of Cillian's curls behind his ear. He twitched, one eye opening and fixing on her. A slow, sleepy smile spread across his face.

"Look at that," he said, his Irish accent much more pronounced, and sexy as hell with that deep, throaty, sleepy voice. "We got some rest after all."

Sofia smiled, her hand still lingering on his face, yearning to run her hands through his curls some more. "I think I just needed you next to me to help quiet my mind."

Cillian opened both his eyes and fixed them on her, his expression sobering. "So you're saying I'm your anchor?"

Sofia's smile widened. "I'm saying you're my lighthouse, calling me home when the storms try to take me."

Heat and desire burned in Cillian's gaze. He leaned in and kissed her, his mouth soft and inviting. Sofia let her hand roam through his hair, her lips tingling from the smooth, gentle movements of his mouth and tongue. It wasn't anything particularly passionate, and she could tell his body was still sluggish from sleep. But the feel of him against her like this, solid and warm and real, set her insides aflame. Her other hand pressed against his cheek, enjoying the tickle of his stubble. His arms wound tighter around her waist, drawing her closer.

When they finally broke apart, breathless and grinning, Cillian pressed his forehead to hers. "I'll rescue you from any storm, Sofia," he whispered.

Sofia closed her eyes, drowning in the bliss of being enfolded in his arms and enveloped in his scent as they drifted back to sleep.

My anchor.

My lighthouse.

～

OVER SCRAMBLED eggs and toast in the cafeteria, Cillian and Sofia made a plan to seek out more Adept children. There was plenty of work to do with those in the Time Catch, but both of them agreed they had to try at least one more time. They had no idea how many more kids were out there, confused and alone, and needed to bring them in safely. If even one child who needed help was snatched up by Ruth or Hans, Sofia would never forgive herself. She knew Cillian felt the same way.

With Seo-Joon and Tamara busy with the Adept children, Amanda gave Sofia and Cillian the green light to go on their mission alone.

"But be careful," Amanda urged. "Ruth and Hans are still out there. If you get into trouble, portal back here immediately and we'll send an extraction team. It's not worth getting your-selves killed over."

Sofia wasn't sure she agreed; she would rather risk her own life than that of an innocent child. Besides, she had more magic than anyone on the extraction teams, and Cillian was a Rogue, but she forced herself to nod before they left Amanda's office.

"This one's in South Carolina," Sofia said, glancing over their notes as she and Cillian made their way down the hall. "Simpsonville." She looked up at him. "You ever been?"

He raised a brow. "Simpsonville, South Carolina? No, lass. Never had the pleasure."

Sofia grinned, knowing full well he'd spent most of his life in Dublin.

The portal was once again set up in Ruger's office. Sofia and Cillian entered, then shut and locked the door before approaching the glowing doorway. Before Sofia stepped through, Cillian grabbed her arm.

"What—" Sofia was cut off as he pressed his mouth to hers. She uttered a small noise of surprise that was quickly swal-lowed up by his desperate kiss.

He drew away, his eyes gleaming with mischief and desire.

"What was that for?" Sofia asked, a little dizzy from the intensity of the moment.

"Just because I wanted to. And also..." Cillian dropped his gaze, his expression turning grim. "Because I want you to be careful. Amanda's right, it's not worth getting yourself killed."

Sofia pressed her palm against his cheek. "I'll be careful."

"Last time was a close call." Cillian shook his head, glancing down at her leg, which had now healed thanks to their abundant time in the Time Catch. "Too close."

A lump formed in Sofia's throat. Cillian was right. She thought of him in his wolf form, fur matted with blood as he faced Ruth's Wraith. God, he could've been torn apart by that monster.

Sofia was willing to sacrifice herself to save a child. But she wasn't willing to sacrifice Cillian. Foolishly, she hadn't even considered until now that her actions would put him in such grave danger. She sighed, leaning her head against his chest.

"I swear, if it gets dicey, we'll portal out of there." She looked up at him to show how serious she was. "I swear it, Cillian."

He nodded and kissed her forehead. "Good." He drew away, lacing his fingers through hers. "Let's go."

Hand in hand, they stepped through the portal, emerging in a dense, wooded forest. In the distance were the sounds of children laughing and playing. A park or a school, no doubt. Sunlight sparkled through the gaps in the trees, and a brisk wind made Sofia sigh with contentment. The weather was lovely here this time of year.

She and Cillian trudged through the forest, avoiding thorns and bristles. A large playground stood on the other side of the woods, occupied by about a dozen children. Sofia shared a glance with Cillian, who frowned and shook his head.

No Adepts here. Cillian would've been able to smell the magic.

Sofia gazed around the park, her eyes settling on another copse of trees on the other side of the sidewalk. This one was denser and would likely hide any glowing lights from their spell.

"There." Sofia pointed. "Let's cast the spell there. With the sun so bright, I don't think anyone will notice."

When Cillian said nothing, Sofia turned to look at him. His body was tense, his jaw rigid and his eyes wide. His arms shook at his sides, and Sofia turned to face him fully.

"Cillian?"

He inhaled deeply, eyes closing as his brow furrowed. "Do you feel it?"

Sofia stilled, opening her magical senses. She tentatively reached out for the Torrent, and as soon as she connected with it, she heard it.

The harmony of their Call spell. It resonated in the air, circulating around them, growing in volume and intensity and urgency.

Someone was calling them. Almost like a distress signal.

Sofia gasped and took Cillian's hand, sending energy into him. "Can you find out where they are?" she whispered.

He grunted his acknowledgment, his hand tight in her grip. His breathing turned strained, and it was all Sofia could do not to wrap him in her arms. Instead, she sent more tendrils of her magic through their bond, feeding power to him a little at a time. It seemed to be more strenuous than usual to pinpoint the Adept's location.

After a long moment, Cillian said, "I've got it. It's half a mile away." He dropped his hand, breaking their connection, and wiped sweat from his brow. "It makes sense; if the Adept is untrained, there's no way they'd be able to send that kind of spell long distance."

"Should we portal there?" Sofia asked, biting her lip with worry.

Cillian shook his head. "We'd have to trudge back into the forest, and we wouldn't be able to portal directly to their location anyway, for safety reasons. But I can run half a mile in three minutes." He shot her a wolfish grin. "Can you keep up?"

Sofia laughed. "Hell no. But I'll try."

Without warning, Cillian broke into a sprint. Sofia barked out a protest before tearing after him.

It took them ten minutes to reach their destination, only because they had to stop often as Cillian sniffed out the Adept's location or listened for their song once more. But at long last, panting and covered in sweat, they reached a small row of houses tucked behind the park where they'd arrived. Cillian slowed to a brisk walk, and Sofia followed suit, allowing him to lead the way. She kept the Torrent close, her fingers flexed at her sides, ready to summon a spell at a moment's notice. She kept expecting Ruth's horrifying gargoyle creature to jump out of the bushes and tackle them.

"It's this one." Cillian stopped in front of a tan house with a dark brown roof. As he gestured to it, a shout echoed from within, followed by the sound of breaking glass.

They both surged forward, Sofia's mind already concocting the worst of scenarios. *Ruth and Hans are already here. They're siphoning the kid's magic. We're too late. Oh God, oh God...*

The front door was already cracked open as they burst inside. A man's voice was shouting something unintelligible. The boy who responded sounded older, like a teenager instead of the young child Sofia was expecting.

They hurried down the hall, and Sofia draped a quick Shield spell over both of them as they followed the sounds of the fight.

A pair of figures stood in the kitchen, shards of broken glass surrounding them. One was Hans Kaufmann. The other was a boy with dark blond hair, tall and gangly, his dark eyes fixed on Hans. He looked to be maybe fifteen years old.

Hans whirled at their approach, gold light shimmering from

his fingertips. At the sight, Sofia's magic surged, glowing gold in the small space, blasting him with an Attack spell before he could react. The magic hit him squarely in the chest, sending him flying backward in a shower of gold sparks.

Cillian shifted to his wolf form, baring his teeth and prowling toward Hans, who struggled to rise to his feet.

"Where's Ruth?" Sofia demanded, hands up, ready to strike with another Attack spell.

Hans wiped blood from his lip and groaned. "Gone. I've lost her. Whatever is controlling her has taken over completely, and I can't get her back."

"Liar," spat Sofia. Her gaze roved over the small house, expecting Ruth to pop out at any moment.

"Ask your Rogue!" Hans snapped. "He'd be able to smell her."

Sofia glanced at Cillian, whose fur quivered slightly. His ears lifted, and he cocked his head. After a moment, his voice sounded in her head.

"He's right. She's not here."

"So what are you doing here, then?" Sofia snapped. "What do you want with him?" She gestured to the teenager, who slowly backed away as if ready to bolt from the room at any moment.

"His magic, of course!" Hans said. "He's a Guardian."

Sofia stiffened, eyes shifting to the boy, who froze, his face paling. He shook his head vehemently. "No. No. I don't have magic. I'm not like those kids on the news. I s-swear."

"We aren't going to hurt you," Sofia said, trying to make her voice gentle, but with Hans in front of her, it was difficult to snap out of attack mode. "Cillian, stay on Hans. Don't let him get away."

"You got it," said Cillian, baring his fangs at Hans and backing him into the corner of the kitchen.

Sofia lowered her hands and slowly approached the boy. He

stumbled away from her, eyes wide with fear. She raised her palms in surrender. "Hey, it's okay. We're here to help. We heard you call for us. Did you cast a spell?"

The boy's mouth fell open. "You heard that? I thought it was just my imagination. Just my panicked thoughts."

"Your magic responded to your fear," Sofia said. "That's a good sign. It was trying to protect you." She tapped into her Guardian powers, and gold light shone from her fingertips. It reached toward the boy, who cringed away.

Sofia frowned. She didn't feel the same sense of awareness and kinship she felt with other Guardians. Ordinarily, her magic would ignite, sensing the same energy shared between them. But with this boy, there was nothing. An empty void of nothingness that felt hollow and strangely familiar to her. It made her stomach churn with dread and agony.

She shook off these emotions, and her Guardian magic receded. "If you come with us, we can help you. Do you have any parents or siblings? Anyone who might be endangered by all this?"

The boy's eyes cut to Hans behind her as he slowly shook his head. "No. I don't have anyone. I've been on my own for a while."

Sofia knelt down. "Do you want to learn how to control your powers? I won't force you to come with us, but if you don't, he'll just keep coming for you."

The boy bit his lip, considering. "Come with you where?"

"We have a safe house nearby. I can portal you there. There are a bunch of other kids, most of them younger than you. We're training and educating them, teaching them how to harness their powers and defend themselves. You'll be free to leave whenever you wish."

The boy's eyes narrowed. "How can I trust you?"

"If I wanted to harm you, I would have helped him." She jerked a thumb over her shoulder, her face twisting with disgust. "That's the difference between him and us. We'll give you a choice. He won't."

Clarity burned in the boy's eyes as if something about this statement resonated with him. He lifted his chin slightly. "And I can leave anytime?"

"Yes."

The boy exhaled through his teeth, his expression thoughtful. He opened his mouth to respond when Cillian's voice rang out in Sofia's mind.

"Shit!"

Sofia whirled to find Hans pinning Cillian down with an assault of gold magic. Cillian snapped his teeth, trying to break free, but Hans poured more of his magic, caging Cillian, suffocating him with his magic.

Sofia slammed a Blood Choke spell on Hans, who stumbled backward, clutching at his throat, his eyes turning red. She raced to Cillian's side, but he was up in a flash, pouncing on his foe. Hans roared with fury as Cillian's jaw clamped down on his hand.

Hans's foot connected with Cillian's snout, and he whined in pain. Hans kicked again and again, baring his teeth. "I've had enough of this...goddamn...*dog!*"

His foot slammed into Cillian's cheek, and Hans sent a gold flame straight into the wolf's eyes. Cillian howled in agony, but Sofia was there, leg swinging with a powerful roundhouse kick that sent Hans flying over the kitchen counter and toward the dining table. Papers and dishes fell with a clatter of broken glass.

Sofia glanced over her shoulder to find the teenage boy, petrified, backed against the wall as he watched the fight.

A burst of gold light emanated from the dining area. Sofia rounded the corner and found traces of a vanishing portal. Hans had disappeared.

"Damn!" Sofia growled, slamming her fist on the counter. If

they had brought Hans into the TCO, that would have been a huge win for them—and a huge blow to Ruth.

Seething, Sofia hurried to Cillian's side, helping him up on all fours. His face and snout were bloody, and one of his ears looked like it had almost ripped clean off. "God, Cillian, are you all right?"

"Just some minor wounds. I'll stay in wolf form for a bit longer—I heal faster that way."

Sofia nodded, scratching under his neck. "I'm sorry. I shouldn't have taken my attention off him."

"I'm fine, Sofia. Just take care of the boy."

She rose to her feet and approached the boy, who flinched at her nearness.

"Hey." Sofia raised her palms again. "It's all right. He's gone. We're ready to get you out of here if that's still what you want to do."

The boy pointed to Sofia, then to the space where Hans had vanished. "He turned...wolf... Will you...will you be able to show me how to do all that?"

Sofia smiled. "In time, perhaps." If he truly was a Guardian, like Hans claimed, then there was a whole realm of possibilities for what his magic could do.

"I'm Sofia," she said, weaving her fingers in the air to conjure the portal back to the TCO. "What's your name?"

"Matthew."

"Nice to meet you, Matthew." She brought her hands together, and a gold portal appeared. He gasped and drew back a step.

"It's all right," Sofia said. "I'll let Cillian go first to show you it's safe." She turned to the wolf and nodded.

Cillian hobbled forward, sniffing in Matthew's direction with mild curiosity, before vanishing through the portal.

Matthew's eyes widened. "Where did he go?"

"To our headquarters," Sofia said. She waved her hand toward the doorway. "After you."

Matthew gulped, fisting his hands at his side, his brow furrowed with uncertainty. After a moment, he nodded as if to convince himself, then vanished through the portal. Sofia cast one more disappointed glance toward the wrecked kitchen, angry with herself for letting Hans escape, before she stepped through the portal after Matthew.

FORTY-FOUR

TWO WRAITHS ARE BETTER THAN ONE

The menacing crowd surrounded them, and a few feet away, Jayne found Tristan and Ruger also cornered. Though the Disciples still wore the ancient costumes, they didn't wield weapons this time. Perhaps they thought that was too conspicuous, given the civilians roaming casually about the square.

If they wanted inconspicuous, maybe they should've rethought their choice of wardrobe, Jayne thought as a few tourists passed by, giving the Disciples an odd look.

The man in front was someone Jayne recognized from the fight in the street. He had long blond hair tied back in a ponytail and a short beard covering his chin. He pointed a finger at Jayne, his eyes dark with rage. "You shouldn't be here."

She lifted her palms and forced a smile. "We're here to see the museum. No need to get hostile. We aren't breaking any laws."

"You are breaking the sacred law by bringing your disease with you." The man's voice was soft as he drew closer to her.

Jayne's skin prickled from his words. "What disease? I'm perfectly healthy."

The man's eyes drifted down to her arm. Though it was covered by her sleeve, Jayne still felt the urge to itch at the stretch of graying skin hidden underneath. Her blood chilled from the certainty in the man's gaze. He didn't know. He couldn't.

"Don't make this messier than it needs to be," Ruger said. "There are innocent people nearby. Let us go peacefully, and no one will get hurt."

The man shook his head vehemently, jabbing his finger at Jayne again. "She has already made this a disaster! It's only a matter of time now..." He gazed around the square, his face taut with sudden terror.

Jayne frowned. What the hell was this guy talking about? "A matter of time before what?"

"Do you think you are the only ones to seek the power living within the museum?" The man's voice was hushed. "The power has already corrupted many. Including you. Like calls to like, and you are drawing them to you even as we speak."

A chill of foreboding swept over Jayne. She shared a look with Vivienne, who shook her head slightly as if to say, *No idea what he's talking about.*

"Leave!" the man pleaded, his hand flicking toward the blade belted at his waist. "I will do what I must to protect my people and the people of this city, even if it means hurting you."

"I'd like to see you try," Jayne said, anger rising up inside her. "Look, we aren't leaving. What we're doing is too important, and like you said, we aren't the only ones after the power that's hidden here. If you don't let us through, someone else— someone worse will snatch it before we do. Trust me when I say you won't like what they'll do with that magic."

"You aren't hearing me," the man said impatiently. "We are in Croatia for a reason. There is a beast that roams freely, tainted by the ancient powers that turned on him many years ago. He is drawn by raw magic. Magic like yours. And he senses kindred creatures like himself. Our job is to keep him away from the populace and protect the city from his destruction. We have failed recently. The earthquake caused by the last magician seeking the grimoire caused so much damage we are still trying to recover.

"And now you are here, a burning flame in the darkness, guiding him straight to us. Go back through your portal before he comes and kills us all." He drew his knife and gestured at her. "I will not ask again."

Horrified, Jayne's eyes flicked from the knife to Ruger and Tristan, who both wore befuddled expressions. Could this possibly be true? Was there a Wraith living in Croatia?

It couldn't be Ruth. Jayne had encountered her in Rome not long ago, and judging by what this man was saying, the creature had been living in Croatia for quite a while.

"Jayne," Vivienne said quietly.

The other Disciples each drew their weapons, some jagged hunting knives, others spears or staffs. This was about to get ugly fast.

"Look, we are here to help," Jayne said, trying again. Her heart thundered madly in her chest, her instincts raging inside her, preparing her to fight. "We just—"

A piercing screech echoed in the square, followed by the intense flapping of wings. Jayne squinted into the bright sky, her blood chilling as a winged figure took shape above her. It drew closer and closer before slamming into the concrete before them, only a few yards away from her.

Oh, God, no! Jayne's heart lurched in her throat as she took in the Wraith's appearance. It was similar in size to Ruth's, but this one had cracked, crimson skin and deep, blood-red eyes. The wings stretching behind it were skeletal and all bones, no leathery skin covering them at all. Fangs dripped blood from its lips as it snarled at them.

It looked like a devil. Something summoned from Hell itself.

"You've doomed us all!" roared the blond man, whirling to brandish his knife at the Wraith. "Disciples, *attack*!"

Screams echoed in the square as the crowd of Disciples rushed the creature, surrounding it and raising their weapons. Around them, civilians fled the scene in terror. Jayne could only watch in horror as the horrified tourists reacted to the creature's presence.

"The Torrent isn't hiding this from the non-Adepts," Jayne shouted to Ruger. Normally, during a magical battle, the entire thing was shielded from innocent eyes, protecting the magic of the Torrent.

But not this. It was as if the Torrent wanted people to see this. Or it didn't have a choice because the Master within was too powerful.

Jayne reached for the Torrent and threw a Shield spell over the creature, layering it with a Cloaking spell. Ruger and Tristan were also weaving their own spells, warding the area from prying eyes. The damage might have already been done... But they couldn't afford to cause mass panic. Not when they still needed to get inside the museum.

The creature roared, swiping clawed fingers at the Disciples. Several of them fell, blood spraying from their injuries as the Wraith took them out one by one.

This one was powerful. Each blow was fatal. All it took was a single swipe to end a man's life.

Jayne summoned Medb's staff and surged forward, slamming an Attack spell straight into the creature's chest. It grunted but was otherwise unaffected by her spell.

"Damn," Jayne hissed, swinging her staff again to slam the flat end into the beast's skull. This time, it did stagger backward, but Jayne was only pissing it off.

She glanced over her shoulder and met Vivienne's gaze. "Shift," she commanded.

A flash of white light, and Vivienne was in her sphinx form, standing nearly as tall as the Wraith itself as she bounded toward it. Her claws flashed as she raked them down the creature's red flesh. Black blood bloomed from the injury, leaking onto the ground. Jayne wielded her staff, connecting it with the Wraith's throat.

Tristan and Ruger followed suit, sending well-aimed strikes at the creature's more sensitive parts. Just like with Ruth, magic didn't work on this thing.

So how the hell were they supposed to kill it?

Jayne summoned the Torrent, envisioning an armory. In seconds, she stood before a long array of weapons. Thinking quickly, she grabbed a dagger and an axe. When she returned to the battle, Tristan shot her an incredulous look.

"This is no time for tree-felling, you old lumberjack!"

"We need something," Jayne argued. "This thing might be able to heal from the wounds we're giving it." She raised the axe. "But can it heal from a severed head?"

Tristan's eyebrows lifted. He ducked as the creature swung his claws toward him. "At least this one doesn't have a tail, eh?"

Jayne couldn't help but laugh.

Vivienne pounced, tackling the Wraith to the ground. Around it, the Disciples stabbed and struck, hitting the beast over and over again. Jayne plunged her dagger into the Wraith's arm, slicing through muscles and tendons until she had it completely pinned. The beast roared, thrashing against the blade, but it held fast.

"Get the other arm!" she shouted.

Ruger stepped hard on the Wraith's other wrist while Tristan summoned a blade and buried it into the beast's skin.

"Move!" Jayne bellowed.

The crowd parted as she raised the axe, then buried it into the creature's thick neck. She barely sliced flesh at all. Growling in frustration, Jayne withdrew it, raised it again, then struck. Once. Twice. Three times. Like a lumberjack indeed, she hacked away at the beast's neck piece by piece. Each swing made the Wraith thrash harder, its legs kicking and connecting with a Disciple, sending him flying.

"Come on, Jayne!" Tristan shouted, struggling to keep the beast's arm pinned down.

"I'm trying!" She struck again. Black blood gushed along the concrete.

Several Disciples rushed forward, recognizing what she was doing, assisting her with trying to sever the head from the body. The Wraith managed to free its other arm and knocked several of them down. A sharp pain pierced Jayne's shoulder, and she cried out, her skin burning as the beast's claws shredded through her. She wanted to collapse, to sink to her knees, but she had to keep going.

She had to kill this thing.

Vivienne lunged, claws extended, and slammed her paws straight into the creature's chest. It roared again, but the sound was wetter. Feebler.

It was dying.

Jayne tried raising the axe again, but her shoulder was on fire. She could only lift it one-handed, but that wouldn't be enough force.

"Give it to me." The blond Disciple extended his hands. Blood ran down his forehead, but his eyes were steady and clear.

Jayne nodded, handing over the weapon. With a mighty shout, the man lifted the weapon, which was now burnished with shimmering red power, and buried it in the creature's throat. The skin severed completely, and the Wraith went still, its head rolling away from its body.

A searing, blinding white light filled the square, and Jayne shut her eyes against the intensity of it. Magic exploded in the air, washing over her like an ice-cold tidal wave. The air rippled and shifted, reminding Jayne of the Time Jumper. Had Henry activated it?

No, this was different. The air smelled crisper and cleaner, clearing away the rotten putrid smell of the Wraith and its blood. Gradually, the light faded, and Jayne squinted as her eyes adjusted to the scene before her.

The Wraith was gone. In its place was a man with long, curled but matted black hair and a frilled shirt with a cravat as if he'd stepped out of the court of Louis XVI.

And, as if taken by a rusty guillotine, the man's head was removed from his body.

This was who the Wraith had possessed. This was the last magician who had tried—and failed—to take the Liber Linteus.

Jayne was breathing heavily, but she still felt like she wasn't getting enough air. Mutters and whispers surrounded her as the Disciples took in the sight of this strange man, but all Jayne could think of was Ruth.

She and her Wraith could be defeated after all. And if they took Ruth down, they would weaken the Master who controlled her.

But that meant killing her mother.

Ruger had pulled out a cell phone and was speaking quickly in hushed undertones with someone, no doubt calling the clean-up crew to dispose of the body.

The blond Disciple approached Jayne, who tensed. He lifted his hands to show he meant no harm. "We owe you a debt. We have been trying to end this creature since it came into being hundreds of years ago." He stuck out his hand, which was sticky with blood. "I am Josiah."

"Jayne Thorne." She shook his hand. "So, does this mean you'll let us pass by? Peacefully?"

Josiah's face turned grim, and Jayne knew she had pushed her luck. "We may be indebted to you, but we cannot simply turn over this immense amount of power. Not when you, too, are tainted. You are on the same path as the beast." He gestured to the headless corpse on the ground.

"I am enslaved to no one," Jayne insisted. She lifted her arm. "This isn't the same thing!"

"Isn't it? You are a slave to some great power, Jayne Thorne, even if it is not what you think. Tread carefully, lest you find the same fate." He raised his hand, and the crowd of Disciples gathered behind him. Jayne scanned the square, her heart twisting at the sight of so many lifeless bodies. So many dead...

"We cannot stop you from entering the museum," Josiah said. "But our magic is tethered to the Liber Linteus, and we will do whatever it takes to protect it if that magic is threatened." His eyes were steely, the threat in his words obvious. *Go sightseeing, sure. But don't get near that grimoire.*

Jayne gritted her teeth. Would it do any good to tell him that nothing would stop her? That the gods themselves had asked her to perform this assignment?

But no. They had already wasted enough time. Vivienne approached, now in human form, looking sweaty and red-faced but otherwise unharmed. "Let me look at that."

Jayne winced as Vivienne rolled down the collar of her shirt, exposing a bloody red gash. "Yeah, can't exactly walk around with that, can I?"

Vivienne summoned a tendril of fire on her pointer finger, and Jayne stiffened. "What are you doing?"

"I have to cauterize it." Vivienne offered an apologetic grimace. "Sorry."

"What—" Jayne broke off with a strangled yell as the flames burned into her, scorching her. The smell of sizzling flesh stung her nose, and the pain was so intense she almost blacked out.

When Vivienne withdrew, Jayne was covered in sweat and ready to murder her Rogue. "That was rude," she said hoarsely.

"It had to be done. See? No more bleeding. You need a bandage, though. And a new shirt."

"Where are they going?" Tristan asked.

Jayne followed his gaze. The Disciples were dispersing, vanishing among the crowd. Some of them circled toward the back of the museum, while others spread in the other direction.

"Setting a perimeter," Jayne said darkly. "They won't attack us now, but they will as soon as we get to the grimoire."

"Let them try," Henry said, lifting his chin. "Time itself will stop them from following us."

Jayne raised her eyebrows. She had never heard her father sound so fierce and intimidating before. Then again, with the fresh cut dripping blood on his cheek, perhaps the battle had brought that out in him.

"Cleaners are on the way," Ruger said, pocketing his cell phone. "Let's tend to our wounds and get changed while the area is still cloaked. We need to get inside that museum before anyone comes looking for us. This has already drawn too much attention."

Jayne scanned the crowd. Some people were speaking in wild, hysterical tones, gesturing with their hands. But for the most part, the crowd looked at ease. Some exchanged dubious looks as if those who'd seen the Wraith were completely out of their minds.

Hopefully, it would stay that way. But they couldn't afford to wait and find out. The Liber Linteus was near, and Jayne could feel the pull of its magic.

FORTY-FIVE

THE HEIST

Luckily, there was a shop just down the street from the museum, where Jayne bought herself a new shirt. It was not her style, much more appropriate to backpacking students and totally clashing with the clever librarian look she was going for—but at least it would help her blend in with the masses.

After Jayne had finished changing clothes, Vivienne pointed to her shoulder. "Are you going to be okay with that?"

Jayne lifted her bad arm and winced. It was bandaged and no longer bleeding, thankfully covered by her new shirt, but it still throbbed. "I'll be fine. I can still lift it." She didn't add that it hurt like hell to do it, but they had no other choice. They had to get the Liber Linteus today. With the Disciples on high alert and the Kingdom not far behind, they couldn't afford to waste this opportunity.

Vivienne's lips thinned as if she could sense Jayne's discomfort, but she said nothing. After ensuring Henry was beside them, the cut on his face now nothing but an angry red line, Jayne led them to the museum. She didn't see Ruger or Tristan, but she knew they were there, taking their positions.

Jayne and Vivienne entered the museum with Henry close

behind. They paid their entrance fee just like the other tourists, and Jayne forced a pleasant smile on her face, trying to blend in. She elbowed Vivienne, who wore a permanent scowl.

"You're a cheerful patron of the museum, remember?" Jayne muttered under her breath.

Vivienne rolled her eyes, smoothing her expression into something neutral. It wasn't perfect, but at least her resting bitch face was gone.

The museum itself was a winding maze. The rooms zigzagged, narrow and twisty, with displays covering the walls. Staircases were roped off with signs about the earthquake damage. Civilians paused in each room on the ground floor to closely observe the items on display. It took all of Jayne's restraint not to join them, to drink in all the history and culture available in this place.

As if sensing her curiosity, Vivienne grasped Jayne's elbow, guiding her away from the displays and toward the red-carpeted staircase. Jayne ensured her father was behind them, then cast a Cloaking spell so they could climb the stairs unmolested. When she was sure no one could see them, they clambered over the rope and took the steps to the second floor, and then the third. The renovations were nearly finished, but there were still obvious cracks in the plaster and mismatched paint on the walls. It broke her heart knowing that the Wraith had caused this damage.

Below, Jayne heard Tristan's voice echoing with his obnoxious American accent, "What do you mean, I can't touch it! That's ridiculous!"

Jayne snorted, and Vivienne even cracked a smile. If everything went according to plan, Tristan's argument would draw as many museum security personnel as possible so Jayne, Vivienne, and Henry could snoop around undisturbed.

Once they reached the third floor, Jayne drew in a breath at the sight of the pharaohs and mummies, the displays of ancient hieroglyphics, and the magnitude of history and stories preserved over thousands of years. The lights were off, and she couldn't make out the details, so she brought her hand up and let the glow of her golden Guardian magic fill the room.

"God, it's beautiful," she whispered, approaching an intricately carved sarcophagus.

Vivienne steered her forward. "Focus, Jayne."

She dropped the spell and kept her gaze pinned forward. "Right. Focused."

The three of them wound their way through the halls, Jayne's eyes glossing over the displays and the deep blue wallpaper surrounding them. At long last, they reached an ordinary black door tucked into a corner. The wall label read *Zagreb Mummy*.

Shooting a glance over her shoulder, Jayne cloaked them, then approached the door. Vivienne positioned herself strategically in front of Jayne, tensed and ready. For good measure, Jayne started by jiggling the handle. Locked, of course. A keypad next to the doorknob blinked an angry red as if annoyed she'd even tried opening it.

Jayne waved her hands, summoning a Sensory spell from the Torrent, then pressed it into the door frame. Her fingers meet the cool surface of the door as she listened carefully. A faint humming noise emanated from within. She closed her eyes, waiting for her spell to take root.

There it was. She sensed a built-in alarm, set to activate if the door was opened without the proper security clearance. Ripples of energy danced around her spell, an unfamiliar form of magic attempting to mingle with hers.

The Disciples. It had to be their protection spells. Jayne squinted, trying not to let the magic touch her, but it felt like her tiny spell had triggered the magic of the Disciples, drawing them closer.

Jayne jerked her hand away from the door as if she'd been

burned. It was too soon to attract their enemies. They were here to canvass only.

"Everything all right?" Vivienne asked quietly.

Jayne nodded, guiding her and Henry away from the door as a few security guards appeared down the hall.

"Just as we suspected," Jayne said under her breath. "Magical and nonmagical measures in place. But nothing we can't handle."

"I felt their magic," Henry muttered from behind them. "That's powerful stuff. More powerful than I'd realized."

Jayne agreed, but she didn't want to seem too pessimistic. "This mission will be in and out. By the time the Disciples of Gaia are even aware of us gaining access to this room, we'll be long gone."

She only wished she believed it would be that easy.

WITH TIME TO KILL, the team perused the lower levels of the museum, then grabbed dinner at a restaurant nearby. Jayne was pleasantly surprised by the tangy *Zagrebački odrezak*, a fried, breaded sandwich consisting of ham, cheese, and sliced veal.

When dusk fell, they meandered down the street, keeping close to the museum, but not so close that they would attract unwanted attention.

At long last, the museum closed. Darkness fell on the square, and the team was ready to act.

This had to work. It had to.

Before they parted ways, Tristan turned to Jayne and wiggled his eyebrows. "Any chance I could get another goodbye kiss?"

Jayne punched his arm, her face heating. "You ass." When he only grinned roguishly at her, she added, "For the record, that wasn't a goodbye kiss. That was a to-be-continued kiss."

His eyebrows lifted, his smile turning more sincere. More genuine. More Tristan. For a moment, Jayne just gazed at him, reveling in this rare display of true emotion from him. Not the mask. Not the sarcastic partner. But Tristan.

He leaned close to her, pressing his forehead against hers. "To be continued, then," he murmured. His deliciously soothing voice sent a ripple of pleasure over her, but before she could respond, he was gone.

Vivienne appeared at Jayne's side, and Jayne flinched, expecting to be teased for her brief moment with Tristan. Instead, she asked, "Ready?"

Jayne nodded. She pulled a Cloaking spell and a Shield spell from the Torrent and draped them in it, then shared a solemn glance with her father before the three of them approached the museum doors. Jayne pulled out an Unlock spell before pressing it carefully into the glass doors. A click sounded, and the door swung open. Jayne glanced around the emptying plaza once before holding open the door for Henry and Vivienne to pass through. She carefully eased it shut behind them without a sound.

The darkened museum surrounded them, lit only by a few small lights built into the ceiling. An eerie emptiness filled the air, making Jayne's nerves twitch.

"Come on," she whispered, guiding Henry and Vivienne up the stairs. Their steps felt far too loud for the still and quiet space, but there was nothing to be done about it. No one outside their Shield could hear or see them anyway.

They followed the same path to the third floor, then to the locked black door that housed the Liber Linteus.

When they reached it, she turned to Vivienne. "I'll give the command to shift as soon as I'm in. Be careful, and try not to be seen."

"I know what I'm doing," Vivienne insisted. "You be careful, too, Jayne."

311

Jayne offered a small smile before approaching the black door. Waving her hand, she summoned another Unlock spell layered with a Jammer that would halt the magical threads that denoted the Disciples' magic. Moments later, a soft metal click sounded. Jayne swung open the heavy door and slipped inside with Henry close behind.

The lights clicked on automatically, and a flashing red beam in the top left corner of the room indicated a silent alarm had been triggered.

No matter. They would be in and out in seconds. Hopefully.

The chilled room looked exactly like the simulated Time Catch. There was the mummy, calmly encased in her vitrine, and across from it, the linen strips of the Liber Linteus. As Jayne's eyes rested on the grimoire, a buzzing built in her bones, humming through her blood and awakening the goddess magic inside her. Effortlessly, Medb and Vesta's powers came to life, igniting the flow of ice and heat from within her. Jayne gasped from the intensity of it.

"Good," Henry muttered behind her. "I can feel your power, Jayne. It's ready."

"Right. Here we go." She withdrew Quimby's battery pack from her pocket, and carefully stepped across the room. When she stood in front of the glass case with the Liber Linteus inside, she glanced over her shoulder at Henry.

He lifted the Time Jumper in his hand. "All set?"

Jayne steeled herself before giving a sure nod. She held up three fingers.

"Three. Two. One. Mark." She pushed the button on the battery pack just as Henry activated the Jumper.

The world slowed around Jayne, the air shifting and tightening around her chest, squeezing the breath from her body. She inhaled a rattling gasp, struggling to breathe.

An explosion of green light burned against her vision. She jolted, squinting against the brightness of it.

This was new. It definitely had not happened in the simulation.

But she had to push forward. Maintaining her grasp on the goddess magic within her, Jayne reached for the Torrent and found the Carry spell. She weaved it through her hands before returning to the vitrine before her, only to find it encompassed in that same green glow.

Oh, no... This had to be the work of the Disciples.

"What do I do?" Jayne shouted, her gaze still fixed on the vitrine. "Is it safe?"

"I—I've never seen magic like this before," Henry stammered. "But it feels like Guardian magic, Jayne. Be careful."

Guardian magic. The Disciples of Gaia used earth magic. Just like Medb. Just like Jayne.

Would it interfere with the Time Jumper?

Jayne shook her head, her body sluggish. She was running out of time. She had to trust that the Disciples weren't prepared for time travel. This plan could still work.

Sweat beaded on her forehead as she pressed the Carry spell against the cool vitrine. The glass on the wall quivered, the green spell flaring as if angry that Jayne had interfered with it. She closed her eyes, willing Vesta and Medb's powers forward, hoping to appease the Disciples' magic.

I'm one of you, she told it. *I have earth magic, just like you. Let me in.*

The quivering faded, as did the green glow. Jayne urged more of Medb's icy magic inside, just to be safe, before wrapping the vitrine in the Carry spell.

The weight of it immediately pulled her down, making her groan. It took all her effort not to sink to one knee, her back bowing and her shoulders hunched from the effort.

A small beep filled the air, and the world shifted and tilted, dragging Jayne with it as the Time Jumper deactivated. Her head spun, her vision darkening as the strength of the grimoire threatened to swallow her whole. Whispers filled her mind, some in languages she didn't even understand.

Then, in the distance, a language she did.

"Ovdje!" someone shouted from the other side of the door. *Over here.*

A loud screech. Then, pain lanced through Jayne, sending a path of fire down her arm. She hissed against the throbbing ache, glancing down to find her arm untouched.

But deep down, she knew—it wasn't her; it was Vivienne. The Rogue was in trouble.

"Portal," Henry said urgently. "Now."

Something beeped next to her, and Jayne glanced at the now bare wall where the Liber Linteus had been. A flashing red light gleamed from a device built into the wall.

The motion sensor had been activated. Jayne had seconds before the explosives detonated.

Another loud screech just outside. Several men were shouting in Croatian.

"I can't leave her out there," Jayne said, moving toward the door. But each step was like wading through molasses, the grimoire still trying to bring her to her knees.

"Jayne," Henry said urgently. "The explosives... There isn't time. Vivienne can take care of herself. Stick to the plan."

Jayne shook her head. "I'm not leaving her, Dad." Her hand grasped the handle of the door, just as Henry snatched her free hand.

"If you are caught, this whole mission is a failure," he said sharply.

Jayne clenched her teeth, meeting his gaze. In a flash, she snatched the Time Jumper from his hand and pushed the button.

"No—" Henry's words were cut off as Jayne wrenched her hand free of his grip, leaving him frozen with the rest of the world. The battery grew hotter in Jayne's pocket, and sweat kept pouring down her neck.

She pushed against the door with all her strength, groaning as it finally fell open. Before her was a crowd of people. Some wore security uniforms, hands raised, faces taut with determination. Above them, wings flared toward the ceiling, was Vivienne. But something wasn't right. One wing was bent at an odd angle, and her feathers were stained with blood.

Jayne squinted, surveying the figures in front of her before her gaze fell on a face she recognized. Blaine. And there, next to him, was another goon Jayne knew by face but not by name.

The Kingdom was here. And they had Vivienne cornered. They must have tipped off the Croatian security guards; Jayne knew for a fact that only three men were on duty tonight, but there were far more here now. As if they'd expected to encounter trouble on this shift.

A beep sounded from Jayne's pocket. Her battery was drained. She was out of time. Beyond out of time.

Her dad was going to kill her.

She shot a guilty look at Henry, still immobilized in the doorway, his face a combination of confusion and horror.

Thinking fast, Jayne weaved her hands together, summoning a golden portal next to the open door. She found her Lasso spell, then tossed the glowing rope toward Vivienne. It wrapped around one of her talons, then tightened. Jayne tugged gently, pulling the Rogue down. As she did so, she pushed the button on the Time Jumper, deactivating it.

The world erupted into sound and chaos. Vivienne screeched again, then jerked downward with Jayne's rope. Still holding onto the lasso, Jayne used her free hand to pull on her father's arm. A high-pitched beeping sound rang out, and a deafening *boom* exploded from within the mummy room. Heat and ash burned the back of Jayne's neck as she dove through the portal with Vivienne and Henry in tow, narrowly avoiding being squashed by a collapsing shelf of ancient relics.

The ground tilted as Jayne fell face-forward, tumbling into nothingness. Her scream was lost in the spinning vortex that surrounded her. With a heavy *smack,* she landed flat on her face on something coarse and rough. Rocks and gravel scraped against her flesh as she pushed up from the ground, her cheeks stinging and her arms burning. The ground was still spinning, making her dizzy.

No...that wasn't the ground. That was something else.

A flash of white light, and a hand gripped her arm. It was Vivienne, eyes hooded and nose bloodied. "Jayne... What did you do?"

The earth shook. Cracks formed in the concrete beneath them. Squinting in the darkness, Jayne made out the shape of the museum about half a mile away. The portal had taken them far enough away to avoid being seen, but something else was happening to the building. It trembled violently. Glass shattered, concrete crumbled, and the surrounding civilians lingering in the street began to scream.

Jayne lurched to her feet, then stumbled, her head swimming. Vivienne was there in an instant, steadying her.

"What's happening?" Jayne asked. "An earthquake? Or is this from the detonator?"

But in her gut, she knew this wasn't natural. A strange purple light hovered above the museum. It shimmered and twisted like a kaleidoscope, and from within the light, Jayne could make out flashes of lightning.

Oh, God, no...

"It's the time vortex!" Henry roared. "Jayne, give me the Time Jumper. Now!"

Jayne handed the device to him, and to her surprise, he threw it to the ground and stomped on it, crushing it into a million pieces. Something zapped and sizzled in the air, smelling of hot sage and fresh soil.

Earth magic.

"Why did you do that?" Jayne cried.

"The device was linked directly to the time vortex," Henry said. "By destroying it, I destroyed that link. But I don't think it's enough."

Jayne stared, horrified, at the museum. The flashing purple light remained, but the ground wasn't quaking anymore. Several people pointed to the light, shouting in alarm.

They could see it. Everyone could see the time vortex.

"What do we do?" Jayne cried. "How do we stop this?"

Henry's eyes were blazing as he looked at her, shaking his head slightly. He didn't know.

Without thinking, Jayne crouched to the ground, burying her hands in the gravel beneath her. Her eyes closed as she called on Medb's power. *Heal this place,* she commanded. *Please, Medb. Bring life to this place once more. Heal what is broken.*

Something stirred inside her, before flickering like the dying flame of a candle.

"No," Jayne whispered, shaking her head. "No!"

She pressed her fingers harder, allowing the rocks to dig into her skin, to push underneath her fingernails. She focused hard on the icy chill of Medb's powers inside her.

The rocks shifted, and Jayne felt a presence beside her. It was Vivienne, her hands next to Jayne, eyes closed as she whispered a spell in French.

Heat burned in Jayne's blood. Vesta's power.

Then, Henry was there, his hands next to theirs, eyes closed. Jayne sensed his Guardian magic flaring to life.

Together, the three of them crouched, hands touching, buried in the earth as they called on the ancient powers of the gods.

To Jayne's amazement, the purple flashing lights above the

museum subsided, collapsing in on itself like a black hole in space. She sucked in a dry gasp as, with one last flash of lightning, the time vortex vanished, leaving the sky as clear and beautiful as it had been seconds ago. Civilians still cried out hysterically, pointing to the sky where the lights had just been. But for now, the museum and the area were safe.

Gasping, Jayne removed her dirty hands from the gravel and sank backward on her ass, beyond exhausted.

But the drama of the night wasn't finished yet.

"You have no idea what you've done, do you?" Henry's voice was hollow and full of despair. Jayne had never heard him speak like that before.

"Dad, please—"

"I warned you, Jayne. And you broke the rules! You're like a —a child with a weapon! I can't trust you with anything anymore."

Seething, Jayne jumped to her feet, ignoring the nauseating dizziness that overcame her. "A child with a weapon? Dad, I didn't make some careless decision. Vivienne could have died. I wasn't about to abandon my partner."

She felt Vivienne's eyes on her but couldn't bring herself to meet the Rogue's gaze. Instead, she stared hard at Henry, who was visibly shaking with anger.

"If you can't respect the delicate boundaries that keep the time vortex secure, then I don't know if I can trust you."

Hurt and fury filled Jayne's chest. She took a step toward Henry, prepared to yell some more, but Vivienne caught her arm and shook her head slightly.

"Leave it," Vivienne muttered. "You both need to cool off."

Jayne heaved a deep sigh, turning away and running her hands through her hair. Her mind felt like mush, and she still couldn't see straight. The grimoire still weighed her down, but they couldn't leave until Ruger and Tristan showed up.

"There they are." Vivienne pointed, and Jayne made out two figures moving toward them from the plaza.

Jayne exhaled with relief, wiping sweat from her forehead. God, it was so hot.

"Jayne."

She glanced up to find Vivienne watching her with a conflicted expression. "You—you sacrificed everything to save me. I won't lie and say I had it under control. I didn't. The Kingdom caught us by surprise, and I was unprepared. Your father has a point—it was terribly careless." She paused, biting her lip. "But I'll be forever grateful to you. Friends?"

She stuck out her hand. Jayne shook it firmly.

"Friends. And partners," Jayne agreed.

"*Oui.* Partners." Vivienne smiled slightly before turning back to the plaza. Tristan approached, followed closely by Ruger. Thankfully, neither of them looked injured.

But Jayne's relief was short-lived. Darkness pricked the corners of her eyes, spreading across her vision like ink bleeding through a page. She blinked, hard, but she couldn't regain clarity. All she could do was surrender to the darkness as it took over completely. Fatigue claimed her, fueled by the intensity of the grimoire still contained in her Carry spell. She slumped over, eyes rolling back. She heard Vivienne's shout of alarm, felt a pair of hands on her as someone tried to lift her up.

Then all was black.

CHAPTER

FORTY-SIX

WARRIOR GODDESS

J ayne stood in the small room with the grimoire, facing the glass vitrine with the mummy enclosed inside. But there wasn't a soul in sight. The black door was wide open, but the museum was empty. Silent. No blaring alarms. No shouts. No screeches from Vivienne's hawk form.

Jayne spun around, heart racing as she tried to figure out what had happened. Why was she back here? Was she in the Time Catch?

"Jayne Thorne."

She whirled and found a familiar red-haired woman standing next to the case with the Liber Linteus. She wore the same armored helmet, the same battle gear.

The warrior goddess.

Jayne felt oddly weighted, looked down only to realize she was wearing similar garb as the goddess before her, full battle dress, with fur-lined gauntlets and leather corset and a wide belt buckled at her waist ready for weapons. She held the staff, and she could feel the power of lightning sparking along the wood. Her throat went dry. "Am I really here?"

"You are here in your dreams, as before, Jayne Thorne. I haven't much time. But I must impart this prophecy to you."

"Who are you?" Jayne blurted.

"I am Freyja."

Jayne's heart stuttered in her chest. Freyja, the Norse goddess of war. Freyja, the prophetess. "Nice to meet you. Um...the prophecy?"

Freyja's voice reverberated through Jayne's body.

"Long ago, I once foretold the downfall of our great king and god. He became desperate and paranoid, believing his own army of winged soldiers would turn against him and betray him. So, he waged war, destroying the Valkyries and imprisoning those he believed to be disloyal. My sisters and I had to act. We crafted a prison for him, to contain his power before it consumed the world. We trapped him...but he exacted revenge against us, binding us to grimoires around the world. The first of these was myself, caged in the Liber Linteus."

Jayne shook her head, struggling to keep up. "So, it's an old prophecy? From thousands of years ago?"

"Yes. This is the Prophecy of Wind. Our great king fulfilled the prophecy himself when he turned against my sisters and me. He betrayed everyone who had once allied with him." Freyja's eyes filled with a deep sorrow that had seen thousands of years of injustice and misery.

"What does this have to do with me?" Jayne asked.

"You are the key, Jayne Thorne. Our sacred vessel. With you, our power can be reborn, merging together to defeat the great god once and for all. We cannot wield it ourselves, you see, for we are cursed. But we can bestow these gifts for you to wield on our behalf." Freyja extended a long, slender finger and gently brushed the tip of it against Jayne's forehead.

A surge of energy pushed against her, making her cry out. She wanted to jerk away, but she forced herself to remain still. Wind whipped against her, tousling her hair, raising goose bumps along her arms. The lightning arced into the sky, turning it blue.

When Freyja withdrew, the wind vanished, and Jayne gasped, feeling an unfamiliar sensation take hold of her. It wasn't ice, like Medb, or fire, like Vesta. It was...sound. Like wind chimes. Faint, but distinct. Sharp, pure peals against Jayne's eardrums. It resonated against her bones as if a tiny musician were playing the xylophone along her body. Every limb quivered with the energy of that song. Freyja's song.

"The Air totem is yours, Jayne Thorne," Freyja said with a smile. She stepped back, and Jayne panicked.

"No! You can't leave yet. I still have so many questions. How do I wield this power? How do I stop the god in the Torrent? And my mother... She has one of the totems. How do I get it from her?"

Freyja gazed at Jayne patiently. "I know there is much you do not understand. But I do not have all the answers. Ruth Thorne is not our chosen vessel. The power of the totem will reject her as a host, in time. But you must be there to retrieve it when it does, lest it fall into the wrong hands.

"As for the unmerciful god in the Torrent, you cannot face him until you have our full arsenal of magic. My sisters are waiting for you. Their power, their magic, calls to you."

"Sisters? The Valkyries?" Jayne shook her head. "But...the Master of Shadows was a guy, right? Or was he also a Valkyrie?"

"We began as a tribe of women, but over the years, more joined our ranks. We needed all the allies we could get to defeat our king and god. Just as you will need as many allies as you can get, Jayne Thorne. Even the most unlikely of magic-wielders."

Jayne frowned at this. Who was Freyja talking about?

"My time has come. But I have one last prophecy to impart to you." Freyja drew closer, her eyes like liquid fire. "The powers contained within you are too strong for this world, Jayne

Thorne. You and the Torrent cannot coexist. One of you must perish, or risk the destruction of our world."

A chill skittered down Jayne's spine from the solemnity of Freyja's words. *One of you must perish...*

"I'm going to die?" Jayne whispered.

Freyja said nothing, her eyes still burning. She withdrew a step, bowing her head to Jayne in respect. "I know you will do the right thing, Jayne Thorne." Her form flickered, and the walls around them began to melt away. Jayne recognized the telltale sign of her dreamscape fading, and she desperately reached out as if to grab Freyja and keep her here.

"No, wait!" Jayne shouted. "Am I going to die? How do I stop it? What do I do?"

The scene vanished, and with a bone-rattling gasp, Jayne sat up, eyes wide open, heart thundering madly in her chest.

"Jayne!" Something shifted nearby, and Henry's worried face came into view. He held her shoulders steady, peering into her eyes. "Can you hear me?"

"Yes," Jayne said, her voice strangled. She was lying on the couch in the Zagreb safe house. Someone must have brought her unconscious body through a portal to get here. She climbed to her feet, groaning as pain shot up her limbs. She glanced down—she was in street clothes, not the battle gear from her dream. She felt oddly naked without it.

"Is everyone okay? Where's Ruger?"

"Checking in with Amanda," Henry said, jerking his thumb over his shoulder toward the closed bedroom door. "He made sure we'd all portaled safely out of there first, though. Thankfully, the media is more concerned with what happened with the time vortex than with anything going on inside the museum." Henry shook his head. She knew he hadn't forgiven her misstep.

But now wasn't the time to dwell on it.

The door opened, and Tristan and Vivienne came through.

Seeing Jayne upright, Tristan rushed to her side. The relief on his face told her how scary it must have been when she went down.

"You're awake," he said. "What happened?"

"I got the grimoire," Jayne said. As she thought about it, the weight of the Liber Linteus no longer pulled on her. Perhaps with Freyja's message delivered, the magic inside the grimoire had subsided. "The warrior goddess is Freyja, and she gave me the prophecy. I know who the Master in the Torrent is."

Vivienne straightened. "Who? Who is manipulating us and our friends?"

"It's Odin," Jayne said. "The Norse god. The All-Father."

CHAPTER

FORTY-SEVEN

JUSTICE IS SERVED

A manda waited in the parking garage in McLean, arms folded over her chest, fingers drumming an erratic rhythm along her upper arm. She stood between a posh red Porsche Cayenne and a black Tesla SUV. Two rows down, her tactical team waited, ready to intercept Pierce.

She was filled with a mixture of anxiety, satisfaction, and pure rage.

This was it. She would finally confront Pierce for his crimes. Part of her wanted to laugh in his face. The other part of her wanted to strangle him for all he'd put her through. For all he'd put the TCO through.

After everything they had done for him...

Amanda shook her head, gritting her teeth. Ever since her conversation with Rebecca, it was like a floodgate of emotions had opened up inside her, exposing all the raw and festering parts she'd tried to keep buried for so many years. And she couldn't shut those gates. Not anymore.

Footsteps echoed nearby, and Amanda ducked behind the SUV in case Pierce spotted her too soon and bolted.

As the figure drew nearer, Amanda caught a glimpse of

Pierce, his expression taut with concern and fear. He was worried about why he'd been summoned on such short notice. Perhaps he thought Ruth was here to punish him.

Good. He deserved that fear.

Pierce hesitated mere steps away from the SUV, but still Amanda waited. Then, he called out hesitantly, "Firebird?"

Ruth's code name. Amanda knew this from the emails she'd intercepted. But still, she remained silent.

"Ruth?" Pierce called out more firmly.

There it was. Verbal affirmation. Even though Amanda had plenty of proof already, hearing him voice the name like a colleague instead of an enemy jolted her entire body, making her see red.

Unable to help herself, Amanda stepped out from her hiding spot.

Pierce gave a sharp gasp and staggered back a step, his face going bone white. "A-Amanda! God, no, I—"

He whirled to run and the tactical team emerged, surrounding him completely. Pierce spun in place, his face taking on a greenish tint as if he might be sick. He fisted his hands in his hair, gasping for breath. "No—*no!* This isn't—I swear to God, I—"

"It's over, Pierce," Amanda said, her voice biting. "I've been collecting evidence against you for weeks now." She took a step closer to him, and he flinched, his entire frame trembling. "We would have fought for you. Died for you. Because our loyalty runs that deep. But theirs? They would have discarded you in an instant. They probably will, now that you've been caught." She shook her head, her chest swelling with a combination of anger and sorrow. "How could you have been so foolish?"

Sudden disgust twisted Pierce's features, making him look unrecognizable. "Foolish?" he spat. "You say you would have fought for me? That's not true for a second. Maybe if I were on your precious team of field-trained officers, but no. I'm just an assistant. Just someone who does the grunt work. Another blank face for you to pass by every morning. My career was going nowhere. I've worked for you for years, Amanda. And you never gave a damn about me."

Amanda kept her face perfectly composed, though his words sliced right through her. Part of what he said was true. She hadn't given much thought to him, his personal life, his aspirations. But she would have protected him. And had he approached her about advancing his career, she would have done her damnedest to make opportunities available to him.

Instead, he'd sought out Ruth.

"I'm sorry you felt that way," Amanda said softly. "But treason wasn't the answer." She flicked her fingers toward Pierce, and two men from her team drew closer, cuffing his hands behind him. She watched solemnly as the officers marched him from the parking garage. The fire seemed to have left Pierce; he hung his head, and Amanda swore she saw his shoulders shaking with sobs.

She thought she'd feel a sense of rightness, of satisfaction from finally seeing justice served. But instead, all she felt was a pang of sorrow. Pierce's betrayal had been a result of several factors. But one of those was her own ignorance. Her own neglect of someone under her care.

And something deep inside her told her that, with war brewing on the horizon, this would not be the first betrayal she would have to endure.

Her cell vibrated in her pocket, and Amanda whipped it out and answered, "Newport."

Chris Panna, the head of her research team, spoke in a staccato hurry. "We've just finished analyzing Henry Thorne's data."

"And?"

"And he's right."

Amanda's insides turned cold. "Right about what, exactly?"

"We've gone through his data and run tests of our own based on the samples we took from the Torrent and Officer Thorne's Guardian magic. There are signs of life within the Torrent. Multiple Adepts in peril. Their magic is sending huge spikes of energy, almost like distress signals. We didn't see it before because we weren't looking at the right frequency."

Amanda sucked in a shaky breath. Goddess, she couldn't believe it.

Henry Thorne was right.

Jayne's grandmother—and her daughter from the future— were trapped inside the Torrent.

And now they had to do something about it.

CHAPTER

FORTY-EIGHT

FOR BETTER OR WORSE

Jayne sat in her apartment in Nashville, which she hadn't seen in weeks, enjoying a slice of apple pie à la mode and a glass of wine as she read over the notes Henry had made based on his research of the Liber Linteus. Her father was still knee-deep in deciphering everything contained within the grimoire, but she wanted to stay up to date with everything he found. As promised, he'd sent her the data he'd gathered from the past two days alone, and it was quite a lot. It made her eyes itch with exhaustion just reading it.

Honestly, she was glad he was sharing any information with her at all. After his outburst and everything that happened in Zagreb, she feared she had permanently driven a wedge between them. But Henry was still cooperating with her, if a bit coolly, for which Jayne was grateful. Even if he refused to discuss his technology with her anymore.

But that was fine. Baby steps.

He still hadn't discovered a backdoor access to the Torrent, but he was hopeful. Based on some of the translations, there were hints that whoever had written this grimoire knew far more about the Torrent than anyone else. It made Jayne wonder who the author had been. Was it Freyja? Or one of the other Valkyries?

An ancient god. Norse mythology. Jayne shook her head, taking another long sip of wine. She still couldn't believe it. Odin, the All-Father, was the heinous monster who had trapped her family in the Torrent, feeding off their energy like a vampire.

She set her glass down and sighed, rubbing her temples. She couldn't stop thinking about the prophecy Freyja had given her. *You and the Torrent cannot coexist. One of you must perish...or risk the destruction of our world.*

She hadn't told anyone about it except for her father. Somehow, she felt like he would understand.

To her surprise, Henry had only nodded grimly and said, "I was afraid of something like that."

The words shocked and horrified her. Because, not only had her father suspected this and hadn't told her, but it also meant it was *true*. If Henry Thorne, who would do anything to protect his daughters, had accepted that one of them would die to save the Torrent, then Jayne truly was doomed.

Not to mention the international kerfuffle their little heist had caused. Amanda was knee-deep in it with both the Croatians and the director. It didn't matter; magic continued to explode everywhere. More and more children were showing up for Sofia and Cillian's new school; more and more adults were asking for assistance with their newfound, and unfathomable, power. At this rate, the magical folk were going to outnumber the nonmagical, and what kind of world was that going to be? Jayne wanted peace and harmony, but she knew in her soul that the world would have to be broken in order for it to be remade. There would be casualties. She would be only one of thousands, in the end.

Well, *those* were happy thoughts.

When a knock sounded at her door, she welcomed the distraction, rising to her feet to open it.

Tristan stood on the other side, hands in his pockets, his hair a mass of thick waves that hung to his shoulders. He offered her a crooked smile. "Hi."

Such a simple word, and yet it evoked an explosion of butterflies in her stomach. "Hi." Guilt wriggled through her. After the events in Zagreb, she'd parted from him without a word, too exhausted and overwhelmed to process her feelings and what was left unsaid between them. But here and now? Anything could happen. And she'd kept him waiting long enough.

She reached forward, gripping him by the collar to drag him into the apartment. The door shut behind him, and he laughed. "Well, that's one way to welcome someone inside."

"I want you," Jayne said without preamble. "All of you. I don't want to do this halfway or on-again off-again. I want the whole Tristan Lowell package. The good, the bad, and the ugly."

Tristan's smile turned feral. "Not much of the *ugly*, I'm afraid."

Jayne swatted his arm. "God, you're so full of yourself."

"But you love it."

"Yes, I do. I love *you*."

Shock flared in his eyes. "You—what?"

"I love you, Tristan." The words had never felt more right. More sure.

His mouth parted, his expression momentarily frozen with surprise.

Jayne laughed and poked his cheek. "Uh-oh, I think I broke him."

He shook his head, his face splitting into a wide smile, his eyes crinkling in that way she loved so much. Then, his mouth was on hers. She kissed him back fervently, meeting each stroke of his lips and tongue with one of hers, their bodies writhing against each other with urgent desire. He backed her against the wall, hips pinning her, and she gasped from the delicious weight of him pressing into her.

"*Mon amour,*" Tristan murmured, his lips trailing a path of fire down her jaw and toward her neck. His tongue flicked at the hollow of her throat, and she moaned. "*Je t'aime.*"

I love you.

The words had once frightened her, but now they were a promise. A token for her to grasp onto. A vow for their future.

She was grateful he didn't ask what had changed. He would eventually, and she would have to be honest. *Time is running out.* But for now, she wanted him, badly.

She slid off his jacket and worked at the buttons of his shirt. His hands ran up and down her thighs before hitching her legs up, his hardness pushing against her core. She threw her head back, relishing the solid feel of him. His mouth was on her neck again, devouring her. His shirt came off and fell to the floor. His hands found the bottom of her tank top and wrenched it upward, exposing her bra. With a groan, she wriggled out of the tank, discarding it along with his shirt.

His fingers were everywhere. The warmth of his body mingled with hers, bringing a delicious heat that she only wanted more of. Jayne's hands fiddled with his belt, undoing it and unzipping his pants. They slid off, and he stepped out of them. She could see his arousal straining against his underwear, and it made her knees go weak.

"See something you like?" he whispered, flashing her a grin.

Ah, so he wanted to play? Well, so could she.

Jayne dropped her legs, shooting him a coy smile as she slowly backed away from him. Surprise flared in his gaze, but he watched her hungrily like a predator. She edged away from him, still staring at him with beckoning eyes. Her hands drifted below the waistband of her pants before tugging them lower. And lower.

Tristan's eyes were on fire as he watched her undress. The pants fell to the floor, and then Jayne's fingers slid along her underwear. She stilled, watching him, relishing the frenzied look in his eyes. "See something you like?" she teased.

He drew closer to her, making her blood thrum. "I will devour you, Jayne Thorne."

"Is that a promise?"

In one swift movement, much faster than the average human, Tristan hoisted her up, wrapping her legs around him. Her bra was off, baring her chest to him, and he kissed each of her breasts hungrily, making her shiver. His hands cupped her rear as he gently deposited her onto the couch before sliding off her underwear. Jayne used her toes to tug at his boxers, and Tristan laughed, helping them the rest of the way off.

Both naked and fully aroused, their bodies tangled together, limbs and hands and teeth and tongues. Jayne was about to urge him onward, to finally have him fill her completely, when a tiny logical voice sounded in her mind. She stopped, looking into his face.

"Think you could conjure up a condom?" she whispered.

He blinked, momentarily jolted from the hazy stupor of their intercourse. "I...um, yes..." He turned away, then faced her again, both eyebrows raised. "Jayne."

"Tristan."

"Maybe we shouldn't. In case..."

She knew exactly where he was going with this. Jayne's breath caught in her throat, alarm pulsing through her. *My daughter.* The one trapped in the Torrent.

Could she possibly be Tristan's daughter, too?

And was Jayne ready to meet her? No. No, she was not.

"Knowing what we know," Jayne said quietly, "about the prophecy and the totems, I understand you not wanting to risk it." He didn't know about the prophecy of her death, but how could she tell him that? Besides, even if she *did* die in this war against Odin, she knew one thing: she *would* have a daughter.

He kissed her gently. "This job has taught me is that life is short. It's dangerous, and uncertain. So I will tell you this. I want to live my life now. With you. For better or for worse."

Affection surged inside her, so fierce and gripping that tears pricked at her eyes. She pressed her hands against his cheeks, bringing his mouth to hers. When she drew away, she whispered, "I want that, too. So let's be careful."

He nodded, kissing her again, his mouth pressing harder, bringing the urgency back with it. For a brief moment, he drew away, digging into the pocket of his discarded pants before pulling out a condom. She was relieved it was real, not magical. Just in case.

Then their bodies were moving again as if nothing had changed. And yet everything was different. Here were two people who loved each other deeply, madly, insanely, talking about a future. And that possibility scared the hell out of Jayne, but the thrill of it, the beauty of that knowledge coursed through her, stronger than any arousal or desire. Stronger than any magic she possessed.

Her legs wrapped around his middle as he hovered over her, nudging against her entrance. His eyes met hers with one last question. *Are you sure?*

She nodded, clenching herself around him.

And then he was inside her, filling her so completely that she cried out with pleasure. He slid in and in and in, so deep she thought she saw stars explode in her vision. They found a rhythm together, his thrusts meeting hers, his moans matching her gasps. Her fingernails clawed at him, raking down his shoulders and chest. His hands tangled in her hair, his face buried in her neck as he whispered her name again and again. As sweet release poured through them both, their mouths met in a clash of desperation, solidifying their union, physically and emotionally.

"*Mon amour,*" Jayne murmured.

"*Mon amour,*" Tristan echoed.

And together, they fell into oblivion.

JAYNE WOKE to a soft tapping noise. Blinking sleepily, she extricated herself from the warmth of Tristan's arms, leaving him sleeping in the bed as she followed the sound.

It was coming from her door, but it sounded too soft to be a knock—almost as if a bird were tapping on the wood. Frowning, Jayne looked through the peephole, then sighed.

"Hi, Dad," she said as she swung the door open. "Do you know what time it is?" She gestured to the window where the pitch-black sky hadn't yet lightened with the incoming dawn.

Henry stepped into her apartment without a word, wringing his hands together, his curls more disheveled than usual. Which was saying something.

Jayne closed the door and scrutinized him. "Are you all right? What's happened?"

"If you want to kill a creature, you cut off its source of food," Henry said.

Jayne rubbed her forehead. She was too tired for this. "I'm sorry, what?"

"Ruth. The secret to her undoing."

Jayne straightened, suddenly alert. "Yes?" Her heart drummed nervously in her chest. Was he really about to disclose this information?

"You were right," Henry said, running a hand through his hair. "Seeing that Wraith in Zagreb made me realize how foolish I'm being. Ruth will inevitably become that creature. Entirely. And she won't stop until she's destroyed everything and everyone." He shook his head. "I can't keep holding on to the idea of her. Not anymore."

Jayne actually stopped breathing, her skin prickling with anticipation. "All right. So, what's this about cutting off her source of food?"

"When we first arrived in Zagreb, Quimby used this device to temporarily disable an Adept's magic."

Jayne nodded, remembering the grenade-like object. "Right."

"I don't think it would be too hard for Quimby and me to put our heads together and develop a serum that will permanently disable an Adept's magic."

Permanently. A knot worked its way into Jayne's throat. If Henry was right, and this fell into the wrong hands, their enemies would potentially have the ability to render the entire TCO powerless. She thought of the Tiriosis Tristan had injected her with that had done something similar.

"The research team has been working on that," Jayne said slowly. "They haven't made much progress, though. With the Tiriosis, the risk of infecting the Torrent itself was too great."

"If we focus less on the Torrent and more on a person's blood and genetic makeup, I think we can make it work."

"But I don't understand. You want to develop this serum and infect Ruth with it? It would solve a lot of problems, yes, but what if the Master just gives her that power back? What if she makes another bargain with him?"

"No, you don't understand." Henry took a step closer to her. "Ruth has been enslaved by Odin's power. She has become dependent on it—so much so that if she goes without it, her body will break down. She is reliant on that magic like a drug. Dependent."

Jayne's hand unconsciously went to the stretch of gray skin on her arm as panic rose inside her chest. *Dependent on the magic. Like a drug.*

Her arm itched. Was that Jayne? Was she risking following in Ruth's footsteps?

Henry, oblivious to where Jayne's thoughts had turned, went on, "If we cut off her source, and she is unable to get that connection back, the loss of that power will slowly kill her."

Like a drug addict wasting away one day at a time. A slow, painful end. No wonder Henry had been so reluctant to share this information. It was one of the worst kinds of deaths, to be helpless as your body slowly decayed and you were powerless to stop it.

"So that's the big secret?" Jayne asked numbly. "Remove her magic, and she dies?"

"Not just that. But her bargain, her connection with Odin, dies, too. She's been feeding him for years. He, too, will be cut off from a source of food."

Jayne's mouth went dry as she processed these words. "So, we inject Ruth with this serum. It weakens Odin. She dies. Then, we track down other Adepts who have entered into bargains with him?"

"If we can develop this serum, we can successfully cut off every tie Odin has to our world. We can end him, Jayne."

CHAPTER
FORTY-NINE
BLOOD IS THICKER THAN WATER

S ofia stood in the back of the classroom in the Time Catch, watching Hector go over the basic logistics of the Torrent for their new students. Her eyes were on the teenager they'd rescued, Matthew, and the hollow, empty sensation surrounded her once more. The strange feeling she'd gotten when she'd first met him in South Carolina hadn't abated; if anything, it had only grown stronger since then. It brought up a well of memories she'd tried so long to suppress: the cancer, eating away at her body one day at a time. Chemo treatments, ripping her body apart, burning her from the inside out. The exhaustion, the trauma, the grief and pain...

But *why*? Why did this boy evoke those feelings so power-fully? Sofia shook her head, trying to rid herself of the onslaught of memories, but they were too powerful.

A hand pressed into her shoulder, and she looked up and found Cillian watching her with worried eyes.

"Still feeling off about Matthew?" he murmured.

"It's not Matthew, it's just...there's something about him. His aura, his magic. I don't know." She bit her lip, shaking her head. She wasn't making any sense.

"Is it because he's a Guardian?"

"I've met other Guardians before, and none of them felt like this."

"Maybe there's something unique to his magic. Something that resonates with yours."

Sofia considered this, watching as Matthew raised his hand to ask Hector a question. The sleeve of his shirt rolled down, revealing a thin, leather bracelet. Sofia's eyes homed in on this, something snagging in her memory. She'd once had a bracelet with a powerful Suppression spell built into it, a strong magic that weakened her day by day, festering and growing, bringing about cancer and sicknesses, draining her of her magical energies entirely. She'd chosen that, begged for it, in an attempt to keep Jayne safe. When she took it off, the cancer within her disappeared, and her power had flared to life.

Sofia gasped, the sound so loud that every student in the classroom turned to face her. But she didn't care. She stormed toward Matthew, a mixture of horror and fury pulsing through her. Before he could back away, she gripped his wrist and snapped the bracelet off him.

"What the—" Matthew objected, but a flash of magic exploded in the air between them, sending them both flying. Sofia collided with a desk, her shoulder on fire, while Matthew was sprawled on the floor, groaning.

"Sofia!" Cillian helped her up, inspecting her for injuries.

"I'm fine." Sofia rolled out her shoulder, wincing in pain. But it wasn't anything serious.

She hurried over to Matthew and extended a hand to him. His eyes were wide, his face ghostly pale.

When his fingers met hers, a bolt of awareness shot through her, familiar and foreign all at once. She saw a baby with white-blond hair and blue eyes. *Her* blue eyes. She saw Ruth, clutching the baby to her chest, sitting next to Hans Kaufmann. She saw a boy watch with wide, frightened eyes as Hans cast a spell on the bracelet, enchanting it with his Guardian magic, before thrusting it on Matthew's wrist.

Matthew was on his feet, but Sofia jerked away from him as if she'd been burned. Around them, the other Adept children were also on their feet, watching the interaction with curiosity and confusion.

"Sofia, what's going on?" Hector asked.

"I—you—we—" Sofia broke off, unable to breathe as she pointed to Matthew. The boy was shaking his head vehemently, as if begging her not to expose this truth, to vocalize what passed between them.

But she had to. She couldn't deny it. "You're my *brother*."

A ripple of gasps echoed around them. Cillian growled, and Hector staggered back a step. Several children whispered excitedly with one another, including Gregory and Hazel.

"How?" Kendra, the girl with pigtails, exclaimed. "How could you two be related?"

"You're Ruth's son," Sofia said. "*Hans's* son." She stepped toward him, eyes narrowing.

Matthew waved his hands, his expression frantic. "No, no, no, it's not what you think! I mean, yes, they are my parents, but—but I'm *not* loyal to him. We were fighting when you found me. He was trying to get me to go with him, to go after my mother, but I refused. I didn't want to be his weapon anymore. He forced this bracelet on me, cursing it so I would be unable to remove it myself or speak of its true purpose. He bound me, Sofia. I was caged by his magic, too powerless to resist it. I—I was nothing more than his slave." His voice broke on the last word, his eyes brimming with tears.

Sofia swallowed hard, unable to shake the sheer unbelievability of it all. Hans's son was her half-brother.

Hans's son.

Ruth's son.

Could she trust him? What if he was lying?

But his face was so stricken with grief and trauma. His Guardian magic still called on her, drawing her forward. She hadn't sensed it before because of the bracelet; if his powers hadn't been blocked, she would have known immediately he was her brother.

Would she have brought him here if she'd known? Ruth and Hans were monsters, capable of all kinds of horrors. What would they do with a son? Could he have been planted here intentionally, to spy on them? Did he need to be incarcerated before he took them all down?

"Sofia," Cillian said quietly, reaching toward her. "He's just a boy."

Just a boy. Just a child.

In a flash, Sofia's mind turned to young Jayne, flinching away from Ruth's magic.

She had to believe Matthew was a victim. Just like she had been. Just like Jayne. Another victim in Ruth's bloodthirsty search for more power.

And Sofia knew better than anyone that you couldn't help who your parents were.

As her panic faded, a resolute determination took its place. Sofia nodded slowly and drew closer to Matthew. "Yes. He's just a boy. And he's my brother." This time, the words weren't an accusation; they were a promise. A vow.

"You're my brother," she said again, "and I swear I'll protect you."

EPILOGUE
OPEN THE GATES

R uth braced herself before the swirling current of energy, the ethereal whispers of the gods and ancient ones washing over her, making her skin prickle.

The entrance to the Torrent itself. The last time she'd been here, the Master had taken hold of her.

And she'd let him.

But it was far too late to dwell on regrets. What was done was done, and she was here for a reason.

She pressed the blade into her palm, drawing blood, before raising her hand in the air. Her blood burned against her flesh as the Torrent absorbed it. She whispered the word he'd seared into her mind, in his language, the old Norse.

"Hnjga!"

She flinched against the scorching pain but held fast, allowing her blood—the blood of Odin's servant—to unlock the gate.

Now is the time, he'd told her. *My army awaits.*

A deep grinding grated against her ears, a heavy portcullis being lifted. She drew back a step, chest swelling with fear and unease.

She would follow Odin anywhere, to the ends of the earth—because the alternative was her own destruction. She was bound to him, and if she disobeyed, the power of his spell on her would devour her whole.

But this? This was different. She was opening the realm to all manner of creatures whose thirst for blood knew no limits.

No one was safe. Not even her. Odin wouldn't blink if he lost her to the fury of his army. His *blóðtöku-maðrs*. The blood-letters.

My path is set, she reminded herself. *No turning back.*

Even so, she backed up another step, just to be safe. The grinding halted, and a quiver of dark energy rolled over her, making her slightly nauseous. The stink of death and decay filled her nose, awakening the creature inside her.

Brothers, it seemed to say.

Ruth gritted her teeth against the Wraith inside her, shoving it away for now. She needed to be in control.

A screech rang out, followed by the flapping of wings. In front of her, three Wraiths appeared, gray and scaly, with blood-red wings. They soared toward her, and Ruth clenched her fists to resist the urge to flee from them.

Behind them was a horde of Wraiths, all of them slightly different. One was tall and skeletal, with no wings but claws that extended all the way to his feet. Another was thick and bulky, with two sets of wings that shone like silver.

Odin once revealed that every Wraith manifested itself differently. There were various classes and races, all depending on the Adept they once were and the spell that had entrapped them.

Ruth lifted her chin. *I am not like them.* She had not fully succumbed to her Wraith.

Not yet, at least.

But it was only a matter of time.

Ruth spread her arms as the army of Wraiths poured out

from the Torrent, flinging themselves into the sky, ready to wage war and wreak destruction on the mortal realm.

No one would be safe from Odin's wrath.

Dearest Reader,

Are you as breathless as I am??? Things are getting serious for our team, and I can't wait to share the next installment of this series with you. THE BOOK OF SPIRITS will be available in 2024. Stay tuned to my newsletter for news on the release.

In the meantime, if you're interested in more from Jayne's world, I suggest checking out the Guardians mini-series, which provides supplemental stories about all the secondary players in this world. Guardians of Power is the latest installment, where you'll meet a young Henry Thorne and his friend Valeri Rudik as they make their first attempts at time travel.

I am so grateful for your time and support. Thanks for reading, and for being a part of my magical world!

Blessed Be,
Joss

ACKNOWLEDGMENTS

This book has been an epic undertaking, and so many people held my hand as I navigated its turbulent waters. My agent, Laura Blake Peterson, who has always been a huge supporter of me refilling my creative well in this fantasy realm; James Farrell, who kindly shepherded this novel through the audio process; Erin Moon and the fine folks at Tantor Audio, who bring Jayne et al. to life; Kim Killion, artist extraordinaire, who took a leap of faith with me as this world transitions from reality to fantasy and created a spectacular set of covers to reflect the change; Phyllis DeBlanche, for the naughty jokes and ellipses hunting; and can I give a shoutout to the Vellum team, who makes making a book so incredibly fun and easy? There, I just did. And my teams at Ingram and Amazon, as well, for all the help over the years getting these books into your hands; and my friends at Poisoned Pen, Murder by the Book, and Parnassus Books who love to hand-sell these beauties—I adore you!

Laura Benedict, Ariel Lawhon, Lisa Patton, Patti Callahan Henry, Paige Crutcher, Jayne Ann Krentz, Barbara Peters, Boyd Morrison, and Honorée Corder were constant cheerleaders; my awesome parents listened to every plot twist as they came with bated breath; my exceptionally cool team of beta readers gave such incredible feedback and really helped this book level up, especially Jennifer Jakes, Claire Bartlett, Renee Butler, Sherrie Saint, Sara Weiss, Erin Alford, Lana Turner, and Joan Huston; and my Readers and Rogues FB group are wonderful.

To my permanent franchise love interest, Randy: you make

every day magic. You bring me to life, and you give me so much power. My creative spirit soars because of you. Je t'aime.

When it comes to a personality as big as Jayne's, two heads are always better than one. My deepest thanks to R.L. Perez, who helped craft the initial rough draft of this story before she departed the co-writing gig to attend to her growing family, and Alisha Klapheke, who helped develop this magical world in the first place, and is always on the other side of the phone with an answer or banter, or both. Thank you, friend!

And finally, my forever gratitude to you, for taking a chance on these books. I hope you love reading them as much as I love writing them.

ABOUT JOSS WALKER

Joss Walker is the fantasy pen name for *New York Times* best-selling thriller author J.T. Ellison, where she explores her love of the fantasy genre and extraordinary women discovering their power in the world.

With Jayne Thorne, CIA Librarian, Joss has created a light-hearted urban fantasy series perfect for lovers of books, libraries, romance, and of course, magic.

Photo credit: KidTee Hello Photography

Join Joss Walker's newsletter
https://josswalker.com/subscribe

ABOUT R.L. PEREZ

R.L. Perez is a YA fantasy romance author, perfectionist, anxious Type A worrier, and proud Hufflepuff. She's published three series set in the same world, featuring witches, romance, and time travel. When she's not working on her books, she's either napping, diving into a good book, obsessively watching Netflix, or playing with her two kids. She loves chocolate, loud laughter, and alternative rock music.

Join R.L. Perez's Newsletter
www.rlperez.com/subscribe

About Two Tales Press

Two Tales Press is an independent publishing house featuring crime fiction, suspense, and fantasy novels, novellas, and anthologies written and edited by *New York Times* bestselling author J.T. Ellison, including the Jayne Thorne, CIA Librarian series under J.T.'s fantasy pen name, Joss Walker.

To view all of our titles, please visit

www.twotalespress.com